For Candy

Prologue

Vietnam, 1970

"Snipers up!"

PFC Augustus Overbridge hustled forward, while his spotter, Benje, jogged two steps behind. Satch and Sam were already hunkered down next to the lieutenant.

"Point saw something in the tree line across the paddy." He pointed at Satch. "You two up and left. O and Benje, up and right."

The platoon flattened out as the sniper teams melted into the forest. Benje muttered, "We were practically home. Must be less than three miles." O said nothing. They crept forward, Benje leading out, silent in the jungle. Twenty minutes later, they were in position on their bellies, five hundred meters forward and just at the edge of the trees to the right of the rice paddy. Benje swept his gaze along the edge of the field with his 9x50 binoculars, his movements as unhurried as a sloth. O waited patiently, the big Remington 700 held almost lovingly at the ready. *Come on, Benje, work that Filipino jungle magic.*

A shot rang out on the far side of the paddy. Benje swung his field glasses smoothly around to where Sam and Satch were set up directly across from them behind a fallen trunk. Satch's right arm hung awkwardly, but he had his binoculars up, and he and Sam were both intent on something up ahead. Benje followed Sam's sight line to a small rise at the far side of the paddy. At first he saw nothing, then jabbed at O. "Check out that knoll. There's a patch."

O focused through his scope at the small hill. There was indeed a rectangular patch of ground, slightly dryer than the surrounding foliage. *Just where I would have set up.* His rangefinder showed eight hundred meters. "Got it. Check out the same spot on our side."

"Nothing there," Benje reported. "The ground slopes down on this

1

side, no good for set up."

O waited, breathing slowly, his scope fixed on the leading edge of the hide. *Breathe in, breathe out, melt into the ground.* His pulse slowed and all the tension drained from his body. The patch of ground tented up and the tip of a muzzle showed, followed by a telescopic sight. O fired at a spot a foot back from the sight, and chambered his next round immediately. A second later, a cloud of pink mist erupted and the covering tarp blew up into the air, exposing another man. He started to squirm back, but O's second shot was already on its way, aimed center mass. It caught the second man in the right shoulder, sending his detached arm careening into the air. O turned to Benje. "Did ya get that? That's 77 brains and 54 bodies. Put that in the book! Who's the best damn shot in the Corps!"

Benje grinned and started to pull out his notebook, but a bullet ripped through his helmet from their right, covering O with a gory shrapnel of metal, brains, and bone. O scrambled around on his belly, and spotted movement barely two hundred meters forward in the trees. He grabbed Benje's M16 and fired two shots into the back of one man, knocking his body into a tree. A second man melted into the jungle. O slung his Remington over his shoulder and went after him, adrenaline pumping him up so tight he thought his head would explode. "A solitary marine is a dead marine," floated into his consciousness from basic training. He pushed that thought down, and followed deeper into the jungle, no longer interested in rules or tactics or safety or anything other than killing.

He ran hard, following the noise of a man who was clearly more interested in speed than stealth. After a few minutes, he started to slow. There was something wrong with his right leg. He looked down. Blood was spreading from a tear in his pants, adding to the blood and bits of Benje spattered over his fatigues. He stopped long enough to tear away the fabric, revealing a jagged gash in his thigh. A splintered piece of white bone poked out of the wound, and for a moment he felt cold, sure that his leg was broken. *Like I could run on a broken femur,* he mocked himself. He grasped the bone and pulled, ignoring the pain as it came loose. It was about three inches long, with a couple of teeth in it. *Benje.* He tossed it aside, pulled tape from his pack, and strapped it across the torn flesh, slowing the bleeding. *No time for pain,* he thought. *Focus.* He listened intently. His quarry was still crashing recklessly away through the jungle, best guess three hundred yards ahead.

Three hours and several kilometers later, the adrenaline was gone, and his thigh screamed with every step. The noises of the fleeing Viet Cong had become slowly more distant, and the sun was low on the horizon. *I'm going to lose him.* But then the trees were gone and the world opened into a plowed field which sloped gently down to a hut village. O stopped short and squinted in the sudden light. His quarry was in view, running hard, getting closer to safety with every step.

O sprawled at the tree line and slid back the bolt of his Remington, chambering a round. He felt the caress of the walnut stock on his cheek as he lined up the target. Almost nine hundred meters. He ran the numbers. *Nine hundred meters. Just over a second. Running man, ten feet. No wind.* He held off three feet above and ten feet in front of the target, still a hundred yards from the huts. *Hasten slowly*, he reminded himself, and invested four seconds in slowing his breathing. *Breathe in, breathe out, melt into the ground.* The trigger broke crisply at three pounds of pressure, and the .308 round sped at nearly three times the speed of sound into the back of his enemy's head, rewarding him with another beautiful spray of pink mist. *78 brains.*

After the rush of the kill, O suddenly came back to himself. He pulled a few feet back into the jungle and sat against a tree, watching the village. *Nothing.* He looked down at his leg. He grit his teeth and pulled off the tape. The edges were already getting red. He could almost hear his CO. "Third purple heart. Automatic ticket home. Sorry we had to cut off your gangrenous leg." His aid kit had some antiseptic, which he poured into the wound and scrubbed hard with his toothbrush. A new personal high for pain. He shook his canteen. *Not enough.* Still, he poured a little in to rinse the wound, then taped it again, and took a sip.

Night fell quickly in the tropics, and soon his world was an almost inky black. He put a patch over one eye, and continued to scan the village lights for movement with the other, as he moved laterally about two hundred meters through the jungle. Six silhouettes retrieved the body, but there was no other sign of extra-village activity. *At night all the villages were Communist.* He sat motionless against his tree, so quiet that the night creatures of the jungle went about their usual business, small bodies rustling along the ground or through the canopy above.

The waning gibbous moon rose over the hill and he checked his luminous watch. Ten o'clock. He could now see dimly in the moonlight. And be seen. Good for moving, bad for hiding. Still no movement from the village. *Home's gotta be south and west, but how far?* he thought. *Could be a dozen miles.* He rose stiffly and started to move through the jungle, the moon behind his right shoulder. *Hasten slowly*, he reminded himself. Every hundred paces or so he stopped and listened, then moved on. At three, he came suddenly out of the trees and onto a well-worn dirt road curving to the southwest. He started down the road, but stopped after a hundred meters and shook his head. *I must be getting delirious.* He went a few feet into the trees and pulled his sniper tarp out of his pack. He spent twenty minutes weaving in some fallen branches and leaves, then lied down to watch the road from his hide. *Hope the boys are out on patrol this morning. Preferably a whole armored division.*

Soon after sunup, some villagers passed by with an oxcart. No hurry, just a day in the life. O did not move. His leg throbbed. Next came a VC patrol, moving quickly and almost silently. Not actually *on* the road, but just inside the jungle on the far side. If they had been on his side they would have stepped on him. O's finger twitched, but six was about five too many for the Remington. It would have been different if he still had Benje's M16. They passed uneventfully.

The pain from his thigh was getting worse, and after six motionless hours, it had stiffened up, even a slight movement causing searing pain. He had to look. First, he listened. No human sounds, just the normal jungle noises which assured him that no one was near. He pushed back the tarp and sat up, examining his leg in the sunlight. Pus oozed from under the tape, and the surrounding redness was now wider than his hand. He listened. *Still no noise.* He dug at the end of the tape with his fingernail, and yanked it off. A strangled groan hissed out through his clenched teeth. *Yes, definitely pus.* He rummaged in his pack and found the remaining antiseptic, which he then dumped into the wound. This time, the pain was too much, and darkness closed in on his vision, accompanied by a loud roaring in his ears.

He was awakened by the sound of the villagers with the oxcart, hurrying now, going back the other way. The sun was noticeably higher in the sky, and was beating down on his exposed face. His lips were burned and cracked, and his eyelids hurt with each blink. *How long had he been out?* He reached to pull the tarp back over his body, but stopped himself. *They won't see me unless I move.* They appeared intent on speed in any case, urging the ox along with cajoling cries and a switch. They passed, and he scrubbed the wound once more with the last of his water, and re-taped it.

Barely two minutes later, he heard a rumble which got slowly louder.

Trucks! Soon they came into view, two U.S. Army deuce-and-a-half's and about twenty soldiers on foot. He yelled, "Hey!" but only a harsh croak came out of his parched throat. The truck noise was enough that it would have probably masked a whole platoon of VC in any case. O pulled himself forward on his elbows the few feet to the tree line and started waving his Remington in the air. One shot passed over his head and then someone yelled, "Stop shooting, idiot, that's one of ours." Moments later two soldiers grabbed his shoulders and started dragging, but were stopped by his screams and the irritated barking of the medic.

"What the hell happened to you?" he asked.

O was barely conscious, and was only able to rasp out a whisper.

"78 Brains. 78 Brains. 78 Brains."

Chapter 1

Barbuda
Friday, September 23, 2016

Frank awoke with a start. Somebody was pounding on his door, the sound barely audible over the drumming of the rain on the metal roof. He sat up in the total darkness, groggy with sleep. *Who the heck?*

"Go away!"

"Please, Dr. Frank, it's Constable Peters. It's rather important."

Frank fumbled for the lamp. *Still no power.* With the storm shutters closed, the room was dark as pitch, and his flashlight had long since given up. The wind was still rattling loudly, but was no longer the screaming siren of the last two days. He rolled out of bed, tangling his leg in the sheets and falling heavily to the ground.

"Umphf. COMING," he shouted.

He made it over to the door and opened it. The constable was standing in his yellow slicker on the porch. It was raining steadily, but to the east the clouds had cleared and the morning sun was blinding. In the glare, he could make out his neighbor's house, a hundred yards away and down the bluff. It was missing most of its roof, and had collapsed sideways off its stilts onto a wrecked thirty-foot sailboat, stenciled with the name *Serenity*. The pink sand beach was littered with debris and dead fish.

Paradise. I'm sick to death of paradise. This week, particularly.

"Hello, Peters. Here to tell me 'I told you so,' I expect. Fine, I should have evacuated when you told me to get out on Monday. There. You were right."

Peters did not even smile. "No, sir, nothing like that. I wondered if you might come give me a hand with something." He peered through the door into the gloom. "I thought you said you had a generator."

"Yeah, something crashed into that side of the house about an hour into Hurricane Marge. It was not like I could go out and try to fix it. How can I possibly help you?"

Peters shifted from one foot to the other. "I was hoping you could come with me. There's something, er, someone, I should say, washed up on the beach. I've got coffee in the Rover," he added.

"It's a little out of my jurisdiction, wouldn't you say? What's the urgency?"

"Well, we don't have a coroner on the island, I doubt anyone will be able to come over from Antigua today, and I would really like some help moving it so as to keep it from floating back out. I was making the tour of the island when I saw some birds pecking at something, and, well, I would really like you to have a look, being a coroner back in the States and all. Please, sir."

"Assistant coroner. But hot coffee sounds good." And he really did love dead bodies. He pulled on his tall rubber boots and followed Peters out.

* * *

They drove north and west about a mile and a half. Frank saw birds poking at something tangled in the seaweed that was up near the normal high tide line. They parked at the side of the road about twenty yards from the body, and sloshed over.

Approaching the body, Frank started analyzing immediately. *Bloated and green,* he thought, *but the skin hasn't burst. Probably between one and two weeks in the water.* As he got closer, he could see a length of chain looped around the waist, cutting in deeply with the swelling. The fingers, toes, and genitals were partly gone and had ragged edges. *Crabs,* he thought. *Tall, probably male.* Then he saw why Peters had wanted help. The top of the skull was gone. Neatly. As if cut off with an autopsy saw. The brain was missing, of course. *The scavengers of the deep would have eaten that soft morsel right away.*

"Did you take photos yet?"

"No, um, I actually had a quick look and thought I would get someone." Peters was nearly as green as the body.

"You have a camera in the Rover? Run get it, and I'll take the shots. You're right, we can't leave this here. Where can we take it?" But Peters had already bolted for the car.

They decided that the only place would be the garage at the constabulary back in Codrington. Frank took about a dozen pictures, and Peters got a tarp and spread it next to the body. They rolled the corpse onto the tarp, which caused a large amount of noxious gas to bubble out of the throat, and a pool of brown fluid seemed to ooze from everywhere.

"Rope," Frank directed, and Peters fetched some from the car. Frank pulled up the corners of the tarp and secured it, and only a little fluid leaked out when they heaved it into the back of the Rover. Frank drove, Peters hanging his head out of the window like a dog to escape the stench. Frank laughed to himself. He was immune to smells of all sorts, after decades of exposure.

The constabulary had a generator, and Frank found a couple of floodlights and illuminated his subject. *Getting an ID on this body is going to be tough.* The eyes, most of the nose, and the ears were gone, and he could not even hazard a guess as to the original skin color- certainly not the greenish yellow he was presented with. There were teeth, but in poor repair, and no sign of any dental work, so no help there. Frank was not really sure how much he should even do. *After all, they have their own medical examiner in Antigua, and they probably won't respond kindly to my meddling. I know I would pitch a fit if some foreigners touched one of my bodies.* "I'll just look," he announced out loud, "but not start an actual autopsy." No answer. He looked back over his shoulder. Peters was at the far side of the garage, cleaning the back of the Rover with some bleach. Frank started to whistle cheerily.

He looked at the chain. It had broken off a short length from the body.

"Someone must have weighted him down and tossed him in the sea." he muttered to himself. He laughed. He missed his morgue, with the bright lights, bright tools, and foot-operated dictation recorder. He would try to keep his musings internal. *A couple more weeks and he would have been picked clean,* he thought. *Probably an anchor – the chain has that white corroded look that you see in the holds of small sailboats. Pretty generic.*

He then looked at the skull. Under bright light, he saw something very odd. "Take a look at this, Peters, look, here at the edge of the skull." Peters was not enthusiastic, but he came over. "The bone edge is *healed*. He must have been alive for at least a month after this was done."

"What, alive with the top of his head off!?" Peters had had enough, and went over to the sink in the corner and began to heave.

Frank shook his head. *Cops. The same everywhere.*

The pathologists' greatest joy was to torture the cops. Frank thought back to one Saturday morning when he was a student working part time in the Medical Examiner's office. They brought in a week-old suicide victim who had been discovered in his apartment due to the smell. His skin was dull green, and bloated with gas to the point of bursting. The smell had been unimaginable, and the detectives smeared mentholatum on their lips, wore masks, and stood as far back from the autopsy table as possible. Dr. Kovac was about 4'10" and 90 pounds, wrinkled like a gnome from smoking two packs a day. She had winked at Frank, and asked the cops, "Do you know why they swell?" Just some head shakes. "Methane," she said. She then grabbed a large syringe with a giant needle, and with a sharp jab thrust it in the victim's chest. The force of the gas blew the plunger out of the syringe, and Dr. Kovac fished her lighter out of her pocket. "Look, it burns," she called out, and lit the gas that was hissing out of the cadaver, making a fountain of flame four feet high. She doubled over with laughter as both detectives vomited into the sink. Frank decided then and there that Forensic Pathology was his thing. He laughed to himself and got back to work.

He ran his finger around the outside of the skull. There were four holes in the skin, symmetrically arranged. He broke his resolve to not meddle, and used a box cutter to incise through one of the holes. The bone beneath had a neat, sharp hole drilled into it. NOT *healed. Clearly he had had something screwed to his skull.* He then looked more closely at the inside of the skull. There were tiny linear grooves, spaced about a quarter of an inch apart, all around the inside of the skull, with deeper indentations about a half inch down, where the other grooves ended. Frank closed his eyes and thought about it. The bone had an interesting erosive wear. Perhaps something metallic, like a screen or mesh had been attached all the way around.

"Peters, get over here. Look, this guy was kept alive with the top of his head off for at least a month, and with some sort of device attached. We need to call your superiors at Antigua. Something very strange has been going on here."

"It's no good, we have no phone service, and the radio antenna was wrecked with the storm. I can probably repair it, but it will take me a couple of hours."

Frank itched to keep working, but decided he better stop cutting. Still, he wanted a look at the back. "Come help me roll him over," he called. Peters sidled up, and ran as soon as the feat was accomplished. There was some sort of a wire connector coming out of the small of the man's back. Like an old thirty-prong computer printer cable connection. He wiggled it with a finger. It was solidly mounted to the lumbar vertebrae. "What the hell is that?" he muttered. He was definitely going to get the locals to let him at least watch this one.

"Get working on that antenna, Peters. Let me take the Rover up to the north end. Jacobs has a satellite phone, if he is still there. I'll see if we can borrow it."

"Oh, he'll be there. Too stubborn to evacuate, same as you." Peters surrendered the keys.

* * *

Frank drove the few kilometers north to Jacobs' cottage as quickly as he dared, dodging the debris. A far cry from his own modern house, which was built on the bomb-shelter principle, this was a traditional wooden beach hut, with thick plywood screwed over the windows for the storm, instead of Frank's motor-driven category-four-certified shutters. Jacobs was there all right, busily engaged in removing the plywood over his seaward window. Frank honked loudly to get his attention, then got out of the Rover. *It would not do to sneak up on Jacobs. Like as not he would be carrying a revolver to 'protect against looters'.* He walked over.

"Mornin', William."

"Ah, Frank, come balance this plywood while I get out the screws. Be about ten times easier."

Frank obligingly helped him remove the remaining plywood sheets from the sides of the house. William Jacobs had been living on Barbuda for about twenty of his eighty years, and was the stereotype of the American ex-pat in the tropics, with his leathery skin, straw hat, and flowered shirt. They were on amicable terms, despite Frank's use of sunscreen, which Jacobs considered an abomination.

"Is your sat phone working? I need to call over to Antigua about a body Peters found on the beach."

"Battery's dead. No power for the past couple of days."

"The constabulary has a generator, we could charge it there."

"Okay, I'll grab it and ride over with you."

By now the rain was pretty much over, and it was easier to see the mess created by the hurricane. Mostly tree limbs and leaves strewn everywhere, but down along the coast there were many beach houses which had clearly not been up to it, with parts of roofs peeled off or porches ruined. One house was at about a thirty degree angle, the foundation washed partly away on one side.

"Morons," Jacobs muttered, "gotta be prepared if you want to live in the Caribbean. Also, DRIVE ON THE LEFT!" he shouted.

Frank moved over. Not that he was worried much about traffic.

* * *

When they arrived at the constabulary, Peters was still up on the roof. Frank shouted up to him, "Any luck?"

"Probably take another hour or more. Still trying to sort out the mess."

"Come on down. I have Jacobs and his phone. Just plugged it in."

Peters tried the main constabulary number in Antigua. After three tries just went to an out-of-service message, he shook his head and headed back up to the roof.

Frank had a thought. "Mind if I call my daughter?" he asked Jacobs. "She may be worried."

"Go ahead, if you can get through. I'm going out for a smoke."

Frank dialed Mitzi's number in New York. After what seemed a very long time, it started to ring and she picked up.

"Hello, who is this?"

"Hi Mitzi, it's Dad. Wanted to let you know I was okay."

"That's good to know. Why would you not be okay?"

"Well, with the hurricane passing over my house and all."

"Oh, I guess that means you are on your island. And there was a hurricane. I hadn't heard."

Frank was not surprised. He spoke with his daughter about once a month, usually when she called to tell him about one of her cases. She had followed in his footsteps, and was a forensic pathologist with the New York FBI office. Which was really why he had called. Mitzi was well down the spectrum towards Asperger's syndrome, and although she loved her dad in her way, it was not exactly a fuzzy relationship.

"Listen, we found a body I wanted to talk to you about."

"Really? Go on, then." He could almost hear her perking up. He described what he had observed in detail.

"So, you think he had this hardware, then died or was killed and someone *removed* all the hardware and dumped him. Then the storm broke him loose from the anchor or whatever, and deposited him on shore. That really is interesting. Any ideas on what it was all about?"

"None."

"Interesting that they left the spinal hardware. I'll bet the cranial set up was unique, or at least expensive. Let me know when you know more. Gotta go." She hung up.

* * *

Peters came down from the roof. "That should about do it. Let's give it a try."

He fired up the radio set, and started transmitting. "St John's, this is Codrington, come in." No response. He repeated a half dozen times, with no response.

"They must be down over there. I'll try again in an hour." He stood up and turned away, but the radio crackled to life. "Codrington, this is St John's. What is your situation?"

Peters sat back down at the mike. "Peters here. We've a body over here that is pretty unusual. We need to get transport to take it over there."

"Unusual, how? We've got at least fifty dead over here, another seventy-five or so missing."

"This victim was not killed *in* the storm, more like washed up *with* the storm. The whole top of the head is cut off. Quite grisly. We have an American medical examiner over here, he had a look, thinks it quite fishy."

"What is this American's name?"

"Frank Lenz. Lives midway down the coast. Normally works for the state of Minnesota, I believe."

"Let me check with the Chief Inspector about getting someone to come collect the body. Expect a message in two hours. Be at your transmitter at eleven o'clock sharp. In the meantime, keep it quiet. No need to start any rumors."

"Sounds good. No one else really around, anyhow." He signed off.

William was anxious to get home, so Peters drove him and Frank back to their cottages. Frank said he was going to get cleaned up a little, then come back over to the constabulary. His curiosity was in high gear.

* * *

Over on Antigua, Edward Simmons was on the roof making a call on *his* secure satellite phone. This was not one supplied by the police force. He placed a call to the Compound.

Santiago, Simmons' contact at the Compound, was a fixer. He took the report, then in turn called upstairs to *el jefe*, who listened to the story

13

silently, and when it was finished said simply, "Clean it up. Now. Include Simmons. Be thorough." Santiago smiled. He loved his job.

* * *

The Compound was on Isla Sofia, a small privately held island in the Caribbean, about forty miles west of a point midway between Antigua and Barbuda. Santiago sent one man to St John's. He was an unimaginative but very dependable fellow who simply met Simmons in the alley around the corner from the Constabulary, ostensibly to give him a message from Santiago. The message was straight-forward, and consisted of a quickly broken neck. His launch made it back to the Compound before lunch.

* * *

Santiago himself went to Barbuda. As he boarded the boat, which was painted to look exactly like the Antigua police patrol boats, he made a mental list. *Body. Constable. American.* Each had its own potential for complications. He had radioed Peters at eleven, and told him he would be arriving at the dock at 11:45.

Peters met them at the dock. Santiago stuck out his hand. "Dr. Melendez, assistant coroner. These are my assistants, James and Sebastian." Peters shook his hand. He could see that there was also a pilot who stayed on the boat. The rest of them piled into the Rover to ride the five hundred meters to the constabulary, bringing along a large duffel bag.

Codrington was nearly deserted, but they passed a couple of people on the street, who waved and greeted Peters. Santiago was not happy. The number of loose ends on this job could become unwieldy.

"How are things on the island as a whole?"

"Not too bad. Ran over to check on the two resorts while I was waiting on you. All the guests had been evacuated, of course. No one hurt, but the west face of the Flamingo is really beat up, and the cellar is flooded. Both of their generators are functioning, and the staff is starting to clean up. Old Geoffrey, who manages the Caribbean Jewel, was in fine fettle, strutting and swearing like a martinet."

So much for just making it look like Peters was lost in the storm, Santiago thought, *he had been seen by far too many people to sell that. Well, well, first things first.* Back at the garage, Santiago looked over the body quickly, and his men pulled a black body bag out of the duffel and manhandled the slimy corpse in. They loaded it into the Rover, cursing as brown fluid poured down the front of their pants.

"Say, Peters, did you take any photos?"

"Oh, yes, er, well Frank, I mean Dr. Lenz, did. The camera is in the back of the car." He rummaged around and pulled it out. Santiago took out the memory card and put it in his pocket.

"How did the island roads fare?"

"Not too bad, overall, but there is a big chunk washed away just south of here. Dr. Lenz nearly drove into it and killed us earlier this morning. Would've, if he hadn't been driving on the wrong side."

They went back to the dock and the assistants carried the body onto the boat. No one was around to see. *First bit of luck this whole day.*

"Can you take me over to see this Dr. Lenz?" Santiago asked. "I would be interested to hear his observations."

They drove south down the coastal road. "Does this Dr. Lenz have a nice place?" Santiago asked.

"Gorgeous. Big cement house painted bright blue, nicest house on this stretch. About another kilometer."

Good to know, thought Santiago.

As they went around the next bend, Santiago could see that the road had really taken a beating.

"See, there is where the road is partly washed out." Peters pointed. It looked like a forty foot drop off the bluff.

"You really should put up some warning triangles," Santiago remarked.

Peters blushed slightly. He should have done that hours ago. "Right. I'll just do that."

As they came to a stop, Santiago reached his hand behind Peters, and with a sudden powerful motion flung his head into the windscreen, cracking the glass. He gripped the hair of the limp man, and cracked his head several more times into the glass. Peters was now bleeding profusely. Santiago pried open his eyelids, noting with satisfaction that the pupil of the left eye was dilated. He got out and went around to Peters' side of the Rover, reached in through the window, and put it in gear, turning the steering wheel to the right. It started to move slowly towards the washout. *Hurry up,* Santiago thought. He watched for a few seconds then went around behind the Rover and pushed, sending it over the edge. It landed very convincingly nose down. No airbag deployed. *This Rover must be at least fifteen years old,* Santiago thought.

Santiago pulled a compact radio out of his pocket, and gave some instructions to his men. He jogged down the sand to the sea, and swam out fifty yards, where his "assistants" picked him up in a black rubber boat. They motored down the coast until Frank's house came into view, then switched to paddles for the last bit, beaching out of sight behind a small dune. Santiago crept up the beach and around towards the back of the house.

Frank was just drying off from his cold-water shower when Santiago came in silently through the back door. Frank had used the manual crank to raise all the hurricane shutters when he got home, and opened all of the windows and doors to let the wind blow through. Santiago simply walked up behind him, reached around and thrust a thin blade up under the left rib cage. It took Frank about three minutes to die. He could feel the pain, and could imagine his pericardium filling with blood, making his heart's contractions become slowly more and more useless. He wasn't really surprised, somehow. *Excellent knife placement*, he thought. *There'll hardly be any blood to clean up. Nothing beats professional handiwork.*

The men put his body in the rubber boat and set to work on the house. They busied themselves tidying up the place, washing and putting away dishes, sweeping the floor, putting away all the clothes that were strewn about. A well-used suitcase was in a closet, which they packed with clothes, toiletries, and underwear. They found Frank's passport in a fireproof box in the bedside dresser. Santiago closed the storm shutters and locked the door behind them. They took the suitcase with them as they pulled the boat back down the beach, sweeping the sand behind them with palm fronds. The phony police boat was now just out past the surf, and they loaded everything in and headed for the Compound.

Halfway there, in the middle of the Caribbean, they spent an hour dismembering Frank and the other body, putting the pieces into a dozen wide-mesh bags with rocks, which they then dumped overboard at intervals on the remainder of the journey. *As should have been done in the first place.* Santiago was annoyed. He would have done it right if he hadn't been on the mainland that day. It was surprisingly difficult to get good help.

Back at the Compound, Santiago went to see Blaylock, the computer geek. He tossed the passport on his desk. "I need it to look like this guy went back to the States before the hurricane."

Blaylock looked up. "When is he actually going back?"

Santiago shook his head. "He's not. We just don't want an investigation here."

Blaylock picked up the passport. "What do we know about this guy? I can show him on passenger manifests and through passport control, but what makes you think people back home in – "he looked at the passport, " – Minneapolis will believe he was there if no one saw him?" He shook his head. "Give me some time to check it out. Come back in an hour."

Santiago left. Blaylock sighed and turned to his computer.

An hour later, Santiago was back.

"Okay," Blaylock started, "We've had some luck. Looks like he lives alone, no relatives in town. I got into his home and cell records, definitely a loner. Been on Barbuda for the past three months, only made a couple of calls off island, most recently a couple of weeks before the storm to another guy who works at the Minnesota State Medical Examiner's Office, same as our guy. From his Netflix account it looks like he watches TV all night, every night. Orders a lot of pizzas. I hacked into American Airlines and inserted him onto the passenger manifest from Antigua to Miami four days ago, with connections to Minneapolis arriving at 11:50 p.m. His passport shows up as cleared in Miami, but if anyone checks the security tapes, he won't be there. Nothing I can do about that. Here are the boarding passes." He handed Santiago a Ziplock bag.

Santiago thought a minute. "What kind of pizza does he like?"

Blaylock started typing. "Ham and pineapple. In June, he ordered pizza from Dominos eleven times, all ham and pineapple."

"Okay, can you insert a ham and pineapple pizza the day after his arrival at noon?"

"Piece of cake," Blaylock replied.

Santiago picked up the passport. "What about the passport stamp?"

"The U.S. doesn't stamp citizens coming home. It's all in the computer chip."

Santiago gave the passport, boarding passes, wallet and suitcase to one of his men, and sent him in the launch to Antigua to catch the next flight to Miami. He then called upstairs to *el jefe*.

"Cleaned up," he reported simply.

Chapter 2

Monday, October 3
Minneapolis

Alice looked up as Jeff tapped on her door frame, his white lab coat filthy, as usual. "Still not here?" she asked. Jeff shook his head. Alice glanced at the clock. 8:31. She had been supervising the Medical Examiner's office for nearly twenty years, and in all that time, Frank Lenz had never been more than ten minutes late without calling, and THAT had only happened once or twice. She tried his home phone and cell yet again. Still nothing. Finally, she called Frank's job-share partner, Hal Jensen, on his cell.

"Hi Hal, it's Alice."

"Alice, terrible to hear from you. I'm supposed to be off for three months."

"Frank didn't show up this morning, and he's not answering his phones. I wondered if you knew anything."

"Nope, last I talked to him was about a month ago. He said he would be back in town the end of last week. Maybe I should go check on him. I have a key to his house."

Hal grumbled to himself on the way over to Frank's bungalow overlooking the Mississippi. *I should have known Frank would screw me on this. I should have taken the first three months off,* he thought. He had been planning on spending the next three months fishing and, well, fishing. *So much for a job share.*

No one answered when he knocked, so he let himself in. The house felt empty. Stale. He went into the kitchen. There were some Domino's boxes in the trash, with a couple of old slices of pizza. Hard as boards, must have been at least a week old. His bed was un-made, and there was a towel on the bathroom floor. Bone dry. Frank's wallet was on the bathroom counter, along with his passport and an American Airlines boarding pass, Miami to Minneapolis from two weeks previously. *Curious,* he thought. *Not like Frank to be anywhere without his wallet. OCD that way.* He called Alice on his cell and described the situation.

"Better call Mitzi and see if she knows anything," she advised.

Hal groaned. "Really, you should call her. You know, woman to woman."

"Make the call, Hal. I'm going to call Lieutenant Choi. This sounds fishy, and he and Frank are tight. I'll tell him you're there waiting for him."

Hal had known Mitzi Lenz literally her whole life, and could hardly have been less enthusiastic. He pulled her number off his contacts list, and rang her office. She didn't answer. He found himself in one of those government phone trees designed to push the unstable into a homicidal frenzy. After who knew how many steps, her clipped voice intoned, "Dr. Lenz. Leave a message." He left a simple, "Hal Jensen here. Call me regarding Frank ASAP," and his number.

He sat on Frank's porch enjoying what was likely one of the last warm days of the fall. A blue sedan pulled up, and Dan Choi walked up the path. "Hey Hal, what's up? Alice said Frank is missing. Thought I'd come by myself and check it out."

Hal took him on the tour. Choi was careful, treating the house like a crime scene. After twenty years in Homicide, he treated EVERYTHING like a crime scene. He looked at the boarding pass. "How long do you keep YOUR boarding passes?" He asked.

"Not a clue. Usually toss them when I get home and empty my pockets, I guess."

Choi pulled an ivory pair of chopsticks from his jacket pocket and manipulated the passport open. "Great picture. Makes him look ten years younger."

Hal looked over his shoulder. "It's almost ten years old. From before when Jill died."

Hal's phone rang, or rather whistled. The theme song from *The Andy Griffiths Show*. Lieutenant Choi rolled his eyes. Hal answered on speaker. "Hello."

"Mitzi Lenz here. What's the problem?"

"Hi Mitzi, it's Hal Jensen. Frank didn't come into work today, and we are getting worried. Have you talked to him lately?"

"Friday morning ten days ago."

"So, he was home in Minneapolis?"

"No, on his island, riding out the hurricane. He called to discuss a case that turned up there."

Choi broke in "Are you sure he was on the island? His boarding pass says he came back to the U.S. the Monday before that."

"Who are you?"

"Lieutenant Choi of MPD."

"Yes, I'm sure he was on the island, he was calling on a friend's satellite phone. Tell me exactly what you are finding there."

Hal described the place.

"Dad would never walk out of the house without his wallet. EVER. Not even to take out the garbage. And he always put his passport in his firebox the instant he got home. ALWAYS." They could hear her typing." I am flying out this afternoon. Process the house, Lieutenant. What's your fax? I'll send you a formal missing person's report, he's been missing more than forty-eight hours, along with a copy of my power-of-attorney to access all his records. He signed it to me right after Mom died." She hung up.

Choi raised his eyebrows towards Hal. "She seemed, uh, forceful."

Hal laughed grimly. "Oh, you have no idea."

* * *

United had a flight out of Newark at 10:40, and Mitzi landed in Minneapolis at 12:55. She was at the house by two. There was a uniformed cop barring the door, but he was able to get Lieutenant Choi on the phone, who drove over. Mitzi was seething.

Choi shrugged. "You asked for a crime scene, you got a crime scene. You can come in with me, just don't touch anything."

She looked at him. "I have been working FBI crime scenes for a dozen years. I know the drill." They put on the lint-free shoe covers and went in. There were two techs dusting the kitchen and bathroom for prints. "What about the boarding pass?" she asked.

"Sent to the lab with the wallet and passport."

They went to the bathroom, where the towel was still on the floor. "Dad always threw his towel over the shower door, never on the floor." Choi showed her where the wallet and passport had been. "Impossible, impossible, impossible," she muttered. Next she asked to look at the garbage. The two slices of mummified pizza were still there. "Ham and pineapple. That's not right. He only ate ham and pineapple in the spring. Fall is pepperoni. Look," she pointed, "no receipts stuck to the boxes. These were carry out, not delivery. Dad ALWAYS got delivery. I've seen enough. Let's go to the lab."

Choi obligingly drove her down to the crime lab, where the items from Frank's house were still in bags. She pitched a fit until the tech examined the boarding pass. Clean, no prints. "Fresh out of a printer," she muttered. The wallet and passport were covered with smudged prints, as expected.

Choi's cell rang, and he picked it up. "Choi." He listened. "Thanks." He hung up.

"That was one of my detectives who was following up with immigration. The system shows him coming in through Miami at the right time. He's checking with the airlines now."

"Waste of time." Mitzi was annoyed. "He was never here. I spoke with him on the island four days after that flight. The real question is why someone bothered to make it look like he was here. What was the point? Thanks for your help. I'm heading back to New York. I'll be flying to Antigua tomorrow."

Choi watched her leave. She was probably right, but he still would run down the few loose ends in Minneapolis. Definitely an enigma.

* * *

Cameron Hansen sighed as he looked at his phone. *Mitzi. What now?*

She was exhausting. Most people with that level of intensity burned out quickly, but she seemed to just go on and on.

The text was simple enough. "Pick me up 11:42 p.m. EWR Delta 5573 from MSP. Boarding now. No excuses. Phone off."

He checked the time. 7:45. Maddening. He HAD a life, after all. And it was not like she was his girlfriend. THAT thought brought a shiver. He was not even sure that "friend" really described their relationship, although he was certain that Mitzi would quote some definition that she would claim proved it did. Go-to-colleague-who-you-can-depend-on-to-have-your-back would be a good descriptor. Which, on reflection, he had to admit sounded suspiciously like "friend," after all.

In any case, there was no question of not picking her up. It really was not like he actually *did* have a life, anyway.

As he sat in the cell phone waiting lot at Newark, Cameron asked himself how it had come to this. Working as an analyst in the New York Homeland Security Anti-Terrorism Unit was boring. He had not joined the CIA with the plan of sitting in an office. He stretched out his right foot, testing the ankle. Still, every day above ground was a good thing. So, here he was, waiting for Mitzi.

He had met Mitzi working on a joint FBI-CIA team on a case involving a cell of would-be bombers who had succeeded in setting their own apartment on fire. Mitzi was the forensic pathologist, and they became acquaintances. The kind that discussed both cases and personal issues professionally and with complete objectivity. Mitzi's mother had just died, and to hear her talk about it, the only thing that really bothered her was that she had not been able to do the autopsy herself. She was beautiful, in an icy blond nordic way, and he had tried to flirt. Her apparent immunity to his usually persuasive charms initially convinced him she was gay, but eventually he had decided that she was simply asexual. He had finally come to the conclusion that embracing her would have about the same satisfaction level as embracing a floor lamp, except with less warmth. More like a bookshelf. So, when she invited him to come to her apartment after their third autopsy, he had been completely unprepared for her raw passion. He was even less prepared for the fact that, afterwards, she never changed her demeanor towards him whatsoever. Just a half-dozen sporadic encounters over the course of a couple of years. Weird. Like some Vulcan who was a robotic android except during mating season. He finally told her "no more," which also did not seem to change their relationship in any noticeable way.

His phone chirped. Mitzi was at the curb. He sighed and drove up to the terminal. Mitzi jumped in. "Something happened to my dad. Someone tried to make it look like he was in Minneapolis when I know he was in Barbuda and I'm sure it had to do with the body he told me about when he called."

Cameron interrupted. "You're welcome, nice to see you as well." Mitzi did not look amused.

"Fine, forget the amenities, but please start at the beginning."

Mitzi took a deep breath and recounted the events of the day. "There is no way he was ever back in Minneapolis."

"Fine, I'm convinced. It certainly seems plausible that something happened in Barbuda that someone is covering up. You said you talked to him. What do you remember about the conversation?" Mitzi glared. She then repeated what Frank had told her, verbatim. Cameron mused.

"What would be the point of mounting a connector to the spine?"

"Nerve stimulation. It is the only thing that connects the dots. Some sort of cerebral harness used to transmit signal to the lower spinal cord.

Like for lower limb reanimation."

"Does something like that even exist?"

"I'd bet you a dollar."

Cameron was silent. He NEVER bet against Mitzi.

* * *

He drove to her building. "Come in," she ordered. He tried to object, it being one a.m., but she was having none of that. She booted up her computer and logged into her Verizon account, checking the call log. "He called me from Barbuda on the morning of the twenty-third."

"*If* he was even in Barbuda. With a sat phone, there is no way of actually knowing where he was," Cameron pointed out.

"He *told* me he was in Barbuda. There is no conceivable reason he would have lied about that."

"That we know of."

Mitzi opened her mouth, then shut it again and turned back to her screen. She retrieved the number of the satellite phone. She dialed the number, but it went straight to a message stating it did not accept messages.

"It's 2:30 in the morning in Barbuda," Cameron noted. "Plus, most people only turn them on when they are someplace with no regular service. Did he tell you the name of his friend?"

"I'm quite sure I already recounted our entire conversation in detail. All 796 words, 812 if you count contractions as two words." She did not add "idiot," for which he was grateful. And a little surprised.

She grabbed her bag. "Let's go downtown. You can get to the phone records at the office." Before he objected, she continued, "And since the provenance was outside the U.S., and involves falsifying immigration documents, this clearly falls under ATU jurisdiction. Let's go." Cameron followed her out.

* * *

The Anti-Terrorism Unit never slept, but there were only a relatively few analysts there, since nothing in particular was brewing. Cameron went to his desk, and logged into the system. The satellite phone was registered to Bill's Beach Bar in San Diego. No answer at the business number, just a cheery recording stating that they opened at eleven. Twenty minutes later he had tracked down the number for the bar's owner, Gabe Sinclair. No answer on his land line, just a message that said "Don't leave a message, we never check this phone." Cell phone went straight to voice mail, which was full.

"We'll have to wait for the bar to open," Cameron remarked. Mitzi did not answer, just scowled and went to the break room, curled up on the couch, and was instantly asleep.

* * *

Mitzi was up at eight, and started calling Gabe's home and mobile numbers every ten minutes. She was fuming. "Who doesn't answer their phone?" she demanded. Cameron foolishly started to answer, "People who run bars," but her glare was a clear indicator that there was no need. She busied herself booking them on the 10:55 a.m. non-stop to Antigua, arriving at 4:10.

Cameron was unsure. "I think we should verify the phone owner's whereabouts before racing off. Could be a waste of time."

"That was clearly Dad's last known location, so we will need to go there regardless."

"I still think that talking to witnesses is more efficient than literally flying off half-cocked."

By nine, there was still no answer, and it was time to go. "Look," Cameron said, "if we are off line on a plane, we won't be even able to talk to anyone in California, and the plane takes off before the bar opens."

"Fine." She canceled their reservation. "I'll book the next flight." She tapped and waited. Then howled and pounded her fist on the desk. "The next flight does not get there until 12:10 in the afternoon tomorrow, going on Air Canada via Toronto!" She continued to tap. "AND I can't rebook this close to the one you just made me lose." More typing. "We are on the last flight that makes the Toronto connection, 9:00 p.m. out of Newark. We will be on that flight. Info or no info." Her tone did not encourage further discussion.

Gabe himself finally answered at the bar at 1:45, fifteen minutes before opening time in San Diego. Cameron snatched the phone from Mitzi. "Hello Mr. Sinclair, this is Federal Agent Cameron Hansen calling regarding a satellite phone registered to your name." Mitzi was trying to grab the phone, but he batted her away. "Yes, sir, there is a missing person who was last heard from on that phone on September twenty-third. We think he was in Barbuda." Cameron was nodding and writing. "Have you spoken to him recently? Uh hum, uh hum. Is your wife available to speak to us? Thanks." He covered the mouth piece. "It's his father-in-law, William Jacobs, lives on Barbuda. His wife talks to him every Sunday. Doesn't have any other phone, only turns the satellite phone on to make calls. Been living there for twenty years, finally agreed to the weekly calls a couple of years ago." Cameron was back on the phone. "Hello, Mrs. Sinclair, yes, this is Agent Hansen calling. Did you speak with your father this past Sunday? Good, good. Did he mention any friends or acquaintances on the island? Is that so. Anything else? Do you have any other way to contact him? No, ma'am, we have no reason to believe he is in any danger. Do you have another number that we can use to reach you?" He scribbled it down. "Thank you so much, have a nice day."

"Apparently it was the usual quick call, more a 'proof of life' than a conversation. She asked about the hurricane. He said he was fine, but the whole island was a mess. Nothing about any friends or any further details. I guess we're headed to the island."

"Wasted a day," Mitzi replied.

Chapter 3

Wednesday, October 5
Antigua

Cameron was still grousing about his night trying to sleep in a chair in the Toronto airport when they landed in Antigua. "We would have only been two hours later if we had left this morning through Miami," he grumbled.

"We would have been here yesterday if you hadn't pushed me to cancel that flight."

He had no further response.

They went straight to the St. John's constabulary, showed their credentials, and were introduced to the duty officer.

"Look," he said, after listening to Mitzi, "I'm sorry about your father being missing, but the islands were hit hard by the hurricane on the twenty-first and twenty-second, things were a major mess both here and on Barbuda."

"Were you in touch with Barbuda on the twenty-third?" Mitzi insisted.

"As I said, the phones were out." He consulted a log book. "And the duty officer did not record anything about any wireless transmissions that day."

"Can we speak to him?" Mitzi asked.

"That would not be possible," came the reply. "Afraid the poor chap died that day. Neck broken. Still under investigation, but it looks like a homicide."

"Are there a lot of homicides here? Seems like a tropical paradise to me," Cameron asked.

"Well, we had ten last year, all but one related to drug trafficking."

"How about on Barbuda?"

"Last murder there was in 2007. Tourist-on-tourist crime."

"Who do we talk to on Barbuda?"

"McCabe is the constable there now. May not be too much help, though. He took over after the hurricane. I'll ring him up for you."

"Just let him know we're coming to see him," said Mitzi. "I want to get over as soon as possible."

"Well, the boat heads over at nine in the morning. Unless you charter a helicopter, which is about a thousand dollars, you won't be going until then."

"Where do I charter a helicopter?"

* * *

Mitzi hated helicopters. The noise was bad enough, but the way it felt like her bottom slipped around as they left the ground always made her queasy. As they climbed to a thousand feet, the pilot, a chipper fellow with a shocking mass of orange-dyed dreadlocks, offered to give them an aerial tour of Antigua. "Just get me to Barbuda ASAP," Mitzi snapped. He shrugged and pointed out a dot barely visible near the horizon to the north. "There she is, missy, about fifty kilometers away. Have you there in a jiffy."

* * *

As soon as the pilot dropped them off at the tiny Codrington airfield, he radioed the Compound. Santiago took his report, and went upstairs to talk to *el jefe*.

Juan Carlos Perez was in the pool, swimming with powerful strokes from his massive arms. Santiago waited at the shallow end. One did not interrupt *el jefe* during his swim. Perez did six more laps, then waved him over.

"Speak."

"Two Americans, a man and a woman, urgent helicopter jump from Antigua to Codrington. Didn't seem like a couple, did not go to the resorts. Seemed from their conversation that they were going to speak with the constable about someone who went missing after the hurricane. The pilot didn't get much more, but he thought he should call it in."

"Who do we have on Barbuda?"

"Marcello is working at the Caribbean Jewel. And Alyssa is there, I think."

"Marcello is clumsy. Leave him out of it. Have Alyssa watch for them at the constabulary, see if she can learn anything. Tell her to keep it simple." He resumed swimming.

* * *

"You've got to be kidding!" Cameron folded himself into the Fiat 500. "This is really all you have?"

The rental attendant smiled and shrugged.

"Ignore him," Mitzi said to the man, waving a map. "Do you know William Jacobs? Lives north of town?"

"Sure, everyone knows Mr. Jacobs. He was here before me, and I was born here." He pointed on the map. "His place is about here, painted bright yellow about ten years ago, so now kind of dull yellow."

They drove south first to Frank's place. The cottage was buttoned up tight, hurricane shutters closed, storm debris strewed over the property.

Mitzi hammered on the door. "Dad, are you in there?" There was no answer. "We should break in."

"Let's go get the property manager and her keys. Nothing's going to change in a half hour, and breaking in would be a chore."

* * *

Jenneane Collins was several hundred pounds of sweaty loquaciousness. "Frank is such a dear."

"Have you seen him since the hurricane?"

"No, I thought he left before then. I don't have renters for his cottage until the end of the month, so I really didn't have any particular need to call on him. I was planning on going over next week to get things ready. I'll drive over with you. But not in that," she said, wagging her finger towards the Fiat.

Cameron was more than happy to hop into her mammoth Lexus SUV.

As they drove down the coast road, she pointed out a large sink hole. "That's where poor Peters was killed."

"Who was Peters?"

"He was the constable here. He died the day after the storm, drove straight into that hole. Such a tragedy. I had seen him earlier that day with the folks from Antigua, always such a nice boy."

"Which folks from Antigua?" Cameron was suddenly alert.

"Not sure. The police boat docked at the main pier, and then I saw them get into the constabulary's Land Rover and head towards the station."

"So this was on Friday the twenty-third?" Cameron checked. "Were they policemen, then?"

"Yes, the Friday. Not policemen, no, something else. I think they were fetching something, because they came back through a while later and loaded a large bag onto the boat. The man who appeared to be in charge left again with Peters. I went over to the Flamingo about then to have a bath, my power being out and all. The boat was gone when I got back."

"Did you talk to the police about all this?"

"No, no particular reason to."

* * *

"What a mess," Jenneane said as they came around the bend. There was debris everywhere, including an entire palm tree smashed into one wall of the shed. "Generator was in there," Jenneane remarked, "Have to get someone in to fix that."

She unlocked the front door and flipped the switch to raise the storm shutters. "At least the power has been restored here. Some parts of the island are still out," she remarked.

Mitzi looked around, suddenly sad that she had never come down to visit her father here. Everything looked normal enough, like he had closed it up and left. "Anything look out of order to you?" she asked Jenneane.

"Well, as a matter of fact, Frank always locked up his clothes and personal things in the back closet when he left. He must have thought he would be back. Awfully clean if he was coming back, though."

Mitzi and Cameron spent an hour going through the house while Jenneane watched House Hunters International on TV. Mitzi called to Cameron from the kitchen. She was kneeling on the tile floor. "Look at this. There's blood in the grout."

She scrounged in the drawers and came up with a Ziplock bag, and then scraped in some of the discolored grout. Cameron was impatient. "Even if it is blood, even if it is HIS blood, people bleed in their own homes all the time. Wouldn't mean anything." Mitzi ignored him.

There was an old but clean Jeep Wrangler in the garage, keys hanging on a peg. "He leaves the car for his renters when he leaves," Jenneane explained, "gets a taxi into town."

They found nothing else, and rode back to Codrington in silence.

* * *

"Constable or Jacobs?" Cameron asked.

"Jacobs." If we see the constable first he may insist on going with us, and I would rather talk to Jacobs on our own. You know, American to

American. In fact, I'm not sure I feel the need to let the locals know about Jacobs at all."

* * *

Jacobs was casting into the surf, but did not seem to be disturbed at the interruption.

"Yep, Frank came up that day, and we went down to the constabulary. Island was even more of a mess then than it is now. You his daughter? The one he called that day?"

"Yes, Mr. Jacobs," Mitzi started.

"Please, William. Mr. Jacobs makes me feel old," he interrupted with a wink.

"Mitzi. Have you seen him since then?"

"Nope. But that don't mean nothing, no reason I should've. Plus, he said he had to go back to the mainland to get back to work."

"What about the body you saw?"

"Pretty grisly. Bloated up, top of the head cut off, all the small parts gnawed away and all. Seen worse in Korea, though. Peters was green."

"Peters the constable?"

"Yep. Killed in an accident later that same day. Drove straight into a sink hole off the road south, from what I understand. Roads are still a mess, as I'm sure you saw. I've only gone into the post office once. Sorry, don't know anything more."

"Thanks for your help," Cameron said before they squeezed into the Fiat and headed back to town.

* * *

"They did not mention on Antigua that Peters was killed." Mitzi was indignant. "Don't you think that would have been something they should have told us?" Cameron didn't have an answer.

Constable McCabe was at the constabulary waiting for them.

"They called and told me you were coming. Expected you hours ago, to be honest."

"We went to look at my father's place first. It took a while to get the property manager and all. Do you know her? Mrs. Collins?"

"No. I just transferred over here, really don't know anyone yet."

"Yes, we heard that your predecessor was killed in an accident."

"Yes, that's right, one of the residents discovered him dead in his

31

Rover in a sink hole the Saturday before last. Looked like he'd been dead a day or so."

"Anything odd about the accident?" Mitzi asked. "What did the autopsy show?"

"There was no autopsy. We don't do autopsies for motor accidents. Particularly with all the mess after the hurricane. I did the examination at the scene. Nothing to say. He took a nose-dive into a sinkhole, broke his skull on the windscreen. Poor blighter."

"What about the corpse he and my father had found? The one that washed up?"

McCabe stared. "What are you talking about? I don't know anything about any corpse."

Mitzi started to tell him what she knew, but stopped as Cameron gripped her arm. "We had heard there was a body they brought here," he broke in.

"Someone must have been telling hurricane ghost stories. There was nothing here, everything was ship-shape."

"Probably so," Cameron laughed. Then added, like a new thought, "Could we see the Rover?"

"I don't see why not. But look, it's getting dark, and you won't see much. How about tomorrow morning? Say noon?"

"Perfect," Cameron replied.

They drove out to the Caribbean Jewel. Mitzi was fuming. "You certainly did not push him on anything."

"He doesn't know anything, he wasn't here."

"Oh, so now you know that Daddy disappeared on the twenty-third? It could have been any time since then, as far as you know!"

"Possible, but by the time McCabe got here the next day, there was no body and no Peters, so it makes more sense that, IF there is something fishy going on, that was the day."

"Jacobs is still there," Mitzi observed.

"Maybe whoever they are didn't know about him."

They booked into a two-room suite. Mitzi went straight into her room and slammed the door.

Chapter 4

Thursday, October 6
Barbuda

First thing in the morning, Cameron was on the phone with the Chief in St. John's. "We talked to a woman who says a police boat was here in Codrington on the twenty-third. What was that about?"

"Not possible," he replied. "We were fully engaged in rescue operations here, about four hundred people were stranded in areas not accessible by land after Hurricane Marge came through. The whole force, including all our boats, was tied up. I would have had to personally approve a trip over to Barbuda, and that never happened. She must be mistaken on the day. We sent a boat over the next day, when Peters was found. That must be what she saw."

"What she saw," Cameron replied, "was Peters driving them towards the constabulary, and then returning with a large heavy bag that they loaded onto the police boat."

* * *

Breakfast at the Jewel was what Cameron thought of as thoroughly British, with eggs, toast, and thick ham steaks. Then they headed back to Codrington. "Park near the dock," Mitzi directed. They got out and started into the small shops along the road, looking for anyone who had seen anything that day. Some of the shops were still closed, and after a couple of hours of talking to cheery shop owners who turned cool as soon as they picked up the interrogation vibe, they found only one person who had been there at the time in question. He was the proprietor of a driftwood art shop, a tiny, round, red-faced man, and he was pretty sure that the constable's Rover had been up and down the street a couple of times that day, but he was somewhat near-sighted, and he did not have any recollection of seeing who was in the car.

They continued walking along the street to the constabulary. As they got close, a trim brunette with deeply tanned skin popped out from a doorway, nearly bowling Mitzi over. "Sorry," she puffed, "I wasn't looking out well. Always rushing about for no reason."

"No problem," Mitzi replied, "were you around the Friday after the hurricane?"

"Oh, I'm always around. Can I help you with something? And how do you do, my name's Alyssa."

Cameron took her offered hand. "You'll have to excuse Mitzi, she has had a bit of a shock. My name is Cameron."

"How do you do."

"Anyway," Mitzi continued, "on that Friday did you see Peters driving around in the Rover, like to the dock?"

"No, I don't think so. Poor Peters, such a tragedy."

Mitzi was impatient, "And how about a police boat coming into the dock? Anything else unusual that day?"

"Pretty much everything was unusual that day, but no, nothing like a police boat. Your husband said you had a shock?"

"He's not my husband and I am not prone to having shocks. Thanks for your help." She darted into the constabulary.

"Sorry for the trouble, ma'am," Cameron added, and followed her in.

* * *

Alyssa crossed the street and ducked into a doorway fifty yards down, where she could watch the constabulary. She called the Compound, reporting what she had heard. A few minutes later the garage door opened and McCabe drove out with Cameron and Mitzi in the back. They turned right and headed up the street out of town. Alyssa darted around the corner, re-emerging seconds later on a moped, a blond wig showing under her helmet as she went up the road.

She was expecting them to head south on the coast road, and so hung back to avoid detection. When she finally crested the hill, to her surprise, there was no sign of the brand new Rover. She was puzzled, but disguised or not, she did not fancy driving up and down the side streets looking for them. She went back to her second-floor apartment overlooking the street, with a view of the port as well, and sat at her window to watch.

Three blocks away, Mitzi was scrutinizing Peters' wrecked Rover. "Why are there three separate cracks in the windshield? And why are they all in the lower third? If Peters took a dive into the sink hole, you would expect one break, and probably in the upper third, if you think about the trajectory. Unless he was belted, but you say he was not, and I would think even you would know whether you had needed to unbuckle him. Where is the body? I want to do an autopsy."

McCabe was overwhelmed. "You'll have to talk to the authorities in Antigua. His body was released to his family the following day. I have no idea what happened to him after the service. Buried, no doubt."

"Let's get back to Antigua," Mitzi snapped to Cameron. "Call the helicopter."

"Forgive me ma'am," McCabe cut in, "but the ferry leaves in an hour, save you hundreds."

"Perfect." Cameron was ready for some sanity. They rode back to the dock, where they turned in their car and purchased tickets for St. John's. Just before the boat left at four, Alyssa jogged up the ramp, spotted them, and headed their way.

"Hullo again," she beamed at Cameron. "Didn't know you were heading over to Antigua. Find what you were looking for?"

Mitzi turned. "Do you spend much time in Antigua?"

"Just popping over to do some shopping and visit a friend," she replied.

"Must be a close friend. You have no bag." Mitzi turned away and said nothing more for the entire ninety-minute crossing.

* * *

When they docked, Mitzi grabbed Cameron's arm to stop him from getting up. The awkwardness was finally too much for Alyssa, who got up with a cheery "Bye, now," and disembarked. Mitzi watched her as she slowly made her way up the landing, and did not rise until she rounded the corner at the top of the hill.

"Close enough friend to keep her underwear and toothbrush, but not close enough to meet her," she remarked.

They jumped into a taxi at the wharf and had the driver take them up to the lookout before calling the chief inspector.

Cameron inquired after Peters' remains. "Buried on the twenty-eighth. I was there, we all were."

"I need to have him exhumed to do an autopsy." Mitzi was emphatic.

"I'll need a little more than your say so for that. His people won't like it. What do you think you are looking for?"

Mitzi explained the windshield.

"Listen, I think it is time you told me what you think is going on. I can't just have two Americans poking about my islands willy-nilly."

"We're staying at the Blue Bay Inn, Bungalow 4. Meet us in thirty minutes."

* * *

When the Chief rapped on the door, Mitzi popped it open and fairly dragged him in. As they laid out the whole situation, he started to nod.

"Right, let's say that your father never left Barbuda, but was taken or worse by someone who did not like him having seen this alleged corpse, and that same someone somehow killed Peters and made everything disappear. Why did they leave this Jacobs?"

"It's possible they did not know about him. He may not have been mentioned when Peters contacted this conveniently dead Simmons, so they did not know about that loose end. What are the chances someone on the island has a phony police boat?"

"Not likely. We are constantly patrolling, trying to interdict the narcotics trafficking."

"Do you have any thoughts?"

"Well, as a matter of fact, there is a small privately held island north and west of here. Very private, mysterious almost. I've long been concerned there was something going on over there. The fishermen have reported seeing men patrolling the bluffs with rifles. It is out of my jurisdiction, and there has not been any traffic between here and there, other than small launches buying food and such. Lots of food, actually. There are likely forty or fifty people there, by our estimates. If there is something going on, my money would be on Isla Sofia."

"Who owns the island?"

"We really don't know. Sixty years ago, some Cuban developers were building a resort, but it was damaged in a storm, and then, after the revolution, it was abandoned. Rumors are that now it is used by one of the drug cartels."

"Which one?" asked Cameron.

"Like I said, rumors. Some say the Hidalgo, others the Ojo del Diablo."

Cameron was about to ask another question, but saw a movement out of the corner of his eye. He spun and jerked open the French doors to the veranda. The silhouette of a lithe figure jumped over the rail at the far side of the deck and ran across the grass. He started to give chase, but stumbled as he tried to vault the fence, and landed heavily on his bad ankle. The shadow melted into the trees.

"That was Alyssa," he stated.

"How could you possibly tell that?" Mitzi asked.

"I watched her walk for quite a while earlier. I have a, er, talent for remembering gaits."

"You mean asses." Mitzi rolled her eyes. "Well, she's gone."

Cameron jumped up and opened the door. "Thanks, Chief." The Chief rose slowly to his feet, and before he knew it, Cameron was shaking his hand and letting him out. "I don't think we need bother Peters' family. You've been a big help."

The Chief found himself outside. He considered banging on the door, then decided against it. "Cheeky blighter," he thought, then got back into his car and drove off.

* * *

Cameron made a phone call, gave a code and their address, and twenty minutes later they were picked up by a trim man in golf shirt and chinos. He had driven in via the west entrance, passing an unseen Alyssa who was watching from the tree line by the side of the road. They left to the east, and drove in total silence to a lovely home overlooking the harbor. He escorted them upstairs, where a steel door opened into a loft with thick green window glass and metal blinds. He handed Cameron a bulky phone, asked them if they needed anything, and left, showing them how to bolt the door and operate the intercom to his residence downstairs. "Call me when you are ready to leave or if you need anything. There is food in the fridge and beds in the adjoining rooms."

"Okay spymaster," Mitzi said at last, "who was that, where are we, and what are we doing?"

"That was the U.S. Consul to Antigua and Barbuda, who works for the East Caribbean Embassy in Barbados. This is his secure communications room, and this," he waved the phone, "is a secure scrambled satellite phone. I'm calling Langley." Which he proceeded to do, holding up a finger at a fuming Mitzi who was trying to get his attention. "Just listen, I'll explain more later."

It took a few minutes, but after giving the duty officer his code and sending his left thumbprint, he was connected to the Deputy Director of Operations. "This better be good, Hansen," the DDO started, "where are you and what have you got?"

Cameron started at the top and gave him the whole story, the body, Frank, Peters, the phony police boat, and finally got to Isla Sofia and Ojo del Diablo. The DDO perked up. "Is this island definitely privately held, not part of any of our sovereign neighborly neighbors?"

"I have no way of verifying that, Director."

"Okay, stay put. I'll contact you when I have something."

"Okay, give," Mitzi was nearly apoplectic. "What is going on?"

"Ojo del Diablo is a Mexican drug cartel. I've known for years that it is actually controlled by Juan Carlos Perez."

"Juan Carlos Perez, the Mexican telecom billionaire?" Mitzi was confused. "He's like a poster boy for the successful self-made Latin American businessman."

"Well, to be honest, many people at the Agency think the whole connection to Perez is dubious. Based mostly on the work of one agent who was working undercover in the organization. His cover was blown, and he failed to get any actionable evidence. But the DDO is a believer, and an anti-drug raid is the perfect excuse – we have reasonable cause to believe that a U.S. citizen was kidnapped and taken there, and 'there' is not part of any country, so minimal opportunity for blowback. The DDO is going to re-task satellites to get more information, verify the status of the island and so forth."

"What are *we* going to do?"

"Just like the man said. Stay put. I'm getting some sleep." He went into the left bedroom and stretched out on the bed, falling asleep instantly. Completely back in operative mode. And it felt great.

Mitzi wanted more information, but could tell that was not happening tonight, so she took the other room and tried to sleep. Less successfully.

* * *

When Alyssa re-approached the bungalow, it was evident that no one was there. She called the Compound and explained to Santiago what she knew. Which was, basically, nothing. He looked at the time, weighing whether *el jefe* would want to know "nothing." He decided that all he risked by reporting was a tongue-lashing, but if *el jefe* felt less than informed, he might lose trust. Which, here on Isla Sofia, was the same as death.

He knocked on *el jefe*'s door, and when he heard the bark, went in.

Perez listened quietly, staring out the window, the light of the thin crescent moon glinting off of the waves below.

"I think it is time to move the project out of this facility," he said after a pause. He picked up a phone from the desk and punched in a long number. "We are leaving. How long to get the *Cortez* to Isla Sofia?" he asked. He listened, nodded. "Yes, the entire complement. That should be fine." He hung up and turned to Santiago.

"They are just approaching Caracas, where there is some cargo which must be unloaded, so the *Cortez* will be here on Saturday in the early afternoon. Ready the *Turtuga Marina* to go immediately, I will leave now with Blaylock and the data. Load the subjects and all the research equipment into the containers as we discussed. The *Cortez* will take everything to Veracruz. The drug operations stay."

Thirty minutes later, Santiago stood on the dock. Perez motored his wheelchair up the ramp onto the yacht. Blaylock followed him, towing a large roller bag. As the hands stowed the gang plank, Perez wheeled around. "Finish up here, and meet me in Basseterre. If anyone comes looking, I want this to look like any other drug facility. Nothing must be left to connect any of this to me. Everyone left here is completely expendable."

The *Turtuga Marina* slid into the night, its wake glowing a phosphorescent green.

Chapter 5

Friday, October 7
Isla Sofia

As soon as it was light, Santiago had the four containers brought up from the dock and placed at the far end of the parking lot behind the loading dock at the east end of the old resort hotel. Two were blue, one red, and one yellow.

"All of the medical equipment and supplies and the computer equipment need to go into the blue containers," he instructed. "Yellow needs to be set up for the subjects. They can be put in tonight so everything is ready for tomorrow."

"What about Red?" asked the crew foreman.

"Extra space if we run out. Nothing must remain of the research equipment."

The twenty men set to work. The biggest challenge was the MRI machine. It was massive, and the only way to remove it quickly was to tear a hole in the side of the building. It filled most of the first blue container. That accomplished, everything else proceeded apace.

While the crew continued to work, Santiago checked his guards in the hallway leading to the other wing. "Remember, NO ONE comes into this wing." The guards all nodded. They had no idea what went on in the east wing, but knew that too many questions led to dead soldiers. He continued into the central part of the hotel, which was completely devoted to the cutting and packaging of cocaine and other illicit products. Out in the old courtyard were the barracks, where the rest of the men were loafing about, just another day in the life of a foot soldier.

* * *

By mid morning, Mitzi was raw. "We have to DO something! How can you just sit there? This is killing me."

Cameron looked up from his novel, a grimy old Ken Follett he had found in a pile of worn paperbacks. "Because there is nothing to do until we hear back."

"Can't we go out? Talk to some more people? At least call Langley for an update. Or how about giving me more of the story on Perez."

Cameron sighed and picked up the sat phone. After going through the same rigmarole he got to the DDO's assistant. "Hansen here. Any news?" He nodded. "How about permission to brief Agent Lenz fully. She's with the ATU in New York. Yes, call me back." He hung up.

"Your FBI status is good and bad," he explained. "Helpful due to your high clearance level. But except on actual joint operations, and sometimes even then, my bosses don't really trust the FBI to do the right thing."

"You mean we like to obey the laws."

"See, it's comments like that which lead to all our problems."

By noon, the crackers and cheese were gone, and they had started to consider making some real food. The phone chirped. Cameron picked it up. "Hansen. Well, that's something. Thanks."

"What?"

"Nothing yet on the target, but I have been authorized to brief you."

"Great, so tell me about Perez," Mitzi started.

Cameron held up his hand. "The first thing you need to know is there is somewhat of an, er, personal aspect to this." He pointed at his leg. "I'm sure you've noted the limp?" Mitzi rolled her eyes and nodded. "My last field operation, six years ago, involved Perez. I'm the guy. My cover was blown, and I was pulled into analytic work. Picked up my limp in the process."

"That's something you won't forget."

"Perez was wounded as well. My shot hit him in the spine, left him paraplegic. Something HE undoubtedly has also not forgotten. Which is why we are staying here, incommunicado. Can't take the chance that he finds out I'm asking questions about his operations. Could lead to complications."

"So, he knew who you were?"

"I was in Ojo del Diablo, undercover. He did not know my real name, but a photo would definitely be a problem, and Alyssa could have easily taken one. I thought I had turned his mistress, but when I pulled out a gun, she must have had a fit of loyalty. She barreled into me, which spoiled my aim and knocked me off a balcony. Shattered my ankle. It may also have saved my life, as it turned out, since the truck I landed on happened to be the surveillance van. They pulled me in and we were gone before his goons had time to react. That was when we first discovered that "*el jefe*" was Perez. And even now it is really only my word. I've managed to build up a pretty good circumstantial case against him, and the DDO seems to buy it. What do you know about him?"

"Isn't he a communications magnate in central America? Worth into the several billions?"

"Yes, MexiVox – phones, computing, plus real estate and shipping. All of that very public, very legit. Except that a surprising number of his contracts turn out to have been one-person bids, all his competitors just seem to mysteriously withdraw themselves from consideration. He also owns a shocking number of politicians, judges, and the like. I'm pretty sure that his underground income from drugs and other criminal activities dwarfs his legitimate holdings, but we are missing a few vital connecting pieces. We have not known his location now for over a year. He has been somewhat reclusive since the "para-sailing accident" that led to his paralysis, and he dropped out of view after a brief appearance at a para-athletic competition last summer when he demonstrated a rudimentary exoskeleton, sort of like the one we saw in Rio."

"Oh yes, I remember that. Pretty much failed completely, as I recall."

"Yes, I'm sure he was not happy with the press." Cameron grinned crookedly. "Did me good to see him, really. I had finally gotten to the point where I was able to run fairly well again, and his pathetic attempt to walk made me feel like I had at least gotten the best of the deal."

"Okay, but how does this relate to the body my father found or his disappearance?"

"Well, obviously there is some sort of spinal research happening, but from the CIA standpoint, this is an opportunity to hit a drug compound and possibly link it to Perez. I hope they are going to let us take it."

At about five, the secure phone rang. It was the Deputy Director himself, and Cameron put him on speaker.

"We're in business. Expect a team to pick you up at 0200 on the southeast side of where Marble Hill Road turns east to become Weatherall's Road. You will rendezvous six kilometers east of Isla Sofia and plan on landfall at 0330. Leave Dr. Lenz in the safe room." The line went dead.

"I'm coming," Mitzi spoke with authority.

"You will stay here. If you play nice, I may be able to get you over there afterwards. And if you even *ask* again, that will NOT be playing nice. I'm getting some sleep." He hit the intercom, told the Consul to be ready to drive him somewhere at 0130, and signed off. He headed into the left-hand room again and closed the door, leaving Mitzi staring. *He's like a completely different man,* she thought. She considered banging on the door, but after analyzing for a few moments, she decided she would do exactly as requested.

* * *

It was well after dusk when the foreman reported to Santiago. "Everything is done except moving the subjects."

"Show me."

Blue 1 was completely full, and some of the medical equipment had been put into Blue 2 with the computers. Yellow looked like a hospital ward room, with everything except beds and patients.

"Looks good. And you are sure that the others don't know anything about this?"

"One hundred per cent. Only my men."

"Perfect. Have the nurses help you move the subjects into Yellow, then assemble everyone at the loading dock for further instructions."

* * *

Santiago sat on the loading dock and watched as the six subjects were rolled into Yellow on their beds, which were secured into position so that the pitch of the ship tomorrow would not be problematic. The men closed and locked the doors of Blue 1, Blue 2, and Yellow. The subjects were sedated, and the two nurses locked in with them were completely reliable.

The twenty workers gathered below him. "Excellent work," Santiago smiled. "I have prepared a surprise." He pulled out a machine pistol. "All of you into the container." He waved the gun towards Red. Two of his guards stepped out of the building, similarly armed. The workers, stunned, shuffled into the container. "All the way back, please." The guards followed them in, guns held at the ready. When everyone was herded to the back, the guards opened fire. They then went back to the hotel and brought down the rest of the medical staff, consisting of an anesthesiologist, a neurosurgeon, and several nurses. Once to the loading dock, they were also shot, and their bodies tossed into Red. The guards looked around. Everything was in order. "Go stack those bodies better," Santiago instructed. We have several more people to take care of." The guards obediently went back into Red. Santiago shot them in the back and swung the heavy doors closed. "Everyone left here is completely expendable," he murmured quietly.

Santiago called the captain of the *Cortez*. "Everything is ready. Four containers. The two blue and the red should be dumped in deep water. Deliver the yellow one to Veracruz as we discussed. What is your estimated arrival time?" He looked at his watch. Barely ten o'clock. The ship should be to Isla Sofia the next morning before noon.

* * *

The whisper-quiet stealth helicopter picked Cameron up at precisely 0200, and lifted off immediately. As they arced north and then west out to sea, he changed into tactical gear, checked his weapons, and was briefed by the mission commander.

"We have eight teams of six timed to be in position at 0315. Satellite recon shows a dock with a couple of small fast-looking boats." He had a schematic up on his tablet, and was pointing as he talked. "There's a compound with one large building about four stories above ground, heat signature indicating more underground elements, and two smaller buildings west of the main structure. We've identified one tunnel egress at the boat dock, and two on the far side above the beach. The above ground complex is surrounded by a spiked wall. We'll land two teams here at the dock, another at the mouths of each of the other two tunnels. The other four teams will deploy inside the compound, two on the ground, two on the roof. The two low buildings are most likely barracks, there would be room for up to fifty men, and there could be additional soldiers inside the main building. We should be able to quickly neutralize the outside forces, and once we have control of the tunnels and the compound, tear gas down the ventilators should be effective in flushing out any resistance. Assuming there is resistance."

"Rules of engagement?" Cameron needed clarity.

"The DDO cleared it through the congressional ops committee. We go in cold. If they fire on us, we are authorized to use all necessary force."

Cameron studied the photos. "What is my assignment?"

"You're with Team One, northern barracks. There would be room between the building and the wall to land, but be prepared to rappel."

Cameron settled in for the flight, massaging his ankle. The commander returned after checking his other men. "How good is the stealth on this thing?" Cameron asked.

"These pilots are the best. We're just clearing the swells by a few yards. These are Black Hawk UH-60's and should be next to impossible to pick up until the last thousand meters or so. At that point, we will be traveling at a hundred and twenty knots and should cover the remaining distance in about twenty seconds. Annoying that we can't go in guns blazing, but I guess we don't have 'hard evidence.' Not that that had always stopped the Agency in the past."

"Have you been in on a lot of Agency activity?"

The commander squinted at Cameron. "Now, you know that if I told you, I'd have to kill you." He laughed and punched him in the arm.

The eight helicopters were at the rendezvous point at 0245, and they proceeded to their assigned points surrounding Isla Sofia.

By 0310 everyone was in position, five thousand meters out, arranged like the spokes of a wheel. "Confirm status," barked the commander into his com. The replies started to come back. "Ready Three." "Ready Six." After getting ready signals from each team leader, he transmitted, "Oscar Mike," and with a chorus of "Roger"s, they started their run.

At 0317 the Compound's security officer was alerted to simultaneous noise from ALL of the outer surveillance buoys surrounding the Island, four thousand meters out. He checked the radar. Nothing. When the inner buoys likewise transmitted noise simultaneously, fifty seconds later, he hit the alarm despite the negative radar.

Santiago was instantly awake, and raced to the window in time to see men rappelling into the Compound. Earsplitting loud speakers from the helicopters screamed out commands to come out with no weapons, delivered in English and Spanish. There was a brief delay, but then there came the deep pounding of machine gun fire out of the barracks buildings, pinning the assault teams to the ground.

Santiago dialed *el jefe*, who, as usual, was calm.

"I did not expect this type of assault. Nor this soon. I will divert the *Cortez*. Destroy as much as you can." The sat phone went dead.

Santiago ran to the loading dock. The noise outside was deafening, but there was pounding from within Yellow. He was taking small arms fire from the roof, and was grazed along his left chest, a burning pain that throbbed and made every breath painful. There was no possibility of getting to the containers, and he sprinted back into the building.

Out in the courtyard, the helicopters' double 7.62 mm machine guns returned fire, shredding the roofs of the small buildings, which had brick walls to a height of about four feet. The machine gun from the south barracks was silenced, but there was still sporadic small arms fire from within the wreckage. The north barracks gunner continued to fire, and the helicopters banked away.

Cameron's team was exposed, deployed into the open space north of their target building. The man next to Cameron was hit full in the chest, throwing him violently onto his back, where he lay writhing in pain despite the body armor which had absorbed the round. The rest of the team inched their way towards the roofless barracks until the leader was close enough to lob in a grenade. The guns inside stopped momentarily, but then resumed.

Santiago ran to a door in the back of the concrete storeroom and opened it, revealing a huge propane tank lying at the core of the building. A large block of C-4 was nestled under the tank, and he set a timer for twenty minutes. He locked the steel door behind him and ran to a manhole-type cover in the floor. He pried it open with a crow bar, and climbed down the long steel ladder to an underground cave. He fired up the waiting mini-sub, and headed out, gliding silently into the Caribbean.

The main building exploded in a fireball, and burning debris rained down on the fighting men. The south barracks was on the receiving end of a large section of wall, which set the remains of the structure on fire, and the surviving defenders crawled out to lay on the grass face down.

The north barracks was still defended, and Cameron inched his way closer. He rolled against the base of the stone foundation, and listened carefully to the gunfire. *Sounds like three shooters,* he thought. The brick wall just ahead of his position was cracked and partly crumbled. He moved closer, then eased out one of the loose bricks. He took three breaths, then brought his eye up to the opening. There were about ten men in the ruins, all but three cowering in a relatively intact corner, with only two actively firing. He maneuvered into a crouch, then stood up quickly and shot them both, as the rest of his squad came up and over the wall. The fighting stopped, and it was eerily silent except for the quiet whoosh of the stealth copters.

The Agency was left with about twenty-five prisoners from the outside barracks and the tunnel guards, who had given up without a fight. Two of the men from Cameron's team had been hit with rubble, and he helped apply field dressings.

47

The mission commander stood alone, staring at the burning ruins. He did not turn when Cameron walked up to him. "Fourteen of my men dead. Both the roof teams were annihilated. Three dead on the ground. Seven wounded." Now he turned and looked straight at Cameron. "For a spook mission. Unbelievable."

"Something important must have been going on here. Otherwise, why destroy the building?"

He just shook his head and walked away.

Divers were deployed in the harbor at first light to check for mines, and finding none, their support ship docked. The U.S. casualties had already been helicoptered to the ship, but the enemy fighters, living and dead, were all still in the compound, where medics were treating their wounded.

The main building continued to burn, and would have to do so, since they had no effective way of fighting the fire. Cameron was unhurt, and was sitting on a piece of rubble when one of the team leaders approached him.

"Agent Hansen? Come with me." He led Cameron around to the back of the east wing.

There was a loading dock, and in the adjacent lot were four large shipping containers. On the left was a red one, which had been opened, and appeared to be filled with bodies. "All shot," the SEAL said simply. Most were in simple work clothes, but two wore fatigues and had rifles, and there were several women and a couple of well-dressed older men. The floor of the container was slippery with blood. To the far right was a blue container, which had been crushed under a large mass of concrete, corresponding to a large defect in the back of the building. Next to it was another blue container, completely intact, and the open door showed a large amount of computers and other technical gear.

Finally, there was a yellow container, which looked like it had been cut in half by a large metal panel of some sort. The entire roof was covered with holes, from the size of a softball to as big as a basketball, with additional debris sprinkled everywhere. The front half had been pried open and was smoldering. There were two badly burned bodies on the floor, and three more, their charred arms still handcuffed to the remains of what looked like hospital beds with rails. The back of the container was blocked by the metal panel, but there was definitely someone alive on the other side, as a steady stream of weeping and Spanish shouting testified.

"There's someone there," Cameron exclaimed. "Let's get him out!"

"Not that easy," came the reply. "That steel panel is wedged tight. It must have confined the fire to the front half. There is a tractor down at the dock, we're bringing it up to see if we can move it. Also there is no guarantee this guy is a friendly."

Cameron couldn't argue with that.

Eventually the tractor was successful. Cameron watched as the panel was dragged free, while three men observed with rifles up and ready. He was greeted by the sight of three more men cuffed to beds. Two were dead from being struck by debris which had rained down through the roof. The third was alive, but there was a large triangle of metal protruding from his belly, and the bed was soaked with blood. He was jabbering mostly incoherently, but Cameron was able to identify the word "diablo."

He tried to calm the hysterical man, and asked in Spanish what had happened.

"They brought me here from my boat, and pounded a chisel in my back, and my legs no longer work," he finally sputtered out in *campesino*-accented Spanish.

"Who brought you here?"

"I don't know, they were like pirates, attacked my fishing boat, and my two brothers and I were all brought here. That was months ago, and there were eight of us here at first, all paralyzed with the chisels. It was horrible. They held me down and screwed something to my back. Then a man hit the chisel with a hammer. I fainted, and when I woke up my legs were dead. Four of us were taken away and I did not see them again until last night, when they brought us here. Two of the ones who had gone away were put in the container with us, but at the front, far from me. I could tell one was my brother. My other brother was next to me, but he no longer answers."

And then, just like that, the man died.

Cameron went back around to the front of the building and found the mission commander. "I have an FBI forensic pathologist over on Antigua. Let's get her over here to help sort out the bodies out back. This is no drug operation."

"I need authorization."

Cameron got on his secure sat phone and was connected to the DDO.

49

After he was briefed on the events, he noted, "Doesn't sound like you have a hard link to Perez."

"Not yet, but we have a container full of computers and equipment, and a bunch of dead patients or experiments or something. We could really use Dr. Lenz over here to help sort things out. She's already involved, and it will take a while to get any other experienced pathologist."

"Fine, give me the commander." Cameron handed over the phone. The commander said simply "Yes, sir," and jogged over to one of the helicopters.

"Thanks," Cameron said into the phone.

There was a long pause, and he was afraid they had lost the signal, then the DDO spoke. "Just find that link, Hansen, and make it solid. I want something besides dead Americans to report to the Committee."

Chapter 6

As Mitzi was en route to the island, Cameron was watching the equipment from the undamaged container being unloaded onto the blacktop of the parking lot. It was mostly computer workstations and several racks of server boxes, but there were some interesting finds. First was a lower body exoskeleton similar to the one Perez had demo'ed at the para games. *Bingo,* Cameron thought. There were several long, thick cables with multi-pin connectors, a complicated carpentry rig, and assorted medical equipment, including an operating table fitted with heavy leather straps.

A generator and a couple of computer techs were brought up from the support ship. After a few minutes, one came over to Cameron. "No hard drives in any of the cases," he reported. "They were all in a box at the back, smashed to pieces. Nothing recoverable." Over the man's shoulder, Cameron could see a helicopter approaching. *Mitzi.*

Mitzi quickly organized the four corpsmen. "Take a million pictures, then bring out all of those bodies from the red container and lay them out on the lot. Search their pockets, put anything you find in one of these Ziplock bags next to the body you find it on. I think that I'll start with the bodies in the hospital beds."

The two bodies on the floor of the yellow container looked like they were female, whereas all the ones in the beds were male. Two of the charred corpses in the front of the container were wearing odd metal helmets. Mitzi felt a rush of adrenaline. She rolled the first one onto its side, and there it was. "Cameron, get over here," she yelled.

"What did you find?"

"Look, these two have helmets, and look on the back." She pointed to the lower spine, where Cameron could see a connector protruding. He stared, then ran out to the pile of computer equipment, returning with one of the cables. It fit. They rolled over the other helmeted corpse, revealing a similar connector. They moved on to the other bodies. Of the four remaining, none had either helmets or connectors, but all had ugly scars over their mid lower backs. Three, including the one Cameron had spoken to, were not burned, and in addition to the scars in the middle of the back, she noted four small healed puncture wounds in identical positions over the pelvic bones. That also clicked for Cameron. He went out again, and came back with the carpentry rig. He placed it on one of the backs. The pelvic wounds lined up with the holes on the sides of the rig. "These look just right for framing screws," he remarked. When placed on the back, there was a short piece of pipe which centered over the spinal wound. "I think that they screwed this on and then pounded a chisel through to cut the spines." Mitzi nodded.

They had put up a large tent in the lot, designed to be a mobile hospital unit, complete with operating tables and lights. Mitzi supervised as the corpsmen moved the bodies in from the yellow container.

She started with one of the unburned bodies, putting it face down on the operating table. She incised carefully around one of the wounds, tracking it down to the spine. It transected the spinal cord at the L4 level, not cleanly between the vertebrae, but rather right through the middle of the bone, with the bone in that area splintered. She showed Cameron. "This is very curious. It would have required significant effort to make a wound that specific. Much easier to let an instrument slide between the vertebrae to sever the cord."

"Do you know what else is curious," he asked. She looked up. "We have dozens of bodies, and so far have not found so much as one cell phone."

"They probably don't have service here."

"Probably not, but my experience is that even the poorest laborers have them, usually a smart phone, and they would never leave them anywhere, even if they could not use them. They are simply too valuable to lose."

"So they must be forbidden."

"Exactly. Someone wanted to make sure there were no photos."

"I need to get a look under these helmets," she said, and looked at the two burned bodies with the headgear. One was a little less charred, and she examined the helmet carefully. She tried to feel around the edges, but could not find a way to get it off. Frustrated, she poked her head out of the tent and called to one of the men outside. "I need a band saw. Is there one down on the ship?"

"Probably, there is a full shop."

"Bring one here. Now."

"What are you going to do?" asked Cameron.

"I have two specimens, so I am going to take an aggressive approach with this one."

When the band saw arrived, she got a couple of the corpsmen to help her saw through the skull a couple of inches below the helmet, taking off the top of the head at the level of the eyebrows, then just over the ears and through to the back. That left about two inches of bone, brain, and burned flesh showing below the helmet. She then set it upside down on a work table. As she worked the brain out around the edges, it was easy going for the first few centimeters, but then the brain was very tightly stuck to the skull. She showed it to Cameron. "This is very unusual. In my large experience with burn victims, brains do NOT fuse to skulls." She worked at it for quite a while, but it would not separate. "Fine," she muttered, and started to scrape the brain away with a scalpel. "Of course," she exclaimed. "Look here. There's no skull under the helmet. There's a fine metal mesh, like a screen for a window, and the brain is firmly stuck to the screen. Like it had healed there."

Cameron was watching, transfixed, unable to move. "Like your dad said. The top of the head was cut off. How long do you think he had been like this?"

"Hard to say, given the burned state, but at a minimum, several weeks. This mesh is fixed to the inside of the skull remnant with what look like tiny staples. The skull edge is nicely healed, at least eight weeks. Yes, completely consistent with what Dad told me." She shook her head slowly. "I guess there's no chance of him being here."

Cameron shifted from one leg to the other. The building behind them was still burning, no one could be alive there. If he had been on the island, he was dead. "No, I'm afraid not."

She turned back to her work.

Once she had the brain completely removed, she could see that the screen or mesh was like a smooth helmet, and the brain was stuck to it wherever it was in contact, but the deep folds of the brain's sulci were not in contact with the mesh at all. "Go find me an electronics expert," she directed Cameron.

He went over to where the techs were still sorting through the computer equipment. "Need a little help over here. Got some interesting stuff." Sandy, a tall, almost wispy man from Cedar Falls, reluctantly followed him back over to the autopsy tent, and after one look, took a few minutes to vomit repeatedly.

Mitch, the corpsman, started to laugh, but stopped when Mitzi casually tossed him the helmet with the attached bone and gristle. "I saw a barbecue grill out front. There will probably be a wire brush. Scrub away all the brain and flesh remnants, then let Sandy here see what he can make of the connections."

Mitch gulped, but pride demanded he not show weakness, and soon, he had just the ivory ring of skull and the bare wire mesh inside the helmet. He brought it back to Sandy.

Sandy could now see that the helmet was secured to the mesh with four snap clamps. He popped those open and the helmet separated easily from the mesh. He was greeted by a mass of wires, attached to the mesh at perhaps a hundred and fifty points, each with five individual strands, for a total of around seven hundred and fifty connections. These all exited at the back of the helmet, ending in a round socket connector three inches across, bristling with connector pins. He showed it to Mitzi and Cameron. That was it, as far as he could tell. Wires attached to mesh. Stuck to brain.

Mitzi resumed working on the back, Cameron watching from a few feet away. "Come look at this," she called over her shoulder, waving him forward. She had cut back the skin above and below the connector. She pointed as she talked. "See, there is this metal plate screwed into the bone of L3 and L5, nice and solid. It looks like basically all of the main body of L4 has been removed. I'm gonna cut out this whole section so I can turn it over and look at the other side." She had acquired a Ka-Bar from someone, and sawed through the ligaments and disc between L2 and L3, then between L5 and S1. Then through the muscle tissue about four inches each side of the spine. She rocked the whole segment back and forth, then was able to get her knife in front of the spine, cutting down to release the block of tissue. She flipped it over and started poking around in the burned tissue. "There is some sort of a box on this side of the plug, and about a hundred wires that look like they are attached to the nerve roots." She called Sandy back over. He pried open the box. Inside were a couple of green circuit boards and a black processor. He poked at it.

"Bet that's a Snapdragon 410 processor," he said, almost enthusiastically.

"What's that?" Cameron asked. "Is that a powerful unit?"

"I'll say," Sandy was nodding, "That's the one Samsung used in last year's Galaxy A5. I mean, sure, they went with the Exynos 7580 this year, but this little baby could probably run command and control for a battleship."

The second body was more badly burned, and the spinal connection was almost completely destroyed. Mitzi turned her attention to the head. Now knowing what to look for, they scrubbed the flesh off the bone and the helmet with the wire brush, found the connecting clamps, and freed the helmet. They were greeted with the same hundred and fifty wires, five strands to a wire, connected to the mesh. "See the difference?" she asked Cameron, pointing at the screen. He stared at it for a minute, then shook his head. She in turn shook hers. "This mesh, instead of being a flat dome, is wrinkled and folded like an actual brain. The first one was just a bowl on top of the brain, but this one has these furrows to contact more of the cortex." She peered at the edges of the skull and ran her finger along it. "This was also attached much more recently, perhaps in the past two to three weeks. It looks like they are making progress."

Another tech poked his head in. "Something you guys will want to see. Turns out that the well-dressed dead guy in the other container actually did have some electronics. His tie tac had one of those novelty spy cameras. One of the guys recognized it from one his uncle has. We've recovered some video."

They went to a workstation where a jewel stud tie tac was attached to a computer with a USB cable. "There are two video clips," the tech said, pointing to the monitor. The first one had a man in a lower body exoskeleton, with a thick cable array coming from a metal helmet like the ones on the burned corpses. He was fairly successful in taking some slow steps across the floor. It then cut to the same man, still with the same helmet/cable apparatus, but now with another large cable attached to a metal plate on his back, no longer in an exoskeleton. He was standing, wobbly, holding onto a bar on a mirror wall, such as you would find in a ballet studio. He was laboriously lifting first one leg, and then the other, nearly falling each time he brought up a leg. Fear and effort showed in equal parts on the man's face, which was covered with sweat.

"Run it again," Sandy directed. They studied the video several times. The cable went off screen, so they did not have any way of knowing how large the control device was. Anything from a laptop to a room.

The mission commander appeared. "New orders. Put everything back in the containers. We're going to take these four boxes with us and go."

"Go where?" asked Cameron.

"The containers and prisoners are going to Guantanamo. You guys are going home."

"But I've got a lot more work to do!" Mitzi was indignant.

"Someone upstairs has decided different. Sorry."

The containers were closed up and loaded onto trucks, then taken down to the port and transferred onto the support ship. Mitzi and Cameron were directed to the Captain's quarters. They waited for several minutes, then a monitor came alive and the DDO was on screen.

"We've decided it is best that this little operation never happened. The Navy pathologists will finish the work on all the bodies at Gitmo, and hold the equipment there securely for now. As far as I can tell, it was an unmitigated disaster. Fourteen men and a helicopter lost, and a bunch of prisoners who have no clue what went on there. So far, the ones who are talking all think it was just a drug processing station." He pointed towards Cameron. "You have nothing to link Perez." He pointed at Mitzi. "You have nothing to link your father. Neither of you can tell me what was going on there."

Mitzi spoke up. "We have proof of secret brain-spinal cord research, and we know it is all directed at a very specific, very unusual spinal injury. Like one made by a bullet. This is all pointing at solving a specific problem. Perez's problem. And my father stumbled onto it!"

"Plus," Cameron added, "we have the lower body exoskeleton like the one Perez had at the para games."

"All circumstantial, all conjecture. You actually have nothing. I believe you, but I need more than faith. We are done here." The screen went blank.

Chapter 7

Monday, October 10
Basseterre, Saint Kitts

Santiago found himself waiting again as the man with that precise bullet wound swam, this time in an infinity pool behind his small villa overlooking the harbor. When he was finished, two burly guards hoisted him into one of his custom-made chairs, and he waved Santiago over.

He gave his report as quickly as he dared.

"So, you were unable to destroy the containers." Not a question. Perez mused for a minute. "Were all the hard drives destroyed?"

"Yes."

"And we are sure no one in the east wing had cameras?"

"One hundred percent."

"So, that leaves the nurses and the subjects."

"I think the containers were close enough to be destroyed in the explosion."

Perez shook his head. "We cannot assume that. They were all from Veracruz. And the subjects were mostly Mexican. We need to wait a while before trying to get any work done there. No matter, we are ready for Phase Two. Go to New York. Have Maxwell contact Overbridge. We have the Poet ready, correct?"

"Yes, he is training intensely."

"Excellent. Tell Maxwell we are ready to present to Overbridge. Have him at our facility in Queens on Saturday."

Santiago turned to leave. Just as he got to the door, Perez called him back. "And Santiago, my friend, remember. Overbridge is not like the Brazilian surgeons. He will not be intimidated, nor bought. He needs to be persuaded, seduced, convinced. He needs to be a believer. Let Maxwell do it his way."

"Understood."

* * *

After Santiago left, another man came in from the next room. James

Maxwell was a slight man, with almost white hair, and a voice that sounded perpetually like he had been punched in the throat, breathy and strained.

"You were listening, yes?" Perez's English had only the slightest accent. "Is the Poet's mesh ready?" He raised an eyebrow.

"Yes, but why are we doing such a limited implant? We could do a complete cortical mesh and really accomplish something here."

"Proof of concept. We need something that will show Overbridge the potential, with a high likelihood of success. If we lose this patient, we lose the surgeon. Who we would then have to eliminate. And our pool of approachable surgeons that I would find acceptable is small. Besides, the limited implant will be more than adequate for the spinal interface. Take the G-5 and get to New York. Santiago does not need to know you were here."

As Maxwell left, Perez had a sudden stab of pain in his belly that took his breath away for a moment, and left him exhausted and sweating. It was indeed time to accelerate the process.

* * *

Mitzi and Cameron flew to D.C. that same day, where a grim driver picked them up and drove them to Langley. Mitzi was kept in a surprisingly comfortable waiting room, while Cameron met with the DDO.

"Ah, Agent Hansen," he started, "Thank you for convincing me to organize the worst black ops disaster in a decade." He turned a pen slowly in his fingers. "So, as an analyst, what do you think was so important about spinal cord research, even illegal, involuntary research, that would make it necessary for Perez, assuming it was Perez, to destroy the entire facility and kill his own researchers and soldiers?" He waited for an answer.

"I really don't know, sir."

"Very helpful. Let's see if Dr. Lenz is similarly useless." They called in Mitzi. She had, of course, been pondering that very question.

"The mesh is simply too big, "she began, "If you want to animate the legs, you would put an interface on the part of the cortex which controls the legs, which is actually a very small area on each side. Certainly not enough reason to cover the entire top of the brain. The second mesh, newer, not only had wrinkles corresponding to the actual shape of the brain, but it did that for the WHOLE cortex, not just the motor area. At first I thought it was simply more convenient to do the whole thing, but once I thought some more about the folds, it was clear they wanted either a way to detect brain activity over the whole brain, or potentially stimulate activity over the entire brain."

"What would be the goal of either of those, in your opinion?"

"I really don't know. Maybe some way to exert mind control, or something."

"There you go," Cameron interjected. "Perez will kidnap a politician, whisk him off to a secret island, implant a mind control screen in his head, and send him back to run for President. All you need to do is make up a good story as to why he always wears a metal helmet with a cable out the back."

The DDO snapped, "Don't be an idiot." He stared at the wall for a minute. "No, this seems more personal. From what you tell me, Dr. Lenz, all of the spinal cord injuries were made to be identical, and likely correspond exactly to Perez's own injury delivered by Agent Hansen here. And yes, I still believe it is Perez. With that and the video clip showing attempts at walking, I think it is clear he is spending his resources to help himself, and is not willing to waste time on animal experimentation. I just don't understand the need for the complete destruction of the facility. Along with our men. I had the Secretary of Defense in a near apoplectic fit this morning. Plus, in reality, we still have nothing on Perez. He has complete deniability."

"But he owns Isla Sofia," objected Cameron.

"No, Ojo del Diablo owns Isla Sofia. The proof that HE controls Ojo del Diablo is thin."

"He *is* Ojo del Diablo," hissed Cameron, "my bullet in his back is the proof."

"Plus," added Mitzi, "the exoskeleton we recovered is the same as the one he demonstrated at the para games."

"Look, I'm on your side, and I want this guy, and as far as possible I will continue to act on that *as appropriate*, but please do not confuse your solo testimony with actionable proof. We have no actual evidence that Perez even *has* a bullet in the back, and was not in a para-sailing accident, as has been reported around the world. Keep digging, but don't expect further action short of something substantial. Get out of here."

* * *

"Bureaucrats," Cameron spat. "I had hoped for more." The same driver was taking them back to Reagan National, where they would catch a shuttle for New York.

"I can see his point. We need to get more information. Or you do. I'm sure that the backlog of work for me after this impromptu week off will be enough to more than keep me busy."

"So, you're just going to let it go? There's something really important - and bad - going on."

Mitzi sighed. "Look, my main focus was finding my father. At this point, there is no reasonable chance that he is alive, so my motivation is dwindling. The DDO told you to keep digging, so Perez is still your job. Let me know if you come up with anything, or want to run something by me, but I've got to get back to work."

They rode on in silence. *Keep digging*, Cameron thought. *But how? Where?* He stared out the window as they approached the airport. *I wonder if Perez actually spent time on the island,* he mused. *Yes.* For something like this, this big, this personal, the man he knew would have wanted to monitor the progress himself. *Okay, so how did he get there? There was no runway to accommodate a plane, so by boat or by helicopter.* He looked at the rotating radar tower. *No, there would be no reason for us to have watched movements in and out of Isla Sofia.* Then another thought. *Not on purpose, but how about by accident? Satellites. They photograph everywhere.* He sat back, nodding slightly to himself. *I'll check with the reconnaissance guys. Somewhere to start, anyway.* He considered sharing his idea with Mitzi, but he was more than a little annoyed. *Sure, drag me suddenly off with no notice, then just as suddenly lose interest. I think I'll just do my thing, my way, from here on out.*

Lacking anything specific to discuss, Mitzi was characteristically silent. She had no interest in small talk, and spent the flight going over the notes of the cases waiting for her in New York, which had been emailed to her by her assistant. *My boss is not going to be happy,* she thought. The DDO's words gave her an out. *I'll just tell him that I was on a classified operation, and he can talk to CIA if he wants to know more. He would rather talk to a scorpion,* she thought with satisfaction.

Mitzi knew she was considered a "difficult" employee. And relished that knowledge.

Chapter 8

Tuesday, October 11
New York

Augustus Overbridge opened his eyes and sat up, swinging his legs off the left side of his bed. He looked at the clock. 5:30 precisely. His mouth pulled back in a satisfied half smile, and he reached out and flipped the switch on his ancient clock radio to OFF. Then ON, OFF, ON, OFF. The alarm was set for 5:31, as it was every night, but it had not gone off for several years. Two thousand, nine hundred and seventy-eight days, to be precise. Dr. Overbridge prided himself on his precision. He wished to arise at 5:30, and it was his subconscious' duty to awaken him appropriately. He was no more likely to tolerate sloppy sleeping than he was sloppy waking.

He rose and stood in front of his bedroom window, gazing over the East River. It was still dark, but the lights of the Manhattan psychiatric center slightly to the north on Randall's Island and the great expanse of Queens across the river were beautiful in the pre-dawn. *A lovely day to be alive,* he thought. He snapped on the light, and instantly the window became a mirror. He looked critically at his naked body. Sixty-six years old, at six foot two and one hundred sixty pounds, a little on the gaunt side, he had a large, round, nearly spherical bald head, lean but defined muscles, and just enough belly fat to hide his toned abs.

He walked down the hall to his home gym, and worked through his weight routine for thirty-nine minutes, showered, shaved, and opened his closet. On this, as on every morning, he put on white boxers, black socks, and a starched white shirt. He then donned the dark gray suit at the far right side of the rack, carefully moved the other nine suits one spot over, and hung the hanger on the far left, ready to receive today's suit in the evening. He checked again to make sure the suits were evenly spaced, and then turned to the right and opened his tie closet. Two hundred and sixty-two bow ties and two hundred and seventeen standard long ties were displayed on pegs from ceiling to floor and on the backs of the closet doors. He had twenty-three empty, available pegs. The ties were arranged chronologically, starting with his prep school tie from Exeter in the upper left, down to the lurid chartreuse and magenta paisley purchased three weeks ago on the bottom right. Tie choice was the only variable in Dr. Overbridge's routine. Today was a surgery day, calling for a long power tie, not the bow which he would have favored on a clinic day, worn with a starched white lab coat. He considered his surgery schedule. He had a particularly difficult aneurysm scheduled. He decided to go all out, and reached for his favorite. Bright yellow, with tiny red-and-blue Supermen in a diagonal pattern. It was a Super tie. For a Super surgeon. Dr. Overbridge considered himself to be the finest neurosurgeon in the City of New York, and therefore the world. The odd thing was that many in the field would agree with him. The mystery was why he practiced at Our Lady of Salubrious Penitence.

Our Lady of Salubrious Penitence was known as OLSP, which was often distorted mockingly to Owl's Pee, and was emphatically *not* where you would expect to find excellence in neurosurgery. Nestled in the middle of East Harlem, with virtually no community support and abysmal practitioners in almost every field, its administrators spent their days at Town Hall lobbying against the posting of city hospital mortality rates on the government website. It was a teaching hospital, but only in the sense that medical students and residents from real academic programs were forced to rotate through. The emergency room was a catastrophe, the support staff close to criminal.

Except in neurosurgery. Dr. Overbridge attracted patients who paid. A lot. There were certain types of aneurysms for which his success rate was nearly twice the national average, and twenty percent better than at the prestigious Neurological Institute of New York. People flew in from all over the country, and in fact, the world. Dr. Overbridge had come to Our Lady over twenty years previously, with the proposal that he be allowed to run his own department, his own way, funded exclusively by his patients. Administration jumped at the opportunity, and he had been there ever since.

So, the Superman tie for today.

His housekeeper had arrived at 6:30, and at precisely 6:45, he breakfasted on two eggs, over easy, with two strips of bacon and buttered wheat toast. The same as on every weekday. He walked out his front door at precisely 7:15. Which is when he had to start counting.

Four steps to the elevator. Good, he was the only passenger going down from the 44th floor. That was better, fewer variables. Two steps in, turn and face the doors, press the button for the lobby three times. Eight steps across the lobby, nod to the doorman, six more steps out onto the street. From his front door at 1819 2nd Ave (at East 94th Street) to the front door at OLSP on 3rd Avenue and 111th was exactly one mile. He walked every day, rain or shine, slipping on rubber overshoes for inclement weather. After all these years, he was pleased that he could now almost always succeed in making it exactly one thousand paces, or two thousand steps. After all, that was the origin of the word mile. The Romans would be pleased. Up six steps to the main entrance, four steps past security, and sixteen more to the elevator. Today the elevator was full, necessitating a very awkward one-half step and turn. The elevator rose sluggishly. Finally, thirty-eight steps down the corridor to his office.

Surgery was scheduled for nine o'clock. Today's was a large and particularly difficult aneurysm on the posterior aspect of the circle of Willis. He was reviewing the angiogram on the high-definition monitor at his desk, when the door burst open and a somewhat ruffled-appearing, very short man with brown curly hair and a round belly, which threatened to burst the buttons on the midsection of his wrinkled white coat, popped in, breathless.

"Dr. Overbridge," he sputtered, "there is a skull fracture in the emergency room!"

Overbridge blinked at him slowly. "First, who are you, second, I am never on call for trauma, and third, never, ever, come into my office without knocking. Go out and try again."

He stood, gaping for a second, then went back out the door, closed it, and rapped gently.

"Come in."

"Dr. Overbridge, there's …"

Dr. Overbridge held up his hand. "Hello, young man, my name is Dr. Overbridge. And whom do I have the pleasure of addressing?"

"Uh, I'm Dr. Brentwood. I'm the new surgery resident on your service. You can call me Bill."

"Not at all likely. Why are you here?"

"Uh, there's a skull fracture in the ER," he said slowly.

"How does that concern me?"

"Oh, yeah, Dr. Castle was injured playing racquetball this morning, and Dr. Pearlman is away this week, and that leaves you.

Dr. Overbridge sighed deeply and turned his gaze to his computer screen. "Name?"

"Um, Bill Brentwood?"

"No, the patient's name." The word IDIOT was left unsaid.

"Jimmy Moretti, M-O-R-E-T-T-I. Date of birth 5-16-73."

Dr. Overbridge had the patient's scan up on the monitor in a few moments. "Hmm. Tell me what you see."

"Well, there is a depressed skull fracture on the left parietal skull, near the middle meningeal artery, lots of soft tissue damage over the fracture, but no hematoma intracranially."

"Quite correct. Mechanism of injury?"

"I don't know."

"Did you ask?"

"I haven't seen him yet, just got the call from the ER."

Overbridge stared at him blankly for a full, and very uncomfortable, thirty seconds.

"In the future, kindly see the patients before presenting them to me." He sighed deeply. "Well, I guess it can't be helped. Shame to waste a good tie on a routine trauma case. By the time we get to the aneurysm, I will have changed into scrubs, and my patient will not know I was prepared."

Once again, Bill just gaped.

They walked down the hallway to the elevator. Bill could not help but notice that Dr. Overbridge's lips were moving slightly, as if he were counting.

In the emergency room, the patient was awake, but was not saying anything intelligible. The ER doc came over. "Thanks for coming down. I don't know if he is loopy because of the head bonk or his blood alcohol level of 0.24. Apparently, he had had some sort of a disagreement with his local Korean grocer, who ended it by cracking him on the head with the butt of his gun. Jimmy went down, and the cops soon arrived, followed by the paramedics, and here we are." He shrugged. "Happened down on the lower East Side, but, as usual, all of the up-scale hospitals between here and there were inexplicably 'on diversion', so Jimmy got a ride all the way up the island to annoy yours truly."

Dr. Overbridge looked at the patient. The left side of his head was caked with blood, and there was also a large bruise on his cheek bone. He did not touch him or speak to him. He turned to Dr. Brentwood. "I will go and make sure all is in readiness upstairs in the OR. Make sure we have someone competent to give consent when I return."

Today would be operating room A-7. Out of the elevator, six steps, turn right, twenty-eight more steps, and into the room. They were setting up. He saw his usual circulating nurse, Vicky, and some scrub assistant on whom he had never before laid eyes. The usual, at Our Lady of Salubrious Penitence. At any rate, the scrub tech was not the problem. The problem was Felix.

Felix was the anesthesiologist.

Felix was the Anti-Overbridge. Felix was ANNOYING.

"Mornin', Augie!" Felix was always jovial.

Clearly, there must have been more to his name than Felix, but he had done his best to deny that fact. His name badge was carefully covered with black tape so that neither his title nor his last name was visible.

"I am Felix," he would always say, "and Felix means lucky."

"Whatcha got for me today? What happened to your aneurysm?"

"Unfortunately, there is an emergent depressed skull fracture in the Emergency Room."

"Depressed? Why don't we just give him some Prozac?" He laughed. No one responded.

"Ah, come on Vicky, laugh a little! You know I love how you jiggle when you laugh." She glared and went to the far side of the room.

Felix was always inappropriate, and openly disdainful of anyone who was PC.

Felix had been written up for inappropriate behavior so many times that Administration had a special filing cabinet just for him. Yet, here he was, still working. He said it was because of his file of photos from the Board of Trustees' summer retreat.

To him, Our Lady was always Owl's Pee. Even when he had been interviewed on the nightly news about his role in saving a drowning victim from the East River.

Everything looked in order, so Dr. Overbridge made his way back to the emergency room. There he was treated to a piercing, keening noise, which appeared to be emanating from a creature at Jimmy's bedside.

Jimmy's wife, Stella, had arrived.

Stella was trying very hard to be Barbie. Lower East Side Barbie, to be sure, but Barbie nonetheless. BIG bottle-blond hair, giant enhanced breasts overflowing a tube top, mini skirt, and spike-heeled sandals. *The perfect ensemble for eight o'clock on a brisk fall morning,* Overbridge thought. *In*

Harlem. At the hospital.

"I should nevah ov sent him out for coah-fee! I knew he was too drunk to play nice. And that Mr. Ahn gets soooo cranky."

"I am Dr. Overbridge, and I can assure you that your husband will be given the finest of care. I will have him taken to operating room A-7, where he will be placed under general anesthesia, following which the scalp will be prepped and draped in the usual sterile fashion. I will then extend the laceration as necessary, elevate the depressed skull fragments, fixate them as needed using micro titanium plates, irrigate the lacerations, and close. The risks are infection, brain injury, bleeding, and death."

"DEATH!" Barbie's sobs crescendo-ed. "It's all my fault! I've killed my Jimmy!"

Felix poked his head around the corner. "Hang on there, gorgeous, we're not gonna let anything bad happen to Jimmy- He's got something to LIVE for with a hot number like you at home. This Doc here is an odd-ball, but he is the best. We'll have Jimmy upstairs and fixed up in a jiffy, so just don't you worry your sweet tushy about a thing. I am Felix, and Felix means lucky. But not as lucky as Jimmy, from the looks of you!"

Stella stopped crying, smiled, flipped her hair back, and winked at Felix.

He got her to sign the papers, and shooed her away with just the most friendly little pat on the hiney.

* * *

The surgery went off without a hitch. Well, almost. When Dr. Brentwood scurried into the OR, he announced, "Hi everyone, I'm Bill Brentwood, The new surgery resident."

Felix looked him over. "Are you sure that the "BB" doesn't actually stand for Bilbo Baggins?" he asked with a chortle.

Bill blushed and stammered, "N-not funny!"

"Oh, come on, we all just want to know what part of the Shire you hail from. And would you mind taking off your shoes so we can see those famous hairy feet? And are you in love with the fairies like all the other Hobbits?"

"You mean elves," responded Bill. "Bilbo fancied elves, not fairies."

Felix laughed so hard, he could barely breathe.

By now, Bill was so frustrated that his voice squeaked and he stomped his foot. When Felix caught his breath, he apologized. "I'm so sorry, I made a mistake. It is clear you are NOT a Hobbit. In fact, I can see now that you are actually that strange little man, Rumpelstiltskin, and I just want to warn you that if you keep stomping like that, you risk the floor opening up and swallowing you."

Bill wisely shut up.

Once the surgery was finished, Dr. Overbridge went to the waiting room to talk to Jimmy's wife. There he was greeted by no less than twenty-five family members, including two brothers, three sisters, assorted cousins, and, most importantly, the matriarch of the family. It was loud. There was no doubt about the love that surrounded Jimmy.

"How is he?"

"Will he be okay?"

And the inevitable comic, "Will he be able to play the piano?"

Dr. Overbridge ignored all of the questions impassively, giving no sign that he actually heard a thing. When the cacophony ebbed, he gave his report.

"The patient is in satisfactory condition in the recovery room. He is unconscious, and will likely remain so for the next four to six hours. Although there is still a risk of infection, meningitis, or death, I feel his prognosis is good." He turned and left. He had only progressed seven steps down the hall when Stella caught up to him, wrapped her arms around him, and kissed him on the cheek. His only reaction was to blush a red reminiscent of Rudolph's nose to the top of his bald head, giving him the look of a cherry Tootsie Roll Pop.

He then headed up to the pre-op area. He briefly considered changing back into his suit, so as to present himself to the family of the aneurysm properly, but decided that, as the operating room schedule was already far behind due to the emergency, he best hurry along.

The aneurysm was a twenty-three-year-old princess. Literally. She had been flown in from the Middle East, accompanied by a fat donation to the Our Lady of Salubrious Penitence Neurosurgical Foundation. More had been promised if the operation was successful. Dr. Overbridge was supremely confident.

"The risks of surgery," he intoned, "include infection, bleeding, permanent brain injury, and death."

* * *

After his surgery was brought to a successful conclusion, Dr.

Overbridge spent the remainder of the afternoon in the clinic, checking several patients who had already had surgery, dictating his detailed operative reports, and working on his latest journal article. He had already authored more than two hundred.

In a profession known for emergencies, unexpected complications, and irregular schedules, Dr. Overbridge was unique. He left at six p.m. This morning's case notwithstanding, he rarely took emergencies, and never after noon. They were simply too disruptive.

Although he walked through arguably the city's most uninviting neighborhood for an older middle-aged white male, it never occurred to him to be afraid. When people asked him about his walk, he would simply blink at them, and state that he had always walked in New York, and always would.

Chapter 9

Wednesday, October 12
New York

By Wednesday, Cameron was exhausted. He had spent the last two days staring at satellite images of Isla Sofia. Although it was not any kind of a surveillance target, Cuba was nearby, and since the satellites transmitted 24/7, the island had been well photographed. Just not *intentionally* until the last week. On average, there were flyovers about twice a week, and the techs had been able to send the files to a high resolution monitor in his New York office at the Anti Terrorism Unit. All he had to do was to go through the footage, slowing down to enlarge and examine the pertinent frames in detail.

Three years earlier, the small island had been uninhabited, with an abandoned, unfinished hotel built in the Fifties near the natural harbor on the east. Then large ships had appeared, the dock was rebuilt, and over the course of about six months, the structures they had encountered were in place. Which had not really told him anything he didn't already know, other than the time line. Not once was a helicopter seen on the island.

He then focused his attention on the dock, and made a chart showing the number and types of boats. There were usually several vessels in the thirty to forty foot range, which looked like working boats, as for fishing. Larger container ships were frequently there at first, but then more and more rarely. One specific boat caught his eye. It was a big boat, about a hundred feet from stem to stern, and looked more luxury, less utilitarian, with a swimming pool on top. He called down to Langley, and was put in contact with Melrose, their yacht guy. He sent him the photo.

"Any chance you can identify this boat?" Cameron waited. About a half second.

"Closest guess would be a Baia Yacht. Looks a lot like the Astro." Melrose was enthusiastic. "She's one hundred four feet long, triple turbines, speeds up to fifty knots. Almost eight thousand horsepower. Awesome."

"Are there many of these?"

"Hardly. These are one of a kind. The Astro lives in the Mediterranean, rents for about a hundred grand a week." Cameron could hear a keyboard clicking. "Looks like she's been up and down the French riviera most of the time for the past year. Where and when was this picture taken?"

"Two weeks ago in the Caribbean."

"So, clearly not the Astro. I'd still check with Baia. It sure looks like the Astro. You may have some trouble getting them to say much, though. When a client gives you ten million dollars for a pleasure boat, some discretion is expected."

"Any idea on the cruising range?" Cameron heard more clicking.

"Looks like about five hundred nautical miles at forty-five knots. Remember, though, these are custom-made, and you could outfit a ship this big with tanks to go three times that far at speed, or farther if you were willing to go slower. Best guess is Baia has built about a half dozen in this range, and total of all builders worldwide about fifty or fewer in the past twenty years. That hull shape would put it somewhere in that age range."

"Thanks, Melrose." Cameron hung up. He stared at the opposite wall for a few minutes, then called Baia Yacht's main number. He got a machine, which informed him in Italian, English and probably Chinese that the office would be open in the morning at eight. He glanced at the clock. Five o'clock made it eleven p.m. in Italy.

He opened the Intelligence directory and got the name of the chief agent at the Naples consulate. Howard Jenkins. Didn't ring a bell. He picked up the phone, tossed it back and forth for a minute, then hung up. Better to wait until morning. Nothing to do for the moment.

He then called down to the satellite surveillance office, and got the chief tech.

"Can you get me all the links to images of the Caribbean ports surrounding Isla Sofia for the past few months."

"Sure, but can I ask what you are looking for?"

"I found a particular boat, and I want to see if I can tell where it has been going."

"What kind of boat?"

"Pleasure yacht about a hundred feet long."

The tech laughed. "Email me a photo. I'll just run it through recognition software. Should be able to get all we have. It could take you months to do it yourself."

"How big an area can you look at?"

"The whole world if you want, but that would take a couple of weeks."

"How long for the Caribbean and the eastern seaboard for, say, the past six months?"

There was a long pause, then the tech replied, "Umm, I would say maybe four to six hours."

"Perfect. I'm sending the photo now." He hung up and shot an email. He pulled out his mobile and called Mitzi.

She answered with her usual grace. "WHAT?" she snapped.

"There is a luxury yacht that has been coming and going from Isla Sofia for the past while, I've been checking satellite images. If I can trace the boat to Perez, it would be direct evidence of his involvement. I'm also getting info on the boat's movements for the past few months."

"Sounds interesting. I'm still stuck on the 'Why.' Why does he need mesh over the entire cortex? That is a really big deal, and from what we saw, the system would not be anything you would voluntarily have done."

"I haven't even thought about it," Cameron admitted. "I need the proof of Perez's tie-in or I can't do anything else, anyway. I'm gonna take a nap and then check the satellite data and call over to Italy once it's a decent hour over there." He hung up and stretched out on the couch in the analysts' break room.

* * *

Cameron woke around midnight. There was a large file in his inbox. Seventy-two photos of the boat, stamped with the dates and coordinates. He pulled up a map and started plotting. Over the past six months, it had been everywhere from Miami to Veracruz to Caracas to Havana. In the past month, however, it had only been seen in two harbors. Most of the time, it was at Basseterre, St. Kitts, and the rest at Isla Sofia. Looked like they were about a hundred and fifty miles apart, a quick three-hour cruise.

He pulled up his main file on Perez, and searched for Basseterre. St Kitts and Nevus was, like Antigua and Barbuda, a Commonwealth former British colony, and had been independent since the early Eighties. Perez openly held property there, including a villa where he was suspected to spend time each year. In point of fact, Perez's last definitely known location was in Mexico City six months previously, where he had been present for a stockholder meeting. Since then, he had been lost to view, and with several private jets at his beck and call, he could easily be anywhere on earth.

The satellite data was not continuous, and the most recent photo was from last Monday at Basseterre. He called down to the duty officer in satellites.

"Can you tell me when the next pass over the Basseterre, St. Kitts' port will happen?"

"You the guy that had Jeff run the trace on that boat?"

"Yes, Agent Cameron Hansen."

He could hear keyboard tapping. "Looks like tomorrow about 1300, so two p.m. local. Weather looks clear, should have a good view."

"Great. Can you email me with a yes or no on the boat's presence in port?"

"Sure thing."

He looked at the clock. Just after one a.m. *Close enough,* he thought, and called Jenkins.

"I need you to run over to the Baia shipyard and see what you can find out about a boat. I just sent a satellite photo to your inbox."

"Where is the shipyard?"

"About a half-hour drive from you, according to Google. I need to know if it actually is one of their boats, and who bought it and where it was delivered."

"What are you hoping to find?"

"I'm trying to establish a link between this boat and Juan Carlos Perez."

"MexiVox Perez?"

"Yes, that's the guy. Can you go over this morning?"

"I suppose. Nice day for a drive."

"Call me the moment you get something."

* * *

Cameron stretched out again, but had not slept much when his phone rang at three-thirty.

"Thanks for a waste of a morning," Jenkins started.

"What did you find out?"

"Not much. There actually was a lot of activity there – they are pushing to get some billionaire his newest toy delivered on time next week. No one in the main office would even talk to me, but I found the foreman out in the yard and showed him the photo. He recognized the boat at once, said they had delivered it about three years ago to one of their middle-men in Florida. Said that the rich come in two varieties – some want everyone in the world to know when they have a new yacht, the others want no one to know, and so use a broker to make the arrangements. The foreman had made the arrangements himself, what with refueling needing to occur crossing the Atlantic and all."

"Did he mention anything about the way the boat was fit out?"

"Yes. One large master stateroom, two smaller guest suites, crew quarters for six. Large salon and galley. Oh, and the whole thing was set up accessible, you know, ramps, wide doorways, and an elevator between decks. Also extra fuel tanks for longer cruises."

"That's gotta be Perez," Cameron exclaimed. "Thanks, Jenkins, I owe you one. Did you get the name of the broker?"

"He said I'd have to get that from the main office, he couldn't remember. And like I said, they weren't talking"

Cameron drummed his fingers for a minute. Waiting for satellite confirmation would cost him a day. He went online and booked a flight from La Guardia at seven-thirty on American, and just had time to go home and pack before heading to the airport.

* * *

At about the same time, Santiago was talking to his man at the Baia Yacht facility. "There was an American here asking the *capo* about your boat," the man told him. "Seemed like something official." Santiago promised to send him an extra five hundred euros, then called *el jefe*, who was still in Basseterre.

"The Americans are tracing the *Turtuga Marina*."

"Where are you," Perez replied.

"At the facility in Queens. The Poet is in training several hours a day, strengthening his legs."

"Good. Prepare my apartment. I will be arriving this afternoon." He hung up, then rang for his man downstairs, who, in turn, called the pilots and had them prepare the G-5, which had just returned from New York the day before.

Cameron did not know it, but somewhere between Miami and St. Kitts, Perez's Gulfstream 5 passed almost directly over his American Airlines 737. Perez, as usual, was using a false passport, and the executive airport personnel at both ends of his journey were amply rewarded for silence. And, of course, threatened with unimaginable consequences for leaking information. Carrots and sticks.

Chapter 10

Thursday, October 13
Basseterre, Saint Kitts

When Cameron landed in Basseterre, he booted up his phone and saw there was an email from Langley indicating that the Baia Boat was still in the harbor. As he had seen it himself on the plane's approach, that was no surprise.

There were also about two dozen voice mails from Mitzi. He listened to the first four or five, all of which simply said, "Call me," or "Call me now," or "Call me immediately." He decided the rest could wait. Just like Mitzi to be certain she had to talk to him NOW. *I'm not jumping through your hoops today*, he thought. *Maddening woman.*

He realized his options here in Basseterre were actually quite limited. He had no official status, and certainly could not simply knock on Perez's door. "Hi Juan Carlos, remember me? I slept with your woman, betrayed you, and shot you. Enjoying your wheelchair? Oh, and I have a few questions about your sick human experiments on your private island."

Instead, he took a taxi to the main constabulary, where he asked for Spencer Lewis.

Lewis had, at one time, been instrumental in St. Kitts' upset all-Caribbean rugby championship. Now he was the Island's top cop, and ran a small but well-regarded police force. He was generally known to be friendly to the CIA, and Cameron hoped at a minimum for some local information, if not direct assistance.

At his current girth of over three hundred pounds, Lewis bore only a passing resemblance to the lithe open-side flanker from twenty years previously. He had a genial, easy manner, and a laugh that seemed to bubble up from the depths of his massive torso. Cameron liked him immediately.

"How can I help my friends from Uncle Sam?" he almost chortled. "Not much happening here, you know. Still kind of a mess after the hurricane." St. Kitts had been hit almost as hard as Antigua, and it showed. Basseterre meant "low earth," and much of the low earth was covered in wrecked houses and mud.

"I am here about Juan Carlos Perez." Cameron had decided to be direct. "We have reason to believe he has been engaged in some rather unsavory activities in the area."

"Hmm, always thought there was something fishy there." Lewis was doing his best to frown, but the muscles of his face seemed to rebel at the attempt, treacherously turning up the corners of his mouth in a comical caricature looking much like Humpty Dumpty. "As you might guess, he is popular here. Throws out a lot of money. Hosts fancy parties at his villa or on the *Turtuga Marina*, his yacht. Don't actually know if he is here, haven't been down to the harbor. He comes and goes a lot."

"I saw the boat in the harbor as I was coming in," replied Cameron, "if that means anything."

"Doesn't prove anything, but it is hopeful. Let's ride up to the villa and have a look."

"Er, I can't approach him directly," Cameron interjected hastily. "We have a history."

"Let me guess, an affair of the heart?" Lewis winked, a massive movement that was as contorted as if Cameron had squeezed lemon juice into his eye. He laughed and clapped a fleshy paw on Cameron's shoulder, practically snapping his clavicle.

"Something like that. How much time does he spend here?"

"Well, the past six months, he has been here a lot, leaves in the *Turtuga* for a couple of days at a time, but mostly here. He was definitely off-island for the hurricane, rumor has it that his people hired over a hundred men to get his property back to normal before he came back."

"He went out on his boat during a hurricane?" Cameron was surprised.

"Well, the boat left a couple of days ahead of the storm, and the house was closed up. I would imagine he headed down south out of the path, but I don't really know."

In the end they decided to take the constabulary van up the mountain to the villa. Lewis would knock on the door with the pretext of delivering an invitation to the Governor's upcoming gala, while Cameron hid in the back. Accordingly, when they were a couple of blocks away, Cameron got out and climbed into the cargo area, and Lewis slammed the door.

Cameron was suddenly claustrophobic. The van was, in point of fact, designed to carry prisoners. The back had thick padding on the walls and floor, and a steel cage separating it from the passenger compartment.

There was no handle on the inside of the door.

His discomfort increased when, instead of parking at the curb, Lewis drove directly to the gate and honked twice. The gate swung open, and Lewis maneuvered up the drive and around to the side, where he pulled the van under a carport and got out. A lean whip of a man was approaching from the front of the house.

Cameron started to sweat. The driver's window was open, and he was able to hear the two men clearly.

"I've brought you a present," Lewis boomed, "tell *el jefe* that I've got a nosy American for him."

"*El jefe* is gone, flew away this afternoon." The voice was harsh, almost a hiss.

"Wish I had known that," grumbled Lewis, "I would have just let him nose about. Now we'll have to take care of him." He heaved a massive sigh.

"I'll need to check with *el jefe* first," said the thin man.

Cameron had pulled out his phone, only to find it had no service. At first he was surprised, but then glanced up and saw that the roof and sides of the compartment were covered with the chicken-wire-like jamming net.

Lewis opened the back door and snatched the phone from Cameron, laughing. "No, no," he tutted, "can't have you calling in the cavalry." He slammed the phone on the edge of the bumper with such force as to almost bend it in half, then tossed it back into the van.

Cameron had been tensing his muscles, and as Lewis' arm was extended, he uncoiled a viscous blow to the big man's neck, hoping to smash his larynx. His fist landed hard, but felt just like punching a memory foam pillow, sinking slowly into the massive fat, probably not even causing a bruise. Lewis' eyes lit up with surprise, but he simply swept his extended arm into Cameron's head, the force cracking him against the side of the van. Dazed, he tried to deliver a second blow, but Lewis grabbed his fist with a massive hand, and yanked Cameron out of the van onto the ground, put his knee into his back, and deftly applied handcuffs. He then jerked him to his feet.

The thin man snapped a photo, and sent a text. Less than a minute passed, and the phone buzzed. He answered, listened, nodded to himself and said simply, "Yes, *el jefe*," and hung up.

"*El jefe* wants him taken to New Jersey. I'm to take the *Turtuga* to

Florida, where I'll be met." He turned to Cameron. "A luxury cruise for you," he grinned, showing bad teeth. "Apparently *el jefe* wants to talk to you. He told me to give you a message. Enjoy your legs while you can."

At 36,000 feet, Perez was pleased. It had been six years since the man he had known as Anderson had shot him, and despite his network of informants, he had been unsuccessful in discovering who he really was. He had almost despaired of ever finding the man. But all he had to do was wait, and the rabbit hopped right into the fox's den. He dialed Santiago.

"Meet Gonzales in the cove south of Miami on Friday at nine p.m. He will have a package for me. Bring it to the number two facility. I much prefer that you inflict no damage. I mean to take care of it personally."

Santiago made plans to leave for Miami with his special truck. He would drive up the coast with "the package." Piece of cake. Except for the part about no damage. He preferred to have options.

He really did love his job.

* * *

It was nearly midnight, and Mitzi was annoyed. She had been trying since morning to reach Cameron, but his phone had been off. It had occurred to her that Perez had to be drawing his talent from somewhere, and she wanted him to see if he could find out anything about any Central or South American neurosurgeons who had disappeared. All of her contacts were stateside, and she hoped to have a research assistant assigned down at Langley. She must have called twenty times, each time going straight to voice mail. Finally, as afternoon turned into evening, she became concerned, and took a taxi over to his apartment. No answer at the door, but she had a key and let herself in. No Cameron. The apartment felt stale. *Where was he?*

She thought about asking over at his Anti-Terrorist Unit office, but decided that whoever was there overnight, they would not be likely to give out anything, FBI credentials notwithstanding. No, her best bet there would be in the morning, when she could talk to Harris, who had the office next to Cameron. He happened to be FBI and was on cordial but cautious terms with her.

Cameron was also annoyed. He could not believe his stupidity. He had been so excited to get back into the field that he had managed to forget everything he knew about fieldcraft. He was currently handcuffed to a chain attached to a sturdy cleat over the headboard of a luxury queen-sized bed, with a toilet and sink within reach, and a large TV with a selection of movies. So things could have been worse. Of course, he was in the middle of the ocean heading for a rendezvous with a man who had every cause to detest him. So clearly things could have been better.

He had no reason to believe that anyone even knew he was missing. Certainly he had not told anyone he was leaving town, another unforgivable blunder, and he had had no meetings scheduled. He kicked himself for not having returned Mitzi's calls. Even if he were missed, which was by no means certain, he had not left much of a trail. The thing was, he knew better, which was why he was annoyed, but given the fiasco at Isla Sofia, he had been wary of letting anyone know that he was continuing to pursue Perez until he had something concrete. He should have checked in, left notes of his plan, checked in on arrival to Basseterre. That was what the secure email was for, after all. The techs in satellite surveillance could certainly help, but only Mitzi would know to ask them. He perked up a little, remembering her repeated attempts to contact him during his flight. Mitzi would be looking, and she would look harder because she would be angry.

He was also berating himself for having gotten into the back of the van. After six years behind a desk, his operational readiness was way below par. He should have been on alert for the possibility that officials on a small island like St. Kitts would be likely to be on the Perez payroll. He felt like a fool, and knew he was likely going to die for his foolishness.

At least he was eating well. The *Turtuga Marina* was only stocked with the finest food, and he was brought meals at regular intervals. Plastic cutlery, obviously. He had searched in vain to the limits of his manacles for any scrap of metal to use as a pick, but the room was very sparsely decorated, and very clean. He wondered a little about the stateroom. It was certainly an odd mixture of luxury and confinement, and he thought more than once that he was probably not the first unwilling guest on board.

* * *

The ship cruised surprisingly quietly. He had a porthole, and he estimated they were making at least thirty knots. Malcolm had said the Baia Boat could cruise at forty-five knots, and he guessed that the slower speed was to conserve fuel. He thought it was over a thousand miles to

Florida, so maybe about thirty hours. Not that he was in a hurry. He doubted he would like the next part of the journey, which would likely be the last one he ever made.

Chapter 11

Friday, October 14
New York

Dr. Overbridge reserved Fridays for new patient consultations. At this point in his career, only patients already known to require his expert surgery made it through his staff's screening process to actually see him. He scheduled one new patient per hour, and saw four each Friday morning starting at eight, and three in the afternoon, starting at one. Patients were required to arrive a minimum of fifteen minutes early, so as to be in the consultation room when he walked through the door at the top of the hour. If they were not there, they were not seen, and would have exactly one opportunity to reschedule, with a five hundred dollar penalty fee. He himself, of course, was never late. Not even a minute. He considered physicians who ran late to be poor managers, and could not fathom why any patient would trust such a surgeon with their life and health.

The pre-surgical visits were long, albeit with very brief conversations. Essentially, he would put the scans up on the monitor, and, after staring intently (and silently) at each and every one of as many as six hundred frames in an MRI, CT-angio, or angiogram, he would then simply tell the patient the name of the operation proposed, a rough success rate, and the risks, which were always infection, bleeding, permanent brain injury, and death. He did not like to explain options and alternatives. In his world, the only options were to do it his way or to find another doctor. His reputation and statistics were compelling, however, and there was always a long waiting list for his services.

At precisely three o'clock, Overbridge opened the door to his consulting office, wearing his white coat and an orange and red polka dot bow tie.

Maxwell sat in the visitor's chair, and Dr. Overbridge greeted him and pressed his thumb on the pad next to his monitor. The screen lit up, the CT-angio already loaded in by his assistant. He scrolled slowly through the films, stopping every now and then to go back and check a prior frame.

He spent several minutes going back and forth over one specific area. There was a small aneurysm of the anterior communicating carotid artery, with a broad neck, and arteries branching near its dome, making it poorly suited for a non-surgical approach. He then looked up at Maxwell.

"Have you had any headaches or other symptoms?" he asked. Maxwell shook his head.

"No, not really."

"And how about the patient? Does HE have any symptoms?"

Maxwell sat up with a start. "What makes you think I am not the patient?"

"Well, for one, it is extremely unlikely that this particular aneurysm would have been discovered without some symptom to prompt the CT-angio. And secondly, your brows and cheekbones are significantly less prominent than the scan would indicate. Thirdly, your eyes are much closer together. I look at a lot of scans, and a lot of patients."

Maxwell looked at Overbridge. "You are, of course, correct. I am representing someone who wants to make sure you will do the procedure prior to seeing you."

"I think we are done here. I have patients who are kings and billionaires, politicians and celebrities. I do not do business this way. You are wasting my time." He started to stand.

"COULD you do the surgery?" Maxwell hadn't moved.

"Of course. You knew that before you came. There was no need to play games."

"There are two reasons for this unconventional approach. The first is that, in addition to the aneurysm, there is something else we need you to do for this patient, something that may interest you enormously."

Dr. Overbridge was walking towards the door.

"The second is that the patient is Pierre Lemieux."

Overbridge froze, then turned rigidly and returned to his chair.

"I need you to come to our research facility in Queens to show you what we are working on. I promise it will be worth your while. More importantly, it will be worth it to Pierre. A car will pick you up at your apartment tomorrow at eight a.m. sharp. I trust you will be at your curb." He rose and left the room.

Overbridge remained, rigid, in his chair. He sat there, motionless, until precisely four o'clock, then rose and removed his white coat, which he placed in a hamper in his office closet, put on his suit jacket, and started his walk home. His secretary stared, stupefied. She had worked for Dr. Overbridge for seven years. He always left his office on Fridays precisely at five. She tried calling after him, asking if there was something wrong. He did not so much as acknowledge her existence.

* * *

In lower Manhattan, by three o'clock, Mitzi had been busy raising hell for almost seven straight hours. Her office in the FBI complex was a couple of blocks from the ATU, and she had been there most of the day. She went in to see the Special Agent in Charge of the ATU, Agent Kevin Crawley.

"Sir, I need some help with Agent Hansen."

"I heard you were over here irritating everyone. Tell me what you've got."

"Well, when I spoke with him Wednesday night, he was tracing a luxury yacht suspected to belong to Juan Carlos Perez. He found it in Basseterre, and we have him on a flight to St. Kitts' yesterday morning. He cleared customs, but then nothing. I called and talked to the Chief of Police himself, a friendly fellow named Lewis, who assured me that Cameron had not shown up at the constabulary. He knew all about the yacht, and even went down to the harbor to check, but it was not there. We have no idea where the boat is now, and there is thick cloud cover that rolled in over the Caribbean this morning, so it might be days before the satellites give any more information."

"So, what do you want?"

"I want you to authorize me to go down there and look for him!"

"Hansen is CIA. I'll have to call Langley first."

An hour later, she was called back into Crawley's office. "The DDO is sending two agents down in the morning. No one goes down alone, and we will be sending field agents. Not pathologists. No more amateur sleuthing is going to be tolerated. Understood?"

"Yes, sir," she agreed immediately. But what she said to herself was, *In a pig's eye.*

* * *

The *Turtuga Marina* had droned along steadily all afternoon and all night Thursday, and all day Friday, then stopped abruptly about sunset. Cameron looked out the porthole, and saw nothing but ocean. He wondered idly if they were waiting for another boat, but after a few hours the engines came back to life, and the boat powered up to what must have been near full speed. The night sky was inky black, and unlike the prior night, there was no reflection of running lights on the water. After about twenty minutes the boat slowed to a crawl, and he sensed more than saw the irregularity of land. Another half-hour's slow, nearly silent running, and the boat stopped. The thin man appeared at the door, and secured his hands behind his back, while another man kept a gun leveled on him. Next, two heavy weights were attached to his ankles. He gave a quizzical look.

"These will discourage you from trying to escape by jumping overboard." Cameron could see the logic in that.

They loaded him into the Zodiac at the stern, and Cameron could see that they were in a small bay. A set of headlights shown from on shore, which otherwise was completely dark. The small boat powered across the quarter mile separating them from the beach. He definitely would have jumped had it not been for the leg weights, but as it was, he stayed put. As they approached the shore, he could see that the headlights belonged to a pickup truck or SUV. Two men, both large, were standing on the sand in front of him. They beached the Zodiac, and he walked slowly across the sand, the labor of an extra fifty pounds on each leg exhausting him quickly.

The pickup truck had a Leer cap on the bed, and inside there was a wooden crate the size and shape of a coffin, padded on the bottom, with heavy leather straps for his ankles and wrists, and one across his chest. He was loaded in, leg weights and all, and the straps cinched tight. The leg weights were removed and the two men from the boat carried them away. He heard the Zodiac's engine start up, then fade into the distance.

"If you make noise, which would probably be useless anyway, we will stop and tape your mouth. We will also pull over and tape your mouth prior to stopping for gas. Enjoy your ride." A straw was put between his lips, and he drank deeply. A lid was then placed on the crate. Not tight, breathing was not a problem, but he could barely move. All in all, he had preferred the *Turtuga*.

He could hear the liftgate being secured, and the cab doors closed. They reversed up the beach, then spun quickly around and bumped along for several minutes before the road became smooth and the truck powered up to speed.

The truck stank of sweat, urine, and gasoline. They rolled along steadily, stopping every few hours, first to tape his mouth, then at filling stations, then a few minutes later to remove the tape and give him more water. He asked to relieve himself, but the response was a laugh, "Why do you think it smells like piss? Feel free to wet yourself." As dim daylight filtered into the crate, he did just that.

It was getting dark when they stopped again, barely an hour after the last gas stop, and replaced the duct tape and checked all the straps. After just a few more minutes of travel, the steady highway noise was replaced with the stops and starts of city traffic. Cameron assumed they were approaching his destination. He struggled with the straps, as he had from time to time along the journey, but was completely incapable of getting any slack. Finally, the truck came to a stop, and he heard a large overhead door lowering. Both doors slammed, and he heard footsteps on concrete. Nothing was said to him, he was simply left in his crate. After the first fifteen or twenty minutes he started to lose it, and twisted and turned with all his might, but to no avail, accomplishing nothing but wearing bloody abrasions in his wrists and ankles. He screamed against the tape until his voice was reduced to a hoarse whisper, and his throat was as raw as if he had used a bottle brush to scrub his tonsils. He had nothing left, mentally or physically. He was sure he would die. And afraid that wouldn't happen anywhere near soon enough. Finally, exhausted, he fell asleep.

Chapter 12

Dr. Overbridge was at the door to his building at precisely eight a.m., as a black town car with tinted windows rolled smoothly to the curb. A man climbed out of the passenger seat and opened the rear door for Overbridge, who walked the seven steps to the car, and got in.

"Wait," he directed. He clicked the safety belt in place. Then removed it. Replaced it. Removed and replaced it once more. The driver watched him.

"Okay to go now?"

"Proceed," he nodded. The car moved into traffic, then headed east. Overbridge stared out the window, counting the doors on the right side of the street. Once they merged onto FDR drive, he was able to close his eyes and think.

His thoughts were not pleasant.

Over thirty years ago, he had been a clinical fellow in advanced neurosurgery at the UniversitätsSpital Zűrich. Monique Lemieux was from Grenoble, a brilliant neurobiologist, beautiful, and passionate in a casual way that provided the perfect counterpoint to the intense study at the Center. When he left to return to America, the goodbye was simple, with neither of them expressing regret, nor any thought of continuing their association.

Ten years later, at the Neurological Institute of New York, a small elderly man approached him. Monique was dying, ravaged by ovarian cancer, and had asked her father to bring him to her. Overbridge had heard nothing from her in the intervening years, but M. Lemieux had insisted, and he had flown to France.

Monique had been almost beyond recognition, bald, emaciated, sallow. She introduced him to her son, Pierre. Their son. No, Pierre did not know.

She asked him to take them for a picnic in an alpine meadow, where she proposed to tell Pierre of his parentage. She had wanted to take the

87

téléphérique de la Bastille, to the top of the mountain near the ski jump built for the Olympics. Pierre loved the tram ride high over the city. Overbridge, however, had insisted on driving, excited to take the rented Aston Martin Volante convertible up the beautiful winding road. They never made it, Overbridge failing to negotiate an unmarked hairpin curve. Monique's face was crushed into the dash, and shards of the wine bottle in her lap had lacerated her chest and neck. Her left carotid was open, pumping. Overbridge tried to control the hemorrhage, pinching the vessel between his thumb and index finger. She was slippery with blood, and he would first succeed, then slip, then succeed again. At first she was conscious, calling to Pierre, telling him it was okay, but slowly she faded, and was gone. The rescuers arrived to find Monique dead, Overbridge still gripping her neck although barely conscious. Pierre was whimpering in the back, crying for his *Maman*.

Overbridge was taken to surgery to remove his ruptured spleen and control the internal bleeding.

When he awoke M. Lemieux was in his room.

"I think," he said, "that we should not meet again."

Overbridge struggled to comprehend.

"Where is Monique? And Pierre?" he was finally able to croak out.

"She is dead," he answered evenly. "Pierre's spine was broken. He is paralyzed."

"When can I see him."

Lemieux' eyes were hard. "You are not understanding. You fathered him and deserted him. Then you killed his mother. Now you have paralyzed him. You will be returning to New York as soon as you are able, and you will not ever return here, you will not contact us or him. Ever." He rose and left the room.

Overbridge stared at the ceiling. His whole body had been full of grief and tension. His heart pounded, and the bile rose in his throat. He began to feel that his heart would explode. Suddenly he saw the holes in the ceiling tiles. He had started to count them. The guilt somehow became less acute as he counted. He had been able to slow his racing heart, breathe normally. Numbers were pure, perfect, true. As he continued to count, he realized that order was the key to overcoming chaos.

Order had become his friend, his talisman, his deity.

Pierre Lemieux was now an internationally recognized poet and para-Olympian. Overbridge had seen numerous pictures of him, watched him roll his wheelchair up to receive the *Grand Pris de Poésie* from the *Académie française*. He had not tried to contact him.

As they crossed the Triborough Bridge into Queens, Overbridge wondered whether repairing the aneurysm would exorcise the demon that had gripped him for the past twenty years.

* * *

The car pulled into a nondescript alley off a nondescript street several blocks from Elmhurst hospital. The overhead door in the back of a large brick building went up, and the driver rolled in and parked in a cavernous empty garage. The door rolled shut behind them. Neither Overbridge nor his escorts had said a word.

Maxwell was waiting and opened his door, and Overbridge followed him to an elevator. Nine steps, then up three stairs, then six more steps to the waiting elevator. They went up to the third floor, where the elevator opened into a corridor lined with doors, looking very much like a small hospital wing, except that the floor was covered with a rich chocolate carpeting, and the walls were decorated with museum-quality impressionist paintings.

Twenty-six steps down to the end of the hall, double glass doors opened onto a conference room, with a large walnut table, over-sized overstuffed chairs, and sixty-inch high definition screens on both side walls. Maxwell waved him to a chair.

"I'll get right to it," he said, pressing a button which lowered shutters and dimmed the lights. The screens lit up.

First came a scene of a man in a complete lower body exoskeleton, laboriously moving along a walkway with side rails. His head was shaved, and the top was covered with wires inserted into the skin, coming together in a thick cable that led to a work station, with a similar cable going back to the exoskeleton. A narrator was explaining that this was the first generation, with needle EEG electrodes detecting brain activity, external signal processing, and simple robotic legs.

The next scene showed the same man, this time with a tight-fitting cap, again with many wires, now going directly to a unit on the top of the exoskeleton. The voice explained that the interface had been miniaturized to allow for on-board processing, and that, instead of needle electrodes, a special cap with surface electrodes had been used. The walking was not as smooth as before, which was due to decreased signal clarity from the brain.

The image next showed a different man, again with the needle electrodes on his shaved head, the same cable and workstation, but now the return cable went not to a lower body exoskeleton, but into a plate on the man's spine. He was able to walk, slowly, and with support. The narration explained that this man had been fitted with a spinal nerve stimulation interface, and that the impulses generated by the computer were used to stimulate the actual muscles of the legs and feet. The voice described the laborious process of determining by trial and error which nerves stimulated which muscles, and the immense initial processing required to program the movements.

Overbridge sat passively through the presentation.

"Well," Maxwell asked, "what do you think?"

"Interesting," Overbridge replied, "but why am I here?"

Maxwell stood up and escorted Overbridge back to the elevators. They went down to the second floor, the elevator opening into a single large room, with an operating setup in the center, and with dogs in cages down one wall. Maxwell guided Overbridge to the cages. In each was a dog, all Labrador retrievers. They all appeared healthy, and wagged their hind quarters enthusiastically as the men approached.

Maxwell pointed to the plates on each cage, showing "Interface Implant," and indicating dates of up to five months previously. He opened a cage. "Here," he invited Overbridge, "examine the animal."

Overbridge looked at the dog. There was a connector on the back of the animal's head, which he touched, first lightly, then gripped it firmly and wriggled. It was apparently fixed to the skull. The connector was like an old computer cable plug, with perhaps thirty pins. The casing appeared to be titanium.

Maxwell tossed the dog a kibble, and strode across the room. He opened a large cabinet, where there were plastic models of brains, which Overbridge noted to be about the size of a dog's. Maxwell took one and handed it to Overbridge.

He looked closely and saw that there was something on the model. There was a plug similar to the one he saw on the dog attached on the back side. He looked carefully at the plug. It was indeed titanium, with a finish similar to the osteointegrated implants the dentists used. At Maxwell's urging, he grasped the connector and peeled a nearly invisible fine mesh off of the brain model. It was perfectly fit, following the contours of the brain into all of the folds. It had about the consistency of a spider web, and became nothing but a torn cobweb as he removed it.

"This mesh," Maxwell said proudly, "is my work. It is made from a new semi-conducting fiber, which we are now using in a wide range of applications in computers and communication, and can be spun into a web with several hundred individually addressable electrical gates per square centimeter, which can be used for either detection or stimulation of impulses. We go from a high resolution MRI, through 3-D printing of a precise replica of a dog brain, to spinning a perfectly fitting mesh in about two days. All of these dogs have had mesh applied to their brains, and the skull replaced, with the connectors you saw integrated to the back of their skulls."

Overbridge was interested. He thought about the difficulties in performing such an operation, which would involve removing the skull, opening the dura, placing the mesh, closing the dura, and getting a seal where the fibers connected to the plug. "It would be impossible to place something that fine," he remarked. "How do you overcome that?"

In response, Maxwell opened an envelope and dumped the contents on the lab bench. A mesh with enough stiffness to maintain shape was revealed, and sat on the bench like the ghost of a brain. "I have engineered a special sugar-based coating. Once in place, water, or saline, or blood will almost instantly melt the coating, and the mesh will settle into the folds and crevices nicely."

"What is your success rate?"

"About sixty per cent of the dogs survive through recovery. Less than satisfying." He sighed. "If we can get them out past a week, they do fine. It seems to be mostly a matter of getting adequate dural seals to prevent leaks and infection."

Overbridge was annoyed with the incompetence of the surgeons. *It would certainly be a difficult procedure,* he thought, *but I am sure my success rate would be close to one hundred per cent.* The right corner of his mouth twitched up slightly. He then turned to Maxwell with the obvious question.

"If your goal is to re-animate legs, why do you need such a large implant? A smaller implant to go over the lower body motor cortex would be adequate. And again, why am I here?"

Maxwell opened another cabinet and pulled out another model, this time a human brain. It was marked to show the motor cortex, that part of

91

the brain that originates the impulses to cause movement, and specifically from the waist down. This was a strip about three centimeters wide, starting in the middle of the brain in the cleft between the right and left hemispheres, and arching just over the top of the brain on both sides. He then took another coated fiber mesh in the shape of a large "M," which fit precisely into the hills and valleys of the model, covering the motor cortex completely on both sides.

"You are quite correct, this is what we need for lower body re-animation. This model is a perfect replica of Pierre Lemieux' brain, 3-D printed from an MRI, and although the mesh I am holding is just for demonstration, we have spun a mesh precisely to fit his lower body motor cortex. Most conveniently, the approach to his aneurysm can be made through the center of the brain adjacent to that area, so the placement can be easily done at the time of his aneurysm repair. He had his spinal implant placed three months ago, and has been working every day on computer-assisted leg motion. He is ready for the direct cerebral interface, which will give us a hundred times more accurate detection of brain impulses than the external interfaces, and should allow return to near normal motor activity. You are here because we want – he wants – you to place the mesh."

Dr. Overbridge wondered exactly who "we" were.

"What about his aneurysm? The approach is similar, but the chance of disaster when doing this at the same time is substantial." Overbridge realized with a start that he had actually started to picture the procedure, and he pulled up short on the thought that he was actually being drawn in to consider doing such a thing.

"There is no aneurysm. Those images were faked in order to provide a reasonable cover story as to why he was having surgery."

"So, what we have here is a new, clearly not-FDA-approved device, the product of clandestine research and development, which you would like me to surreptitiously implant in an internationally famous literary figure. Preposterous. Why would I ever consent to such a scheme?"

"For one thing, you would be part of history. This has the possibility of solving one of the most vexing problems of modern medicine. But you and I know it would be more than that. This is about redemption, Dr. Overbridge. You paralyzed Pierre. You break it, you fix it. Gives a new meaning to child support."

Again, Overbridge wondered who "we" were. Although he assumed that his name would have been in the accident reports, only Pierre's grandfather would have known he was the boy's father. The fact that they had this information was unsettling.

"Pierre will be in your office on Tuesday for his pre-operative visit. By the way, we have not told him of your relationship. Probably best not to bring it up. Think it over, Dr. Overbridge. Here is my number." He handed him a business card. No name, no logo, nothing except a phone number. "I also wanted to ask you a question. How many dog cages did you see in the lab?"

Overbridge stared at him. "I have no idea."

"Think about that. You did not count them."

Maxwell escorted Overbridge back to the elevator, which they rode down to the garage. The same two men were there waiting, and they loaded him into the car and headed back to Manhattan.

* * *

Overbridge's head was spinning. He ran through the data over and over, trying to decide if this was more completely an opportunity or a disaster. It was, as he had pointed out, illegal. If he were discovered doing such a thing, that would be the end of his career, and could conceivably actually mean arrest and imprisonment. That really did not bother him. He would only get caught if surgery did not go well or if there was a complication. He did not tolerate complications in any case. And it was true that as he had become absorbed into the presentation, he had lost the compulsion to count.

Somewhat to his surprise, he was noticing a feeling that had been missing in his life for many years. Passion. Passion like that which had once consumed his life. To ride motorcycles. To teach residents. And, most of all, to save brains. Passion that had started to ebb several months before the accident, and had finally been extinguished in that hospital in Grenoble. He felt a thrill. His decision was made.

Chapter 13

Sunday, October 16
New Jersey

Cameron was awakened by the sound of the tailgate being opened. The lid of his crate was pulled up and he was greeted by the same face he had seen on each stop of the journey. He had lost all track of time, but surely had been lying there for many hours. He was starving and thirsty.

"You stink." The man wrinkled his nose. He removed the chest restraint, and then took a large box-cutter from his pocket, and expertly cut through Cameron's clothes, leaving him naked except for his shoes. The laces were cut through, and the shoes pulled off and thrown to the ground. Three more men helped to pull the crate out of the truck bed, so that it and Cameron were upright on the floor of the garage. The wrist and ankle straps were then removed, and he was efficiently propelled across to a steel door with a small window, which was opened and he was thrown inside. The room was tiled, with a drain in the floor and shower head in the ceiling, too high for him to reach. Without warning, the shower started, and a loudspeaker instructed him to clean himself. He was willing. At first the shower was warm, almost hot, but after a few minutes the water turned to ice, and he was shivering when it stopped.

The door opened, and a large towel and a paper jumpsuit were tossed in, along with a pair of slippers. Cameron dried himself and dressed. Immediately the door opened and the four men pulled him out and frog-marched him into another room. This room looked exactly like the jail cell in a hundred prisons, stainless-steel toilet with a sink built into the top, steel cot bolted to the floor, thin mattress, thin blanket, thin pillow.

"*El jefe* will see you in a couple of hours, so just relax." His captor tossed a sandwich on the cot. "Enjoy."

Cameron was not about to argue. He was pretty sure it was Sunday, and he had not eaten since Friday on the boat. He wolfed down the sandwich, and drank from the sink. He then stretched on the cot and closed his eyes.

As he had for the entire trip, he berated himself repeatedly for his stupidity. His only real question was why he was still alive. The clue was in Perez' message to "enjoy your legs." He thought back to the "patient" discovered in the Isla Sofia facility, with his story of having had his spinal column severed. Maybe Perez would be satisfied to paralyze him, and would then let him go. Somehow he doubted it. It was more a question of how long he would keep him alive and tortured. No, if he did not escape, he was a dead man. That much was clear.

His current quarters did not present many opportunities for escape. He figured he would be taken to see Perez in a couple of hours, and if they maintained their pattern of moving him un-manacled, with just four men, he would at least have a chance. Particularly as he was being fed, and was reasonably rested. Despite his recent stupidity, he was a fit, trained operative, and if he could keep his wits about him, favorable options might present themselves.

By evening, the promised audience with Perez had not eventuated. Instead, Cameron had been treated to some entertainment, so to speak. His cell was fitted with a flat screen attached to the ceiling, well out of reach, placed so that when he was lying on the bed, it filled his vision. Up to now it had been dark, but now it sprang to life.

The first video showed a man being roughly strapped face down on an operating table. Cameron recognized it from the island facility. He also recognized the rig which was screwed into the back of the man's pelvis with two-inch framing screws and a drill. The man was writhing and screaming, clearly wide awake. Once the rig was in place, a large hammer was used to give a powerful blow to what looked to be a standard one-inch wood chisel, driving it deep into the man's spine. He shrieked, then apparently fainted. This video repeated over and over for what seemed to be a couple of hours, the volume loud enough that Cameron was unable to distract himself, and he found that he was mesmerized by the horror in front of him.

Next was a scene similar to what he had seen from the tie-tack camera, with the same man, his bald head covered with needle electrodes, the wires snaking into a cable that disappeared off camera, and another cable attached to his back. He was clearly trying to move his legs, with some success, but the movements were clumsy and tentative.

The final video started with a smiling Perez, who explained that, although promising, the needle scalp electrodes simply did not give the quality of signal needed to really optimize the spinal interface. Fortunately, another solution had been found.

An operating room appeared, the now-familiar man lying on an OR table, clearly anesthetized. The room looked like any modern operating theater, with the usual anesthesia machine, several computer monitors, and a team of surgical staff in blue sterile garb. The head of the bed had a semicircular ring attached, and the patient's head was being scrubbed with betadine, following which it was lowered into the ring. Four stainless-steel bolts were then applied, just above the ears and at the back of the head. The surgeon tested for stability by attempting to rock the skull, but it was firmly in place. The back of the table was flexed, and the patient was put into a seated position. The entire table was then lowered so that the head was at waist height. More betadine was applied, and sterile drapes were attached to the frame, so that now all that was visible was the top half of the head, which reflected the brilliant overhead lights, and the face down to the upper lip.

The camera shifted to directly overhead, and an incision was made just above the frame, going neatly around the back of the scalp from temple to temple. An electrical device was used to stop the bleeding, which was initially considerable. This same instrument continued the cut all the way to the bone. First with a metal scraping tool, and then with thumbs and fingers, the scalp was peeled off of the skull from back to front, and inverted over the top of the head inside-out, covering the face. This reminded Cameron of one of his junior high school friends who used to invert his eyelids to gross out the girls.

The skull gleamed brightly. A vibrating saw, like the one Cameron remembered his orthopedist using to remove his cast as a child, made a cut all the way around the skull. The skull was then separated from the tissue below, surprisingly easily, Cameron thought, and removed. Again, the bleeding points were burned with an electrical device.

A white membrane, which pulsated slightly, was all that was left covering the brain. Cameron knew this was called the dura. This was slit open, and peeled back to reveal the entire top half of the brain. The wire mesh cap that Cameron remembered all too well was then snugged down over the brain, and the rim tucked under the inside of the skull, where a complicated device was repeatedly fired around the circumference, apparently securing the screen in place, the thick cable protruding out the back. Running down the center of the cap was a white plastic strip an inch wide, and the dura was pulled over the mesh to that strip, where it was glued in place. The scalp was flipped back into place, and sewn back together, followed by staples finishing the skin. Cameron noted that the skull was not replaced.

The scene then cut to one of the man, now fit with the helmet Cameron recalled, again working on his walking.

Perez, still smiling, appeared, and explained that, although the concept was good, there were technical difficulties still to be worked out, and so far, none of the subjects had been able to survive more than a few weeks after the placement of the wire-mesh implant. He was delighted to have a new patient to help with the research. He was confident that the next several months would be more than Cameron could have ever anticipated.

The remainder of the night, he was left to sleep, which, surprisingly, he actually did, determined that he would be alert and ready when they came for him.

* * *

Monday morning breakfast came. So did lunch. Between them, Cameron was treated to another showing of the videos of the night before. He supposed it was designed to make him afraid, hopeless. Instead, he was able to look inside himself and find a calm, assured power that fired his will.

The four men opened the door to the cell, and he saw the truck across the garage, tailgate open, man-box waiting. A burly man grasped each arm, and he felt the nose of a pistol in his back as the fourth man led the way. He was hyper-aware, taking in every detail of his surroundings, feeling the cadence of their gait. He struggled slightly, feeling the power behind the iron grips holding his elbows, rigidly preventing escape, and he saw how it would work. They would be expecting him to twist, or to fall, or to kick. All of their collective strength was aimed at preventing those moves. Instead, calling on his old gymnastics training, and using the guards' arms for support as he would have the parallel bars, he suddenly slammed his body back, crashing the back of his head into the following man's face with a crunch of nasal bone and cartilage, while flinging his legs forward and up, all the way over the top and back around onto the man who was now sprawling backwards. The force of the motion in this unexpected direction tore his arms free, and as he came down on the bleeding man, he was able to roll in a smooth motion and wrest the gun from his hand, firing into the two other men, who were trying to twist back towards him. They were down before they could reach for their own guns.

The lead man, however, was spinning and drawing his weapon. Cameron was already rolling to the left, the truck shielding him from the other man's aim. He crawled around a support pillar, and took stock. They were in a standoff, with no clear offensive move available to either man. One of the side guards was definitely dead, having caught a round full in the face, and the other was making a terrible gurgling noise as he breathed. The pistol's owner was groaning and bleeding, but starting to move. Cameron had a clear field, and put a round into each of the two men. No use having some half-dead hero making him all the way dead.

The other man was behind the truck, and out of view. Cameron was considering his options, when the truck suddenly came alive with a roar, and accelerated towards the overhead door, which had started up. The driver did not wait, but crashed through the half-open door, losing the top half of the cab in exiting. Which was fine with Cameron. He could already hear sirens, and figured the local police force would be arriving with all sorts of annoying questions forthwith. He quickly rifled through the three dead men's pockets, and to his delight found his wallet and ID. He ran out through the ruined door in his ridiculous jumpsuit and slippers just as the Newark PD arrived.

Two hours and ten thousand phone calls later, the FBI contingent of the Homeland Security Anti-Terrorism cooperative unit had secured the building and taken over the investigation. Newark PD had been politely booted out.

Santiago had dumped the ruined truck a few blocks away, and was on a PATH train into Manhattan before the police had the wherewithal to button up the area. Not that shutting down public transit in greater New York during rush hour was a viable option.

He made the call to Perez. It was extremely unpleasant. Extremely.

Chapter 14

Dr. Overbridge walked into his consulting office at precisely 10:00 a.m. Pierre Lemieux was seated in a wheelchair, a sport/racing model, and he was wearing thick gloves. He had the immense arms and shoulders of the para-athlete.

Maxwell was in a chair next to him.

Lemieux pulled off a glove and extended a hand. "Hello, sir. Thank you for agreeing to do this. I have been dreaming of walking again since I was ten. Let me show you what I can do." He pulled a laptop from the satchel next to him, and booted it up. He put on a glove with a thick cable, which was tethered to the laptop, and also reached around and fished another cable from behind his back, which he also attached.

Using complex hand gestures, he demonstrated first extending one leg, then the other, and after standing with some help from Maxwell, he used the gaming glove to cause his legs to move into an awkward shuffle-step forward.

"This was how I prepared, how the computer learns which nerves move which muscles. I can walk these short, wobbly steps with computer commands. With scalp electrodes, I can walk all the way across a room. I know that, with a direct cerebral interface, I will be able to walk. Maybe even to run. After twenty years of being tied to this thing." He splayed his fingers and his right leg kicked at the chair.

Overbridge stared at him a long minute.

"The risks of surgery are infection, bleeding, permanent brain injury, and death."

He rose and left the room.

* * *

Autopsies were Mitzi's business, and she spent all of Wednesday with the three corpses supplied to her by Cameron's efforts before meeting up with him at a surprisingly depressing Starbucks.

"What did you learn?" he started.

Mitzi waved her hand like she was swatting a fly. "Boring. Other than that they were healthy men in their late twenties of probable Latino lineage, who died as a result of very obvious gunshot wounds, there's really nothing to say. Their prints did not show up in the computer files. Their teeth were not well cared for and did not have any interesting dental work. One of them had had an appendectomy, and from the look of it, not in the States, but that's not very specific. More importantly, what have you learned?"

"Learned?" he snorted. "I learned, after several hours of intense study, that the DDO's outer office is a room even less interesting than a prison cell. I learned that I am no longer to have anything to do with Perez or this case. I learned that my next several months will be spent analyzing TSA efficiency reports, looking for ways to improve through-put at airports without using any kind of profiling. I'd say that I learned more today than I have in any prior single day of my career."

"So," Mitzi asked, "have you got any ideas regarding what Perez is really up to?"

"Yes, he is using Nazi war criminal methods to do human experiments to figure out how to walk again."

"That just doesn't add up," Mitzi leaned forward and jabbed him with her finger. "Why is he covering the entire cortex with his mesh? And given what you told me, I can't see how it would work anyway. There is no way the operation you described would ever be viable long-term. All that foreign material in the brain, no skull, no way to control the leakage of the spinal fluid. This can't be the endgame. I can't imagine Perez is really getting ready to have the top of his head opened up in order to walk. And walk poorly."

"I can't talk about it anymore," Cameron said. "I nearly died this week, not to mention last week on Isla Sofia. I'm done. I'm doing as I'm told."

"You do that," Mitzi snapped. "Just make sure you answer your phone when I call." She rose and hurried out into a cold rain, pulling her thin raincoat around her.

She kept turning it over and over in her mind. There had to be a reason for the whole-cortex mesh. Certainly it was to provide an interface to a computer from every area, but why? What practical purpose could there be to cover everything? Motor and sensory functions really only took up a small portion of the surface of the brain, less if your focus was only from the waist down. This mesh covered it all – audio cortex, visual cortex, even the pre-frontal cortex, where complex reasoning took place. To need all that was simply illogical, and certainly Perez himself did not need anything of the sort. But this kind of criminal obsession could only be for personal gain. Nothing else would motivate the vast expenditures of money and resources they had encountered.

At this point, she absent-mindedly stepped into a puddle which hid a pot-hole, and before she could stop herself, she was flat on her face in the street, drenched, and was barely able to crawl back to the curb before a taxi sped past, sending up a rooster tail that covered her again with frigid spray.

Shivering, she pulled out her phone to call for an Uber, but it was cracked and soaked and would not turn on. She stomped and cursed, then smashed the phone repeatedly against the corner of a nearby building, over and over until the glass front was completely destroyed and the delicate innards were leaking out like the circuits of a damaged Terminator robot. When she could think clearly again, she stared at her ruined phone. There was a Verizon store on the next block, and she sloshed her way over, and spent the next ninety minutes obtaining a new, waterproof Samsung, vowing to leave Apple behind forever.

When she came out, the rain had stopped, and she walked home, still puzzling.

Chapter 15

Perez's motorized wheelchair rolled smoothly off the van's lift, and up the ramp to the elevator. He went up to the third floor and installed himself in the conference room. He stared out the window, thinking about Santiago. The failure was incontrovertible. He had had his old enemy in hand, and let him slip away. Inexcusable. Except, he had to admit, he himself had also let the man escape all those years ago. Still, inexcusable. He picked up the phone, gave a few terse instructions to Maxwell, and told him to send Santiago in as soon as things were ready.

A few minutes later, Santiago arrived with two other men. He was sweating, just enough that the odor of his anxiety made Perez's nostrils flare slightly.

"Let's go downstairs," Perez said evenly. "We need to discuss our next steps."

Santiago said nothing as they moved down the hall to the elevator. This time it went down all the way to the first sub-basement below the garage. They entered a room with a large glass wall, where Maxwell was waiting with three other men. On the other side of the glass was an emaciated man, walking slowly, holding a handrail. He was wearing the helmet which indicated a metallic mesh implant, and cables were attached to the helmet and his spine. He was making good progress, his steps close to natural. Loud rhythmic music was playing, and he was trying to step along with the beat. They watched for a few minutes, then Perez turned to Santiago.

"This man is dying. We are barely keeping ahead of the infection. The man who you brought up from Florida – what did you say his name was?"

"Hansen," Santiago said, his throat dry.

"Yes, Hansen. Cameron Hansen." Perez smiled ruefully. "He had another name when I knew him. In any case, I was going to use him as a replacement. Your failure has made that impossible. Regrettable."

He waved his arm, and five men grabbed Santiago, flipping him neatly and effortlessly onto his stomach on a table to the left of the glass. His arms and ankles were handcuffed to the legs of the table, and thick leather straps were tightened around his thorax and buttocks. Santiago's head was turned towards the glass, where the mesh man was still walking slowly back and forth, clearly oblivious to what was happening on the other side of what was, to him, a mirror.

Maxwell brought in a rig, and two of the men used a Craftsman drill to secure it to Santiago's pelvis with four long screws. Santiago bit through his lip, but made no sound as blood dripped from his mouth. One of the men took a small sledge, and at Perez's nod, brought it down hard on the center of the rig. Santiago gasped as his breath was forced out. Then gasped again as he realized that there was no real pain. The chisel had not been placed in the rig. He turned his head the other way, where he saw Perez, who had a pencil-thin smile on his lips, and a deadness to his eyes.

"Never fail me again. The next time, I will not be merciful."

Perez and Maxwell left the observation room through a side door. "It's a question of value," Perez said once the door closed behind them. "I did not become who I am by wasting resources, financial or human. I am confident that I have made my point. Santiago is still a useful asset. For now."

Maxwell had also understood the lesson, and it was now the stench of *his* fear that Perez was inhaling as they entered a room filled with computers and servers. Blaylock was seated in front of a desk with a small monitor showing the man walking, and a large monitor with several dozen rows of irregular lines which were scrolling from left to right. There were labels down the left side, grouping the lines into sections, including left and right frontal cortex, motor cortex, sensory cortex, Broca's area, visual cortex, auditory cortex, hippocampus, and so forth.

"Show *el jefe* what you've got," Maxwell directed Blaylock.

"Progress, definitely progress," Blaylock enthused. "What you are looking at is real time. Let me show you some of what we've put together." He tapped rapidly on his keyboard, and the screen split into five columns.

"Each column is about three seconds of activity, but that is enough to get the idea. The first column is just walking. Note that the auditory line and frontal lines are almost flat, most of the activity is in the motor areas. The second column is when we added music – see how not just the auditory lines become much more active, but also the frontal and speech-center areas and even the hippocampus, as he processes and remembers the sounds. The third column is after about fifty repetitions of the same piece of music. See how the auditory line is about the same, but the other areas are quieter? Once the music is memorized, it does not get everything going in quite the same way." He pointed at the fourth column. "This one is really interesting. You know how we were concerned about how to get, shall we say, less-cooperative subjects to actively remember things? Well, after the fifty repetitions, we play a few seconds of the music, then stop it. The subject will always actively remember the next few seconds." He superimposed the fourth column over the second. "See how the auditory and frontal areas are almost identical in the memory phase to how they were in the acquisition phase? It's beautiful." He was beaming.

"And the fifth column?" Perez was leaning forward.

"Okay, so the fifth column was done in a silent room, where, instead of recording from the whole brain, we *input* signal into the auditory cortex identical to what we recorded when the music was playing, and record from the rest of the brain. You can see that the recording from the rest of the brain is similar to when there was music. Again, the subject is less than cooperative, but when we watch his gait and how he bobs to the rhythm, it appears that he is having the same experience from the mesh as from actual music."

"How does this compare to prior subjects?"

"On the one hand, beautifully; on the other, not very well. The broad activity is similar, but nothing specific enough to allow for, say, playing a song into a new subject's brain and having it be immediately recognizable as music. Each brain has to be analyzed and programmed individually. Vision is much easier, better subject-to-subject conformity. I can stream visual almost as easily as showing a movie."

"What about tapping into the subjects' memories?" Perez kept his tone level.

"*That* is a major cooperation problem," Blaylock shook his head. "If we had been able to keep subject F3 going a little longer, we may have had more. He really seemed to want to help with the project. Anxious, almost. We got to the point that if he actively remembered something, we could see how the memory diffused across the brain and we could record it."

"Diffused across the brain?" Perez asked. "What do you mean?"

"Well, it turns out that memories are not lodged somewhere in the temporal lobe like a lot of people think. That is more like a trigger area, but the different parts of a memory are stored in the cortex where they originated. For example, if you are remembering a day at the beach, the feel of the sand is in the sensory cortex, the view in the visual, the sound of the waves in the auditory, the emotions in the frontal, and so forth. We actually got to where we could shock a point in F3's temporal lobe and trigger a memory that we could interpret correctly."

"What about recording the entirety of a subject's memory. A cooperative subject, naturally."

"Well, first of all, I would need the new mesh to do that with any kind of resolution. Next, although the total storage capacity of the human brain is probably around fifteen terabytes, which is manageable, the relationship between various memories and thought would require a similar amount of RAM in order to be useful. That is truly state-of-the-art supercomputing. I now have a combination of eighty-five high speed units, linked in an integrated network of parallel and series combinations. I need about sixty more. My techs are working full time at installation, but it will take about two more weeks to operationalize. Finally, the biggest problem is that, at this point, it would take me about as long to record each memory as it took for it to occur, since we would be depending on the subject to make the connections by thinking about them. So, forty years of work for the memories of a forty-year-old, working full time all of his waking hours. During which time he would have made another forty years' worth. See the problem?"

Perez saw the problem. "I want you to devote all your resources to that particular problem. Experiment with rapid stimulation, amphetamines, depressants, whatever you think might make a difference. I need a solution. And have the computers ready in one week, not two." He spun the wheelchair around, then turned back. "You have off-site back up?"

"Your instructions were to keep all the data off-line, so just the raw data which is written to hard drives and taken to storage every day."

"Set up a second site with the whole necessary array, and configure to transmit all the data on the main project as it is gathered. Backup will be more important at that point than security. I don't want all my eggs in one basket." His fingers drummed. "I think a new CompServ site was just brought on line near Seattle. There should be two hundred servers set up. Have them linked up and configured." He wheeled out, and took the elevator to his fourth floor apartment, intending a swim in his roof-top enclosed pool.

Blaylock turned to Maxwell. "Is the new mesh going to work? I really need the higher resolution."

"Works great in dogs. Don't have a human yet."

"You know, I think I could do some of the memory research on dogs," Blaylock mused. "That might make it a lot easier to get a line on things. How many do you have up there?

"Eleven," replied Maxwell.

"That's a start. I'll get going."

* * *

"The problem with the dogs," Blaylock was telling Maxwell several hours later, "is that, although they clearly have memories, the sense of smell appears to be their biggest trigger, and it is hard for us to really relate to what is going on in their minds. Nonetheless, I think we have come up with something which may be useful. That semiconducting mesh is amazing. I have designed a way to produce thousands of synchronized current loops, which effectively produces a magnetic coil on the surface of the brain, which can be pulsed on and off in fractions of a millisecond. That causes the field fluctuations that I can use to read the signals produced by the brain tissue. So, instead of delivering shocks and looking for surface electrical activity, we can instead look through the entire thickness of the cortex for changes *related* to the activity. It is like functional MRI, only with ten thousand times the resolution. Stimulation of the dogs' olfactory areas leads to activity in the rest of the brain which can only be due to memory of whatever odor is evoked."

"How does that help us?" Maxwell was intrigued.

"Well, if we could calibrate to known memories, we should be able to stimulate these impulses and record the memories at an accelerated pace."

"How accelerated?"

"By a factor of nearly ten thousand. Meaning that we could record a year's worth of waking memories, meaning sixteen hour days, in as little as thirty-five minutes. If we could choose just the waking hours. Which we cannot, but only REM sleep seems to generate actual memories, so let's say about forty-five minutes per year of life."

"Would the subject need to be conscious?"

"Well, yes, for the calibration, meaning the recording of what sights, sounds, colors, odors, pain, touch, etc., look like in that particular subject's cortex. That would probably take twelve to fourteen hours. An extremely unpleasant and painful twelve to fourteen hours, I might add. But for the memories themselves, I don't know yet whether awake or sleeping may actually be best."

"Drug-induced sleep?"

"No, that would possibly lead to altered interpretation of the meanings. Regular sleep. Also, I should point out that this process does not require active cooperation. We could trial on a regular subject. The difficulty would be in verifying the memories. Cross-checking with known events should give us that information, if that were available."

* * *

Maxwell finished explaining Blaylock's findings. Perez, always a quick study, immediately saw the next step.

"How soon can Blaylock be ready to trial the process?"

"His techs are still building the mega-computer, but should be done early next week, as you requested."

"It will take that long to acquire a subject, spin a mesh, and implant it. Good work."

Maxwell was dismissed, and Perez went to his pool, where he was lowered into the water, and began to swim his laps. He thought about the details, turning them over and over in his mind, and by the time he was finished, he had a plan. He was just being helped out of the water, when the pain in his belly returned, more intense. If his man hadn't been right there, he could easily have drowned. As it was, the spasm passed. "Have Santiago here in an hour," he barked as he was helped off the hoist and into his chair. The man pulled out his phone and made the call, as Perez glided down the hall to his apartment.

* * *

Santiago was given very complete, very detailed instructions on exactly what they required. "I need them at the Queens facility by Sunday evening," he intoned flatly. "I don't have to remind you that there will be no further need for your services if you are not completely successful with this assignment."

Santiago nodded, setting his jaw. He would not fail.

Chapter 16

Friday, October 21
New York

Cameron was going crazy. Not figuratively, like being annoyed, but literally, like he was starting to have hallucinations. He had been in a meeting in a large conference room at JFK with the TSA director and representatives from FBI, CIA, State Department, Commerce Department, and, of course, Homeland Security, for just over two hours. Nothing had happened. Nothing. Now if he closed his eyes, he both saw and heard things that weren't really there. Mostly flashbacks of the videos he had been forced to watch in Perez's cell. He could almost feel the point of the chisel entering his spine, hear the sounds of his own lips screaming.

"Hansen!" He did not react. "Earth to Hansen," the TSA director repeated. "Are you with us? Or is the safety of airline travel not a compelling issue for a master spy?"

Cameron sat up with a start. The FBI drone next to him sniggered. He looked like an ad for Middle Aged Spread. They had met that morning while consuming the slightly stale bagels with not enough cream cheese provided by their hosts, and for Cameron, it had been contempt at first sight. Not just the usual CIA vs FBI competition, but something more visceral. Phillips reminded Cameron of the AV guy at his high school who would change the internet passwords during the middle of class, so he would have to be called in to save the day by rescuing a crashed presentation. Or hack into the web cams on the girls' laptops and drool with his buddies while they watched their unsuspecting victims pick their noses or put on deodorant or change their clothes. Now, all grown up, with a badge and a gun, he was able to torture a much broader segment of the population. Worse, Phillips did not seem to be cognizant of Cameron's instant loathing, but actually seemed good-old-boy friendly.

The director was asking him a direct question, which he had clearly missed.

"Sorry sir, could you repeat that?" His face burned.

"What is the current rate of chatter from known terrorist facilities in Tunisia?

Cameron flipped through his notes, missing the pertinent graphic until Phillips stuck his fat middle finger in the stack and gave him the knowing "I saved you, pathetic Muggle" smirk.

"Nothing off of the curve, slightly more than last week, but no significant change."

"Thank you." The director continued his interminable pontification.

Cameron's mind started to wander again. His assertions to Mitzi notwithstanding, after a half day at TSA, he knew he could not just let the Perez matter go. He kept coming back to the same question. What was the goal? What was the ultimate point of the research?

At the coffee break, he walked down the hall and called Mitzi.

"Three hours," she said. "Well done. I was sure you would only be able to hold out for two."

He ignored the jibe. "I can't concentrate on this crap. I keep seeing those videos." He was more than a little embarrassed, worried that Mitzi would think him weak, or damaged, or, heaven forbid, try to connect with him in sympathy. He needn't have worried.

"Not interested," she shot back. "Call your boss and get a couple of weeks off. They should have offered you a leave of absence after this week. I'm going up to Boston to talk to a guy I know at MIT. You can come."

Cameron took a deep breath. The DDO had, in fact told him to take some time. He had refused. "I'll call you back." He hung up and dialed the Center.

The boss' secretary did not even put him through. "He left the papers with me," she said. "He figured you would call. He wants you to check back in two weeks. And no, he does not want to talk to you."

Cameron was about to hang up, grateful to have avoided an encounter, when she said, "And Hansen." Leave Perez alone. If he finds out you have been working on that case, your leave may be extended. Indefinitely." SHE hung up.

He walked back down to the conference room, picked up his things, and started to leave. Phillips was just coming back in, his bulk blocking the exit.

"Leaving so soon?" His smile was so large and so irritating that Cameron almost took a swing at him.

"Change in assignment," he said. "Tell the Director they'll be sending someone else over."

He called Mitzi as he walked to the parking lot. "So, when are we going to Boston?"

"We leave from La Guardia in ninety minutes. My guy has some time this afternoon. Chop chop." She hung up.

"Only Mitzi," Cameron thought, heading for the Grand Central Parkway.

* * *

They caught the 1:00 p.m. American flight to Boston. The meeting was set for four, and they were almost an hour early getting to the MIT campus. Mitzi grabbed Cameron's elbow and dragged him a few doors down Massachusetts Ave to the Flour Bakery, where they split a roasted lamb sandwich at a tiny table by the window.

"I should probably mention that Aidan and I had a thing. Just thought you should be aware."

Cameron was intrigued. He knew almost nothing about her other relationships. "Tell me more."

She looked at him blankly. "Nothing more to tell. He was in graduate school in neurophysiology when I was a medical student at Mayo, and we had a thing. Lasted a few weeks. I've talked to him maybe a dozen times since. He's at MIT's McGovern Institute, and is a specialist in the study of brain organization. I thought he might have some useful ideas." She took a large bite of sandwich.

Cameron was more than a little irritated. She had said almost nothing at the airport, on the flight, or during the cab ride to campus. He had been able to extract the name Aidan Beauchamps, but that was about it. When pushed, she said she had no new ideas, no new information, and wanted to avoid speculation until she had something more to go on. On the flight, she stuck earbuds in her ears and listened to an Audio Digest podcast which summarized articles in the most recent *Journal of Forensic and Legal Medicine*. Cameron had read an article on Dakota Fanning in the *American Way* magazine in the back of the seat in front of him.

* * *

They met Aidan in his cramped office. He was a short, intense man with nearly black eyes and black wavy hair. His speech was a rapid-fire

113

staccato, almost manic. As soon as they sat down, he launched into a monologue on the difficulties inherent in the academic pursuit of grant money, and the need for additional funding for research. Mitzi was only able to listen politely for about four minutes before she interrupted him.

"We came here for some help," she started. He stopped abruptly and sat back.

"Yes, yes, of course. What can I do for you?"

Mitzi described the cranial mesh and the videos they had seen of the subjects walking. He asked some questions, but mostly just listened in a focused way that made Cameron slightly uneasy. When she was done, he gazed up towards the ceiling, then suddenly jerked forward, slapping both hands on his desk.

"I would give anything to have access to this data," he enthused. "Do you realize how much faster we could advance our knowledge with an actual cortical interface? All we have are skin electrodes and functional MRI, and believe me, that is useful for mapping, but hardly for improving our understanding of encoding."

"You do realize that unwilling subjects are essentially being kidnapped, tortured, and killed here," Cameron broke in.

"Oh, yes, of course, forgive me, just saying, from a research standpoint . . . Well, it would be unparalleled."

"Except in Nazi death camps," Cameron finished for him.

"The question," Mitzi asked, glaring at Cameron, "is, what would be the potential practical use for the data which could make the effort worthwhile."

"Well, it could simply be the obvious, that this guy is trying to reanimate his legs. I agree that you would not need the whole brain cortex for that, but, as an experimental interface, you would be able to extract information that would allow you to then refine a smaller, more practical implant. Still, it seems like there would at least have been some subjects-"

"-victims," Cameron interjected through clenched teeth.

"-yes, yes, victims, with smaller implants." He paused, staring at a point just over Mitzi's head. "Or maybe he has a degenerative condition, and is trying to get ahead of becoming locked in. You know, be able to connect to a computer so that as he lost sight, hearing, motor control, etc., he would be able to still interact with the world. You said he was paraplegic. Maybe his disease is degenerative."

"His disease is that he was shot in the spine." Cameron offered.

"Okay, so not degenerative. How about gaming? There are thousands of nerds who would pay enormous sums to be completely connected. You know, just plug in a USB, and have total sensory immersion into another world."

"Seems unlikely," Mitzi frowned. "This guy is already a billionaire. I think he is more about controlling THIS world than some fantasy world."

"So, maybe that is it – incredibly high-speed, high-resolution interface with a computer and of course the internet. In many ways, it is the human-machine interface that is limiting things now. If he were directly connected to a supercomputer, he could access data, perform calculations, infiltrate systems. In theory, access everything, everywhere, anywhere connected to the internet. Like a comic book super villain."

"That actually fits the profile," mused Mitzi. "Still, there is the problem that the interface is not sustainable. No one would want to control the world for a few weeks until their implant killed them."

"No," said Aidan, "THIS implant is not sustainable. He just needs a better implant. That's an engineering issue. Look at atomic bombs. The first devices weighed many tons at Los Alamos, then they got them down to something small enough to actually drop on Japan, and in a few years, the engineers had serviceable high-yield devices in handy backpack sizes. With a better implant, he would possibly have something serviceable in the near future. Of course, developing that could also take years. Depends on how much R&D money you can throw at it. You wouldn't even need human subjects -" he raised his eyebrows at Cameron, "victims. Animal models would be fine for implant optimization."

"What would be the main obstacles with regards to improving the interface?" Mitzi asked.

"Wire size, insulation, and heat. A metal mesh like the one you describe would be fine for detecting impulses for controlling movement, but if there was any significant signal being placed INTO the system, you would develop enough heat to cook the brain. Also, you would need to insulate at least some of the wiring, adding to the bulk. And of course, finer wires would allow for a thin enough implant to put INSIDE the skull, which would solve a myriad of problems. Did you run into anything about research on wire mesh?"

"No," Mitzi replied.

"Good, then you probably have some time."

They took a cab back to Logan Airport. Mitzi hopped out, but

Cameron didn't move. "Let's go," she urged.

"I think I'll stay for a day or two. I have some computer science contacts at Aasgard I want to talk to."

"What's Aasgard?"

"It's an artificial intelligence firm chock full of people who are used to thinking far out of the box."

"I'm staying, too, then." Mitzi started to get back in.

"No," Cameron was firm. "They aren't the kind of, uh, people who would talk to someone they don't know."

Mitzi squinted. "I guess I'm not the only one with old 'friends' in Boston." She slammed the door and stalked into the airport.

* * *

Santiago checked into the resort near San Pedro De Macoris on the southern coast of the Dominican Republic Friday afternoon. He went to his third floor suite overlooking the pool, and immediately set up. He first rolled plastic screens onto the sliding glass doors on the balcony. From the outside, it would be reflective, but he was able to see out just fine. He set up high-powered binoculars, and started scanning the people around the pool. He had enough equipment for five possible subjects, and it took just over forty-five minutes to decide which were the most likely. He put on his swim trunks, and headed down to the pool, a satchel over his shoulder. He walked around the pool area a few times, just another tourist strolling. He stopped several times to sit on the wall around the deck, sipping from a water bottle he took from his satchel as he took in the sights. After a quick dip in the pool, he went back up to his suite.

He booted up his receiver to monitor the five directional microphones he had positioned on the retaining wall, pointed at the five families he had identified. All were also recording for later review. He soon ruled out family number two. They were speaking Portuguese, not Spanish. Five was also eliminated, when four more children wandered by, their conversation clearly pegging them as all being part of the family. Mother number one showed herself to be unacceptable, spending far too much time on her novel, not paying enough attention to her child playing in the water.

That left families three and four. Three was promising. The child, a boy of about ten, was a somewhat chubby, whiny momma's boy, who was obsessed with splashing his parents, who were talking animatedly non-stop. They kept talking about the husband's parents in Guadalajara, and the mother used her cell phone to record Junior's shenanigans a good twenty-five percent of the time. It sounded like they had just arrived for their two-week stay.

Four was similar, although the boy was a little older, a lot thinner, and marginally less annoying. The father was constantly on his phone, and the mother was also talking, but stopped frequently to video the son. There was little conversation between the parents, but the man had told several people on the phone that they would be back to Mexico City the following Wednesday.

A good day's work. He phoned Alyssa. "Hi, gorgeous. I need you here tomorrow." He tried to sound seductive. His heart sped a little as he thought of her hard, supple body.

Alyssa laughed mockingly. "I'll be in at nine p.m. out of Atlanta on Delta. And remember, no funny business." The line went dead.

Chapter 17

Friday, October 21
New York

After his usual Friday clinic of scheduling surgical patients, Dr. Overbridge left the hospital precisely on schedule and began his walk home. Just as he had finished step two hundred and fifty-six, he felt something behind his right eye. Painful, but not debilitating. He knew at once what it was, having waited for this particular moment for over thirty years. He immediately turned, and walked into the Dunkin Donuts next to the 99¢ store. Predictably, there were two policemen, one the beat cop who passed Dr. Overbridge more days than not while making his rounds.

"Officer, would you do me the kindness of calling for an ambulance. I believe my aneurysm is leaking."

The police officer radioed it in, and Dr. Overbridge refused his offer of a donut, stating that he may require surgery and that he preferred to keep his stomach empty.

When the ambulance arrived, Dr. Overbridge refused to lie on the stretcher, but instead climbed onto the seat next to the attendant. As they headed north on 3rd Avenue, the driver said he was lucky, that Our Lady of Salubrious Penitence was only a few blocks, and they had a world class neurosurgery department.

"No," replied Dr. Overbridge, "they do not have a world class department. They have a world class neurosurgeon. And I am he. You will kindly drive away from that fetid pile of incompetent quackery and take me to Lenox Hill. If I become unconscious prior to my arrival, please ask them to call in Dr. Jack Tucker, and only Dr. Tucker. Please also call my housekeeper, and have her go to my apartment and retrieve a packet of films from my tie closet. It is labeled with my name, and addressed to Dr. Tucker. I am sure she has been wondering about it for years. Ask her to bring it to Lenox Hill with all haste."

He then pulled out his wallet, and counted out $1000 to each of them, also giving them a card with his housekeeper's phone number.

And then the world exploded in a bright flash, and he slumped in his seat.

* * *

Jack Tucker was just getting out of a cab with his wife at Lincoln Center when his phone started vibrating. "Who is that?" Cathy asked.

He showed her the text. "Please call Dr. Douglas at Lenox Hill ER for an emergency with Dr. Overbridge."

"I thought that you said you were *not* on call this weekend? Is this another scheme to avoid the Opera?"

"I'm not. This says I need to call for an emergency with Dr. Overbridge. That's like being told to call for an emergency with God. I wonder what the great man could possibly want with me?"

He made the call. Oh, the joys of modern life. In his father's day, if you were on call, you told the service where to find you, or *try* to find you, and if you were not on call, then you simply were not on call. None of this crap.

"Hi, this is Dr. Tucker, I was summoned. Not sure why, I'm not on call."

After a minute the ER doc came on the line. "Hi Jack, sorry to bother you, but I have an unconscious world famous neurosurgeon and a packet of ancient X-rays here, addressed to you. The report is in German, but as far as I can tell, it's talking about an aneurysm. I sent the films down to radiology. Last thing Overbridge said before he passed out was to call you. I know you're not on call, but I thought I'd give you the chance."

"Yeah, I'll come over. Be there in about twenty minutes." He hung up.

"Who the heck is Dr. Overbridge?" Cathy was irritated. "Can't someone else take the case? I don't want to go to La Boheme alone."

Jack had an inspiration. "Text Betsy, I'll bet she's at the church and would love to go." The meetinghouse for their church was across from Lincoln Center, and Betsy was one of Cathy's best friends.

Cathy's fingers tapped on her phone. Barely ten seconds later the phone vibrated.

"Wow, fastest text reply in history. She's headed over. See you later. Let me know when you know something." She kissed him as he hopped into a cab to go back across town.

"Who the heck is Dr. Overbridge?" Jack thought to himself. That was an excellent question. Jack was not sure anyone knew the answer.

* * *

Jack's cab pulled up at Lenox Hill Hospital. He jogged up the ramp to the ER, and was directed to Exam Room 12. There he found Dr. Overbridge, or at least the wraith he had become. Jack would never have recognized him. He had regained consciousness, and Ed Douglas, the ER doctor, was clearly frustrated with him.

"It's on the right, the right, the right, right right right." Dr. Overbridge was chanting as if it were a mantra.

Ed was relieved to see Jack.

"We filled him with decadron and dextran, and he regained consciousness. He's been like this ever since. He either tells us to 'Get Tucker get Tucker get Tucker' or repeats that 'it is on the right,' or tells us, 'It's an aneurysm, look at the films, look at the films, look at the films.'"

"So," said Jack with a smile, "may I look at the films?"

"They're over in radiology. It's an angiogram and a crummy MRI from 1983. From Zurich. I didn't think they even HAD MRIs in 1983."

"Not many," agreed Jack. "Guess I'll go have a look. In the meantime, get a STAT scan to evaluate how much of a hematoma we have."

"It's all queued up, should be ready to go in a few minutes," replied Ed.

Radiology was just across the hall, and Sunny Patel, the neuroradiologist, was looking at the films.

"Hi, Jack. Check out these antiques. Looks like a 4 mm saccular aneurysm of the right middle cerebral artery. At least it was in 1983. Who knows how large it is now."

"I wonder why he never had it clipped?" Jack was curious. "That was a pretty small aneurysm, and should have been successfully treated, even thirty years ago."

"Look at the MRI." Sunny pointed to the other bank of view boxes, where a terrible-quality early scan was hanging. There was a smooth, fluid filled mass just superior to the area where the aneurysm would have been. "They must have gotten the angio to get more information on this cyst and then found the aneurysm. It looks like the cyst would be pretty much blocking access."

Jack agreed. "That cyst would have lowered the success rate from about ninety percent down to perhaps forty percent. Funny he didn't have any follow up studies. You would have thought he would have wanted to know if it was growing."

"Surgeons." Sunny was shaking his head. "If it is YOUR brain, they want to operate yesterday, if it is THEIRS, they just go into denial and take up sky-diving. No offense."

How could he take offense at such an obvious truth? It was like that for hernias. Jack had seen pictures of trusses in textbooks, but the only real one he had ever seen was on one of the general surgeons in the hospital locker room.

"Looks like I may have a long night," Jack said. "Hope the MRI gives us some more information."

He settled down to wait for the scan. Sent a text to Cathy to let her know he would be late, perhaps LATE. Made small-talk with Sunny.

"There's coffee in the next room. Or tea."

"None for me, thanks. Gave that up a few years ago. Joined the Mormons."

Sunny was intrigued. "I heard something about that. How's that working out? Got married again, too, did I hear?"

"Two years now. Working out great. Changed my life. For the better. And Cathy is, well, wonderful."

The stretcher went past, taking Dr. Overbridge into the scanner room. Jack glanced at his watch. 8:30. The opera should go to almost eleven. He went into the control room to watch as they did the scan.

* * *

As they loaded him onto the scanner table, Dr. Overbridge was feeling better. He had stopped jabbering, and was able to think clearly for the first time since the ambulance. He assessed himself. *Okay, thinking clearly. Toes move, fingers move.*

"Please hold still, Doc." The tech was talking to him through the ear muffs. An MRI scan was like lying down with your head and upper body in an old-fashioned galvanized steel garbage can, which someone was tapping. With a sledge hammer. He involuntarily began to count the taps.

He wondered how many MRIs he had looked at in his lifetime. When he was in Zurich doing his fellowship with Schneider, their new scanner had just been delivered, and they were doing scans on all of the house staff just to get used to the machine, and see how it worked. To everyone's surprise, on his they had found something. The radiologists had not seen enough scans to really even know what. Now he would have seen at a glance that it was a simple cyst, really of no consequence. At the time, however, they were concerned, and had done an angiogram. THAT had shown something. A small aneurysm off of the right middle cerebral artery. Small enough that nowadays they would fix it with an angiographic coil. In 1983, surgery had been the only choice. Or ignore it. And wait for it to get larger and burst. He had chosen to put his head in the sand, but he had always known that someday it would leak. Or burst. Well, well, today was the day. He never told anyone, just stole the relevant films and brought them back to the U.S. Aneurysms had become his life, and were likely to be his death. Every few years, he had tried to decide who in New York would be the best surgeon. Besides himself, of course. He would then get a new mailer, re-address his X-rays, and put them back in his closet. There was something that always stopped him from having a re-evaluation. Probably fear. Not just of complications, but of the loss of control. He spent his whole life making sure he was in control of every detail. There was simply no way for him to direct his own operation.

He hoped Tucker was up to it. He had been an admirable resident, working harder than everyone else, plus having better hands and smarts. Overbridge had been pleased when he went to Lenox Hill, although Mt. Sinai would have been closer to both his apartment and Our Lady.

Our Lady of Salubrious Penitence. He smiled. He had gone there to poke them all in the eye. And himself. He was sure to have been the next Chair at Columbia's Neurological Institute of New York. Before Lake. Before Monique. Before Pierre. *What an arrogant fool I had been.* So, penitence at Our Lady of Salubrious Penitence. Founded in 1886 as a sanatorium for "working" women with tuberculosis or advanced syphilis, the nuns had been certain that the Love of God was heavily peppered with Divine Justice for the whores of Manhattan. He felt cursed himself, every day. It had been too far to walk up from SoHo, and so he would walk a mile or so north from his loft, then catch a cab the rest of the way, and the reverse in the evenings. Then he found increasing comfort in walking EXACTLY a mile, and it became clear that the only reasonable thing was to find a place at the proper distance. Exactly. It was better to leave SoHo anyway. Too many distractions, too many ghosts. He had been wrong, however, to think he could escape the ghosts. So, he quieted them by meticulous attention to detail. If he were perfect enough in his routine, they would leave him alone. Or at least be quieter. Less condemning.

Banking had always been the family's plan. His father and his father's fathers before him had been bankers, and were quietly rich in the understated way of the Boston Brahmin. He had rebelled, but only mildly, going west to Berkeley instead of staying at Harvard. There he studied

Economics and co-eds, planning all the while to eventually return to Harvard for business school. Then came Vietnam. And the first ghosts.

He had been an exceptional marksman. He went to Southeast Asia as a well-trained killer. And kill he did. One hundred and thirty-three souls, if people really have souls. Seventy-eight shot in the head. The Brain. How many brains would he have to repair to make up for those seventy-eight? He had saved seventy-eight, and they still haunted him. He had saved seven hundred and eighty, and they still haunted him. Then seventy-eight hundred. Now over twice that. Seventeen thousand, two hundred and thirty-three saves. There had been some deaths, naturally, but they did not haunt him. Except for Lake, the only man he had killed neither by design nor by fate's hand, but by something less forgivable. Negligence.

* * *

The banging stopped, and he was taken out of the scanner. He could see Tucker through the glass of the control room, looking intently at the monitor.

"Kindly ask Dr. Tucker to come look at the films with me in Emergency," he was talking to the nurse wheeling him back. "I need to know where we stand."

Where he stood was actually lying on a stretcher, with a clot the size of a fist in the right side of his brain. Jack showed him the films. "The fact that you are awake and talking tells us that most if not all of that volume must be the aneurysm. Anyone with a sudden clot that large would be dead, or at least paralyzed on half of his body."

Overbridge grimaced. "Clearly. That aneurysm itself must be at least eight centimeters. You, Dr. Tucker, are in for an exciting night. I wish I could be awake to watch."

Irrespective of who the patient was, Jack had the same speech. "The risks of surgery include infection, bleeding, brain injury, and death. Your other options are . . ."

Overbridge interrupted, "You and I both know that the only option is death. Anything else is a fairy tale or a miracle, and I don't believe in either one. Get me to surgery as soon as is possible, if you don't mind."

* * *

The operating room was ready, so Jack headed upstairs. He was a little nervous. After all, this was not only Dr. Overbridge, but it was also a really big, leaking aneurysm, which he did not have the luxury of investigating more thoroughly. Plus, it was Friday night, and he was tired.

He grabbed his iPod from the locker, slammed the door, and headed down the hall to operating room South-3.

When Jack got to the OR, things were in their usual chaotic state, preparing for an after-hours case. A large room, twenty by thirty feet, it had been recently renovated, and was completely up-to-date, including video cameras mounted in the surgeons' headlights so as to be able to record the entire procedure. The on-call surgery staff was bustling around, getting everything set up. The patient was not yet in the room.

"Who do we have for anesthesia?"

"Hi Dr. Tucker," responded a pleasant woman in a Mickey Mouse scrub cap. "We have Dr. Franz tonight. He's in pre-op getting the patient."

"Ah, Alice! I can't tell you how happy I am to see you. You never know who you're going to get on the weekend. And Paul, too? I must have won the lottery."

"Don't get too excited, Dr. Tucker." She looked around. They were alone. "Your scrub tech is Jeremy."

"Jeremy? I don't know Jeremy."

"You wouldn't. He usually works Ortho. I'm not sure he's done a Neuro case since he got here."

Jack groaned. "Perfect." Jeremy walked through the door and gowned up.

"Jack Tucker. Pleased to meet you. Maybe we should go over the instruments I'm likely to use." He put on gloves, and started going through the two-hundred-piece instrument set, indicating which ones he wanted to have available. Jack told Jeremy the name of each instrument, and he kept nodding and saying "got it," but Jack could tell this was going to be a long one.

"Don't worry," Jeremy assured him, "I was in the army, I can handle anything."

Jack was not convinced. He plugged in his iPod, and chose his OR playlist. "The greatest hits of the '30's, '40's, '50's, '60's, '70's, '80's '90's, and Today," he announced.

Paul Franz pushed open the OR door, and wheeled in the patient. "Evening, Jack. This one looks interesting."

Dr. Overbridge was calling to him. "Yes, sir?" Jack asked.

"Can you tell me your plan? Your precise plan? I need to know the details."

"Actually, Dr. Overbridge, what you need to know is that I am faced with an eight centimeter leaking aneurysm, and that I will have to see what it looks like when I get in. The last thing you need is for me to be constrained by a speculative plan based on insufficient information. You made a big effort to get here to be here with ME in MY OR, so now trust me to do my work. We'll talk after, and I'll give you the play by play."

Halfway through his little speech, Jack could tell that his patient had stopped listening, and appeared to be counting the ceiling tiles. Or maybe the little holes IN the ceiling tiles. Or maybe the molecules of oxygen in the air. Counting something, that was certain.

Just before going out to scrub, Jack shot Cathy a text to let her know he was starting a leaking aneurysm, and had no idea when he would be home. Thank goodness tomorrow was Saturday, and he was NOT on call. It was already after ten.

Things started out fine. Jack incised the scalp, exposing the skull, and cut out a good-sized rectangle of bone, setting it aside to be plated back in at the end. The aneurysm was a giant, pulsating mass with a wall as thin as tissue paper. Jeremy was pushing in to look. "Wow, that's a big one. What's the plan?"

"Well, on the far side of that throbbing mass is the aneurysm's neck, probably no more than a quarter of an inch across, coming off of a vital artery not much bigger. If I can clamp the neck, we'll be golden. If I miss, or rupture the thing, we'll have a bloody mess, and I probably won't be able to stop it fast enough to save anything resembling the essence of Dr. Overbridge here. If I accidentally clamp the artery itself instead of the aneurysm neck, then he'll have a major, possibly fatal, stroke. Also, I can't put enough pressure on the mass to move it so I can see. I'll have to do it by feel."

Jack got it exposed as well as he could, then went over and stared intently at the thirty-year-old angios. After a few minutes, Jeremy cleared his throat, "Er, Doc, are you going to do some surgery here?"

Jack turned slowly and looked at Jeremy. "The neck should be coming off the vessel in the same place where it always was. If you will kindly shut up, I am trying to get the position fixed in my mind so I can do this thing." He turned back to the films, and stared and stared, trying to remove all words from his mind, and just become one with the three-dimensional anatomy of his patient's brain. When he felt that his mental

126

picture was perfect, he moved back into place at the operating table. He said a little prayer, and then, with one motion, he gently pushed the aneurysm forward, and slipped a long curved clamp along the side and around to what he hoped was the neck, and ratcheted the jaws together. It felt okay, but there was only one way to know. He opened the mass, suctioned out the blood, and as the wall collapsed he could see that his clamp was very nearly perfectly placed. He adjusted it slightly, applied the permanent clip, and stepped back, sweating.

For the next several minutes, he simply stared into the cavity where the aneurysm had been. Just to reassure himself that the clip was holding, and that there was not any other bleeding. He zapped a few minor oozing points with his bipolar cautery, dabbed gently here and there with cotton sponges. Just watching. Appropriately, Tom Petty was playing on the speakers. The waiting IS the hardest part.

* * *

It was after two when he crept into his house. He went to the guest bathroom and took a warm shower to relax himself, then quietly climbed the stairs and slipped in bed next to Cathy. He was not sure whether she really woke up – she just twined her arms and legs around him and resumed her soft snoring. She had been a little embarrassed when he first had told her she snored, but it truly did not bother him at all, it was just soft and soothing. As he had told her, "I like it when you snore, because then I know you're there."

He was too wired to sleep, just lying there for what seemed like hours, but it was in reality just a few minutes, motionless, enjoying the feel of Cathy breathing beside him.

Chapter 18

Saturday, October 22
New York

Jack woke up to the sound of his phone at a few minutes after seven. He was cranky. "NOT ON CALL," he wanted to shout. But he knew it would be about Overbridge. He had told the ICU nurses that he would be taking calls over the weekend for that patient only.

"Hi Dr. Tucker. Just wanted to give you the update. Your patient in 643, Overbridge, has been stable. Dr. Kelly has kept him snowed and hyperventilated to make sure his intracranial pressure stayed okay. Vitals are all stable. Do you want to try and wean him this morning?"

"Yeah, go ahead and let him wake up. I'll be over around ten. See if you can have him ready to extubate by then."

Jack made his signature goat cheese, havarti and mushroom omelets, with his mother's secret ingredient, corn flakes, added for texture. Cathy was a big fan.

"How long will you be at the hospital this morning?"

"Not long. I just want to make sure he is neurologically intact once we get him off the blower, then I should be good to go. What's on the docket for today?"

Newlywed or not, Cathy had figured out that 'not long' to a neurosurgeon with a fresh post-op in the Neuro ICU meant somewhere between an hour and a half and six hours.

"I was going to get my hair done at two, but there is a message that they had a cancellation, so I think I'll go now. Let's just see when we're both done."

They walked together to Gino's. "Let me know what's happening," she said. "I want to go to the flea market on the West Side later if we have time." She gave him a peck and darted into the salon. He continued down Madison towards the hospital.

When Jack arrived at the ICU, the Intensivist on duty was waiting. He was a large, round, smiling man from Louisiana and had some unpronounceable Cajun name, so was called "Bubba" by one and all.

"He's ready to go, breathing fine, just waiting for you," he reported.

Jack looked at the monitors and checked the ventilator. Bubba was impatient. "Hey, Jack, he's cool. I'm pulling the tube." He cut the straps securing the endotracheal breathing tube, deflated the balloon that was holding a seal in the windpipe, and smoothly drew out the tube.

Dr. Overbridge coughed a couple of times, then looked at Jack. "It would appear that I am alive, so I congratulate you on a successful conclusion. I would like to have the pressure bolt removed, and then leave the hospital at once."

Jack looked at him quizzically. "I would prefer that you stay and remain monitored for at least twenty-four hours here in the ICU. I don't need to tell you the risks we run if your pressure goes up, or if you were to re-bleed. I doubt you would let any of your patients leave twelve hours after the repair of a giant leaking brain aneurysm."

"Certainly not. They would not be able to adequately comprehend all of the potential risks. I, on the other hand, understand them perfectly, and choose to go. Also, I would like to verify that you have not contacted anyone at Our Lady of Salubrious Penitence regarding this episode. I do not authorize you to discuss my case with anyone. Anyone."

"I haven't yet, but it seems like we should let them know you will not be at work on Monday."

"That is not your affair, Dr. Tucker. I will take action if you violate my confidence. Not one word. To anyone. Now kindly remove my bolt and IV, and sign my discharge."

"No, I think you should stay."

"Fine, I'll sign out Against Medical Advice. And yes, I know my insurance might refuse the bill. Please have the papers brought up at once. Don't worry, I'll pay if BlueCross balks. I am most grateful for your skill and service. Truly I am."

"I could hold you on an involuntary commitment."

"It would never stand. I'm lucid, and I am obviously aware of my risks."

Fine, Jack thought, *Let the crazy old goat have his way.*

He watched while the pressure bolt and IV were removed, then followed Dr. Overbridge down to the lobby and watched him get into a cab.

Overbridge rolled down the window. "One more thing, if you don't mind."

"Yes?"

"Would you and your lovely new bride care to meet me for dinner this coming Friday? Perhaps the New York Athletic Club at seven?"

"Uh, I'll check with Cathy, but I suppose that would be okay."

"Very well. Call me to confirm." He rattled off a phone number, which Jack wrote on his hand.

Jack stared as the cab drove off, then turned and walked home.

* * *

After Overbridge left Lenox Hill, he directed the cabby to turn up Fifth and head north. He stared to the side, counting the doorways as they passed. After a few blocks, he spotted a street vendor. "Pull over, please." He unrolled the window, waved a twenty, and called to the man presiding over a large table of knitted hats and scarfs.

"A black knit cap, please."

The man obediently brought over the item. "Ten bucks."

Overbridge handed him the twenty. "Keep it." They drove on north. He next had the cab stop in front of a drug store on 94th. He called over to a teenager. "Young man – would you be interested in making forty dollars for ten minutes' work?"

The kid was interested.

"Please go into the drug store and get me two sets of eyebrow tweezers and a package of super glue. Here's fifty dollars, you can keep the change."

He shrugged, grabbed the fifty, and was back in more like five minutes, carrying a small paper bag. "Thank you," Overbridge said, taking the bag. The taxi continued uptown.

After two hundred and forty-three doorways had passed, they arrived at his apartment. He paid the cabby, took five steps to the door, six more into the lobby, nodded to the doorman, eight more steps to the elevator, up, and then four more to his apartment. He went to the mirror, and checked his appearance. He took off the new watch cap. The large incision was closed with skin staples, and had nothing to hide it on his bald pate. There were orange traces of the betadine prep solution around the ears and forehead.

He called his attorney, gave him instructions on what he required, then called the corner grocer, who sent a delivery order of bread, cheese, and smoked salmon. He was starving. He was also in searing pain. Although the brain itself is not sensitive, having a piece of bone sawed out of the skull is excruciating. He had no pain pills, other than Advil, which he did not wish to take due to risk of bleeding, and Tylenol. That would have to do. He ate, and then arranged himself seated in a high-backed chair, not wanting to lie down and invite brain swelling. After recording a new message on his answering machine, he fell into a fitful sleep.

* * *

Santiago glanced at his watch. Almost noon. Family number four had not made an appearance, but family three had set up, a couple of hours earlier, in exactly the same chairs as the day before. *Okay, then,* he thought, *Family Three, you are the winners on the Price is Right.* He had heard the father, Miguel, tell the mother, Marta, that they should take Jorge to the resort's evening Fiesta at six. Santiago had room service send up fish tacos for lunch, and made reservations of his own for the Fiesta. He then settled in to watch and listen, keeping notes of anything that might be useful.

* * *

By the time Cathy had finished with her hair, it was about one o'clock. Her phone showed a text. "All done. Going home, will take nap. Wake me." She stopped by that French bakery that he liked on the way, and brought him one of their twice-baked almond croissants.

Jack was most definitely sleeping when she got home. On the living room couch. She looked at him for a minute. She tiptoed over and knelt down next to him. She put her lips to his ear and purred softly, "Hungry, baby?" He turned his head to her, and kissed her mouth deeply.

"Mmmmm." He took a deep breath. His eyes popped open and he sniffed, then grabbed the croissant that she was holding over him. "Thanks, sweetie."

"How's your patient?"

That was actually a complex question. Jack was not really sure of the answer. He decided to go with the short version. "Seems okay. Woke up fine."

She had her own mission. "You okay for the flea market?"

Jack and Cathy were just getting ready to head out when the doorbell rang. He opened the door to find a bicycle messenger with a slim ivory envelope.

"John Xavier Tucker, MD?"

"Yes. What's this?"

"No idea. Don't shoot the messenger." He grinned. "Sign here." Jack signed, and he was back on his bike and gone.

Jack examined the envelope. The return address had about nine names and covered a ridiculous percentage of the available space. *Attorneys.* He turned back into the house and tore it open.

The salutation indicated that copies of this had been sent via certified mail and messenger, and listed the Lenox Hill Hospital CEO, Paul Franz, Edward Douglas, Sunny Patel, three intensivists, and "any and all persons involved in the care and treatment of Augustus Overbridge on October 21 and 22" as co-recipients.

"What the HELL is this?!" Cathy came around the corner. She had not heard him swear previously. It was almost a joke with them.

He read on.

"By the hereby, you are served notice that under no circumstances may the private health information of Augustus Overbridge be shared with anyone not directly involved with his care. This specifically and particularly includes administration and staff at Our Lady of Salubrious Penitence. Any violation will be met with a complaint to the New York State Board of Medical Licensure, and will be referred to the New York Prosecuting Attorney for investigation of violation of privacy provisions of the *Health Insurance Portability and Accountability Act* of 1996."

Jack looked up at Cathy. "I guess that, since I read that to you, I'll be going to prison."

"What's he worried about? You said he was fine."

"Well, he *was* fine. I didn't give you the whole story. We extubated him, and then he immediately demanded to be discharged, and left Against Medical Advice. Oh, and he invited us to dinner on Friday at seven."

"You should probably call your attorney."

Jack put in a call to LexMed's main attorney, got an answering service, this being Saturday, and left a message for an urgent call. He then went to the den and scanned the letter, emailed it to the attorney, and cc'd himself so it would be available on his iPhone.

"Okay, let's go."

"What? Where?"

"The flea market. We're losing daylight here."

"Shouldn't you wait for your attorney to call?" Cathy continued to be baffled by his ability to compartmentalize. Jack was the epitome of the mission-driven, single-focus male.

"My phone works all over the city. No reason to sit around here."

So, off they went across the park. It was cold, but sunny, and they walked briskly. Jack was quiet, just enjoying the fall air. Cathy was agitated, and after a couple of blocks she demanded, "Jack, what can you tell me about this Dr. Overbridge? You said it was like getting a call that God was in the emergency room. Do you know him? You've never mentioned him before."

"It's kind of a long story."

"It's a long walk. This whole legal thing worries me. Please?"

Jack sighed. "Okay, when I started my residency at the New York Neurological Institute in June of '92, Dr. Overbridge was one of the attending surgeons. He had been there for, I don't know, seven or eight years. A real superstar, almost a force of nature. His reputation as a surgeon and teacher was one of the main things that had me choose that program. He seemed to operate day and night, had an aggressive research program, wrote dozens of papers, and his talks were always the biggest draw at the big international meetings. Plus, he was cool."

"Cool?"

"Yeah, tall, ripped, thick black hair in a shiny pony-tail, did triathalons. He rode a Ducati from his SoHo loft up to the Columbia Presbyterian campus on 168th street, rain or shine. You would see his picture with some model in the *NY Times* living section about every month.

"Ducati?"

"Italian motorcycle. Think a two-wheeled Ferrari." He laughed. "There was this one story about him actually in the *New Yorker*. One night, he heard a noise in his apartment, so he grabbed this antique cross-bow he had hanging on his wall and went out to investigate. He found a burglar dumping his rare coin collection into a pillowcase. Overbridge flipped on the light and invited the burglar to assume the position. The thief started to walk towards the door, laughing and saying that no one wearing a night shirt would have the nerve to shoot.

"'You don't understand,' Overbridge replied, 'I am a neurosurgeon. These hands kill people every day. I would be delighted to add you to the list. Delighted.' The burglar assumed the position. He was delighted to await the arrival of the police. Delighted." Jack was shaking his head, laughing again.

"That was crap, of course. He was an incredible surgeon. Hardly ever had complications, much less fatalities. He was incredibly intuitive and insightful, and operated with a speed and confidence that was breathtaking. One glance at an angiogram and he would plan an attack. That's what he called it. An attack. Aneurysms were his specialty, he loved the implicit danger of the ticking time bomb, the elegant resolution with a clip. Seriously, he could immediately operate and get to areas that other surgeons would have to spend days planning and contemplating."

Jack stopped and looked at Cathy. "So, you know about Alexander Lake?"

"Yes Jack, I work for the Lake Foundation."

"Do you know how he died?"

Cathy tipped her head. "Some sort of a brain thing, long time ago."

"December, 1994. We got a call that Alexander Lake was on his way from Paris. He was only forty-five, and I can't remember whether he was seventh or eighth on the Forbes' richest list, but a mega-billionaire. He still ran his tech empire, but had already started pouring most of his personal wealth into the Lake Foundation, and had just won the Nobel Peace Prize for his work in third-world health. And, he had an aneurysm. Developed headaches, and the French worked him up with scans and an angiogram. He wanted the best, and that was Overbridge, so he grabbed his X-rays and hopped on his private jet for New York. He demanded surgery instantly, and was in the operating room a few hours after landing.

"I was the junior resident in the OR that day. Dr. Overbridge walked in, stuck his favorite Led Zeppelin tape in the boom box, and went to look at the angiograms which had been placed on the large twenty-panel view box by Jeff, the senior resident. He looked at them, spotted the aneurysm instantly, told Lake it was a 'chip shot', and gave the anesthesiologist the 'get going' sign.

"Once the patient was asleep, Dr. Overbridge marked the incision, which I made, then Jeff cut out the square of skull and we began to retract the brain. Soon Overbridge got down to the offending vessel. It was normal. He looked at it for a minute, then went over to the view box and stared. After a few minutes he saw the problem. Jeff had put the films up backwards, not understanding that the French protocol was the opposite of the U.S. protocol, and not having known enough French to read the labels 'droit' and 'gauche'.

"We were operating on the wrong side of the brain.

"He screamed, and started in on the other side. We had to re-prep, re-drape, new incision, and go back into the opposite side of the skull, which took over an hour.

"During that hour, Mr. Lake's leaking aneurysm had become a burst aneurysm. He died right there on the table."

Jack had stopped walking, and just stood there.

"How horrible. I can see why you haven't talked about it before. What happened next?"

"Well, Overbridge picked up a stool and threw it through the view box, and threatened to kill Jeff, then just left. It was in all the papers, and Overbridge was completely different after that."

"Did they sue him? Or fire him?"

"No, they fired Jeff, and he got most of the blame, but that didn't really change it for Overbridge. He took to this weird over-meticulous planning, limited his operating schedule to one per day, and spent hour after hour reviewing his plans. It was ironic, given that he never changed them – he always knew the right plan from the start. He would come into the OR stating the number of steps planned, and insisted that the circulating nurse check them off as they were completed. And I mean detailed steps.

"'Patient brought to room. Check off number one.'

"'Films placed on viewbox. Check off number two.'

"'Orientation of films and name on films verified by me. Check off number three.'

"'Orientation of films and name on films verified by resident. Check off number four.'

"And so on. By the time we would get to the actual skin incision, usually at around step number seventeen, nearly everyone in the room would be close to psychotic.

"Interestingly, once the operations started, they proceeded at his usual speed, and he showed the same brilliant flair as before. He continued to have the best results of any aneurysm surgeon in the country.

"His cool-ness was also gone. His long hair fell out over about three months, he stopped riding his motorcycle, and actually had a car service bring him to work. No more models. No more social anything. No more lecture trips around the world. No more research, no more papers. No more music in the operating room. Nothing but the surgery itself.

"Before Lake, he was our favorite attending. He had parties at his loft, told us stories from his time at Berkeley in the '60s and literal war stories from Vietnam. After, although I operated with him dozens of times more, we never had another single conversation that was not directly related to the case at hand.

"A few months after Lake's death, Overbridge suddenly left town. He came back a month later, walked into the Chairman's office and announced he was leaving to take a position at Our Lady of Salubrious Penitence in East Harlem. Dr. Knox about had a stroke. 'Owl's Pee!?' he bellowed. 'Have you lost your mind? You could be the next Chairman HERE!' But he left. I had not seen him again until Friday night. He became an eccentric recluse. A recluse who still does more aneurysms, more successfully, than anyone on earth."

They walked in silence the rest of the way to the Flea Market. Just as they got there, Jack's phone buzzed. It was the attorney. "Go on in. I'll track you down after I talk to Vern." Cathy acted like she wanted to wait with him, but he shooed her away. He sat down on a bench.

"What's up, Jack? More HR crap from LexMed?" Jack was president of the large multi-specialty group, and spent a lot of time talking to the attorneys about personnel.

Jack briefly explained the case, and asked him if he had seen the email. He had not, but said he would take a look and get back to him.

Jack texted Cathy, and went into the flea market, where she was examining some truly ratty tapestries that looked like junk to Jack.

"Wouldn't these look great in the entryway?"

He was always honest, so he said "No."

She laughed. "Oh, good. I was afraid you wouldn't be paying attention. The attorney must not have had anything for you yet."

"No, just getting started."

They wandered the market for over an hour. He had developed an uncontrollable urge to buy her some earrings, and they eventually found a simple silver loop pair that looked lovely. As they were walking home, Vern Critchlow called back.

"Well, it's pretty straightforward. Just don't say anything to anyone."

"I'm worried he's going to try to go to work on Monday. It doesn't seem like that would be safe, for him or for his patients."

"Let me think about that. I'll shoot you an email later. In the meantime, at least you have the weekend off. Unlike me."

"What a martyr. I have no sympathy whatsoever. As a matter of fact, it's fun making attorneys actually work on off hours."

"Well, it will be great fun billing you my weekend rate." He laughed and hung up.

When they got home, Jack went to the den and pulled up the email from Vern.

Dear Jack-

The HIPPA regulations clearly protect your patient from any disclosure, UNLESS you can document a threat to health or safety. Here is the relevant passage:

Serious Threat to Health or Safety. Covered entities may disclose protected health information that they believe is necessary to prevent or lessen a serious and imminent threat to a person or the public, when such disclosure is made to someone they believe can prevent or lessen the threat (including the target of the threat).

So, if you can reasonably claim you thought there was a threat, then you could tell whoever was necessary to stop the threat. I would recommend that you document the threat, and you will certainly need to be able to defend your assessment.

I would recommend that you try and have a conversation with your patient to see what his intentions are. Maybe he has some other reason to want to keep things quiet, like a family money issue or something.

I'm available by email this weekend, and you can call me Monday on my cell anytime after six a.m.

Best,

Vern

Jack called Dr. Overbridge's number. He got a recording.

"This is Augustus Overbridge. It is Saturday, October 22, 2016, and I am resting at home. I am in good health and don't need anything. Thank you for calling."

"What're you going to do?" asked Cathy.

"I'll call tomorrow. He has to understand I will be trying to check on him. Plus, I need to confirm for dinner on Friday. If you are willing to go."

"Are you kidding? I wouldn't miss it."

Chapter 19

Sunday, October 23
Dominican Republic

Santiago touched Alyssa's shoulder gently to awaken her, and was rewarded by a lightning fist to the groin that left him gasping on the floor. "Sorry," she grinned, "you startled me."

His first impulse was to throttle her, but he had seen her work before, and was not completely confident that he would succeed.

He considered their relationship complicated. She did not. They HAD no relationship, in her view, and she made it crystal clear that, although their roles sometimes led to expressions of feigned affection in public, in private, she wanted nothing to do with him. He was allowed to look, but not touch. The reason he thought it was complicated was that she gave him so MANY opportunities to look, and the passion in their kisses, played always for the benefit of their marks, was just too real.

"Let's review again," she demanded, sitting up in bed, the sheet barely clinging to her nipples.

Santiago licked his dry lips. "Okay. I sat next to them at the Fiesta, and told them my lovely wife had been detained by work in Monterrey, and that we would meet them for a late breakfast. Here are my notes on everything they talked about for the past two days. I'm sure you have enough to become her best friend."

"The plane is set for this afternoon, right. No screw-ups?"

"It's set. The kid is practically jumping up and down with excitement. He's never been in a small plane, and can't wait for the tour."

Alyssa rolled out of bed, completely naked, skipped past Santiago, and jumped in the shower. She emerged a few minutes later in a bright pink micro bikini with a diaphanous cover that did nothing to disguise her curvy figure. Santiago was having none of that. "We need Marta to *want* to be with us, not be worried about Miguel staring at your boobs."

She stuck out her tongue and put on a striped t-shirt and some shorts. They headed down to pool side, where Marta was busily videoing Jorge as he played with the other children in the pool.

"Holá, Marta," Santiago called. Introductions were made, and after a few minutes Alyssa and Marta had discovered that they had an amazing amount in common, such as Alyssa's fondness for Picasso's "Blue Period" and films by Almodóvar, particularly "Women on the Verge of a Nervous Breakdown."

Through it all, Marta continued to take videos. Alyssa was interested. "My sister takes lots of pictures of her daughter. She is always complaining that she doesn't have enough memory on her phone for all of the things she wants to save."

Marta laughed, "No problem here. I have mine set to upload to Google Drive every night."

"Really? That sounds great. Can you show me how it works? I'd love to show my sister." She pulled out her iPad and handed it to Marta.

Marta obligingly logged on and pulled up the link. "It's a little disorganized," she laughed, "but I must have a thousand hours of video." She then showed Alyssa how she started the upload from her phone. It was quick and the morning's cache was done in under ten minutes.

After lunch, they all hopped into a minivan cab to the harbor, where a Cessna 208 Caravan float plane was waiting for them, a large sign on the fuselage reading "Excursiónes: Costa del Sur." They climbed on board, and soon were flying east along the southern coast of Hispaniola, the views breathtaking. Santiago served champagne to Miguel and Marta, and Fanta orange soda to Jorge, all of whom were in a drug-induced sleep within minutes. Four hours and eight hundred miles to the north, they landed in a secluded bay on Walker's Cay, where they refueled and simply dumped Miguel into the sea, his ankle handcuffed to a kettle bell. They also took the time to peel off the "Excursiónes: Costa del Sur" signs, and changed the call letters on the tail. Marta and Jorge were given injections to keep them asleep, and they immediately took off again, making the thousand mile trip to Sayville, Long Island, in another five hours, arriving just after two a.m. Santiago and the pilot carried the still-unconscious Marta and Jorge to a waiting van. Alyssa returned to the plane, which refueled and took off. Santiago had no idea where she was headed, and knew better than to ask.

* * *

"Why are you so worried about this?" Jack asked.

Cathy had been agitated all day. "Letters from attorneys freak me out.

The only lawsuit I've ever been around was when a worker in Dad's construction company fell off a ladder and ended up with a broken back and ruptured spleen. It wasn't Dad's fault, but it soon became clear that in America, that's irrelevant. That's all my folks talked about for months. The stupid worker had broken company rules with the load he was carrying, and he had been smoking pot, but the ladder manufacturer ended up paying a LOT of money."

"What about your Dad?"

"Oh, his company was dropped from the suit."

"So, no big deal for you guys."

"Are you really not worried?"

"Not about this. Just annoyed. Well, maybe a little worried about my patient and HIS patients, but not about a few letters from attorneys."

After church, he and Cathy usually took a nice, long nap. He called Dr. Overbridge's number just before lying down. He got the recording.

"This is Augustus Overbridge. It is now Sunday, October 23rd, and I am resting at home. I am in good health and don't need anything. Thank you for calling."

Jack left a message. "Please call me back so that I can talk to you. I would like to verify how you are doing. I also need to ascertain that you do not constitute a danger to yourself or others. If you do not respond by six p.m., I will be forced to assume, based on the circumstances, that you are incapacitated, and I will have the police come check on you."

"Let's see if that will get him."

Dr. Overbridge had heard the call, and the message. Since his number was private, he really had not expected calls from anyone other than Tucker. He was sure that Jack would check on him. It was only logical. He was going to have to deal with him at some point before tomorrow, or he would likely try and prevent him from going to work. Which could not be. He had eleven surgical procedures planned for this week, five of them aneurysms, and he had brains to save.

Most importantly, on Tuesday, he was operating on Pierre Lemieux. He was going to compensate for the loss of his son's legs. Nothing could delay that.

Far from quieting his ghosts, the events of the past two days had just raised the volume. Perhaps he had been meant to die, and, having tricked Death, he would be subject to more haunting. Perhaps death was the only way to redemption.

141

* * *

Jack's phone rang at 5:59.

"Hello."

"Augustus Overbridge, responding as requested. I assure you, I am doing quite well. Thank you for your concern, but there is nothing to worry about."

"Are you really planning on going to work tomorrow? After having had a craniotomy on Friday? Seriously? How will you wear a head light? Are you able to stand? Come on, man, be reasonable." Jack was exasperated.

"I am quite competent, and quite serious."

"Why, may I ask, are you so opposed to giving yourself time to heal?"

"I will heal at the same rate at work or at home."

"I insist on examining you tomorrow before you see patients. I have a responsibility to both you and the public. I don't have anything until nine tomorrow. Would you like to meet me at my office at eight? I am on the seventh floor at Lexington Medical."

"It would appear that you are determined. Admirable. Very well, eight o'clock."

Jack hung up. HE was getting a headache.

Dr. Overbridge, in fact, had the mother of all headaches. He was determined that he would be ready to go in the morning. He had a few things to do.

First, the staples. They might catch on my headgear. Jack was right about that. He took a shower, washing over his incision gently with some dishwashing soap he found under his kitchen sink, making sure to clean off all the residual betadine. He had not had any shampoo for years, and did not wish to waste precious energy resources by going out to get some. He carefully dried his head, and checked his reflection. The line of staples over the right side of his scalp looked like a zipper. *Probably not the best look.*

He stood in front of his shaving mirror, and carefully pried out the first staple with the tweezers. He then applied super glue to the wound edges and waited for it to dry. It took him nearly a half hour to repeat the process for the seventeen staples, but when he was done, the incision looked much less shocking. *Jack would certainly have placed a layer of deep sutures,* he thought, *and anyway, super glue is a perfectly safe wound closure material.* Perhaps tomorrow he would inject some local anesthesia into the incision to make it easier to get through the day. *No harm in that. None at*

142

all. He smiled at himself. That felt odd. His facial muscles were not used to that much exercise.

The great thing about New York was that you could have any kind of food delivered at any time. He had a delightful dinner with bouillabaisse, asparagus, bread and cheese, all delivered fresh from Rive Gauche on 88th. His housekeeper should be there in the morning to provide his usual breakfast. He called her, just to make sure. Left a message, of course. They had almost never actually spoken during the dozen years she had been working for him.

Chapter 20

What a crazy weekend, Jack mused as he walked the dozen blocks to his office. *What should I do with Overbridge? Can I really let him just go back to work like nothing happened? And what was so compelling that he couldn't take a few days off?* He jumped back to avoid a bicycle messenger, then crossed the street and into LexMed. The security guard looked up.

"Mornin' Doc. Surgery today?"

"No, just in a little early. Have a nice day."

Other than the surgery center, not much really got going at the clinic until about eight, and the seventh floor was deserted. He went to his corner office and booted up the computer. There was always plenty of charting to do.

Carla, his medical assistant, rushed in at a quarter to eight, saw his door was open and popped her head in.

"Good morning, Dr. Tucker. Need anything?"

"Yes, I have an add-on coming at eight. Name is Overbridge, Augustus." He spelled it for her. "You can get the info from the Lenox Hill system. He had surgery Friday night. Just put him on the schedule as a post op."

"Sure thing. I didn't think you were on call this weekend. Something special?"

"Unusual, anyway. Just get it in the computer, thanks."

Dr. Overbridge entered the office suite at precisely eight o'clock, and Jack took him immediately back into an exam room. *Looks pretty good,* Jack thought. *Walking normally, good color.* Overbridge pulled off his knit cap. *Okay, the staples are gone.* Jack poked at the incision. *Super glue.* Dr. Overbridge was silent, and had grimaced almost imperceptibly. *Nice job, really,* he thought. *No sign of infection or fluid collection. Minimal bruising. Bone plate feels stable. Pulse, respiration, and blood pressure all normal. Coordination and reflex testing normal. Normal, normal, normal.* Nothing about the man other than the incision itself would have indicated that he had been all but dead three days earlier. Remarkable.

"Okay, you win. I have no basis for stopping you from going to work, and therefore I will, of course, not be speaking to anyone regarding your case. For now. I want to see you again tomorrow morning, however."

"Tomorrow I have surgery at eight at Our Lady. It will not be convenient to come down."

"How about if I come up there? Maybe I could come to the OR and see how things are. I would be able to stay until about 9:30."

Dr. Overbridge looked at him carefully, weighing the risks. "Completely unnecessary, but if you have the time and inclination, I will not bar the door."

"Fine, then, that's settled. I will be at your office tomorrow morning at seven-thirty, so I can have a quick look at you first."

"Do what you must." He turned and left. Jack stared after him.

* * *

When Dr. Overbridge arrived at Our Lady, he immediately went to the locker room, changed into scrubs, and put on an OR cap. He then went to clinic and saw his morning patients dressed like that. His nurse must have thought that odd, as he always, always, always changed back into a shirt and tie before donning his white coat for clinic work, but she did not say anything. Dr. Overbridge did not invite conversation.

Although he would never admit it, he was concerned about the surgical case that was starting at noon. Not an aneurysm, but a tumor on the nerve to the patient's left ear. It was a combined case with one of the ear surgeons. The good news was that it was a case done sitting down, which would be easier. The bad news was that it was likely to last for several hours. His head was throbbing, and he was worn. He needed to be sure he could get through the case without Dr. Blake noticing anything unusual. He could not afford questions. Not this week.

He stood at a mirror, and carefully injected bupivicaine, a long lasting anesthetic, into the incision. The pain disappeared. He replaced the surgical cap and headed over to the OR.

* * *

Cathy's day started at just before nine in the headquarters of the Lake Foundation on 2nd Avenue and 44th, near the United Nations building. The Lake Foundation had a twenty-billion dollar endowment, and was

146

therefore second only to the Bill and Melinda Gates Foundation in total assets, with nearly twice the resources of the Ford Foundation. Cathy enjoyed her job immensely. When she had initially taken the job, she had spent nearly a third of her time in-country in Central America, coordinating childhood immunization drives and lobbying with the local governments for improved sanitation. Now, eight years later, she was increasingly in New York. As the Foundation's programs had become more successful, in large part due to her efforts, she had hired assistants in each of her countries who lived there full-time, and she spent more and more of her time trying to get things done at the U.N., or with A.I.D. She still traveled from time to time, but was usually only gone for two weeks or so every quarter.

She pulled up her file on her current project. For the last three months, she had been working almost exclusively on a large sewage treatment project in the southern part of Honduras. Choluteca was a city of around 150,000, which had the infrastructure and hygiene available for about one-fifth that many people.

As was always the case in Central America in general, and in Honduras in particular, nothing was straightforward or easy. International gangs were the middlemen that moved drugs and other contraband through the country. Corruption was rampant, both in the local police and in the national government, and there was semi-open warfare between the gangs and the cops. Honduras was the most dangerous country in the Americas, with a murder rate twenty times that of the US. The going rate for a hit was only three hundred dollars. Although San Pedro Sula in the north was the worst, things were not much better in Choluteca. It was unthinkable that anyone would object to better sewage, but the motivations for the different factions were often obscure and hard to anticipate.

She thought about her upcoming meeting with the Honduran Ambassador to the UN and the Minister of Health, who was in town for an international conference. The governmental permits for her new plant had been stalled by minor bureaucrats who expected bribes. She had long since given up on using any construction company other than the one owned by the mayor's sleazy brother, and that would normally have helped facilitate the process, except that the mayor had just come out against one of the two major gang leaders in that part of the country, and so was living under threat of death, complicating all the negotiations.

She was not about to give up. She had succeeded in building a total of three of these new plants, two in Guatemala and one in El Salvador. The best estimate on lives saved by the improved sanitation was between eight and nine thousand. Per year. She was proud of the Foundation and her part in it.

* * *

The phone in Maxwell's pocket vibrated urgently. He pulled it out.

"Yes, Boss." No one else used this number.

"Is everything satisfactory?" Perez was calm, but Maxwell could feel the tension in his voice.

"Completely. The MRI was done this morning, and the techs are working on spinning the mesh as we speak. We should have it ready by Wednesday around noon, sterilized and ready to go."

"And the videos? Are they satisfactory?"

"Perfect. Blaylock says that they are all time and date stamped, and proud Mamacita did us the favor of labeling most of them. There are more than enough. We have workers looking at all the snippets of five minutes or longer, and should have plenty of material ready by the time we have the subject calibrated."

"Very well. What are you doing with the subject and the woman?"

"The woman was told that they have been kidnapped, and that her husband was returned to Mexico, where he is raising money for their release. She thinks she is still in the D.R. She has been told that if she gives us any trouble, that we will kill her and traffic the boy to a dealer in Thailand. Santiago was most convincing. She just sits and stares at the boy, who is enthusiastically playing video games. All being recorded, of course, for additional data. I do not anticipate any difficulties for the time we need."

"Please convey my satisfaction to Santiago." Perez hung up.

* * *

Overbridge was picked up at his office by a car service at six p.m., and was back in his apartment twenty minutes later. He examined his incision closely. Everything looked fine. He called for Thai food, ate, and sat himself up in bed on pillows. He fell into a restless sleep.

The nightmare was vivid. He was back with Benje in Vietnam. The jungle was hot and humid, and he had just blown the head off of an enemy soldier, when the blood and brains from Benje's own mortal

148

wound sprayed over him. He crawled over to where Benje's body was lying, face down, and rolled him over, only to see the face of Alexander Lake. The dead eyes suddenly opened and fixed on Overbridge. "Incompetent," the dead man mouthed, and then was still.

Overbridge woke up, sweating and trembling. He had rolled off of his stack of pillows and nearly off of the bed. His head was throbbing with every heartbeat, and he started counting the beats as he struggled to his feet and to the bathroom, where he swallowed three Tylenol and gripped the sink to keep upright. Looking into the mirror, he got control of himself, drank a swig of Mylanta, and headed back to bed. He was helpless to stop the parade of images – Benje, Lake, Pierre, and finally Monique, but after what seemed an eternity, he was finally able to fall back to sleep.

Chapter 21

Jack arrived at Our Lady early, just after seven. It was not at all imposing. It did not even have the look of an old beautiful building gone to seed. It simply looked like it had been built as utilitarian, and had gone downhill from there. He went through the metal detectors and signed in with the guard at the desk, who gave him a visitor's badge and directions to Dr. Overbridge's office. Everything about the place was dingy, and from the walls which needed both a scrubbing and a coat of paint to the chain-link fence along the sidewalk guarding the windows, it looked more like a prison than a place of healing.

Why is he here? Jack wondered. Despite the incident with Mr. Lake, Dr. Overbridge had been on the fast track in academia at the Neurological Institute of New York when he had decided to leave. He could also easily have secured positions at New York Hospital/Cornell Medical Center, or New York University, or anywhere else in the country, for that matter.

Jack had certainly never been here before. He had little reason to go into East Harlem, and there was nothing about Our Lady of Salubrious Penitence to attract him.

He waited outside Dr. Overbridge's office. Precisely at 7:30, the elevator doors opened, and he strode deliberately down the hall, stopping six feet from Jack.

"Good morning, doctor. I trust you had no difficulty getting here?"

"No, no problem," Jack assured him. They went into his office, where he removed the black watch cap. Which he had been wearing with his dark gray suit.

The incision continued to look good, and there was, as yesterday, no specific problem that Jack could see.

They rode down to the operating rooms together and walked up to the control desk.

"This," proclaimed Dr. Overbridge, "is Dr. Jack Tucker from Lenox Hill. "He will be observing surgery with me today."

The charge nurse looked up, surprised. "Uh, hello, Dr. Tucker. You'll need to go down to administration and register for temporary privileges. Should just take a few minutes."

"Naturally, I should have expected that." Jack shook his head in self-annoyance. "I probably should have started there.

"I will meet you in the OR," Overbridge said.

There was a barely perceptible twitch of a smile as Dr. Overbridge watched Jack go down the hall to the elevators. Overbridge went to the pre-op area to greet his patient. He had worn a pink power tie today, and had decided that his incision looked acceptable, so he was bare-headed.

Pierre Lemieux was lying on a stretcher in pre-op. He was accompanied by Maxwell, who handed Overbridge a thick envelope, which he slipped into the large side-pocket of his white coat.

Lemieux smiled broadly. "I'm ready. Give me back my legs."

Overbridge glanced around. "We are here to clip your aneurysm," he said, a little loudly. "The risks are infection, bleeding, permanent brain injury, and death." He started to turn.

"Do your best," Lemieux called out.

Dr. Overbridge did not slow or turn. "As if there was anything else," he muttered.

* * *

When Jack arrived in the operating room, after having been delayed at administration for almost forty-five minutes, things were already well under way. The patient had been anesthetized, prepped, and draped, and Dr. Overbridge was just guiding the surgery resident through the skin incision. That was to be the extent of the resident's experience. There was no Neurosurgery residency at Our Lady, and so the General Surgery resident assigned to Dr. Overbridge had the rather uninviting task of opening the skin and closing the skin, and watching Dr. Overbridge do all the rest. Sometimes for hours. He would not even be trusted to do so much as hold a retractor or apply suction.

"Jack Tucker, what in the name of all that is holy brings you to Owl's Pee? I haven't seen you for like twenty years." It was the anesthesiologist. Jack turned, and did a double-take. Felix.

"I could ask you the same thing. I thought you were at Emory."

"Old news, Jack. When I split with Veronica, I wanted OUT of there. I've been here insulting the locals for the past five years."

152

"Sorry to hear you two split."

"You never were a good liar, Jack. You hated that woman as much as I did. I just hope you got smart and got rid of your ball and chain, too."

"Jennifer died." Jack was getting increasingly uncomfortable. Felix had always been a little out there, but now he was showing a real meanness that Jack did not remember from their younger days. He did not want to talk about Jennifer, not with Felix, and really did not want to discuss Cathy with him. He was getting the sense that it would just lead to something unpleasant.

"So, you're free like me! That's great! We should go bar-hopping. I know lots of babes who would love to take a tumble with a rich neurosurgeon. No strings attached."

"I'm not interested, thanks." Jack did not engage. Instead, he walked over to the monitor to look at the MRI scan and angios. The patient had a fourteen millimeter aneurysm in the anterior communicating artery of the circle of Willis, where the large arteries of the brain joined together in the middle of the skull.

"Bad anatomy for a coil," Jack observed. "Makes sense he chose surgery."

"Correct," replied Dr. Overbridge. "Straightforward case." He had finished opening the skull, and was cutting through the dura, the thick leathery membrane protecting the brain. He was grateful that the patient was prepped and draped prior to Jack's arrival. He doubted that Jack would recognize the Poet, but stranger things had happened.

Jack watched him operate, his mind wandering a little. *It was a somewhat strange fact of surgery,* he thought, *that attending surgeons essentially never saw anyone else in their specialties operate. You finished your training, then went out in the world and did your own thing.* In neurosurgery, it was actually difficult to watch someone else work, unless you had a double-headed microscope. This OR had a video feed from the microscope, and Jack was watching on the monitor, but that did not give the stereoscopic view that the microscope provided. Overbridge was working smoothly and competently, and showed no signs of hesitancy or poor coordination. After thirty minutes, Jack was bored out of his mind. It was, indeed a straightforward, although tediously slow, case. It would be at least another thirty minutes before he even got to the area of the aneurysm.

"Satisfied, Dr. Tucker?" Overbridge looked up from the scope.

Felix chimed in "Is THAT why you're here? Checking up on Augiedoggie?" He laughed. "You needn't bother. Even this East L.A. boy can tell you he does nice work."

Jack decided to go. "Thank you for the demonstration, Dr. Overbridge," he said for Felix's benefit. "I would love to discuss the case later. Are we still on for Friday?"

"Indeed, that would be lovely. I will meet you there at seven."

* * *

After Jack left, Dr. Overbridge twisted the base of the video camera as if by accident while adjusting the microscope, and the screen went blank. "Ah, Vicky," he said, "would you be so kind as to see if someone from tech support could come and check the monitor? We seem to have lost video."

She left the room, and he asked the scrub tech to get an instrument from the large set of extras on the back table. While the tech was occupied, Overbridge pulled the mesh implant from under the instrument tray where he had hidden it earlier. He palmed the small device and returned to the surgical field. The tech had not noticed, and Felix was occupied reading a journal article. There was a small clip that attached to the cut edge of the skull, joined by a number of filaments to the mesh. The entire device, including the clip, was made of the new fiber, which Maxwell assured him would not be detectable on X-rays, CT scan, or MRI. He had made sure to keep his body in front of the scrub assistant, and with the camera out of commission, everyone else was blind. He slipped the mesh down the fissure between the two cerebral hemispheres, with the wings going up and over onto the top of the brain on both sides. It fit perfectly, the fine mesh appearing to almost melt onto the moist surface. He did not need to even irrigate. He asked for the aneurysm clip, and then pantomimed placing it on the artery. "Perfect," he said aloud.

Vicky glanced at him. That one word for Overbridge was the equivalent of a receiver doing cartwheels in the end zone. He was not normally prone to any type of display.

He then closed the dura, and asked for tissue glue, which he used to seal the closure, and also to secure and seal the filaments as they came through the dural repair. They were coated with a special fibroblast-stimulating polymer, Maxwell had told him, and would become completely integrated into the closure. He then replaced the rectangle of bone, and secured it in place with the standard titanium plates, the

154

connection socket attached to the long back side of the bone plate. He turned to the resident. "I think I'll close today, doctor. Please go to the recovery room and write orders."

Bill Brentwood opened his mouth to protest. After all, he had been standing in the corner of the room for the past three hours, not even able to watch with the video feed broken. After a pause, he thought better of it and turned towards the door. Overbridge methodically brought the scalp together in layers, using staples for the final skin closure, then carefully taped a light dressing to the skin.

He looked around, satisfied. Felix was clearly playing Candy Crush Saga on his iPhone, Vicky was counting sponges with the tech, who had evidently noticed nothing out of the ordinary. He tapped the dressing gently three times with his index finger.

Pierre Lemieux, para-Olympian and poet, was wheeled off to the recovery room. His name-band and paperwork identified him as one Jamie Wilson, a factory worker from Orange, New Jersey.

* * *

Cameron met up with Mitzi at the *Mad Cow* near Battery Park. Hailed by the *Times* as "New York's most flagrant assault on longevity," it claimed the biggest and greasiest burgers in Manhattan. Mitzi was sold immediately, and the *Mad Cow* had been on her list ever since the *Times* review came out.

Cameron had arrived first, and was contemplating his options when Mitzi rushed in and sat down. "What a weekend," she started, as she waved for the waiter's attention. "Did you hear about the serial killer we brought in?" Cameron shook his head, and Mitzi shot him a surprised look. "Yeah, Arnie Atwood, we tracked him through his porn addiction, brought him in late Friday night. According to the Special Agents making the arrest, he was pretty enthusiastic in his confession, you know, proud crazy psycho, gave our guys the location of his body dump. I went up into the Catskills with the team Saturday morning. More of an entombment than a burial. There was this concrete bomb shelter, and he just tossed them in after a little dismemberment. What a mess. Spent the whole day taking pictures and trying to group them as best as I could. Sunday, I set up in the lab, you know, a separate table for each body. Pretty sure we have eight victims, eight skulls anyway, but some extra arms thrown in. Literally." She looked over her shoulder at the waiter, who had started to tap his pad with his pencil. "Oh yes. I'll have the double blue bacon with avocado. Extra bacon." The waiter looked at Cameron.

"I think I'll just have a Pepsi," Cameron said, unable to face ground beef at this point.

Mitzi had been talking non-stop, but finally she paused. "Okay, Romeo, what did your friend at Assguard have to say?"

"Aasgard," Cameron corrected.

"Whatever. Spill."

"The upshot was that, if you had a seamless interface, you would truly be able to use AI algorithms to manipulate systems in ways that would make the NSA drool, particularly with financial systems, but potentially into military systems as well."

Mitzi was skeptical. "I don't see how it would help you with overcoming encryption, which would seem like more of a problem than the interface."

"That's what I thought as well, but they explained that it was the back and forth between human and computer that was one of the biggest speed-killers. They are actually working on artificial intelligence systems to mock that – you know, cut out the need for the human – but they were very clear that a better interface with an actual human brain would be superior, at least for the next decade or two."

Mitzi was thoughtful. "Let's assume the interface. What else would Perez need to make a system like that practical?"

"First, he would need the right human. Control would be of paramount importance, so you would need someone reliable. Next, assuming the basic interface, you would need a really primo connectivity to the internet. Preferably something immense, like one of the streaming services, or even better, a cable company. Finally, the system you plug into would need to be a truly first-class super computer, in order to process things fast enough to make it worth it. Given those three things, there is no telling what you could accomplish. And Perez owns a telecommunications company, has access to no end of nerds, and can afford to build any computer he wants."

"So, maybe he is not planning to implant himself, but rather one of his computer whizzes. Some of those guys would be so into this they would probably agree, and perhaps longevity would be something that Perez would promise, but not deliver. Can you imagine, having the top of your skull removed for this thing?" Her eyes actually glittered a little as she said the words.

Cameron stared at Mitzi. *I bet she could be convinced to volunteer,* he thought. He shook off the thought. "We need to find his lab."

"Could be anywhere," Mitzi stated flatly. "The guy has assets all over the world."

"I don't think so," replied Cameron. "The kind of access he needs requires that the physical location be where there is extensive infrastructure. All of his assets are in North and Central America, and probably only a handful of cities would be feasible. I think he is here."

"Why?"

"Well, I was brought here, wasn't I? He must have been here last week."

"That could easily have just been last week. For all you know, he is in Mexico City or Vancouver this week."

"No," Cameron was insistent. "The whole attitude of his goons and all, it felt like we were going to the home base. I want to try and find out where high-power-consumption installations have gone in over the past couple of years and start looking."

"How will you do that without alerting the DDO? You're officially off of Perez."

"Not with CIA resources, obviously. What can you do for me at the Bureau?"

"Nothing directly. Let me think about it. I'm sure, as they say, that I know a guy."

* * *

"So good to see you again, Mrs. Tucker." Señor Tapata, the Honduran Ambassador, offered his fleshy hand. She took it a little reluctantly, and, as she feared, he pulled it up to his lips and offered a slight bow. "I believe you have met our Minister of Health, Señor Villanueva," he continued as he passed her hand to his colleague, who gave it a limp shake.

"Of course, we met last April," Cathy responded. *When you were fishing for a bribe,* she thought. She smiled. They were so close to getting everything approved to actually break ground on her Choluteca sewage project. "What do we need to do to wrap this up?"

"The gang problem is so severe in Choluteca," started Villanueva, "are you certain that we would not be better served moving it to Comayagua?" His mouth smiled slightly, but his eyes remained icy.

"Really, Señor Villenueva, we have been over this and over this. The Lake Foundation would certainly entertain a proposal from the Mayor of Comayagua – he is your brother, is he not? However, that will need to be for our *next* project. We have spent literally *years* on the designs and plans for Choluteca, and none of that is transferable directly. Besides, Comayagua's current situation is much better than Choluteca's. Over ninety percent of homes are connected to the current sewage system, including those neighboring your textile factory, if I am not mistaken, as opposed to less than sixty percent in Choluteca."

Villenueva's face paled slightly. *Bet you didn't know we'd found out about your factory in Comayagua,* Cathy thought, more than a little self-satisfied.

"I am sure we can work this all out," smarmed Señor Tapata. "Maybe you would like to come over to the Embassy later to discuss it over dinner and drinks? My evening is free as my wife has flown back to Tegucigalpa for a few weeks."

I wonder, thought Cathy, *if that works better on any of the other women in New York and Washington.* She was always amazed that fat, balding, middle-aged men presumed that what they thought of as power and prestige were such aphrodisiacs. *Particularly with that truly terrifying toupé. Or that weapon-of-mass-destruction cologne.* She decided to zing him. "And I understand that Constanza is in Brazil for a little touch up."

At the mention of his mistress, Tapata smiled broadly. "I see you are well informed. Shall we say seven, then?"

"Just get back to me when you have the final documents. I have a lunch appointment. With my husband." She walked down the hall, away from the two men. She could almost feel them watching her. She was sure that she would have accomplished as much if she had stayed in her office and played Spider Solitaire on her computer.

* * *

In point of fact, she DID have a lunch appointment with Jack. They met at the coffee shop on Third Avenue, attached to the giant used-book store that was such a fun place to spend the afternoon browsing on stormy Saturdays. They also made killer French onion soup, and served it with an unending supply of crispy authentic bread and plenty of butter.

"How was your morning, Sweetie," she asked as she gave him a full body, head to toe hug. Jack, of course, was instantly unable to think about anything BUT simply hugging her, until she finally had to stage-whisper

"We're in public, goose." He laughed and looked around at the bustling lunch spot.

"They can get their own girls." It was his standard response.

He told her about his trip up to Harlem, and about running into Felix.

"You haven't mentioned him before. Was he a good friend?"

"Pretty good, during residency, but he is different now. Less funny, more creepy. Maybe it's me. My tolerance for mean has decreased since you have shown me how wonderful it is to be positive."

"Tell me about him."

Jack rocked slightly back and forth as he thought. "So, Felix was born in East Los Angeles in the late sixties, one of those poor immigrant families that should have guaranteed him a short, impoverished life. But Felix is brilliant. He powered through high school, scored a perfect 1600 on the SAT, which he must have mentioned at least weekly, went to Princeton on a scholarship, graduated Summa Cum Laude, then on with another scholarship to Yale Medical School, and finally to Columbia's residency program. We overlapped by about a year. Our wives really hit it off, but we didn't keep in touch after they moved down to Atlanta where Felix got a staff position at Emory. I have no idea how he ended up at Our Lady."

"Maybe we should have him over?"

"No, I think I'd rather just let it slide."

Cathy could see he was uncomfortable about something, but decided to save it for later. "What about Dr. Overbridge?"

"He seemed like nothing had ever happened. Operated smoothly, quickly, no problems or issues that I could see . . ." His voice trailed off and he stared at the corner of the ceiling, where a spider appeared to be wrapping up a fly.

"One odd thing, though. As I think about it now, he made a really large bone flap, and more anterior than I would have chosen. He got great exposure, though, so I guess I really can't fault him. Everyone's technique is so individual. I was so steamed by Felix's crude innuendo that I was only half watching that part of the procedure."

* * *

Back at OLSP, "Jamie Wilson" was doing very well. Awake, breathing on his own, able to eat a little, overall recovering nicely. No surprise to the ICU staff, as none of them had ever seen one of Dr. Overbridge's cases

159

NOT do well.

What DID surprise the staff was that Dr. Overbridge came by to see the patient. AFTER six. It was as though the sun had risen at two am. He simply NEVER came in after hours. There was also something odd in the way he spoke with the patient. He seemed to want to make sure he was thinking normally, which was understandable, but he also was showing definite signs of possibly caring for the man as a person. When he got the report from the nurse, he actually asked her to tell him about Mr. Wilson. Usually, he had no idea what the patients' names were, referring instead to the "Aneurysm in 315," or whatever. Definitely odd.

The truth was, he was very excited for the next stage of the project, and was anxious for Lemieux to recover quickly so that they could proceed. Redemption indeed. Everything appeared to be in order.

Chapter 22

Wednesday, October 26
New York

Mitzi was counting on the reluctance of the CIA to talk to the FBI for any reason other than a real-time terrorist threat (and sometimes not even then), as she walked down the hall to see Mary Jane, an acquaintance in the cyber crime division.

She pulled open the door, and without any preamble launched in. "I'm looking for a clandestine major server farm in greater New York."

Mary Jane looked at her quizzically. "Hello to you, too. And what, pray tell, would that have to do with forensic pathology?"

"Nothing. I just need it for a project. It's important. Just trust me."

Mary Jane just shook her head. "Well, since I keep that exact list handy, just get me the authorization, and it's yours."

"Really, you keep a list like that?" Mitzi was interested.

"Of course. It is currently showing three hundred and forty-four facilities. We check out about ten a week, that's all we have manpower for. This week we actually had a winner – dark web arm sales. Mostly, they turn out to be dead ends. But I can't just give it to you. How about telling me what you are looking for?"

Mitzi was not sure how to respond. *Crazy megalomaniacal super villain trying to take over the world by controlling computers with his mind,* ran through her head. So she said it.

Mary Jane just stared at her. "Fine, don't tell me, but I really can't get it for you without authorization. Let's do lunch sometime." She turned back to her work.

Mitzi was about to say something, but an idea popped into her head, so she turned on her heels and left.

* * *

"I'm really not in a position to call in any favors," Cameron was saying. "I simply can't get authorization for anything domestic through CIA channels. Not now, not with my recent track record of supreme stupidity."

161

They were in a small coffee shop in SoHo.

Mitzi was exasperated. Again. "Are you finished? Just listen for a minute. If you will pay attention, we'll have that list, no problem." She explained her idea.

Cameron tried to think back to his morning at TSA. Had he burned his bridges with Phillips on the way out? He really was not sure. He sighed. "Okay, I guess it is worth a try. We haven't got anything else."

He called the joint team office over at JFK, and asked for Special Agent Phillips. After what seemed like an eternity, the secretary came back on the line. "Sorry, he's on a site visit at Newark. Try back tomorrow."

"How about his cell number?" Cameron tried to visualize the woman. He had just met her once, when she had given him a packet of papers on his first day. Mid-forties, pear-shaped, mousy hair, desperate eyes. *What the heck was her name?* He had it.

"Listen, Kimberly," he said in what he hoped was his most intimate voice, "you were so helpful the day I started. You remember me, right? Agent Cameron Hansen? This is important." He glanced over at Mitzi, who was miming gagging herself. He stuck out his tongue.

Kimberly's voice went down a half octave. "Well, I guess that would be okay. When are you coming back to TSA?"

"Not soon enough. How's my replacement doing?"

"They haven't sent one yet. Here's that number." She rattled it off.

"Thanks a million. I owe you a coffee." He hung up. Mitzi shook her head.

"You are shameless."

"You're one to talk. Anyway, that was the easy part. I don't know if Phillips will be as inclined to a favor, at least one that requires work." He dialed the number. The call went straight to voice mail. "Phillips, Cameron Hansen here, you know, from CIA. Listen, there's something I need you to check for me. Give me a call." He hung up.

"You know," Mitzi mused, "it occurs to me that we might not have to do anything."

"What do you mean?"

"Well, when they had you, they also had your ID, right? So Perez knows your name and who you work for. Just a matter of time before one of his contacts finds your address and goons show up at your door. I doubt he is any more inclined to just drop this than we are."

Cameron looked at her aghast, as sweat started to form in the small of

162

his back. Images from the videos, which had receded to his nightmares over the past week, blazed up from his memory. He stared at his phone. Perez was a telecommunication magnate. The phone in his hand would be better than any address. He started to take it out of its case to pull the SIM card, when it rang, startling him to the point of nearly dropping it. Phillips' jolly voice boomed over the speaker.

"Hey," Cameron choked out, "thanks for calling. Listen, it looks like there is a lot of high volume data flowing through a Paris cell that seems to be coming from the New York area. We figure there is a big server facility here that is being used to encode and scramble the communications. Can you shoot over the FBI's list of possibles in the metro area so we can cross check it? Sure, just email it to me. I'll look for it tomorrow."

"Make it Friday morning. I'm stuck over here today and tomorrow."

Cameron opened his mouth to argue, then decided to quit while he was ahead. "Thanks. Oh, and this number is going off service, so don't try calling back on it. Bye."

As soon as the call ended, Cameron extracted the SIM card and snapped it in half. He turned to Mitzi. "I'll get a burner and leave you the number." He paused. "Actually, if they get into my phone records, they will be able to see which numbers I've been calling. You could be at risk."

Mitzi pulled out her brand new phone. She shook her head, and pulled out her own SIM card. "Let's go. There's a CVS across the street. They'll have burners."

* * *

Ten miles away in Queens, Blaylock got a call. "Those two phones you've been having me watch both just stopped transmitting."

"Where?" Blaylock asked.

"Somewhere in SoHo, within about two blocks of the intersection of Mercer and Broome."

"Both of them?"

"Yep. The guy's phone had just had calls to a land line at JFK, and then both outgoing and incoming from a cell which looked to be at Newark airport. Their only other calls this morning had been to and from each other."

Blaylock hung up, and immediately called Perez, who listened to the information and turned to Santiago.

"I should have done as you suggested. Looks like Agent Hansen and Dr. Lenz are getting smarter. Send people to watch their apartments. Don't worry about being gentle. Just get them both and bring them here. You stay here and make sure everything goes okay with Cabrera. That is the number one priority. I can settle with Hansen whenever the opportunity presents."

* * *

Halfway down the block towards CVS, Mitzi grabbed Cameron's arm, stopping him. "Why do you think that Perez has not already made an attempt on you?"

"I don't know, maybe he hasn't traced me yet."

"More likely he has been watching you. I think that our phones going dead may have just put targets on our backs." She pointed down the street at a Key Bank. "Change of plan." She hurried towards the bank, pulling Cameron along.

Once in the bank, she asked for the manager, and made a substantial withdrawal. Twenty thousand dollars in hundreds made a stack almost an inch thick. She handed it to Cameron. They then went to the CVS, where in addition to the phones she bought two runners' carry-all packs. They each kept a couple of hundreds out and put the rest inside their pants in the packs.

"I'm due back at work," Mitzi said. "The FBI lab should be safe enough, but we need a plan for later."

They hailed a cab and rode uptown, watching the surrounding traffic carefully. Cameron was brooding when they pulled up at the Federal complex. "Don't leave until I get back to pick you up," he instructed, and Mitzi hurried into the building. After she went in, Cameron dove into the subway and went up to the Bronx. Cash was not what it once was, and he needed a certain type of establishment if he was going to hide out.

* * *

Cabrera had initially been indignant. "I am a veterinarian! I don't operate on people!"

Perez had tried to be patient. "You have implanted over a dozen dogs. This will be the same. In fact the subject is about the size of a large dog. You are an excellent surgeon. The bonus will be considerable, say two million dollars, and then you can go back to Buenos Aires a rich man."

Perez's tone softened, "Or you can refuse and go back to Buenos Aires in a box. And of course, I would not want your large and loving family to grieve, so I would be forced to eliminate them all as well. Not to mention the subject and his mother. Relax. Everything is ready. You will do well." He rolled smoothly out the door and down the hall.

Pablo Cabrera was trembling with fear and rage. He had come to the research facility in Queens to run the dog lab several months ago. He had known the research was secret, but he thought that was just an industrial thing, trying to get ahead of the competition. His key card did not get him to any of the floors in the building not directly involved in his work. It was obvious that the mesh was being developed for eventual use in humans, but, until just now, he had had no inkling that there was anything remotely close to being ready. And now they wanted HIM to work on humans! Not just on a *human*, but on a *child*. He had only been in human operating rooms twice, for the C-section births of his last two sons. Now, here he was, about to be forced to do something contrary to his training, illegal, and, worst of all, offensive to God.

He had no choice. There was no doubt in his mind that Perez would fulfill his threat. After Perez left, that oaf Santiago had roughly torn his ID/keycard from his pocket clip, and told him that, from now on, he would only be able to go from room to room accompanied by him or one of his men. *El jefe* did not want him to consider running. As if he would risk his family by challenging Perez. No, he would get things ready. *I am a fine surgeon*, he told himself, *and really, how much different could it be?*

* * *

In a regular operating room, everything is designed for the safety of the patient, with an anesthesiologist armed with sensitive monitoring devices, carefully sterilized instruments, a whole crew with routines as carefully worked out as a pilot's pre-flight check list. Nothing was even close to being as important as the patient.

In the dog lab, although the animals were certainly valuable, or would be after the mesh was successfully implanted, the truth was that dogs were plentiful, cheap, and easily disposed of and replaced if there were complications. Cabrera had no anesthesiologist, he put the animals out himself, put in a breathing tube, and just left them on a ventilator, counting on the anesthetic gasses to keep them still while he worked. His palms sweat as he thought of the breathing tube. Dogs were notoriously easy to intubate – you could literally open their mouth and shine a flashlight down their tracheas. Piece of cake. Humans, he knew, were different. He had worked some with monkeys, which he thought would be similar, and they were very hard to get tubes in, requiring special laryngoscopes. If he could not get a breathing tube in, that would be game over right there. Dead patient, and, he had no doubt, dead Cabrera. He did not even know what settings to use for the ventilator. He did not want to blow out a lung, but also needed to get enough oxygen in. He did not have sophisticated gas analysis on his machine, did not have any but the most basic EKG for a monitor, and he did not know enough about human heart tracings to even know if there was a problem. It was usually just him and his tech in the room, none of the support staff he really had only seen in movies and on television.

He was actually less concerned about the procedure itself. He expected that he would be able to pull it off. He had, in fact, successfully implanted fourteen dogs, but he had also lost another six perioperatively. That had been good enough for all concerned. He just needed to take his time, get it done.

He went down to his office, intending to look online for some information regarding anesthesia in children. His access to the internet, however, was blocked. Finally, after a very heated discussion with Santiago, he was allowed to open a browser, but Santiago stood at his shoulder, alert for any attempt to make contact with the world outside. After researching the basic parameters, he felt better, and found that his heart rate came back into the normal range. Although he was still sweating, his palms were now dry.

He spent about an hour in the dog lab, which would soon be his operating room, making sure he checked everything. He had a short list of items he absolutely needed, mainly the correct-size tubes for a ten-year old's trachea, and the special laryngoscope he would need to get the tube in. He would use the ketamine that worked on the dogs to put the subject to sleep, as he simply did not have time to learn about more human-friendly techniques. Santiago took the list, and made a call to a contact at the nearby Elmhurst hospital. Everything would be there by six o'clock.

* * *

Cabrera was sweating profusely, and no matter how much he swallowed, the bile kept rising in his throat. It had not started well. Right

166

from the start, he saw that, despite all of his hasty research, he was unprepared. Santiago had indeed made good on getting the equipment, so that was not an issue. Everything else was.

First, the IV. Dogs' veins are about as easy to get into as could be imagined. Not so the flailing, chubby-armed Jorge. He tried and tried, but could not seem to get it in. No problem, he thought, just give him the gas. With the help of Santiago and another guard, he was able to keep the mask on the boy's face until he calmed down, but by then, his hands were trembling from the effort, and it still took him three tries before he finally got the IV.

With the boy asleep, he tried to get the breathing tube placed. From the time he stopped ventilating with the mask until the boy's blood oxygen fell to dangerous levels was only about three minutes, and what with the difficult human anatomy, he ended up with the tube down the esophagus and had to start over. And over, and over. Finally, he used all of his force on the instrument, and got the tube in, breaking off the two front teeth in the process. Grimly, he thought that at least this patient would not be suing him.

Finally, he was ready to start.

A dog's skin, even on the skull, is much looser than a human's, and the head is much more devoted to jaws and snout than on the child. Cabrera had watched some videos on YouTube, and knew that he should make an incision from ear to ear over the top of the head. As he did so, it became obvious that blood loss was an issue. Despite his attempts to cauterize the wound edges, there seemed to be blood everywhere, and by the time he got it controlled, he thought he had lost maybe ten percent of the child's total blood volume. Then, instead of basically pulling the skin back as he did with the dogs, he had to get his fingers under the scalp and almost tear it from the underlying bone. He stretched and strained, cursing his lack of experience, cursing the fact that his tech was less than useless, cursing everyone and everything related to this whole mess. Most of all, he cursed Santiago, who stood in the corner of the operating room, impassive, eyes fixed on him. He had been told that either the patient survived, or else he would be joining him in the cremating furnace they used for the dogs they sacrificed.

The skull itself was much thinner than the dogs', and he nearly cut through the brain's dura with his initial saw cut, which sliced through some dural artery, spraying the room with more blood for the few seconds it took him to control it.

From that point, however, it was just like the dogs. He placed a large needle through the dura and withdrew 300 milliliters of cerebrospinal fluid, taking tension off the bulging tissue, which he then opened cleanly with sharp scissors, exposing the brain. Bigger than the dogs, but that was really all. He placed the mesh, sewed and glued the dura shut, and then put the top of the skull back into place, cutting a notch in the back to bring out the wire bundle. The plates he used to fix the bones were large, clumsy, canine items, a far cry from the fine titanium plates used by neurosurgeons, but they worked just fine. He stapled the scalp incision closed, and was done. He turned off the gas, and after what seemed like hours, but was really only a few minutes, Jorge woke up, opened terrified eyes, and tried to scream. The breathing tube stopped that, of course, and it wasn't until Cabrera was sure he was completely awake that he dared take the tube out. By then, Jorge was more whimpering than screaming.

They did not have an actual stretcher, just a rolling stainless steel cart, which they put him on to roll him to the attached main lab, where he was left in the recovery area, surrounded by the dog cages, whose residents barked enthusiastically.

Marta was brought in. She had been told nothing about an operation, Jorge had simply been taken from her. She had sat alone, weeping, for the five hours he had been gone. Now she saw him, head shaved, staples across his crown, bruises already forming under his eyes, and wires protruding from the back of his head. She was broken, and could do no more than sit in a chair next to him and hold his hand, as he cried in pain and confusion.

Santiago continued his vigil.

* * *

Cameron had gone into the FBI forensic lab to meet Mitzi around seven. He was carrying a large black garbage bag, and they spent several minutes getting ready, before they had flagged a cab and headed cross town. Even in the chill of late October, they were hot to the point of overheating.

They jumped out near Times Square, and ducked into a doorway where they dropped their raincoats, leaving them in evening wear. They walked briskly to the theater, where they went in one door, into the bathrooms where Cameron had been earlier that day, pulled off their

168

formal wear, leaving jeans and sweatshirts with watch caps, then went out the back into an alley. Soon they were on the #1 train headed to Van Cortland Park in the Bronx, which they walked across. The park afforded no cover to hide anyone who might be following, and by the time they reached the far side, Cameron was satisfied. They jumped onto the #4 train back south, and got off at Burnside. He got Mitzi settled into the rooming house where he had bought a week of no-questions-asked accommodations for a couple of hundreds. He handed her a gun. "Do you know how to use this?"

She shot him a look. "FBI, remember?"

"You're a doctor, not an agent," he said in his best Dr. McCoy voice.

She shook her head. "I'm actually both. Where did you get this, anyway? One of yours?"

"Illegal guns are easy to get in New York. It's only legal ones that are hard. Let's say I picked it up in my travels. Sometimes a clean gun is less, uh, complicated." She looked at him thoughtfully, then stowed it in her handbag. She did not mention her service piece that was in the small of her back.

He changed into warm winter clothes and boots, then donned ragged pants and an enormous coat over the top. He stank. Mitzi fanned her hand. "Where did you get those?"

"There was this giant homeless guy who was more than happy to sell his clothes for a trip into Goodwill and an extra twenty."

He took the train back downtown, and walked slowly to a vantage point across and down the street from his apartment, with a good view of the entry. He made a nest for himself in a pile of the ubiquitous trash bags, and settled down to wait.

He was chilled, despite his many layers, when he finally saw two men approach the doorway around three a.m. He was well aware that his entry door was a joke, and indeed, they were into the building in short order. Cameron waited a minute, then threw off the outer clothes and hustled across the street. What the entry lacked in security, it made up for with silence. He slipped in, and started up the stairs to the third floor.

His apartment door, unlike the entry downstairs, would be a challenge. A good Medco deadbolt on a metal door, secure in the metal frame. As expected, the intruders were still in the corridor, trying in vain to pick the lock. He drew his gun and pulled back the slide, a sound which froze them, even before he spoke a word.

What happened next came as a complete surprise. The larger of the two men, who was holding a short crow bar, suddenly pivoted at the waist and swung it into the side of the smaller man's head. Cameron heard the crack of the skull, and the man collapsed in a heap against his door, as the larger man sprinted down the hall away from him. Cameron could hardly shoot him in the back, so he gave chase, awkwardly hurdling the downed man's legs. The fleeing man crashed through the window at the end of the corridor onto the fire escape. Except that he didn't. His foot had caught on the radiator under the window, and instead of going clear through, he shattered the glass, and his neck came down violently onto the shards. He pulled back, flailing and gurgling, as his strong heart pumped a good share of his six quarts of blood in crazy, swirling arcs, until the man fell, first to his knees, and then onto his face.

Cameron considered his options, and decided to simply leave. Despite the noise, he realized that, in all likelihood, no one would have awakened. It was a very solid, pre-war building, one unit to each floor, and the downstairs occupant was deaf as a stone. The upstairs neighbor was an early jogger, and would likely be walking down the stairs in a couple of hours, where the chill from the broken window would cause him to look down the hall. That sort of thing could ruin the start of your day.

After his circuitous route back to the Bronx, he walked into the rooming house at about six, to find Mitzi watching the news on the grainy TV in the corner. There had been a report of a burglary gone bad in Cameron's part of Manhattan, with one man dead on the scene, the other taken to St Luke's in a coma. The police had no other information.

"So, the goons came for you," she stated. "I'm guessing you did not get much information from them." Cameron told her the story. She shook her head. "I think maybe I'll have to call in sick today."

Chapter 23

Cabrera had initially felt pretty good about himself. Jorge had actually woken up, and was even talking to his mother, who had not left from the moment she was allowed to be at his bedside. Neither had Santiago. About eleven, however, the whimpering increased, and the skin over the top of the boy's head started to bulge upward, straining against the staples. Finally, the strain was too much, and with an almost audible "whoosh," a stream of clear yellow fluid shot out of the incision, spraying over Marta, who screamed.

Cabrera was shaking. The cerebrospinal fluid was leaking from the skull under the skin flap. His closure had failed. The same thing had happened with some of the dogs. All of them had died from meningitis, usually within a week.

"What is that?" asked Santiago. Cabrera was slow to respond, so Santiago grabbed a handful of hair and lifted the small man off of his feet and hauled him out of the room. "I asked you a question."

Cabrera stuttered, and squirmed, then told him. "The seal failed. I have no way to prevent a massive infection. He has a few days at best."

Santiago made a phone call, then turned back to Cabrera. "Do whatever it takes to keep him alive and conscious. If he lasts a week, that will be enough. But get us that week."

* * *

Santiago was uncomfortable. In addition to giving his instructions regarding Cabrera, Perez had requested that Santiago come upstairs for a discussion. Given the fiasco at Hansen's apartment, he knew he was once again at risk. He walked into the third-floor conference room. Perez was staring out the window, watching a plane take off from LaGuardia. He did not turn as Santiago entered.

"What," he asked evenly, "happened with Hansen? I understand there is police involvement. Which we don't need. Not at all."

Santiago tried to match his tone. "We gave the assignment to Ruiz. His instructions were to use one of the local runners, and to make sure that, if there was a problem, there was to be no chance of him talking to the cops. From what we are getting from our police contact, he bashed in the kid's skull, and then botched his own escape out the window. Unfortunately, although the kid is in a coma, he survived."

"And Hansen?"

"We actually have no information about whether he was even there, or if something else spooked Ruiz. The police have not spoken to Hansen yet."

"And the woman?"

"Her apartment was entered. She was not there. Nor was there anything to indicate where she has gone. In fact, there was not much there at all. No computer, no phone, no papers."

Perez continued to stare out the window. "My orders were flawed. I should have allowed you to go. What is our potential exposure with Ruiz?"

"We should be safe. He has no record here, and was instructed to go in clean, no papers, no phone."

"And his weapon?"

"From our Argentine military stash, serial numbers filed off completely. No chance of it being traced."

"Take care of the kid at St. Lukes. He must not wake up."

"Of course." Perez said no more, and after a silence, Santiago left the room.

* * *

Dr. Overbridge stunned the Neuro ICU staff for a second time that week by walking into the unit just after noon. He went straight into Jamie Wilson's room. "How are you feeling?" he asked.

Pierre looked up, smiling broadly. "Awesome. Hardly hurts at all."

Overbridge checked the incision, which, of course, was perfect. He then had Pierre go through a series of tests of coordination and arm strength, all of which he passed.

"You are doing very well," he nodded. "I will check you again tonight, and plan on you being able to go home in the morning, as scheduled."

"I don't know how to even start to thank you," started Pierre, but Overbridge raised his hand.

"Just get better. I want this to work as much as you do." He turned and walked past the slack-jawed nurse on his way out of the ICU. He walked down the corridor to the elevator, almost buoyant, and realized that for the first time in years, he had not counted the steps down that hall.

* * *

"We can't just sit here all day," Mitzi grumbled as she paced back and forth in the grimy apartment.

"What do you propose?" Cameron sat up. He had been sleeping for the past several hours. "We're not going to have that list until morning, and I think it is best if I can say I've been out of town. Any ideas for that?"

She nodded. "Way ahead of you. Okay, we took off yesterday, went up to the Berkshires to a cabin, where we have been making feverish love. You were off, I called in sick. Sorry, Boss, but a girl has needs. We show up at our offices tomorrow, fresh in from Massachusetts with smiles on our faces."

"That story could be checked. Easily."

"True. Fortunately I have an address for you, and I happen to know that there happens to be a couple up there. Unless they go to the trouble of pulling prints and DNA from the cabin, the neighbors, such as they are, should corroborate."

"What about the people who are really there?" Cameron asked, impressed that Mitzi had this worked out already.

"They won't be saying anything. Both married. To other people. I let them use the place from time to time. They just happened to need it this week."

"It's YOUR place?" He had never heard her mention anything about a place in the Berkshires. "Since when do you have a secret love nest?"

"Since about five years ago. Sorry, you never made the cut." She gave him detailed directions to the place, complete with tourist info about the nearest convenience stores, etc.

"I think we should actually drive up and back. I need to be completely convincing."

Mitzi could not think of a counter argument, so she just shrugged and grabbed her bag.

173

Chapter 24

Perez called in Cabrera early on Friday. "What is the status?"

Cabrera swallowed. "He is awake, complains of some headache, but definitely awake."

"What about the leak?"

"I have put in a drain under the scalp so he does not build up pressure, but I have to keep an IV running full speed to make up for the fluid loss. We are keeping up for now, and there is no sign yet of infection. I'm pumping in antibiotics round the clock."

Blaylock was standing by the window. "We don't really need cooperation for the sensory programming. As long as he's conscious. Everything is set up downstairs."

"Let's get it started," Perez ordered.

* * *

An hour later, he took the elevator down to the basement and rolled into the observation room behind the one-way glass. Jorge was naked, lying on his back on what appeared to be a form-fitting mold on a table in the center of the room. An array of three robotic arms were rapidly touching the boy, first on one arm, then the other, then on the chest, the legs, the face. The child was squirming a little, but did not seem to be too uncomfortable. Blaylock was at a console, and turned towards the glass. "If you're there, Boss, you are just in time for us to turn him over." He tapped the keyboard, and the mold appeared to soften.

Two men walked over and started to peel first his fingers, then his arms, legs, and finally his torso off of the gel. The gel flattened out, losing the indentation where the boy had been. There was a round hole at one end of the table. The boy was flipped over, and his face was pressed into the hole, then his body was lowered down onto the gel. Blaylock tapped a few commands on the keyboard, and the gel appeared to soften again, as the boy's struggling body settled into the surface, where he soon was unable to move.

"Like a mouse on a glue trap," Blaylock grinned.

The robotic arms started their work again, as Blaylock studied the monitor intensely. "The analysis is improving as we go. I have an artificial intelligence neural network that is learning. This side should only take about twenty minutes."

"Then what?" asked Perez over the intercom.

"Then I think we should give the skin a rest and do auditory and visual."

When it finished, Blaylock released the gel and had the men turn him onto his back again. As the little body was sinking back into the gel, Blaylock placed a set of earphones on him.

"There's nothing really to see here. I first will put in simple tonal stimuli, then progress to more complex sounds, like music, and then to speech. That is where the home videos start to be really useful. We have extracted his mother's voice to start, then after we have fully mapped his hearing and receptive speech processing, we'll add new voices, unknown to the boy. The brain is really good at recognizing speech, which is processed in a completely different area than music or, say, forest noise."

Perez was fascinated. "And for vision?"

"First we tape the eyelids open, then put an artificial tear irrigation system on to prevent drying out. Then the virtual reality goggles, and away we go. First colors, then simple shapes, then recognizable objects, on through to faces. Once again, we start with familiar faces, then move on to random faces. Finally, when we have all of that data, we play movies, lots of action, and correlate sound and vision together. Should take about nine or ten hours for all that. Then back to the skin."

"What does that mean?"

"Well, what we are doing now is simple touch. That gives some excellent mapping, but we need the full range of sensation. After we finish with audio and visual, we need to do cold. And pain. And heat." Blaylock grimaced. "We want to get as much info processed from the touch as we can, as it is likely that his ability to tolerate the pain and heat will be limited. I'm hoping we can get it done in an hour on each side. Come back around seven if you want to watch. Or maybe you don't. Considering."

Perez did not answer, just watched silently for another few minutes, then wheeled around and back to the elevator.

176

Cameron jogged up the steps into the building housing the Anti-Terrorism Unit just after ten. He flashed his ID, then strode purposefully down to his cubicle, where he booted up his desktop to check for email. He pumped his fist as he saw that it was there in his inbox. The attachment was a list of addresses and electrical grid usage for over three hundred locations in the Tri-State area. He spooled it to the printer, and had just picked it up and started for the door when Kevin Crawley, the FBI Special Agent in Charge of the ATU, came out of his office holding a coffee mug and spotted him.

"Hansen!" he called, "a word, if you please." He stepped back to his door, and made a theatrical sweeping movement, inviting him in.

Cameron had no option but to follow him in and sit down.

"I thought the DDO said you were off for a while," Crawley started.

Cameron shifted a little. "Yes, he told me to check back in a couple of weeks. That will be Monday. I just stepped in to check my email, you know, in case there was anything interesting."

"And was there?"

"No," Cameron replied, conscious of the thick wad of paper in his back pocket.

"Traffic bad from the West Side this morning, Hansen?" The SAC was peering over the top of his reading glasses.

"I wouldn't know sir. I've been out of town. Just got back this morning from the Berkshires."

"So you wouldn't know anything about a burglary attempt at your place night before last?"

"What!" Cameron jumped up. "I don't know anything about that! At my place? I haven't been home yet!"

"Yes, we tried to call you yesterday, but got nothing but voice mail. One guy dead at the scene, another taken comatose to St Lukes. Right outside your door. Doesn't look like they got in. The manager let the cops in, just a quick peek to make sure you weren't in there dead. They said nothing looked disturbed. Also said it looked like you hadn't been there for a few days." He scribbled a name and number on a notebook page and handed it to him. "This is the detective on the case. He wants to talk to you. Obviously. Give him a call."

"Will do." He got up to leave.

"No, I meant now," Crawley punched in the number, and put it on speaker.

"Terrence," a voice said. Crawley poked a finger at Cameron.

"Uh, this is Cameron Hansen. My SAC gave me a message to call."

"Ah, yes, Agent Hansen. We need to have a chat. Just routine. How about I come by the ATU at noon? Or would you rather come to me? We could meet at your place. Actually, I think that might be best. Let's say noon." He hung up.

"Great," the SAC smiled. "got that guy off my back. Thinks he's Columbo. Raincoat, false exits, the whole bit. You'll love him." He laughed mirthlessly.

* * *

Cameron was worried about getting to his apartment. He knew there was more than a small chance that the place was being watched. In the end, he decided that a cab dropping him right in front was safer than walking up. He had not seen anyone watching as he entered the ATU, but he waited in the lobby until a couple of agents he knew came down and headed out. "Hey guys," he called, "can you drop me at Grand Central?"

"Sure, thing, let's go," came the reply.

At Grand Central Station, he stood in line, watching the cabs carefully to make sure no cabbies tried to jump the line. He laughed a little to himself. *That would have caused an immediate riot.* He hadn't seen anyone watching or following, but that did not stop him from keeping his gun in hand in the pocket of his overcoat all the way there. He called Mitzi.

"Everything okay?"

"Perfect. Like I said, the FBI offices are about as safe as they come."

He explained where he was going.

"You're clear on all the details?"

"Yeah, no problem." He hung up.

He arrived in front of his building about three minutes late, and scurried quickly through the front door, flashing his ID at the uniformed cop stationed there, who jerked his head in the direction of the elevator. Cameron chose the stairs.

Detective Arthur Terrence was a smallish man in a crumpled tan raincoat, with a mass of unruly graying hair and a mustache. He was leaning against the banister on Cameron's landing. "Agent Hansen, I presume?"

Cameron stuck out his hand. "Pleased to meet you, Detective. Should we go in and sit down? You said they did not get in, right?" Terrence nodded, waving him forward in an "after you" gesture. Cameron unlocked the door, and they went in and sat down.

"So, Agent Hansen," Terrence began, "where've you been the past couple of days?"

"Up in the Berkshires with a lady friend. Just got back into town."

"Hmm. Regular girlfriend?"

"Uh, kind of complicated, really. Regular friend, sporadic, um, date. More like several spaced out one-night stands. Nothing really serious or anything. But she's a close friend." *Way too much explaining,* he thought. He shut up.

"When were you last here?"

"I left the apartment Wednesday morning, haven't been back in until now." He winced inwardly, having answered in a way he could tell himself was truthful. *As if that mattered, given the big lie about the Berkshires.*

"You don't seem worried about anything being missing." Terrence waved around the room.

"You said that they did not come in."

"True, that's how it looks. Still, kind of funny you didn't even look around." He peered intently at Cameron.

"How did it go down?" Cameron tried to sidestep the subject.

"Funniest thing. It looks like the dead guy brained the little guy, then tried to jump out the window and accidentally skewered himself on the glass."

"Sounds awful."

"It looks worse. Wanna come examine the scene, agent?" His eyebrows shot up.

Cameron shrugged, not quite sure whether hesitant or eager would be most convincing. They stood up and walked to the door. "Truth is, I guess with the bodies gone, not much to see," the detective said as he led Cameron out. That was true near the door, just a football-sized blood stain on the carpet. The window was something else. Thick dried blood was on the remains of the glazing, and sprayed on the casement and walls, as well as thick and black on the radiator. The carpet was soaked for about six feet back from the window.

Cameron tried to appear curious as he looked at the scene. "Do you really think this has anything to do with me at all?" he asked. "Seems like a couple of burglars had a fight, one hit the other, then panicked and tried to run. Maybe he was afraid someone heard the noise? Maybe there was yelling?"

Terrence didn't answer, but asked, "What do you keep in your apartment, Agent Hansen?"

Cameron laughed, "Dirty clothes, dirty dishes, pizza boxes and stale burritos, mostly."

"How about documents related to your work at ATU?"

"No, no reason I would bring any of that stuff home, even if it were allowed."

"Any reason anyone would want to harm you?"

"No, I'm just an office analyst."

"Okay, well, let me know if you think of anything." He pulled out a card, started to hand it to Cameron, then pulled it back. "Oh, I forgot, you already have my number." He started towards the stairs. After a couple of steps he turned around. "Curious thing, though."

"What's that?"

"What they were carrying."

"You gonna tell me or make me beg?"

"Get this – they each had a gun, 9 mm, all identifying numbers eradicated, and the dead guy had a taser. And plastic cuffs. And a headbag. And duct tape. What does that say to you?"

Cameron thought quickly. The detective would certainly expect a CIA agent to know what he was describing. "Sounds like they wanted to snatch someone."

"Exactly. Someone here, don't you think?"

"Maybe they were at the wrong place. Maybe that's what they fought about."

Terrence shook his head. "Let's see. CIA former undercover agent lives behind door number one. Downstairs is a retired grocer. Upstairs, a lower echelon stockbroker's assistant. Piano teacher above him. Buildings on both sides, similar nobodies. I even checked the same addresses on the streets north and south. Nothing more interesting than a guy from the chorus in the revival of 'Hello Dolly.' They were at the right place, Agent Hansen. You sure you can't give me a little help here?"

"Sorry detective, I've really got nothing."

"Okay, well, as I say, if something comes to mind . . ." he mimed a phone. He turned and started away again. He stopped again, shaking his head once more.

"I almost forgot. You know how there's often a big pile of garbage bags across the street?"

"I guess. Just part of the ambiance."

"Have you ever seen homeless guys sleeping in the garbage pile?"

"Not that I've noticed. Why do you ask?"

"Funniest thing. The guy next door took his dog out around eleven, noticed a guy sleeping there. Went out again around four. Dog has a weak bladder. Anyhow, no homeless guy the second time. Thursday morning was garbage day, and by the time we got the neighbor's report, the pile of garbage was gone. Pity."

This time, the detective really did leave. Cameron waited a half hour, then also left, walking as quickly as he could to Amsterdam Avenue, where he caught a cab to the FBI offices to pick up Mitzi. Terrence, parked in a car at the end of the block, watched him walk away.

* * *

At exactly seven o'clock, Perez was back behind the glass. Blaylock was slightly ahead of schedule, and the robot arms were busily and apparently randomly touching Jorge with probes a little larger than from the morning. Blaylock explained that cold was less precise than touch, and hence the larger probe. They were just finishing. Jorge was whimpering, but almost completely unable to squirm.

It took the techs about five minutes to change out the tips, substituting slender needles for the blunt cold probes. Blaylock started the program, and immediately small pricks were started, again randomly. Jorge screamed as tiny drops of blood oozed from a dozen, then a hundred, then a thousand needle pricks. Blaylock nodded, satisfaction showing in his face.

"Clean him up," he ordered, and the techs went in and wiped away the blood with clothes wet with a solution that foamed. *Peroxide,* Perez assumed. Blaylock came out.

"This is superb data. It appears that the brain's encoding is even more orderly than I thought. It will take several hours to analyze, but it looks like we don't really have to map the entire body for cold and pain, it is more like there is encoding for position on the skin, then additional brain activity which indicates touch, versus cold, versus pain. Interesting, since the nerve endings for those different sensations are quite distinct. I'll finish with the heat, and then run an algorithm to predict the responses to cold, pain, and heat for the back. We can then see how close we come. If we are close enough, we may find we don't have to do anything but the simple touch, then just enough of the other sensations to calibrate. Could save us a lot of time on future subjects."

While he was talking, the techs had attached squared-off tubes to each of the robot arms, and given Jorge a second cleaning with the peroxide. They then dried him carefully and motioned to Blaylock, who said, "Back to work," and went back into the lab.

Perez watched, fascinated again as the robot arms moved in their pitiless course. This time, a laser emitted by the new apparatus caused tiny puffs of smoke from the boy's skin. Heat. Perez shivered involuntarily. He hoped Blaylock's algorithm worked. It would certainly be nice to shorten the process.

Chapter 25

Friday, October 28
New York

During the week, Dr. Overbridge had quickly regained his strength, and by Thursday was again walking to and from work. He was somewhat distressed that his trip to work that morning took him 2312 steps, over fifteen percent more than his usual. *Most definitely not Roman,* he thought. *If I had been a Legionnaire, I would most certainly have been flogged.* Thursday evening was better, 2235, and he had been confident that he would soon be back on track. His head still hurt, but he was able to simply put that realization in a box to the side of his consciousness, and not be bothered. He finished work on Friday without having canceled a single surgery or patient appointment, and no one at Our Lady had any idea that he had been sick. He was satisfied. Friday evening he walked home, then flagged a cab without going into the building, and headed to the New York Athletic Club to meet Jack and Cathy.

He had discharged his incognito patient on Thursday, and was to see him at the facility in Queens on Saturday. If all was well, they planned to try the device the next week. Dr. Overbridge was very excited. He was helping to solve one of the most elusive problems in medicine, the reanimation of the paraplegic. He was very pleased to be part of the team.

* * *

The New York Athletic Club was certainly an athletic club, but it was also a superb restaurant in midtown Manhattan. Dr. Overbridge had been a member for decades, having not given up his membership when he had stopped going there for racketball and weight training after he left the Neurological Institute. He now went there each week for the Sunday brunch, and on those rare occasions when his father came down from Boston. Rarer and rarer – in fact, the last time had been four years previously. They were not close, and had nothing to discuss. All the elder Overbridge found interesting was money, and although his son made an enormous amount, spent very little, and had, by consequence, literally millions saved, he gave it almost no thought. Which his father did not even start to comprehend.

Cathy was curious to meet Dr. Overbridge, and when they entered the dining room, Jack scanned the room and pointed him out. "He looks like an alien," Cathy whispered as they made their way over. He was already seated and waiting for them, but was situated so that they approached the table, unseen, from behind him. He was sitting perfectly motionless, with the exception that his pale bald head was turning slowly from left to right. As they were coming across the room, she noted that when he was turned all the way to the right, he suddenly turned quickly all the way to the left, then started slowly back again to the right. "What is he doing?" she asked Jack.

"Probably counting something. I have noticed he does that. Hard to believe he is the same man I knew as a resident. Of course, I guess we all have different paths than people would expect." He gave her arm three quick squeezes, and was rewarded with a peck on the cheek.

Dr. Overbridge rose when they arrived at the table. Jack introduced him to Cathy.

"Pleased to meet you," Cathy smiled.

"The pleasure is all mine." Dr. Overbridge was gracious. He called the waiter over. "Shall we start with some wine? No, that's right, you two are Mormon."

Clearly a contrived opener, Cathy thought.

Jack was curious. *Why did Overbridge really want to have dinner?* He had checked around. No one in the medical community had heard of him doing anything social with anyone for decades. This whole week had been extraordinarily strange, starting with that text about this exact time the preceding Friday.

In fact, Dr. Overbridge was completely asocial. He was not connected to society, insofar as he could arrange it. He did not own a cell phone, nor a television. Although he used computers extensively at work, he did not have a home computer or tablet. Nothing. He continued to receive all his medical journals in the mail, and they provided his entertainment in the evenings. He had a large collection of delivery menus, and often his only contact with anyone after work for weeks on end was with the restaurants that he called for meals. And the housekeeper. He had minimized his other contacts as well. All of his income was deposited into an account at

Chase, and his accounting firm made tax payments and sent him a very short stack of checks to sign every two weeks to take care of his utilities and such. He personally stopped into the bank on his way home once a month and drew out whatever cash he needed. He preferred cash, preferred carrying a lot for emergencies, and typically had at least three thousand dollars on his person at all times. If the denizens of East Harlem had been aware of that little fact, it is certain that his walks to Our Lady would not have been so peaceful.

Jack could not have known all of that, but did know enough to realize that this was an unusual event for Dr. Overbridge.

He decided that if Dr. Overbridge was going to bring it up, he might as well talk about his conversion as anything else.

"Yes, that's right. How did you know?"

"Everyone knows, Dr. Tucker. It was big news when you converted." As a matter of fact, Overbridge had overheard the other two neurosurgeons at Our Lady discussing it in the surgeons' lounge. Not that he was talking with them, of course. He considered them so inferior as to not be worth considering. They did not share in his reputation, or his patients, and were relegated to dealing with the normal impoverished patients at Our Lady of Salubrious Penitence, meaning the trauma cases and tumors that walked in off the streets of East Harlem.

He had been curious. It was at about the time Jack converted that Overbridge had decided to re-label his films with Jack's name, as Dr. Peterman at Mount Sinai was getting past his prime.

"Are you a man of faith, Dr. Overbridge?"

That was a question that required some thought. Overbridge stared up at the opposite wall, counting the crenellations in the crown molding of the ornate old room. He was not sure how to answer that. His official internal stance was that he was agnostic, but that did not explain his feelings of being haunted by the dead. If the dead could haunt, logically that would imply an afterlife, which led to consideration of God. He had not attended church since leaving Exeter, as he did not feel that organized religion had anything to offer, and their platitudes tended to interfere with his chosen college and military lifestyles. Since Lake, he had lived an essentially monastic life, but his religion had been the brain. The complexity of that organ itself seemed to imply a higher being, since he had decided that the capacity for art and philosophy which mankind showed did not seem likely to have been the result of any Darwinian pressure that had been observed or that he could imagine. So, he supposed that no, he was not agnostic, but rather that he believed that there must be a higher power.

So, after a delay of a few awkward minutes, during which he had verified for the fourth time that evening that there were indeed three hundred and eighty-one crenellations on the west crown molding, he responded, "I believe that there is a higher power."

"So, you believe in God."

Again a delayed response. The mahogany panels below the crown molding required his attention. There were twenty-four. God was a bit more specific than he was willing to go. God sounded, well, too personal, too contrived. Too "organized religion." Certainly, the God that was variously described and worshiped by the diverse religions of the world. Which God? An Essence? A Person? Singular? Plural? He did not have enough information to be confident in his response.

"I believe there is a higher power," he finally repeated.

"May I ask you a question?" Cathy interjected.

"Certainly."

"What was your motivation for inviting us to dinner tonight. Rumor has it that you are not much of one for social engagements."

Another tough question. He began again to count the panels.

"It would be less off-putting if you could count something more at eye-level," she suggested. "Perhaps the gray hairs on Jack's head, or my eyelashes or something. Just a thought." She smiled and winked at him. He blushed.

"I had not realized it was so evident."

"It makes me wonder what you are feeling, or rather, what you do not wish to be feeling."

He was beginning to think that, with these two, it might be easiest to simply count the difficult questions. Or maybe he was just completely out of practice and had lost his conversational skills.

He decided to answer the prior question. "I wanted to get to know the man who saved my brain, er, I mean, my life. I saw the scans. It was not really possible, you know."

"I guess we both got lucky."

Cathy broke in. "You know better than that." She turned towards Overbridge. "God helped you by helping him. Believe it. But listen, you brought up the whole religion thing. Why was that?"

"After the Lake incident, some things from the past came up that led me to some quasi-religious musings, and so I became attuned to the metaphysical in a way I had not been before."

"What things from the past?" Cathy leaned forward.

"From the war. I had seen a lot of combat. I became cognizant that I was using the practice of medicine to work out my post-traumatic stress, I suppose, and the death of Mr. Lake threw a wrench in my self-therapy." He was startled that he had confided that to this woman he had just met. He must have looked shocked. "I am sorry, that was perhaps more than I should have said."

She smiled. "People often tell me things, Dr. Overbridge. What exactly was surgery helping you work out?"

"I had destroyed a lot of brains. I was trying to save them to make up for that. Losing another through negligence felt like a giant step backwards."

"When you say you had destroyed brains, do you mean you had to kill during the war?"

"I was a very good shot from long distance. The Marines made good use of me. They haunt me, the men I killed."

They ate in silence for a few minutes, then Overbridge turned to Jack. "You did not answer my question, Dr. Tucker. What turned you to religion? Was it this young woman?"

Jack smiled. "No, I met Cathy *after* I was baptized. I guess you would say that I was also perhaps a little haunted. Not actively, but when my daughters and I were invited to visit the church by one of their friends, I was in a place where I was thinking more about God. Once there, the feeling of the Spirit was what drew me in. Perhaps you would like to give us a try."

He did not respond to that immediately. He started to count the crenellations, then stopped himself. He abruptly pushed away from the table and excused himself, "I'm sorry, I need to visit the restroom. I'll be right back." He hurried away.

Jack turned to Cathy. "What do you think?"

"Pretty odd," said Cathy. "What is going on with the counting?"

"A lot of obsessive compulsive behavior seems to be related to guilt. I would guess that it was always there, at least after Vietnam, but he seems to have really gone over the top since the whole catastrophe with Alexander Lake. Most of the time, surgeons are able to get past something like that, ego-maniacs that we are."

"The way he talks about destroying and saving brains is like something out of a zombie apocalypse movie. You usually talk about your cases as people with brain problems, but he seems to think of the brain as the only part that matters.

Dr. Overbridge returned. "So sorry. The joys of the aging male." His attempt at a smile was almost painful to watch.

They finished the meal with no new revelations. As they were thanking him, Jack asked, "How about we have you over? We are having a few friends over on Thursday next. Would you care to come? We are on East 83rd. Say about seven?"

Dr. Overbridge looked as if he were about to say something, but Cathy quickly chipped in, "Perfect, we'll see you then," and grabbed Jack's hand and led him away before he could respond.

"So, who should we invite for next week, Mr. we're-having-a-few-friends-over?" Her eyes twinkled. "He is really kind of fascinating."

* * *

Cameron had napped on the couch in Mitzi's office while she finished her work in the lab. He had given her a report of his conversation with Terrence, and they had agreed that they would stay late at the office, where they would have computer access, before going back up to their hideout in the Bronx.

The list was long – three hundred forty-four addresses, just as Mary Jane had told Mitzi on Monday.

"Okay," Mitzi started, "we have got to do something to filter these. Thoughts?"

Cameron leaned back. "I think we should look at the structures on Google Earth. The place we are looking for is likely a big enough building to house labs and stuff, if it is anything like the place on Isla Sofia. Also, a loading dock or underground garage. And not on a main thoroughfare."

"What if those assumptions are wrong?"

"Then we will miss it on the first go and waste a bunch of time. But we have to start somewhere."

They each took half the list and started to work. Two hours later, Cameron was up to number twenty-four on his list. "How are you doing?" he asked.

"Number twenty-eight. Four reasonable possibilities. How about you?"

188

"Twenty-four," he had admitted, feeling a little out played. "Also four possibles."

Mitzi thought a minute. "At this rate, we will finish in about eight or nine hours and still have fifty or sixty possibilities. I need caffeine." She stretched, and went out to make another pot of coffee.

They actually got to the end of their list around five a.m. Saturday, and had forty-seven structures that met their criteria. Of those, ten were in the Bronx, seven in Brooklyn, five in Queens, three each in Manhattan and Staten Island, fifteen in New Jersey, and three in Westchester county.

"Now what?" Mitzi yawned.

"Now let's get some sleep, then make a plan for eyeballing all of these."

The streets of Manhattan were surprisingly busy early on a Saturday, and Cameron let Mitzi flag down a cab, while he surveilled the area. Nothing suspicious, but he still insisted on taking the cab to Penn Station, then switching to another cab for the ride to the Bronx. This would never do. They needed a car, but getting a rental without a credit card was going to be a problem. A problem for later. For now, sleep.

Chapter 26

Saturday, October 29
New York

The car picked Dr. Overbridge up at his apartment precisely at eight. On the ride out to Queens, he was conscious of an anticipatory excitement. The thrill of being part of such a development was almost overwhelming. When they arrived, he practically leaped out of the car and headed to the elevator. It was on the ride up that he realized he had not counted. Neither the steps from the car, nor the buildings passed en route, nor the intersections. Nothing. He recalled the previous night at the NYAC, and came to the realization that, then, he had been somehow afraid, and now he was not. He had been looking for redemption in the wrong place all these years.

Pierre Lemieux, accompanied by Maxwell, was waiting for him in a well-appointed hospital room on the third floor. Other than a little tenderness at the incision, he said he felt fine.

Dr. Overbridge removed his staples, and verified that the incision was healing well. He then took out a ruler, made some measurements on the incision, and marked a spot near the crown of the head. He injected the area with lidocaine, and after waiting a few minutes, cleaned the area with betadine and made a small incision. The plug was there, just under the skin, protruding out through the gap in the skull. Maxwell handed him the next piece of the device. "This has a special fibroblast-stimulating coating around the outside. It should heal to the skin, and create a water- and bacteria-proof seal," he explained. After deepening the incision and attaching the connector, Overbridge used medical grade superglue to secure it.

"This will hold the skin nicely until it heals, which should just take a few days. We should be able to use it right away, as long as we don't wiggle it too much." He then secured it with a large clear plastic dressing. "And this should keep it stable." He stepped back and attempted a smile, satisfied.

Pierre was impatient. "How soon can I start to walk?"

191

Maxwell looked questioningly at Overbridge, who replied, "I think that either tomorrow or Monday you would be strong enough physically."

Maxwell smiled. "Perfect. That will give us just about enough time for programming."

Maxwell wheeled a workstation with an oversized monitor in from the next room, and carefully plugged the long, thin cable into the connector on Pierre's head. He handed the wireless keyboard/trackball unit to Pierre, and they all waited for the program to boot up. Soon a man's figure appeared on the screen, lying down, and Dr. Overbridge was interested to see that, on examination, the figure's face was that of Pierre. There was a green "start" button in the upper right hand corner of the screen, with a yellow "pause" button and a red "quit" button beneath it. On the left side were a set of legs, front and back, covered with a grid.

"Okay," Maxwell said, "here's how it works. You think about moving your legs or toes or whatever, and the computer interprets your thoughts as commands to the muscles in the avatar on the screen. It will work best if you start with simple things, like wriggling your toe. Click on the part you are going to move, and then concentrate on moving it until you can make it do what you want. Try to map out your legs completely with simple movements."

It took a while for Pierre to get the hang of it. He started with the left great toe, clicking on the grid on the left side of the screen, then thought about moving that part. Obligingly, that part moved on the avatar. He then moved to the ankle, and tried again. That worked fine as well. After a few more areas, Maxwell had him click outside the grid, told him to try again to move the avatar. Pierre hit the keyboard in frustration as the whole leg jumped at once.

"I was just trying to move the toe! Why is everything moving?"

"Your movement commands were too general – it is like you were just telling that whole limb to move when you were trying to program it. I think we should re-start, and you need to really concentrate on moving ONLY the part in question."

Overbridge watched the process intently. After about an hour, Pierre succeeded in programming movements of the entire right leg, which he could then cause the avatar to raise in the air and kick. Pierre was beginning to tire, and Overbridge decreed that he needed to take a break for a couple of hours. Pierre tried to object, but Maxwell agreed and shut down the workstation. He then motioned to Overbridge, and they left the room.

"I will have them take you home," Maxwell stated. "We will pick you up tomorrow at noon."

Overbridge nodded. "Very well. I can see that this will take some time. I am most anxious to observe the progress, however."

Maxwell looked at him. "Speaking of anxiety, how is yours?"

"I don't know what you mean." But, even as he said the words, the compulsive need for order bubbled up, and, although he had not been counting anything all morning, he suddenly needed to know how many ceiling tiles were in the corridor. As his eyes flicked upward, he did his best to pull down and look at Maxwell.

"Exactly," Maxwell smiled. "Solving this problem should help you in ways that all of your years of surgery have not."

Overbridge continued on towards the elevator. After six steps, he stopped, noting that Maxwell was not following. "Something else?"

"Yes," Maxwell replied. "Tell me about that incision on your scalp. That perfect, surgical incision. About a week old, I would say. When we saw you earlier this week, you had on a cap."

"I had a minor procedure."

"With an eight-inch scar?" Maxwell approached and poked a finger around the incision. Overbridge did not flinch or react. "With a large bone plate?"

"I had an aneurysm clipped. It was a minor inconvenience. I did not even miss any work. It really is none of your concern." His expression was completely blank.

"It is very much our concern. We *need* you, Dr. Overbridge. I need to know that you are going to be capable of helping us with this work. When and where was your surgery?"

"Last Friday, Lenox Hill Hospital. I had surgery after work, and was discharged the next day. My surgeon was Dr. Jack Tucker, who, other than myself, is the best neurosurgeon in New York. And therefore, the world. You do not need to be concerned with my abilities, Mr. Maxwell."

Maxwell started to say something, but decided to simply call the elevator. He watched as the doors closed, then went back down the hall to the conference room. Perez was watching Pierre on a monitor.

"Did you hear all that?" Maxwell asked, knowing that there were microphones in the hallway, and that Perez could monitor every space in the building.

"Yes," Perez was thoughtful. He touched a button on the telephone console, and when Santiago picked up, he asked, "When did we stop the full-time surveillance on Overbridge?"

"A few weeks ago. We tracked him night and day for a couple of months, but he never varied his routine in any way, so we put our resources elsewhere."

"I am not criticizing. Resume the surveillance." He hung up and pushed another button.

"Find out everything on a Dr. Jack Tucker, neurosurgeon at Lenox Hill Hospital, and get me the hospital record from Lenox Hill for Augustus Overbridge, who had surgery last Friday. Yes, *our* Dr. Overbridge. And don't make me wait."

Maxwell shrugged. "There's always something."

Perez did not answer, just wheeled around and headed to the elevator. He rode down to the basement to check on their subject.

* * *

Jorge was wearing VR goggles, and had a game controller in hand, which he was working feverishly. Marta was seated next to him, her hand on his knee. Blaylock was in the control room, alternately glancing at the boy and staring at his monitor, where a dozen rows of squirming lines were working their way across. He turned towards Perez, flushed with enthusiasm. "This kid is certainly resilient. After all that last night, as soon as we finished, he was starving, so we gave him small amounts of about thirty foods, got great data about taste and smell and finally filled him up. Couldn't have been better." He pointed through the glass. "Now we are having him play his favorite games. It is like these things were designed specifically with our needs in mind. Eye, hand, sound, cognition, all correlated with easily merged computer data. If he is stronger tomorrow, we will have him do the ones where he is running and jumping and dancing. I think he has almost forgotten the wringer we put him through yesterday. Seems to be enjoying himself."

"How about his physical condition?"

Blaylock looked a little uncomfortable. "Could be better. Still pouring out CSF, but Cabrera is replacing it with IV fluids, and he doesn't have a fever or anything. Cabrera is worried that he is not peeing enough. Wants us to get a pediatrician."

"I don't have anyone set up. It is not like we can go to a local clinic.

Tell Cabrera it is his job. And his responsibility."

* * *

Cameron woke up just after noon, and realized that Mitzi was gone. A little annoyed, a little worried, a smidge panicked, he called her on his burner. "Where are you?"

"Driving around the neighborhood looking for parking."

"Where did you get a car?"

Mitzi did not exactly answer, but rather said, "Oops, there's one. Be up in a minute." She clicked off.

Cameron looked at the silent phone, then jumped up and headed to the shower. He heard the door close just as he was finishing.

Mitzi was sitting at the small kitchen table, eating a banana and sipping coffee from a generic to-go cup. Another one was waiting for him across from her. He sipped it gratefully.

"Okay, so what car do you have?"

"I have friends. I called one and asked to borrow it for a few days. Problem solved."

First off, Cameron thought, *Mitzi does not really have friends.* "What did you tell her?"

"Did I say her? And I didn't explain anything. Somehow people don't expect me to."

Cameron had to admit that was true. Just as he would not bother to ask her if her friend were male or female. She would simply ignore any question she did not want to answer.

"How do you think we should do this?" Cameron asked, suspecting she would already have a plan. Unless there was some major flaw, it would be easier in every way to just go along with whatever she had concocted.

"I think just drive by each spot, see what is supposedly going on there, then approach any likelies directly."

"You mean, like, bang on the door and say 'excuse me, are you the criminals that want to capture and torture my friend here, or just some other criminals growing pot or selling kiddie porn?'" He tried to sound flip, but the reality was that he was more than a little apprehensive. For all they knew, Perez had a hundred foot soldiers looking for them. Or at least him. So far, they had no direct evidence that Mitzi was a target. If Cameron's phone had been tracked, they would have identified Mitzi's phone as a frequent contact, so care was needed, but perhaps they were

195

being a little paranoid. Which he had every intention of continuing.

"Something more subtle, obviously. Tailored to whatever the purported purpose of the place happens to be. I'm not stupid." She glared at him.

"Fine. Where should we start?"

"New Jersey," she said promptly. "First, we have the most possibilities there, second, we know that they for sure had one place there, since that's where you turned up, and finally, that area has the highest ratio of Latinos. Over a third of the population in Newark, which is where most of our buildings lie."

"Okay, New Jersey it is. Where next?"

"Clockwise, so Westchester, Bronx, Queens, Brooklyn, and finally Manhattan."

"I agree, Staten Island is too unlikely for our initial investigation. But why clockwise?"

"Because counter-clockwise is Satanic."

Mitzi's last comment had continued to pop up in Cameron's head as they drove on I-95 into and across upper Manhattan and over the George Washington Bridge. Traffic was a snarl, and it took them almost an hour and a half to get to the first address. Which they immediately eliminated, as it was a T-Mobile service center, with brand-new signage, which was why they had not seen it on Google Earth, their images often being several months old. "Now if that had been Perez's cell company, MexiVox, I would have said 'Jackpot!'" Cameron remarked.

They proceeded on through their list, but the going was slow, the addresses not being very conveniently bunched, and sundown was before six. Cameron wanted to drive back to the Bronx, but Mitzi argued for a local motel. There was an abundance of sleazy-looking candidates near them, and despite his nap, Cameron was bushed, so he went along. As if any amount of discussion would have budged her. In the end, they were only able to get to five of the fifteen addresses, and none of them looked promising enough for a visit.

Chapter 27

Sunday, October 30
New York

Augustus Overbridge awoke at precisely 5:30 a.m., despite a night troubled with a dream he had not had in years.

As a child in Boston, Overbridge had slept in a large room on the upper floor of a stately home – a mansion, some would say. The house had the best of everything; linens, carpets, furniture, servants, food. And wasps. Deep in the timbers of the venerable dwelling, the insects had established their territory, and repeated attempts at extermination had been miserable failures. Somehow, they would creep out of invisible cracks in the moldings, and it was rare for a week to go by without another sighting. It was fortunate that none of the family were allergic, as, several times a year, someone would hop out of bed only to land on one of the creatures, who would promptly deliver a painful sting. Although one was allowed to mention to the housekeeper that another carcass needed to be removed, crying or other signs of weakness were met with grim stares and mocking sarcasm from his father.

Overbridge at age six had developed a very specific fear, namely that one of the insects would land on his eyelid while he was asleep, and blind him with its stings. Soon, that fear had invaded his dreams, such that he would awake in the dark room, certain he was blind, a fear which was not helped by the fact that he would have dug at his eyes with his fingernails in an effort to kill the wasps which he was sure were attacking. He did not dare tell his parents, as that sort of foolishness would likely have been met with discipline of a most humiliating and unpleasant variety. These nightmares became more and more frequent, and he became more and more exhausted, until finally his mother, certain he must have developed a wasting disease, had taken him to the doctor.

Initially too intimidated by the large round man with beefy red skin, young Augustus had not said much, but finally blurted out that he was having nightmares that the wasps were blinding him. His mother looked stunned, and gave a funny little laugh. The doctor, to his surprise, just wrinkled his brow thoughtfully, and pulled out a prescription pad. He wrote two words on it, and handed it to Mrs. Overbridge. "Sleep mask?" she asked.

"Yes," replied the doctor. "Pick one up in the lingerie section. Nothing too fancy," he said with a wink.

So, they had purchased a plain black satin model, and he had worn it every night for as long as he lived in that house. The nightmare went away. Why it had returned now, sixty years later, was not something that Overbridge was about to waste time considering. He would simply acquire a sleep mask.

His Sunday routine was different from the weekdays. First, the exercise regimen lasted sixty minutes instead of thirty. Second, the New York Times Sunday edition had to be read. To this was allocated ninety minutes, and was the sum total of Overbridge's efforts with regards to current, non-medical events. He figured that news which did not make it through a week was not important enough to bother with. In any case, he had little interest in knowing about events over which he had no control. Finally, there was no housekeeper, and so, instead of breakfast at his apartment, he left for the New York Athletic Club at precisely 8:45.

He walked west on 94th Street to 5th Avenue, then south to just above the Met, where he entered Central Park. His standard, slightly circuitous route had him exit across from 7th Avenue at Central Park South, from which it was a short block to the doors of the NYAC. Exactly three miles, exactly six thousand steps, exactly one hour. He dropped his coat at the check stand, then went into the dining room for brunch. He sat at the same table where he had been with the Tuckers on Friday, the same table which he had occupied every Sunday morning, with rare exceptions, for the past twenty years. He had a two-egg omelet with mushrooms, ham, cheddar, and tomatoes, four slices of their excellent bacon, pineapple, four slices of buttered wheat toast, and orange juice. As always. At precisely 10:45 he left the building, retracing his path home.

At his apartment, he made the unusual choice of changing his tie. He had started the day wearing a navy bow tie with lavender polka dots. He removed it and carefully tied a sky blue tie with small red birds. He went into the bathroom and brushed his teeth. He had a special system for that, a unique rotating toothbrush holder with eight slots. He used the brush in the forward position, replaced it after finishing, and rotated the holder one position in a clockwise direction. He thus assured that his brushes would dry completely between uses, for optimal hygiene. His housekeeper replaced the whole set every three months, on the same day that she replaced his worn shoes.

* * *

The drive to Queens was uneventful, but as he rode up the elevator with his driver, the doors opened on the first floor, where he was surprised to see a large waiting room full of people with dogs and cats, obviously a veterinary hospital or clinic. The doors closed again, and continued up to the third floor. Pierre was lying on the bed, some sort of thick tights on his legs, with a wire harness at the top.

"Ah, Dr. Overbridge," Maxwell said, "this is our chief programmer, Blaylock. Pierre was just about ready to start programming his sensations."

"Okay," Blaylock said to Pierre, "the key is to *think* about where you are touching as you touch it." He handed him a long thin pointer. "Start with places that you can feel. Think about the sensation, and where it is." Pierre touched the tip of the probe to his arm, his chest, his face, while Blaylock watched an animation of the areas of the brain mesh which were showing activity. As expected, the stimulations followed the well-known pattern known to neuroanatomists as the 'homunculus.' After about fifteen minutes, he announced that calibration was complete. He went to the bedside, helped Pierre roll onto his side, and plugged the stocking harness into a cigarette-pack-sized box attached to the connector on Pierre's spine, also attaching a long cable from his workstation to another socket on that box. "Start on your legs now. Remember, *think* about where you should be feeling the sensations."

Pierre started, touching the skin of the knees, the thighs, the feet, the toes. Blaylock nodded approvingly as brain impulses were detected in the appropriate areas on the cortical mesh. After he had covered as many points as possible, Blaylock put a blindfold on him, and then asked him to identify where he was being touched as Blaylock used the probe. Pierre's face lit up. "I can feel it," he said softly. "I can actually feel it."

Blaylock then gave him a probe with a round hook, like a cane, and instructed him to work on the sensations of the soles of his feet. "This part is critical," he explained. "You can't balance without it." A full thirty minutes was devoted to each foot, with first light, then medium, then heavy touch. They turned him over, and although it was awkward,

Blaylock insisted that the programming would work much better if Pierre continued to do the touching for his buttocks and the backs of his legs himself.

The next thing Blaylock did surprised Pierre, and shocked Overbridge. First, he drew three "X-es" on Pierre's stomach. He then touched the center of each X a few times, and intently watched the response on the monitor. Then he turned away, and quickly turned back and touched something to one of the targets. Pierre screamed, and the scent of burning flesh filled the air. Before anyone could react, he then stabbed the second target with a pin, and to the third he applied ice.

"Why did you do that?" Pierre whimpered. "That really hurt!"

"Sorry," Blaylock said, "but I needed your response to pain, and heat, and cold. Fortunately, our other research has shown us that we just need one strong stimulus to calibrate, and we can use that to program the rest. The touch sensations we already mapped give us the brain coordinates. At least it was quick. Believe me, I'll make it up to you in just a few minutes. Why don't you show Dr. Overbridge what you accomplished after he left yesterday. It will take some time to integrate the data."

Pierre was a little shaky, but he indicated he was ready. Maxwell booted up the program from the day before, and there was the avatar, now standing in a complex environment, with a curving path, inclines, and stairs. Maxwell clicked on the "start" icon, and the avatar started walking down the path. A little jerky at first, but then more and more smoothly. He was able to climb stairs, turn, and both sit down and stand up. Pierre was sitting in his bed, motionless other than his eyes. Overbridge was fascinated.

Blaylock announced they were ready. He and Maxwell helped Pierre sit on the side of the bed, his legs dangling, and they put a walker in front of him. Maxwell turned to Overbridge.

"I'm sure you remember when Pierre used his gaming glove to stand up in your office?" Overbridge nodded. "He has worked for weeks to get his leg muscles strong enough for activity, and in the process our program was able to beautifully map out his muscles, and the spinal nerves attached to them. There was no feasible way to program the sensory nerves, hence the exercise we just completed. We will now attach Pierre's cerebral cortex, through the mesh implant you were instrumental in applying, into the processing unit, then back into the spinal interface. He will, once we start, have both sensation and motor control to his lower body."

Blaylock raised his brow at Pierre, and, getting a nod, tapped in a few commands. Instantly, Pierre's right leg straightened, kicking the walker across the room. "Sorry," he said, "my fault." He then carefully, slowly, started to swing his legs, first back and forth, then side to side. He stretched his ankles out, pointing his toes, then flexed upwards, and finally scrunched his toes.

"Help me up," he insisted, and Blaylock and Maxwell helped him to his feet and repositioned the walker. He stood for a few minutes, at first grasping the walker tightly, then loosening his grip, just trying to use it for balance.

"Just stand there," Blaylock instructed. "The artificial cerebellum is calibrating."

"What does that mean?" asked Pierre.

"Would you like to explain, Dr. Overbridge?" Blaylock offered.

"The cerebellum," Overbridge started, "is the coordination center of the brain. It is low in the back of the skull, and it takes simple commands like 'bend my knee,' and adds in all the other things that go with it. Like relaxing the opposing muscles, or, if you are standing, shifting the pelvis to balance the weight over the other leg."

"Exactly," broke in Blaylock, "and since your brain impulses are just being taken from the top of the brain, that all has to be done artificially. It just takes a little while to get calibrated."

Blaylock's terminal pinged, and he then directed Pierre to lift first one foot, then the other off the floor, giving the computer additional critical information.

And then, Pierre walked.

Overbridge watched in amazement as Pierre moved slowly across the floor, then turned and walked back, using the walker for balance. He repeated the maneuver a dozen times, then sat to rest.

"What did you decide?" Maxwell asked Blaylock.

"Socks on, no walker first," Blaylock replied.

"What does that mean?" asked Pierre.

"The computer is using both the sensations from your own nerves and the pressure sensors in the stockings to maintain your balance. I want to see if you can walk without the walker. Leaving the socks on. As you are moving, the computer is gathering more and more information and refining the parameters of the artificial cerebellum. I am very optimistic. This is going very well, and soon you will not need the socks, but for now, let's leave them on."

As his son walked slowly back and forth across the room, Overbridge realized that he could feel tears running down his cheeks.

By four o'clock, Pierre was exhausted, and although he wanted to continue to work, Overbridge insisted they shut off the computer and let him rest. Maxwell took him downstairs. "The car will pick you up at seven tomorrow evening."

Overbridge turned. "Why not seven in the morning? I will clear my schedule."

"No," Maxwell replied. "Continue your normal routine." Overbridge started to object, but Maxwell raised his hand to stop him. "Seven tomorrow night." He opened the car door, and Overbridge got in.

* * *

Santiago called Perez from the basement. "Cabrera wants to talk to you. I think it would be good, he is getting hard to control."

Perez sighed. "Bring him up." He hung up, shaking his head.

A few minutes later, the door opened and Cabrera came in. He was shaking.

"What is the problem?" Perez asked, "Is the boy not cooperating?"

"No, nothing like that." Cabrera was talking in a rush, wringing his hands. "He is happy to play the games Mr. Blaylock requested, but after Xbox bowling and then tennis, he vomited, then had a full-blown seizure. When he came out of it, he did not want to play, and now he just sits on the mother's lap. He says he has a headache. The CSF leak is getting worse, and I don't have any good way of keeping up with his electrolyte problems from all the fluid loss. I don't know if I can keep him going. And he will inevitably get meningitis at some point."

Perez raised a hand slightly, and Cabrera shut up.

"You will keep him alive and conscious for another week. I don't want to hear any complaints, nor do I need any details." Perez raised one eyebrow significantly. "Remember, with his survival comes the survival of yourself and your family. Do not fail."

Cabrera opened his mouth, but Perez turned away, saying to Santiago, "Take him downstairs."

* * *

After Cabrera was escorted back downstairs, Perez turned to Maxwell.

"How long do we need to get the data Blaylock needs?"

"More is always better, but he thinks that if he can get three good days working on memory, we should be okay."

"Very well."

Chapter 28

Mitzi and Cameron were up early, and they found a diner serving excellent high-fat food. Just what they needed to prepare for a day's work.

Once it was fully light, they set out again. The first building they looked at caught their interest. A three-story red brick building, looking about thirty years old, it had few windows, and those which it did have were fitted with bars. There was a simple door with wire-reinforced glass on which was painted "Decadent Cake Design." It had closed mini blinds, and the room behind was dark. Posted hours were Monday to Friday, 8-5. A thick bundle of cables came off the corner of the roof to the adjoining telephone pole, and the edge of a satellite dish was visible on the south end.

Cameron looked at his printout. "Why would cake design require the kind of web access and power consumption this place has?"

"Dunno, but we don't have enough here for a warrant. I think we should come back tomorrow and I can try and apply for a job."

"That sounds a little risky."

"Got any better ideas?"

Cameron said nothing.

It took the rest of the day to check the other nine addresses. One more was interesting enough to pursue, an Italian restaurant on the ground floor, four floors above. "I'll go look. Wait here," Mitzi said as she jumped out.

"We really need to talk about our plans," Cameron muttered.

Mitzi simply walked into the restaurant and asked to speak to the manager. Several minutes later, a tall, thin man with sallow skin hustled out. "I am the manager. Is there a problem?"

She flashed her FBI credentials. "Just a quick question. Can you tell me what business is upstairs?"

"I think they call it a server farm," he replied. "There are usually a couple of guys there all the time, they have meals brought in. Maybe total of eight or ten different men. All men." He smiled. "That's all I know."

Mitzi thought a minute. "Do they have a freight elevator? Like from the loading dock around back?"

"Yes and no. There is an elevator, but it doesn't work. They had to haul their equipment up the stairs. Must have taken a thousand trips. I watched them from the back room."

"When was that?"

"About a year ago. Since then, like I say, just a couple of guys at a time coming and going."

"So is someone there now?"

"Probably so. Why don't you knock? Stairs are around back, you can come through the kitchen."

"Isn't there an outside door?"

"Sure, but it's locked, and they don't have a bell."

She thought a beat, then asked, "Do these guys happen to be Latino?"

"More northern European, I'd say. And a couple of Asians. Totally look like computer nerds."

The manager led her through the kitchen and to a staircase next to the loading dock. "Thanks," she said dismissively, "I'll take it from here." He stood there for a minute, then went back into the kitchen.

Mitzi called Cameron. "I'm at the bottom of the stairs, gonna go up and knock."

"Wait, I'm coming."

"No, YOU are the one they are looking for. They don't know me."

"Maybe not, but I should at least be close."

"Fine, come around back and knock on the door next to the loading dock. I'll let you in."

With Cameron positioned at the bend in the stairwell, Mitzi walked up and knocked at the plain steel door. There was no answer right away, so she pounded loudly. She heard some noise, and after a few seconds, the door was opened by a short, round-faced man with thinning blond hair. The scent of marijuana was strong. There was another man sitting at a long table with about twenty computer monitors and keyboards. The whole space was filled with rack after rack of computer equipment, and the floor was thick with cables. Looked just like a server farm.

She pulled out her credentials, and the man paled. He looked like he was going to run, or maybe pass out.

"Easy there," she said. "I just have a couple of questions. May I come in?"

He looked back at the other man, who shrugged. "You have a warrant?"

"No, but the odor of marijuana counts as probable cause. If you talk to me I don't care about your pot, but we can do this the hard way if you prefer. I just have a couple of questions."

He thought a few seconds, then pulled the door open. Cameron came up the half flight and joined them.

They all sat down. A phone rang, and the guy who had been at the table answered it, and started tapping furiously at one of the workstations. He put the phone down and went down one of the rows of machines.

"He's resetting one of the servers," the blond guy said. "That's what we do. We sit here all day and all night, just waiting for a call that something is screwed up, we reset it, and go back to doing nothing."

"Sounds exciting."

"Actually, it's perfect. We are all grad students in comp sci at Rutgers, mostly just study while we are here."

Cameron was waiting for the kid to come back out of the server jungle, his hand on his gun, just in case. He came out and picked up the phone. "Should be good to go," he said, then sat there watching his screen.

"Tell me about your employer," Mitzi was asking.

"Just a big company, ServCorp, that leases out server space and hosts web services. They have about thirty places like this, as I understand it."

"Any others in the New York area? Would you have their addresses?"

"About ten, I think. I can get you the main office number, if you want to talk to them. They could give you the addresses."

"Can we look around?"

"Guess so, as long as you don't touch anything. I'll come with you."

The three of them walked up and down the aisles. Nothing but racks of computers. The other worker was just getting off the phone.

They took the number for the corporate office, and left.

It was getting dark again as they finished the last drive-by. They got another cash room at another abominable motel.

* * *

Back at the server farm, the blond man called a number, and when it was answered, he said, "The FBI was just here." He described the

207

encounter. He listened for a minute, then hung up.

"What was that," asked one of the other grad students.

"I dunno, we're just supposed to call anything unusual in. They told me to call again if they reappear." He shrugged and lit up a joint.

Chapter 29

Monday, October 31
New Jersey

Mitzi strode up to the entry for Decadent Cake Design at 8:05. The space was very plain. Just an old desk with an old phone and an old chair, with an old lady sitting in it. Nothing on the walls, worn carpet on the floor. A single door leading deeper into the building, closed.

Mitzi approached the desk. "I would like to apply for a job," she started.

The receptionist held up a hand. "We're not hiring."

"But I really need a job, and I have a lot of experience with cake design."

The old woman smiled, her cheap dentures showing starkly white. "Leave your name and number. We'll call if anything comes up." She pushed a pad towards Mitzi.

She was just starting to write something down, when the door behind the desk popped open, and a woman rushed through, towing a girl who looked to be ten, but had on eye makeup and high-heeled shoes. She gave hardly a glance towards Mitzi, just steamed ahead and out the door, where she hurried to a car parked on the street in front of Cameron, and took off.

As Mitzi got back into the car, she told Cameron what she'd seen. "I'll bet that place is a child pornography studio and server host. I'll call Mary Jane from the office."

They made their way back to Manhattan. Cameron dropped Mitzi at work, then headed uptown, planning to visit Westchester county and the Bronx today. He remembered to call the DDO.

"How are you, Hansen?" he inquired. "Ready to come back?"

"I think I'll take another couple of weeks. I have plenty of PTO saved up."

"Suit yourself." The DDO sounded neither relieved nor annoyed. "Be ready to go two weeks from today."

"Sure thing, Boss," Cameron replied.

Mitzi cleared up some pending work, then, around ten, closed her office door and picked up the phone, calling upstairs. She got Mary Jane on the line, and told her about what she saw at the Decadent Cake Design. Mary Jane sounded annoyed. "What, no psychotic megalomaniacs? What exactly were you doing there, anyway? I figured it was you that got my list of buildings. Too much of a coincidence, someone else wanting that list. No one had asked for it before, then two requests one after another. Subtle."

"Hey, I'm just doing you a favor. Check this place out." She hung up.

Her next call was to ServCorp's main office. Predictably, she ended up in a phone tree. After several steps and quite a bit of bad techno music, a woman came on the line.

"How can I help you?" The voice was polite.

"I am looking for a server to host my site, but I was wondering if you could tell me where the farms were located."

"I'm sorry, we don't give out that information. There is really no need for you to know where the facilities are located, and we want to limit your data's exposure to criminal activity."

"Listen," Mitzi responded, "I'm actually with the FBI and we need that information as part of an ongoing investigation."

The woman's voice became hard. "Then I suggest you get a warrant and present it at headquarters." The line clicked off

Mitzi called Cameron. "What do you think about that?"

"Sounded pretty reasonable to me. All the way around. I wouldn't give out that information, either, certainly not on the phone just because someone claimed to be FBI and asked. Maybe we can check out ServCorp some other way."

"Mary Jane would be the obvious choice, but I think that bridge is burned for now."

"I'll try Phillips." He called Phillips cell.

"Hey, Cameron Hansen calling again. I need some more information related to that server thing. Yeah, it looks like it may be related to a big server company called ServCorp. Can you have your people find out who owns ServCorp and the addresses of all of its facilities? You can call me back at this number."

Cameron called Mitzi back. "Well, he seemed willing enough."

"I hope he doesn't go back to Mary Jane. She already thinks I'm up to something. Listen, I don't have anything pressing here. Come pick me up and I'll help you with those addresses in the Bronx "

"Okay, see you in an hour."

* * *

Jorge's fever had broken during the night, and by Monday morning he was alert. And surly. Cabrera examined him, then went out to report to Maxwell and Blaylock, who had been watching him on a monitor.

"He is better, but I am afraid, if we stress him again like last night, we might lose him."

"Actually," Blaylock replied, "this next part is low stress. We have his cortex completely mapped, we just need to get him to remember things, and map what happens. Piece of cake."

"How are you going to do that?" Maxwell asked. "Do we even have mesh over the areas where the memories are stored? I thought that was deep inside – the hippocampus or limbic system, or wherever."

"We don't actually know how memories are encoded, but the *consciousness* of the memories happens on the cortex, like all other thoughts. We can't plan on the computers actually storing and encoding memories in the same way as the brain. Instead, the plan is to mimic the effect of the memory encoding system. Similar to the artificial cerebellum we created for Pierre. The hard part is really not the record of the memories, but the brain's way of accessing and relating them. This is where all their home videos come in. We have a bunch ready. It will be easier to show you than to explain."

Maxwell went to Jorge's room. "How are you?" he asked, his Spanish flawless.

Jorge simply turned away. Maxwell spoke to Marta, "Listen, Jorge just needs rest today. We have a bunch of old videos for him to watch, just to remind him of what it will be like when you go home."

"When will we go home?" Marta asked.

"You will be gone by the end of the week."

* * *

Back in the control room, Blaylock was studying the screens intently. Perez rolled in, and looked at all the screens. "Explain," he said simply.

Blaylock turned to four monitors mounted in a column. He pointed to the top screen, which was playing a scene from what appeared to be a birthday party. "This is the video the subject and his mother are watching." He pointed to the next screen down, which showed the same scene, but moved around a little. "This is a camera mounted in the bandages on the subject's head, synced with electrodes around his eyes, so we are seeing exactly what he is looking at." The third monitor showed a similar scene, with some of the colors slightly off, and some of the details rather fuzzy. "This is what we are recording from his cortical mesh, which, as you can see, is pretty much the same." The lowest monitor had irregular lines scrolling across. "This is the same for the audio. The upper line is the sound track from the video, the middle is the room microphone, and the lower the recording from the subject." These lines were very similar, except for every now and then, when the cortical recording would suddenly change dramatically. Blaylock pointed to one of those areas. "That is when there is another noise in the room. See, here he has turned from the video to his mother and she is talking, and the video no longer matches up, nor does the sound. The sound is interesting, in that the cortical recording looks like the room microphone MINUS some of the sound from the soundtrack. His brain has partially repressed the soundtrack. But here is the most important part. He tapped on his keyboard and another monitor to his left started playing video. "This is that same twelve seconds we just saw, where he had turned and spoke to his mother. What do you notice?"

Perez watched the screen. "The scene from the video is there as well. Lighter, in the background, like a water mark. Show me again." Blaylock complied.

"Since he could still hear the video, and this was a familiar scene, he continued to remember the scene, even when he was not looking at it. This is perfect, we can subtract the signal and map the memory. Same for the audio."

Perez watched for a while. "What comes next?"

"We will go and ask him what he watched, and as he tells it, we will again subtract the current sights and sounds, and get more information on memory storage. This is where your investment in artificial intelligence pays off. We have a quarter-billion dollars' worth of hardware and software, and with that, we should be able to determine how and where the recalled memories are experienced. The brain is orderly, and I expect to get enough data to determine that by the end of the day. By morning, it should be analyzed and we will be ready for the next step."

"Which is?"

"We need to access his entire memory and upload it to our system. Then comes the part we really don't know yet, which is how the relationships between current brain activity and memories, and memories to memories, are maintained. In other words, what is the nature of the brain's relational database."

"The artificial hippocampus. How will you do that?"

"Come back tomorrow. I have some ideas."

* * *

In her office at the Lake foundation, the phone rang, and Cathy was told that Ambassador Tapata was on the line. "Hello, Señor Ambassador. So pleased to hear from you." She did not remain pleased for long.

"We no longer require the services of the Lake Foundation."

Cathy was aghast. Months of work on a multi-million dollar project could simply not be for nothing.

"Why not?" she almost shouted.

"There are political considerations."

"What is that supposed to mean? Who does not want to provide safe water for the whole southern third of your country? Is this about that wretched Minister of Health and his conniving brother?" She had lost her filter, despite knowing that speaking like this to a diplomat was unlikely to help her cause.

Señor Tapata was unruffled. "No, we all want clean water. We have simply been offered funding from another source. The MexiVox Foundation will be underwriting the project. I am sure that you can appreciate that the people of Honduras would prefer help from our Central American brothers."

Cathy tried to remain calm. "Señor Ambassador," she started, "please be careful. Six years ago in Nicaragua, there was a similar episode with MexiVox. The sewage treatment plant, which was to be completed in three years by the Lake Foundation, is still less than halfway done, and is not progressing. Meanwhile, MexiVox has made hundreds of millions of dollars with the virtual telecommunications monopoly guaranteed to them in exchange. I am sure your government has made similar arrangements."

"There will be some mutually beneficial aspects of our agreement. The details are not important, to you at least. I'm sure that we in Honduras will be able to avoid the labor issues that have hampered construction in

Nicaragua. Thank you so much for your efforts. Your engineering plans will continue to be most helpful. Goodbye." He hung up.

Cathy was vibrating with anger. Months of work, only to have her project taken and her plans given to Juan Carlos Perez and his gang of hoodlums.

* * *

When Overbridge got off of the elevator that evening in Queens, Pierre was walking, unaided, down the long corridor towards him. He was tethered by a long thick cable to a workstation on a cart, which a technician was pushing behind him. Pierre approached him slowly, a very slight wobble to his gait. His legs and feet were bare.

"Check it out! I can walk. I can feel my legs!"

Overbridge watched him approach, then examined his scalp incision. Everything appeared to be in good shape. They spent the next hour simply walking up and down the hall, side by side. Pierre was talking non-stop. Overbridge had nothing to say.

At the end of that time, the wobble had decreased significantly. Maxwell came to get Overbridge, who again objected to having to wait until the following evening to return. Once again, Maxwell was firm.

Chapter 30

Perez sat in the control room with Blaylock and Maxwell, watching and listening as Cabrera was talking to Jorge.

"What did you do yesterday?" he asked the boy.

Jorge embarked on an enthusiastic description of the videos they had watched, with particular excitement as he recalled a trip where he had ridden on a horse on the beach near Puerto Vallarta the previous summer. Perez watched the screen showing the thoughts and sounds picked up from the cortex, which were similar to the scenes he had seen the boy watch the day before. Not exactly the same, rather from a point of view inside his head. The details also faded in and out as he talked about different aspects; the sky, the horses, the sand, the sea.

Blaylock, on the other hand, was ignoring all that. His attention was focused on a monitor showing the entire brain, with levels of electrical activity displayed as various intensity of color, as on a television weather map showing temperatures across the country. He was wearing a headset and talking excitedly.

"Juan, are you seeing the spikes in areas 267700 to 302400 when he initiates recall? Good, good. See if you can map the pathways to the visual cortex. Jeff, the auditory is yours. Bev, help Juan. Let's stick with the horses. I'll get Cabrera to ask him more about horses." He pushed a button, and Cabrera put a finger in the receiver in his left ear. "Keep talking about horses, ask him everything he knows about horses." Cabrera looked at the monitoring camera and nodded.

Once again, horses were the focus of the child's thoughts, and Perez watched as horse after horse flashed by, different sizes, colors, standing, trotting, galloping, sometimes isolated, sometimes with riders, sometimes in groups.

Blaylock was listening and nodding. "Excellent. Let's go with 266942, modulated with the eight adjacent points." He turned to Perez. "The mesh allows us to map and either record or stimulate at about eleven million individual points, and with phased and coordinated analysis of adjacent points, effectively nearly nine hundred million neurons. There are about sixteen billion individual cells in the cortex, so it is still less than perfect, but I think it will be high enough resolution to get what we need." He tapped a number of lines on his keyboard. "Watch the monitor." He hit return. A rough four-legged form came up on the screen, which took on more shape, almost a dog, then settled down as a horse. The computer at that point detected a spike again at the original point.

"Add in the color and movement areas." The horse started to move, then became first a deep brown, then black, then white, then developed more and more detail. Jorge started to shake his head, then cry. Blaylock stopped the program, and the boy settled down. Blaylock turned to Maxwell, smiling.

"We can do it. The algorithm works. The request for memory is originating in the pre-frontal cortex, then proceeds by deep pathways which we can mimic, and eventually ends up in the visual and auditory and olfactory cortex, at which point the original request point fires, like an acknowledgment of success." He tapped on the button, and told Cabrera to come out.

"Okay," he said to the veterinarian, "here's what you need to do." He handed him a vial of medication. "Give him 12 cc's of this, and put in a breathing tube. It will last about an hour, so you will need to keep dosing him."

Cabrera looked at the vial. Pancuronium. It was a long-acting paralytic agent. Cabrera was familiar with it, as it was part of the cocktail commonly used to euthanize animals. Or to execute prisoners. In both of those cases, it was combined with a powerful anesthetic so that they lost consciousness, and potassium to stop the heart. Given alone, it would completely paralyze the subject, but leave him fully conscious. He started to object, but looked at the unblinking eyes of Perez, and thought better. He left for the operating room to get the breathing tube and ventilator.

Twenty minutes later, Jorge was lying inert, unable to move, but able to see and hear. And feel. The screen showing his visual thoughts worked just fine, as Cabrera first opened, then closed his eyes. The audio line also functioned perfectly.

"Okay," Blaylock said, "Let's get started. Let's start at 266942 again, then move about twenty points, and see what we get."

It was not immediately obvious, but in just a few minutes, it became clear it was a frog, at which point the stimulus point fired, confirming the success. They moved ten points closer to 266942, and quickly were able to resolve a cat. The artificial intelligence neural network took over, and soon each point was quickly followed by an appropriate picture, first animals, then plants, structures, machines, and, in a large separate area, people's faces. The process became faster and faster as the machine learning became more and more efficient. Soon the monitor was changing far too fast for Perez to even have time to recognize the images.

He turned to Blaylock. "How long for this process?"

Blaylock shrugged. "I'm not sure. The way it is going, probably about two hours. The next step is to use that mapping to decode not just static shapes and forms, but actual events. We have all the data that we recorded yesterday, and it should allow us to determine those pathways once we can filter out the static forms. We think that there will be a finite set of pathways, which will then correlate to form the likely ten terabyte memory capacity of the child. The process is more or less automatic now. I think we should be done by morning."

Perez smiled. "I will be here at ten a.m. Have everything ready."

* * *

Cameron and Mitzi had been working tediously from address to address, with nothing that seemed at all promising turning up. Having heard nothing back from Phillips, Cameron finally called him about three.

"Hey, Hansen here. Were you able to get anything for me on ServCorp?"

"Sorry, didn't have time, we had a threat situation this morning at LaGuardia. I'll get someone on it for you."

"I'd appreciate it."

Mitzi glared at him. "You could have been a little more, say, enthusiastic in your request."

"He's only going to do it if it's not a big deal. If he thinks it is urgent, there will be lots more questions."

* * *

When Overbridge arrived, he was taken to the physical therapy area, where Pierre was jogging on a treadmill, still tethered to the workstation. Overbridge jumped as a voice came from a speaker on the wall. "Hello, Dr. Overbridge." The voice was tinny, electronic. Like a computer voice in

217

a low-budget sci-fi movie. "It's me, Pierre!" He looked over at Pierre, who had stopped the treadmill, and smiled at him broadly. "I can just think the words, and the computer speaks!" said the disembodied voice. "At first, when they hooked it up, I had to actually talk, and the computer would come in right after, but with only a few minutes' practice, I was able to do it without speaking. Isn't that amazing?"

Overbridge was, indeed, amazed. He knew, of course, that the mesh he had implanted was large enough to include the Broca's speech area in the left brain, and since that is where expressive speech is generated, it made sense that they could pick it up. What truly had amazed him was the speed at which the program had succeeded in producing speech. He turned to Maxwell.

"How did you generate the speech so quickly?"

Maxwell shook his head. "From the first moment he started speaking, we have been recording his speech and brain signal. It was a simple matter, conceptually, to identify the speech articulation pathways. Conceptually. The analytic processing was very complex, which is why it took until this morning for the program to be ready to work."

Overbridge accepted that, not really being all that computer savvy. Had he truly understood that the process had used a system costing in the hundreds of millions of dollars, and taking up an entire floor in the basement of the building, he would have had many more questions.

Maxwell continued, "The fact that we have access to both Broca's area and the motor cortex controlling the tongue and vocal cords was naturally critical. Next, we are going to have Pierre try and learn to type and use a computer mouse virtually. That should be facilitated by the work we have done on speech, but it will take some time with Pierre using a computer in order to get the program going."

Overbridge was puzzled. "Why are you worried about this? He can already talk, type, and use a computer, after all."

"That actually is a very good question. I will be able to answer it better tomorrow. Shall we say seven again?"

By now Overbridge had understood the futility of arguing for an earlier time. He checked Pierre's scalp, assured himself that there were no complications, and rode back to Manhattan in silence.

It was only later that he noticed that he had felt no compulsion whatsoever to count, and he was not even sure he had used the correct toothbrush. He slept soundly, and for the first time in years, was awakened by the sound of his alarm.

Chapter 31

Wednesday, November 2
Queens

When Perez arrived in the control room, Blaylock was seated at his keyboard, his fingers flying, while simultaneously he was nearly screaming commands into his headset. "I *know* you don't have complete data, do it anyway!"

Maxwell turned to Perez. "We have a problem. The subject became feverish during the night. Cabrera thinks he has full-fledged meningitis. His brain is not working normally due to the infection, so the process is not progressing well. We are having to contend with delirium, and fear, and pain. We would do much better with a cooperative subject. And one who did not have a dog surgeon."

Just at that moment, an electronic alarm started to sound. Perez looked at the monitor, where Cabrera was frantically starting to do CPR on the boy. To no avail. The heart line remained flat, and after thirty minutes of chest compressions, Cabrera looked up at the camera, and shrugged. "He is gone," he said, beaten.

Blaylock threw his coffee cup against the wall, cursing. "We were so close," he said, discouraged.

"How close?" Perez asked.

"Literally a few hours from having had a complete download and relational integration."

"Can you still run the simulation?"

"Yes, but it will not be right."

"Run it anyway. How long will it take to become active?"

Blaylock stared at the ceiling for a few moments. "Probably about two hours."

"I'll give you three. Be ready at one." He pulled out his phone, pressed a button, and when he got an answer, he stated simply, "The boy, the mother, and Cabrera. Use the animal incinerator." He listened for a few seconds. "Good." He disconnected.

Santiago, on his end, sighed heavily. It was not quite that simple.

Although, as a veterinary hospital, they were equipped for animal disposal, to deal with nearly four hundred pounds of remains would require at least four batches, each taking about five hours. It would be morning before he was finished.

His phone rang again. Perez.

"Give that to Francisco. You are needed elsewhere. Come to the conference room." Santiago was both relieved, and worried. Worried that Francisco would somehow screw it up. Worried about what more urgent task Perez wanted him to do.

* * *

At first, Santiago did not understand. When he arrived at the conference room, Perez and Maxwell were busily engaged in conversation. They turned towards him, and Perez invited him to sit. He went to the table, but instead they directed him to a wheelchair similar to the one Perez was using. He sat.

"Spend the next two hours practicing the controls. You need to be completely convincing. As if you have been using it for years."

He fiddled with the controls, and succeeded in getting it turned on. After a few fits and starts, he was able to back it around and out the door into the corridor, but not without banging his knee against the table. Twice. Hard. Maxwell closed the door after him.

"This plan seems complicated. Why not simply pay Overbridge enough to make it worth his while?"

"We have discussed this before. He is not the sort of man to be motivated by money. He has plenty, and has no regard for those millions. He sees himself as a savior of brains. Unless he believes, he will not be suitably engaged."

"Assuming Santiago can do his part, are you sure you can do yours?"

"I have been practicing daily. I am ready."

"I'm not sure Blaylock is. The premature loss of the boy was a setback. Maybe we should obtain another subject."

Perez slammed his hand on the table. "No! It is time to proceed. I don't have any more time. Nor any more surgeons. Not even dog surgeons. Plus, we will have the best chance to recruit Overbridge for the next step if we push ahead while he is in the rush of excitement over the Poet."

Something struck Maxwell. "What do you mean, you don't have any more time?"

Perez blinked, slowly, then rolled over to the keyboard on the conference table. He pulled up an image on the screen. It was an MRI scan, Maxwell saw, but it was not a brain. He looked at Perez.

Perez used the mouse as a pointer. "Did you wonder why I never had my spinal implant? This was found on a scan we did in preparation." He pointed to the lower part of the screen. "Here is my shattered vertebrae." He moved the pointer a little higher. "And here is a large pancreatic tumor. It is inoperable. I have already become diabetic, and my liver has started to fail. By Christmas, I could be dead. The time is now, while I am still mentally and physically strong enough to succeed."

Maxwell stared at the screen. "I hope Blaylock is ready."

"We will know at one."

* * *

Mitzi and Cameron approached the last of their list in the Bronx, having found nothing promising. Mostly server facilities for large corporations. This one was the same, but Mitzi's ears pricked up when the sleepy-looking kid with large, anxious eyes said it was part of ServCorp. They went in and looked around, but, just as before, there was really nothing to see.

"Nothing suspicious there," Cameron remarked.

"Still seems a little weird to me," responded Mitzi. "I think we need to know more about this ServCorp. Where is that data from Phillips?" she demanded as they walked to the car.

In response, Cameron pulled out his phone and dialed. Phillips answered, his voice irritated. "What now?"

"Just checking to see if you were able to get that stuff on ServCorp."

"E-mailed it this morning. Didn't you see it?"

"Sorry, I'm out in the field. Do you remember anything about the locations?"

"Didn't even open the file. That's why we have email. Check your inbox, and stop bothering me."

Cameron looked at Mitzi. "I guess I'll have to go into work." He made a face. "I'll go in tonight, hopefully not run into anyone. I'm supposedly still off."

* * *

The security man at ServCorp took the call. Two visits in three days from the FBI. He pressed a number on his handset. Santiago answered. He thanked the man, and went immediately to see *el jefe*.

"It looks like Hansen and the woman are attempting to tour our facilities in the area." He gave Perez the report.

Perez's eyes glittered. "Perfect. He will soon come to us. Which facility is best suited? I want them both, alive."

Santiago considered. "The Brooklyn offices are all somewhat public. As is the downtown Manhattan facility. Easiest would be the one in Morningside Heights. Isolated area, the approach is easily secured, the neighbors are not likely to see anything. Or at least not likely to admit seeing anything."

"Set it up. But I need you here. Use someone dependable." He dismissed Santiago with a wave.

* * *

Blaylock came into the conference room just before one, setting up a video camera, a speaker, and two microphones at one end of the table. The video camera was mounted on a complicated tripod, and was attached to a tall tower placed behind the camera, with several mounted computer cases, and two large video screens. Blaylock plugged a thick cable into a connector on the wall. He set up his own workstation on one side of the conference table. Perez sat at the other end, opposite the camera.

"Let's put Maxwell at the head of the table. Someone he should recognize. I really wish we had the mother, or at least Cabrera," Blaylock groused. "You should have checked with me."

"Just start the simulation," Perez said flatly.

Blaylock tapped on his keyboard. The red light on the camera lit up, and the lower screen behind it showed the scene in the room. The other screen was blank. Blaylock fiddled with a joystick, and the camera panned around the room.

"Okay, here goes," he said, and tapped in another command.

In a few seconds, the blank upper screen slowly came into focus, showing the same scene as on the other side. The camera started to move, as if looking around the room. It finally settled on Maxwell.

"Where is my mommy!" a voice cried from the speaker. At the same time an image of Marta flashed on the upper screen, as if superimposed on the view of Maxwell's face.

"She went to be with your daddy," Perez responded. At this, another face appeared, a man's face. The camera turned to Perez.

"Who are you, and why did she leave me?" There was no emotion in the computer voice, just words.

Maxwell broke in. "Do you remember your birthday party?"

"No! I want my mommy!" said the voice, but on the screen, there was a scene from what was obviously a child's birthday party.

"What was your favorite part of the party?"

"I don't want to talk about the party! Take me to my mommy!" Again, despite the objection, the monitor was showing a scene from the party, with a large colorful pinata swinging as a stick crashed into its side, spilling candy into a crowd of rushing children. Soon, it was replaced again by the face of the mother, smiling gently.

"Turn off the camera and microphone," instructed Perez. Blaylock complied.

"I can't see!" shouted the voice. "Why is it dark? What is going on?" On the screen passed images of the room, Maxwell, Blaylock, Perez, then more images of Marta and the boy's father, skipping rapidly from one to another, then nothing more than a whirl of colors and shapes, and finally nothing.

Blaylock was looking at his monitor. "Interesting. No activity at all. It might as well be off. There was clearly thought activity for a while after the external input was stopped, but now nothing."

"It is like an isolation tank," remarked Maxwell. "Without some external connection, some stimulus, the thinking slows down and stops. Turn the camera and microphone back on."

Blaylock complied. The side of the screen devoted to Jorge's thinking lit up, showing the same view as the camera. Nothing moved, nothing changed. They shouted, waved their arms, even waved a photo of Marta in front of the camera. Nothing.

Blaylock then reset the program to its initial state, and restarted it. Once again, the camera moved around the room, settled on Maxwell and said, "Where is my mommy?" exactly as before. They had a similar conversation with the computer, but then, instead of turning off the camera and microphone, Blaylock paused the program. When he started it again, the computer continued as if there had been no interruption. Once again, when the microphone and camera were turned off, the program

225

stopped, and could not be resumed.

"It would appear that we have succeeded in producing a sentient program," Maxwell said.

"Yes, that dies if it does not have ongoing stimulation," added Blaylock.

"Make sure that we set up a way to assure that stimulation," directed Perez. "Now, let's explain to Santiago what we need him to do. The good doctor will be here in just a few hours, and I need everything to be ready."

* * *

Traffic was bad, and it was nearly eight o'clock when Overbridge's car pulled into the garage. Pierre was there waiting, walking back and forth in front of the elevator. He was wearing a backpack, and the cable from his head snaked down into it, but there was no external cabling. He greeted Dr. Overbridge with a hug. "Nothing can ever repay what you have done for me," he gushed.

Overbridge looked at him quizzically. "I thought it took a giant computer to run the interface. Now I see just a small backpack."

Maxwell, who had been watching, broke in. "The analysis and programming was extremely complex, but the actual running of the system is easily accomplished with a small but powerful computer. In fact, it is only the artificial cerebellum that requires any real computing. Once the cerebral cortex input was completely analyzed, the algorithm is straightforward. The connections to the spinal nerves are essentially simple wiring. In theory, we could produce a device small enough to be implanted, say in the abdomen, and all the wiring would be internal. It could be charged with a surface induction plate at night."

Overbridge felt a sudden rush of excitement. The magnitude of the accomplishment before him was enormous. There was just one problem. "How can we present this to the world so that it will be accepted? None of the normal protocols have been followed." He started pacing back and forth, something he had not done for many years. He stopped and turned to Maxwell. "Please tell me you have a plan. We must get this out. So many people to help." It did not even occur to him that, contrary to his carefully cultivated detachment, he was thinking of patients as people, not spines, or brains, or aneurysms.

"Indeed, we do," assured Maxwell. "We will perform the first public surgery in a country with fewer restrictions, with records showing plenty

226

of canine research data to back it up. We want you to be a part of that. It is time for you to meet our benefactor, who has provided the literally hundreds of millions of dollars which have been needed thus far. He is waiting for you."

Pierre got off of the elevator and walked down to his room, as Maxwell escorted Overbridge back to the conference room. As they entered, the wheelchair spun around. Santiago's hand stretched up to grasp Overbridge's firmly. "So good to finally meet you, Dr. Overbridge. My name is Juan Carlos Perez."

* * *

"As you can see," Santiago was saying, "I have a very personal interest in spinal injuries since my parasailing accident. I had originally wanted to be the first patient, but with my business responsibilities, I simply have not had the necessary time to have the spinal implant and then the months of rehabilitating the nerves and muscles of my legs. It has been critical to keep me working to assure the ongoing funding."

Overbridge nodded. He also suspected that the billionaire did not really want to be a guinea pig. As out of touch with current events as he was, he still had heard of the Mexican telecommunications magnate, who had dealings that showed up in the Sunday *Times* fairly regularly.

"As we have proceeded with our research, we have also developed a possibility which may be even closer to your heart. Not closer than your son, of course, but closer to your life's work. And even more important to me than regaining the use of my own legs. Come, there is someone else I want you to meet." He led Overbridge out the door and down the corridor to another patient room. There, sitting inert in a wheelchair, was a man.

"This is my uncle, Dr. Overbridge. He was in an industrial accident several years ago. He, like me, is paraplegic. He is also blind and nearly completely deaf." He rolled over to the other man, so that their knees were almost touching under their shawls, and reached out to stroke the man's cheek. Juan Carlos Perez stirred, smiled, and reached up to take Santiago's hands.

"Hello, Uncle Luis," Santiago said gently, at the same time rapidly signing, as Perez kept his hands lightly touching the other man's moving hands. "This is Dr. Overbridge." He spelled the name on Perez's palm. "He is going to connect you back to life."

227

Perez sat motionless for a moment, then spoke in Spanish. Santiago turned to Overbridge. "He asks God to bless you." He waved him closer, putting Perez's hands into Overbridge's. Perez squeezed him tightly, then pulled him close and embraced him, tears streaming down his cheeks from his closed eyes.

"Now," Santiago said, "let me explain what we need you to do." He sat in his wheelchair, holding his "uncle's" hand as he talked.

"To give Luis back his sight and hearing, as well as his legs, we need to put in a complete cortical implant, like the ones you saw for the dogs. Do you think that you can do that successfully?"

"Given an appropriate facility, I can practically guarantee it. But how will we get this approved? I can't simply add a case of this magnitude to a regular operation like we did with Pierre."

"I have a state of the art facility in southern Mexico. Everything will be ready by next week."

"What about the governmental regulations?"

"My stature is immense, and the government will be thrilled for the publicity. We, YOU, will go down in history as the man who made the lame to walk, the blind to see, and the deaf to hear."

Overbridge was still for a moment, just thinking. This was the most important medical innovation in his lifetime. He was ready. He was all in.

"Yes," he said softly, "We should, we *must*, proceed."

Santiago rolled over to him, shook his hand, and left the room, just catching the side of the chair slightly on the door frame as he passed. Overbridge did not notice.

Maxwell took Overbridge back to the garage. "We will not be picking you up tomorrow evening," he said. "Mr. Perez is flying Pierre to France for a surprise visit to see his grandfather, to show him he can walk."

"Can't I go?" Overbridge would have loved to see the look on the old man's face.

"No," Maxwell responded quickly, "keep up your regular routine. Just cancel your schedule for next Thursday and Friday. We will pick you up the day after tomorrow at seven p.m. as usual."

* * *

As Overbridge entered his apartment, he was surprised to see the message light blinking on his answering device. He pushed the button.

"Cathy Tucker here. Just confirming that we are expecting you at our place for dinner tomorrow night at seven."

He had completely forgotten. Well, as luck would have it, he was available. He dialed the Tuckers. Cathy picked up, and he told her he was delighted to be coming.

* * *

Cameron and Mitzi went up to his cubicle, logged onto the system, and printed out the file. ServCorp was a half-billion dollar corporation, which was owned by a Mexican national, Domingo Herrera. The FBI file had no information on the owner, who had no known ties to criminal or political organizations.

Cameron's heart skipped. "I knew a Domingo Herrera. He was the father of Selena Herrera, the mistress of Juan Carlos Perez."

"The girl who nearly got you killed?"

"Exactly.."

"I think that qualifies as a tie-in. How should we proceed?"

"There are a total of seven ServCorp facilities, the two we've been to already, then two in Manhattan, and three in Brooklyn. I say we keep with our pattern."

"So, to Brooklyn tomorrow?" Mitzi got up. "Let's get out of here. I feel exposed."

Chapter 32

It took nearly the entire day to visit the three Brooklyn ServCorp facilities. Each of them turned out to be in the upper floors over ground floor businesses, just like the one in New Jersey, and all were staffed by graduate-student types, who were no more nervous than would be expected for computer nerds being accosted by the FBI. Nothing to suggest anything more than what they purported to be, and certainly nothing in the buildings which would correspond to any sort of command center for Perez.

Each contact was dutifully reported, and Santiago received each additional report with a grim smile. If they kept up their pattern, they should be approaching the uptown office sometime tomorrow. He called Francisco.

"Are you set?" he asked.

"Yes, everything is ready for our guests."

"It will almost certainly be tomorrow."

"Understood." He hung up.

* * *

The bell rang precisely at seven, and Cathy opened the door to find Dr. Overbridge standing rigidly on her porch, his face slightly flushed from his walk through the brisk night air.

"Welcome to our home, Dr. Overbridge," she said. To her great surprise, he gave her a welcoming peck on the cheek as he entered the front hall.

Jack came around the corner, and Overbridge shook his hand warmly. "Am I the first? Sorry to be so punctual."

"You are indeed," Cathy replied. "Why don't you two have a seat in the living room while I help Jean finish the prep."

Jack led Overbridge in and they sat down. *Here comes fifteen minutes of awkward,* he thought, but much to his surprise, his guest started right in.

"Such a beautiful evening. My walk was positively invigorating. And this room is lovely, I can see your wife has excellent taste."

Jack was so taken aback by this normal opener as to be almost speechless himself, but soon they were chatting like old friends. When Cathy stepped in to check on them, the two of them were laughing at the recollection of a prank played on the attending staff by the Neuro Institute residents back when Jack had been in training. The doorbell rang again, and she went over to greet Bill and Amanda.

"Dr. Overbridge, I'd like to introduce you to Bill and Amanda McCullough. Bill is an internist with me at LexMed. We are also expecting Miguel Cardoso, but he will certainly be a few more minutes. He refuses to ever be on time. Says it is a protest against the process of assimilation that is extinguishing his cultural heritage." Everyone laughed politely.

Miguel, a tall man with wavy black hair, swept more than walked through the door a few minutes later. He was introduced as a gastroenterologist from Roosevelt Hospital.

"Really, Cathy," Amanda said in a stage whisper, her eyes rolling loudly, "Four doctors? There goes all hope for polite conversation."

Cathy knew the risks, but had hoped to find guests who could engage with Dr. Overbridge. She needn't have worried about that, as it turned out. There was certainly lots of medical gossip, but Overbridge also regaled them with anecdotes from his days at Berkeley in the Seventies. Or, as he noted, what little he could remember of them. Overall, Cathy was more than pleased with the dinner conversation. Although, at one point, Bill and Miguel got into a detailed discussion about diarrhea and its treatment, for the most part, the topics were socially acceptable.

When Cathy and Amanda came in from fetching the dessert – Cathy's famous pecan bread pudding – Bill and Miguel were engaged in a spirited exchange on the relative merits of medical mission work, versus donations to organizations like the Lake Foundation, versus political activism as a means to promoting better health in less developed countries. Miguel was originally from Brazil, but had also spent several years in Chile, so he spoke both Portuguese and Spanish, and his English had just enough of an accent to be charming.

"These episodic visits by gringo doctors," he almost shouted, "are a waste of resources! The money it costs to do that would be better spent paying local physicians to do the same work. These trips are nothing but imperialist medical tourism."

"You are ignoring the fact," Bill retorted, "that people are much more likely to make contributions if they have been on mission trips, and that they certainly have SOME benefit to the hundreds of patients seen."

"I'm more worried about the safety of traveling to emerging countries," Amanda chimed in. "I am terrified when Bill goes. But he has been on several, and I know he finds them richly rewarding."

"Yes," Miguel shouted, "rewarding for Bill!" He turned to Cathy. "Come on Cathy, you know that the Lake Foundation, working with local resources, can accomplish things that the tourist doctors can't match."

"I used to be more certain. This is a bad week to ask me. Local politics and corruption have blocked us again. At least, if you go do a procedure in Tegucigalpa, you know for certain that that particular patient was helped."

"What happened?" Miguel asked.

"Juan Carlos Perez happened."

She related the disruption of the sanitation plant. "And it's not the first time."

"Go on," Miguel urged.

"Okay, so six years ago, I was on site in northern Nicaragua, going over final plans for a water treatment plant with my chief engineer. A flunkie from the Ministry of Health rolled up in a Range Rover with two men from MexiVox. They told me that THEIR foundation was taking over the project and the funding, and that the Lake Foundation was out. I was mad as a hornet, but when I calmed down, I decided that, as long as the people got the plant, I should be happy I had more money to put into other projects. Fast forward two years, and I heard rumors that nothing was progressing. I tried to go to the site, but the army goons wouldn't let me in. Long story short, it has now been six years, and there is no plant. What did happen is that MexiVox has been given a monopoly on mobile service for that whole sector of Nicaragua, and several high officials in the Ministry have retired to lovely estates and fat bank accounts."

Overbridge had started at the name, and broke in. "Juan Carlos Perez? You mean the billionaire philanthropist? I thought he was very much in support of research and helping."

Cathy shook her head. "That man is only about money and power. The billionaire part is true, but the philanthropy is all for publicity. He promises help, but never delivers, while grabbing up influence with both hands."

"I agree," added Miguel. "The news is all about his beneficence, but the rumors are all about corruption."

"Not rumors, facts. His corruption games *killed* that sanitation project six years ago, and another one this week. Literally tens of thousands of deaths per year could have been prevented, just on my projects. And all so he can control more government officials and wield more influence and power. The man is a monster." Cathy was starting to get worked up, and Jack tapped on her knee under the table. She took a couple of deep breaths and got up to fetch some whipped cream.

The subject moved on to recent changes in Medicare reimbursement, and Overbridge became stiffer and silent. Then the siren wail of Miguel's pager went off. He stepped into the other room to answer, then came back in.

"Duty calls. Some five-year-old with a coin lodged in the esophagus. I think I will go remove it. The evening has been lovely. My only regret is that second piece of bread pudding," he laughed, patting his belly.

Dr. Overbridge also rose abruptly. "I also must say goodnight. I am quite fatigued." He quickly collected his coat and hat, and was gone.

* * *

On the walk home, he ruminated on the remarks made regarding Perez. Troubled, he began to count his steps, which helped. At that point, he noted that he had NOT counted his steps walking *to* the Tucker's home, which was most unusual. He fought the urge to walk back to their door to get an accurate count, telling himself it did not matter, but eventually he gave up and retraced his steps.

When he got to his own door, he found, to his satisfaction, that it was an even two thousand steps. Which could only be a good omen.

As he walked past his doorman, however, he abruptly turned and went back out to the street, heading uptown to Our Lady. The main part of the hospital was quiet this late in the evening, but the Emergency Room was, as usual, filled to capacity. None of that interested Overbridge. He went up to his office to use his computer. He didn't have one at home, and he had resolved to learn all he could about Juan Carlos Perez.

A Google search yielded eighty-five million results. Not very useful. He started with the Wikipedia article. It appeared to have been written by a publicist, although it gave the basic facts. Perez was fifty-five and had grown up in southern Mexico on a farm. He had left for Mexico City when he was fifteen and lived on the streets there for several years, then got a job as a delivery man. He worked his way into running his own messenger service, which eventually was acquired by DHL, netting him a small fortune. This was just as cell technology was starting to take off, and he was able to use his cash to lock up the licenses for the radiowave bandwidth in most of southern Mexico and Central America, leading to a fortune that seemed to grow exponentially. Typical rags-to-riches stuff. Made him look like a scrappy, hard-working, lucky guy. Overbridge looked further.

He logged onto Amazon, and searched for biographies on the man. This was a little more manageable, only about ninety hits, and really several of those were different editions of the same book, so only about fifty to sift through. One caught his eye, "I Have Your Number: The Rise of Juan Carlos Perez." The description mentioned that the author had died under mysterious circumstances soon after the book was published, and that the allegations in the book had been vigorously denied. The book was out of print, but there were some used ones listed. One was from a vendor in Manhattan. He memorized the address and telephone number, then logged off.

He walked home, completely absorbed in his own head, and oblivious to the possible dangers of walking through Harlem at midnight. Nor had he noticed the man in the dark coat who was following him, staying fifty yards behind in the shadows.

Chapter 33

Friday, November 4
Paris

Perez received the call from Santiago in his Paris apartment. Two in the morning in New York, but a reasonable eight a.m. in France. This foray by Overbridge into Harlem at night was well outside his usual pattern. As was the visit with the Tuckers. His isolation had been one of his best characteristics, in Perez's estimation. He was annoyed he had not arranged a camera inside the doctor's office. His men had seen the glow of the computer in the window, but did not have any way of knowing what he had been doing.

Personnel was always the trickiest problem. For some tasks, like the implantation, there were simply too few individuals who were satisfactory. Perez's body would be dead in six months, perhaps six weeks, and for his plan to succeed, it was important that there be no loose ends. World-class neurosurgeons at obscure hospitals with no personal attachments were rare. He would need to step up his surveillance. Since the man walked everywhere, and never appeared to take the slightest notice of any of his surroundings, following him had been easy. Perez simply needed to add monitoring of his phone and office computer. He so instructed Santiago, and was assured that everything would be in place by the time Overbridge's office staff arrived in the morning.

He also wondered about the Tuckers. He had run checks on them, of course. Dr. Tucker was quite public, both at work and in his church activity, and other than apparently being irritatingly ethical, there were no real concerns.

Cathy Tucker was a little more problematic. She had spent a lot of time in his part of the world, and her Foundation dealt with the same governmental and criminal organizations that he had been involved with for the past thirty years. It was altogether possible that she had connections that could be troubling, if brought up.

The real question was whether Overbridge had discussed any of his business with the Tuckers. He would feel him out on the subject, but if there were any question of danger, it may simply be safer to eliminate them. Of course, he could not do anything to alert Dr. Overbridge. It would not do to make your surgeon uncomfortable just before he literally took your head off. Spy shows notwithstanding, Perez knew better than to think that surgeons would perform well under duress. He would not threaten him as he had Cabrera, not with his own life at stake.

* * *

This entire trip to France had been envisioned as a way to pull Overbridge further into Perez's circle. He had had a film crew set up, and had recorded every second of the Poet's walk up to his grandfather's door, the joyful reunion, and the touching gratitude of the old man, which had occurred the evening prior. Perez himself was in the recordings, but would make sure that the version edited for Overbridge showed him only from the side and back, where the resemblance to Santiago was more than acceptable.

Today, they would take the Gulfstream back to New York, and Pierre would be re-installed in his room. His grandfather would die of a heart attack, which no medical examiner would ever suspect was due to an injection of succinyl choline. Perez was not interested in any uncontrolled witnesses.

* * *

One of the biggest hassles for Cameron and Mitzi was parking. New Jersey had not been too bad, but back in the city, it was a nightmare. The ServCorp facility in lower Manhattan, like all the others, was as boring as paint drying, but because they had ended up parking about three blocks away, after a fruitless hour of circling the streets, the process had taken nearly two hours. They had lunch nearby, and talked it over.

"We're wasting our time," Mitzi said. "Even if these are owned by Perez, they may just be what they appear. He does have billions of dollars in legitimate high tech businesses. We need to think of another way to find him."

"I don't know," mused Cameron, "why would he have it set up through Herrera if it were legit? Unless you have another idea, we should at least check out the last address. There's really no downside."

As they drove past the building, looking for parking, Cameron noticed that the street was unusually quiet. Not a business open on the entire block. No parking spaces, either, of course, so around the block they went. It looked like this was a bigger facility than the others, and had alleys on either side, with garbage bins overflowing. As they came around, Cameron could see that there was also an alley that ran all along the back of the building. Three beat-up panel vans were parked there, which bothered him a little, vaguely. Eventually, they found a space two streets over, and parked.

They got out, and proceeded to walk back to the front of the building, planning to knock on the entry door, which was a plain steel door marked only with the address. Still not a soul in sight.

When the door opened, Cameron took one look at the swarthy man inviting them in, and immediately reacted, shoving Mitzi roughly to the side as he used the momentum to propel himself the other direction. The man in the doorway leaped out, pulling a gun from his waistband, and firing it at Cameron. The twin needles caught him in the shoulder, and he fell helplessly to the ground as fifty thousand volts caused him to lose all control. Just as suddenly, the current stopped as the man released the trigger, his own control having been disrupted by his head exploding. Mitzi had understood the threat as quickly as Cameron, and wasted no time in pulling the small pistol from her bag. She liked shooting, and the FBI had always been generous with ammo at the indoor range in lower Manhattan. She fired another shot blindly through the open door, which immediately was slammed shut. Cameron was dazed, but after half a minute, he was mobile, his own weapon at the ready.

The building had windows, but they were barred, and the only street level entrance was the door that they had just approached. They stood flat next to the steel door, protected by the brick wall from potential fire from within. There was no threat from the windows, as the angles were impossible. Mitzi called 911, reported gunshots on their street, then hung up.

"Tasers. They're still trying to capture me."

"Good thing. A bullet would have killed you. Cops will be here soon. We just need to stay out of sight."

"No. We need to go. They could come around the corner in force before the police get here. Besides, the cops will have way more questions than we have answers, and we need to keep the pressure on Perez. Remember, it is only my theory that ServCorp is his. Let's go."

Cameron snaked his leg out, and pulled the taser towards him with his foot. It was the military model, with thirty-foot wires, and would sustain a shock for up to thirty seconds. He tucked it in his belt, his 9 mm at the ready.

They heard sirens.

"West," Cameron instructed, and Mitzi ran, Cameron following close behind. She made it cleanly across the side alley, but shots rang out from an upper window as Cameron passed a dumpster, and he was grazed across the back of his left shoulder, tearing the skin open for six inches and knocking him to the ground. He rolled painfully out of the alley's opening, and struggled to his feet as Mizti turned to help him. The dumpster shielded them as they raced down the street, turned the corner and were away. By now, the sirens were approaching from the east, making a deafening cacophony in the street behind them. There was a hardware store on the next block. Mitzi went in and bought a canvas coat and duct tape while Cameron ducked out of sight in another alley.

Cameron was a mess. He had first been sprayed by the brains of the man Mitzi had shot, then his own blood, then rolled in the dirt. She taped over his shoulder wound, and they replaced his ruined coat with the canvas one. "That wound needs to be cleaned, but shouldn't be much of a problem otherwise," she said. "How are you feeling?"

"The adrenaline is fading. I'm beat."

"Wait here. Don't shoot anyone." She strode off quickly before he could argue. She drove up a few minutes later, and he climbed in the car.

"Did you see anything?"

"About a thousand of New York's finest, I'd say. They did not seem interested in me. Probably because I was walking towards the scene. The vans behind the building were gone. I'm glad we weren't in them."

She was quiet for a minute. "We need to talk to somebody."

"We're a little off the reservation."

"Still, they were waiting for us. Something big is going down, and we need to get the resources we need to stop it. I'm okay with it not being NYPD, but we need some help."

* * *

Friday was a normal work day for Dr. Overbridge. Two aneurysms, starting at eight. The first went more rapidly than usual. The second patient was delayed in pre-op: something about the heart monitor tracing had bothered the anesthesiologist, and so they were doing a quick echocardiogram. Which, at Our Lady, meant at least a two-hour delay. Dr. Overbridge made a quick calculation, and decided to run to the bookstore. He changed and went down the back stairs, exiting on the west end of the hospital. He then walked over to the subway on Lexington, and was down to the bookshop in midtown in just a few minutes. He went in, asked for the book, and was back in a cab and up to Our Lady in well less than the two hours. The book was a "trade-size" paperback, and he had put it in the large inside pocket of his great coat to keep it dry, so his surprised watcher, who was stationed inside the hospital lobby, did not see it when his subject came in and went back up to the surgical suite.

He called it in. "He just came in from outside the hospital. He was supposed to be up in surgery all morning. I did not see him go out. No, I have no idea where he went." The man was sweating. This type of lapse could easily have serious repercussions.

"Stay put. I'll send more men to cover the other entrances."

* * *

Upstairs, the patient was still not ready. Dr. Overbridge sat in the surgeons lounge, reading his new book. The more he read, the more alarmed he became. According to the author, Perez's remarkable rise in prosperity had more to do with his ruthless elimination of competition through intimidation – and possibly murder – than with any innate business genius. Not that there was any doubt as to his intelligence. That was apparently off the charts as well.

The author also discussed his extensive surveillance of business associates and enemies. When the anesthesiologist finally canceled the surgery, Overbridge stayed in the lounge and read. He was a fast reader, with a nearly perfect memory. He finished the book, the last chapter of which contained a prediction that Perez would have the author killed if the book was published.

He considered the situation. The book was alarming, but as he thought about it, he realized that whatever the total scope of Perez's activities, there was also no doubt that he had poured millions into this particular project, which had such enormous potential for the good of mankind. And for him, for his place in history. He would simply be careful.

He would assume that he was under surveillance at all times. He thought about his trip to the bookstore. He had not wittingly taken any evasive action, just taken the most efficient route. Taxis were hard to come by in that part of the city, and the subway was the obvious choice. He had, of course, purchased the book with cash. He smiled to himself. He could not have done any better if he had been a trained agent.

He thought some more about his recent activities. Up until the night of his own aneurysm, nothing had changed in his routine for years. Maybe decades. The aneurysm, as well as his new relationship with the Tuckers, were both changes that a careful man like Perez could find concerning.

He changed and went to the clinic, where he had his usual slate of afternoon patients. He left Our Lady at his usual time, and walked home at his usual pace. He knew it was important to act as ordinarily as possible. Anything else would tip them off that he was aware of their presence. But he *was* aware. Although he had not gotten to the point of wondering why, he had noticed the same man in the hospital lobby every afternoon several weeks ago, and now again today. Noticed would perhaps have been too strong a word. Perceived would be more accurate. He always counted the people in the lobby, and so glanced at each person. With his memory, he was able to dredge up any repeated faces. On the walk home, freed as he was from the compulsion to count, he was able to see reflections in the curved right-side rear-view mirrors of parked cars, which allowed him to verify that the man was following him. He smiled inwardly. Probably the most boring job in espionage.

As he entered his apartment, he tried to ask himself if there had been any changes recently to indicate a bug or camera. He did not know of any, but he resolved to be cautious. He would need to presume that they had placed equipment here as well. It was a bit of a puzzle. Not that he had said or done anything even remotely incriminating in his apartment. Other than the phone calls to the Tuckers, and food delivery, he had not said a word. Also, since they had been surprised by the fact that he had had surgery, their surveillance, at least two weeks ago, must not have been rigorous.

It was also, he thought, a total waste of time. He had no intention of causing trouble. In fact, he was more than willing to participate in the project. He had already accepted the fact that clearly criminal shortcuts had been taken, which he was conspiring to perpetuate. His only concern was for safety. He needed to make sure that his value remained high, and that he did nothing to arouse suspicion. There was no reason that he and Perez could not have a long and fruitful relationship. He was, however, a little worried about the projected trip to Mexico. He needed to think of a way to proceed here, on his turf.

* * *

"Who did you send after Hansen," Perez asked Santiago.

"Francisco."

"So, Francisco is dead." A statement, not a question. "And the police will have his body. That makes five men this Hansen has killed. Six, if you count the street rat that Ruiz left. This is far from acceptable."

* * *

Detective Terrence was interviewing the three nerds in ServCorp's facility. They were all students from City University, and all gave essentially the same story. Six large Latin men had arrived late on Wednesday evening two days ago, ostensibly from corporate, and had set up cots in the break room. Two were always sleeping, the other four sat around a small table near the entry, watching TV and keeping an eye on the security feed from the front door. They said they were there for "quality assurance." That afternoon, they had all jumped up, awakened the two on sleeping shift, and one man had herded the three students into a room and told them to stay there, while brandishing a gun. And there they had stayed, terrified by the gun shots, until the police had broken through the door.

The police techie had immediately gone to the security cameras, and found that, although the cameras were still functional, the recording system had been disabled Wednesday evening at 21:39. Terrence was frustrated. These students were useless, could give nothing better than "big Hispanic guys."

Outside, the forensics team had found fresh blood from the alley – plenty if it – and they already knew it was a different type than was still oozing from the nearly headless corpse on the front steps. He would have to just wait for more information.

One of the uniforms canvassing the neighborhood tapped on the door. "Detective, got something." He held up a cell phone. "Woman at the end of the street was taking a video of her dog when the action started, and then got the whole thing. It's not very good, but it's something."

The video indeed was not very good, as it was from probably two hundred yards away. Initially, in the corner of the frame behind the dog,

243

two vague figures were at the door, then a man came out, and one of the figures went down in a typical seizure-like taser-victim way, then the gunshot could be heard as the new man's head exploded. At that point, the witness had actually pointed the phone at the action, and he could see that the two figures were likely a man and a woman, the woman helped the man up and after a few seconds, they ran away from the camera down the street. More gunshots, and the man went down again, crawled behind the dumpster at the alley, and then there was nothing more to see.

Terrence watched it several times, using his fingers to zoom in on the faces, which were only fuzzy Caucasian blobs. He emailed it to the forensic team downtown, with a copy to himself. He handed the phone back to the uniform. "Good job. We'll see what the folks at the lab can do."

So, not a total waste. Latin guys with tasers. Twice in the past couple of weeks. Detective Terrence did not believe he had seen a taser combined with a homicide in years. He was not much of one for coincidence.

Chapter 34

Saturday, November 5
New York

Mitzi pulled the adhesive bandage off of Cameron's shoulder with a sudden movement. He was lying on his stomach in their Bronx hideout. She looked appraisingly at the wound. "Looks okay. Really just a graze except right here." She poked it, causing Cameron to yelp. "Other than the pain, there is nothing that should really limit you with this little scratch."

"So, I realize that all of your patients are already dead, but I have to tell you that your bedside manner sucks."

"Yes, all of my patients are dead, and so I know this will not kill you. Just hold on while I scrub it out again." She poured some antiseptic soap on, and rubbed it hard with gauze, then patted it dry and taped on a new dressing. That finished, she helped him sit up, and they stared at each other blankly for a few minutes.

"What?" he finally asked.

"Do you want to talk to the DDO or the ATU SAC?"

"Probably doesn't matter much, wherever we start it will end up with both."

"Well, I don't think that going to DC is a good option, and I think we should do it in person. So let's start with Crawley." She pulled out her burner, but Cameron stopped her.

"Don't turn it on."

"What, it's a burner?"

"Right, and you called 911 with it yesterday from the scene. I don't know how good Mr. MexiVox is at tracking, but let's assume the worst. NYPD would also be a problem. We need a new set of burners."

"Fine. I'll go get some." Mitzi jumped up and was out the door without another word.

* * *

Once they had the phones, Cameron insisted they drive over into

Queens before calling the SAC. "For all we know, they are monitoring HIS phone," he explained.

"You are getting a little paranoid," Mitzi retorted.

"No, I'm just starting to act like a field agent on an op again."

Crawley picked up after several rings. "Who is this?" he barked.

"Cameron Hansen, sir. Er, I need to talk to you. In person. Right away, sir."

"I'm in Texas. Henry is covering."

"When will you be back?"

"Late tonight."

"I think I'd rather wait for you," Cameron responded. "This is not something for Henry."

"Who did you kill this time?"

"We'll be at the office tomorrow morning at eight."

"You and Lenz, I take it? Make it nine. If it is not urgent enough to talk to Henry, it is not urgent enough for eight. See you then."

"I hope nothing happens before tomorrow," Mitzi said as they both looked at the phone.

"Toss the phone," Cameron said, as he started the car.

* * *

When his driver picked him up on Saturday, Dr. Overbridge memorized the license plate number before getting in the car. He had no clear idea of what he was hoping to find out, but at this point, he had come around to the mindset that this was a mission in potentially hostile territory, and the more information he had, the more likely he would be able to take some sort of action, if necessary.

Perez watched on a monitor as Santiago and Maxwell welcomed Overbridge and showed him the video his people had put together. It started with Pierre in his wheelchair, winning a race, reading to an audience, accepting an award. As a narrator described the first step, that of implanting the spinal interface, an animation showed how the nerves worked to control the legs. The video went on to show Pierre laboriously learning to use the computer to move his legs, and the months of muscle rehabilitation that were then needed to develop the strength which would be needed to walk. The brain mesh surgery was then explained, followed by snippets as Pierre worked with the computer to program the algorithm, finally culminating in standing, then walking, then jogging, and the glorious reunion with his grandfather. It was a masterpiece, certain to stun the world of medicine. Dr. Overbridge was prominently featured for his part in the success. What was not mentioned was *where* the operation and rehab had taken place, and, in fact, the exteriors were of Perez's private hospital in southern Mexico, complete with interviews with members of an institutional review board that had endorsed the project and granted authority for the surgery in advance.

"You can see," Santiago said, "This will be world-changing, and you will be part of it. Everything is ready for us to take the next step with Uncle Luis next week."

Maxwell added, "Nothing sells like success. With this kind of publicity, any possible ethical objections will be quickly overcome. We have made sure that everyone who knows the actual details of the project is on our team, no one from the outside has any information as to our work."

Suddenly Overbridge knew, deep in his heart, that if he went with Perez to Mexico, he would never return. He was, however, still committed – this was more important than all the work he had done in his career, maybe more important than all the work ever done previously on brain science. Nobel Prize-level work. He would prefer to survive, however. He spoke up, "I need to make sure that Luis survives. I need my own equipment, my own hospital. We need to operate on your uncle here, in New York."

Santiago was suddenly completely out of his depth. His only idea was to play along until he could get instructions. "Tell me how that would work."

"We would bring him in as an emergency bleeding aneurysm early on a Sunday morning. Our Lady is a ghost town on Sundays, and we could manipulate the on-call staff easily. That way, we would have the advantages of my world-class facility and recovery staff, and could maximize our chances of success. With an implant this extensive, I would not want to take any chances we can avoid. Then we simply do as you have done here, add in footage to show it was all done in Mexico, above board, legally and ethically."

Santiago had the presence of mind to simply nod thoughtfully. "Very interesting. Let me think about it while you visit with Pierre. I'm sure he would like to tell you about his trip."

Overbridge was taken down to the rehab room to see Pierre, who was working on a Stair-Master, rhythmically climbing stairs.

* * *

Upstairs, Perez and Maxwell were discussing this latest development.

"This actually makes a lot of sense," Maxwell was saying. "No newly-put-together team and hospital could hope to compete with the facility where he has done hundreds, or actually thousands of cases. We are putting everything on the line, everything needs to be done to maximize our prospects."

Perez was thoughtful. "I am still concerned with witnesses. How many new loose ends would this generate?"

"From what I understand, just an anesthesiologist, a couple of nurses, and a scrub tech. The recovery staff would have no clue other than that they had a patient with a head bandage who had had a brain operation."

"How do we know he is not planning something?" asked Perez, who had stayed alive in a very dangerous world by staying on his guard.

"I think we should make sure there is no time for that. Tomorrow is Sunday, let's have him do it tomorrow."

Perez looked at Maxwell. "Is the mesh ready?"

"Ready, all wrapped up and sterilized."

"Is Blaylock ready?"

"Yes, he told me he has completed the analysis of everything he got from the boy, so he's as ready as he will ever be."

"Get him up here." He rolled over and stared out the window. Tomorrow. Was *he* ready for tomorrow? He fingered the insulin pump at his waistband, thought about the massive doses of lactulose he was taking to stave off the liver failure, the aching pain in his side that was now a constant feature of his day.

Blaylock came in. "What's up, Boss?" he asked.

Perez wheeled around. "We are thinking of doing the implant here in New York. Tomorrow." Blaylock's eyes widened.

"That would be sweet! I'm ready to go, and doing it here would make it so much easier than moving everything to Mexico."

"Did the data from the boy help?"

"Immensely. I will need twenty-four hours of consciousness. Maybe less, if the subject-to-subject variability turns out to be less than anticipated. That's it. Nature made the brain a very orderly place, once you understand the code." His smile was grim. "Of course, those twenty-four hours will consist of what most people would consider torture."

"No matter," replied Perez. "As long as we get the results we need.

That *I* need."

"I can virtually guarantee it," he replied.

"Okay," Perez instructed Maxwell, "Get him up here and tell him to set it up for tomorrow morning." He turned to Santiago. "Just tell him it's a go, tell him to have Maxwell take care of anything he needs, and leave before you say anything to screw it up." Perez left the room.

* * *

When Overbridge returned, the plan to proceed the next day almost threw him, but he remained outwardly calm. "Why tomorrow?" he asked. "Don't you need more time to prepare?"

Maxwell was smooth. "This weekend is perfect. We have everything here, and we are sure you can handle it." He placed a large satchel on the conference table. Maxwell reached in and extracted a plastic skull, with a circular cut around the top, just at the level where a surgeon would remove the bone in an actual procedure. Inside the skull was a plastic brain.

"This," said Santiago, " is a perfect model of Uncle Luis' brain and skull, made from his MRI scan and 3-D printed. I will let Mr. Maxwell give you the details. I must attend to another matter." He rolled smoothly from the room.

Overbridge picked up the model brain. The detail was amazing, and the program used to print the model had colored the vessels brightly, red for arteries, blue for veins, pink for the brain tissue itself.

Maxwell pulled a manila envelope from the case. "Here is a duplicate of the mesh you will be using. Notice the connector on the posterior side. That will help you orient."

Like the mesh he had seen earlier in the dog lab, it was slightly springy, and maintained its shape nicely while lying on the table, despite how fine the fibers were. Maxwell set the mesh in place on the model, and then sprayed it with a fine mist from a bottle. The mesh essentially disappeared completely, just as it had on Pierre's brain. He then grasped the connector, and peeled it back off the model. "See, smooth and easy. In addition to the actual implant, I am sending you with two more practice meshes, so you can get familiar with the placement." He replaced the skull and brain in the bag.

Maxwell picked up the satchel, and carried it as he escorted Overbridge to the elevator. He handed it to him, along with a cell phone. "Just press one to call me with whatever you need to get things set up. It is pre-programmed with me on speed dial. Our resources are nearly unlimited. Don't be shy about making sure everything is correct." The elevator doors closed.

* * *

He was silent on the drive to his apartment. That was nothing new, he was always silent. He was trying to make a list in his mind. He was confident that, if Luis survived surgery, Perez's people would certainly not try anything during the recovery period, which he had already discussed would be fairly long. He came to the conclusion that, for now, his best play was to do all in his power to achieve a successful implantation. Moreover, he *wanted* to do the implant. He was convinced that nothing could be more important. He was, frankly, excited.

In the satchel containing the model of Luis's brain and the several mesh implants, there was also a powerful laptop that, he had been told, had animations of the mesh and its attachments. He would need to study it thoroughly in order to make the surgery appear smooth, routine. There would be no hiding the mesh from the surgical tech and circulating nurse, so he needed to make sure that the on-call team did not include anyone who regularly worked in Neurosurgery. That would unavoidably mean a tech who knew nothing about the procedure. He would be alone, unable to take any of the usual short cuts allowed by having his team around him. He would need to be able to convince the OR staff that the mesh was a new product to deal with some possible complication or other. That should be okay – there were always new things, and only an experienced neuro-tech would be likely to doubt the explanation.

It had been a long time since he last took weekend call, and he was not at all sure of the current procedure for arranging an operating room on the weekend. If he made inquiries too early, they would become suspicious if he did not want to start immediately. If too late, he would potentially have to wait too long to get started. He decided he would need to call in about two a.m. and tell them that he had a Mr. Luis Martinez who had an aneurysm that was showing evidence of leaking, and that he was on his way from New Jersey, and they needed to have the OR ready for him at six. That would be about right. They would whisk him up to the OR, and then. . . .

He stopped. There was a variable he could not control. The

anesthesiologist. Everyone in the anesthesia group spent time in the neurosurgery rooms. They would be able to tell immediately that this was no ordinary aneurysm. They were smart, and they were often so bored that they would watch entire procedures. They knew their brain anatomy, and they were not afraid of him. In fact, they seemed to relish giving him a hard time. He would have to disable the video system completely, and would still be at risk of discovery.

He had a sudden flash of inspiration. He pulled out the cell phone Maxwell had given him and called.

"Hello, Mr. Maxwell?"

"Yes."

"I have some unusual requests."

"Go on."

"Are you able to get into the hospital's computer system? I need to access the surgical tech and nurse on-call list, which would have the names and contact information for the personnel. I am sure it is kept on computer, as they have practically no paper at all in the ORs."

"That should not be difficult. Anything else?"

"Yes, are you able to disable specific phone numbers, so that, if called, they will not go through?"

"Easily."

"Finally, would your people be able to insert an article into the on-line edition of a medical journal. Actually, just the abstract?"

"Interesting, but yes, I'm certain it could be arranged."

"Very good. If you can get the surgical nurse and technologist call schedule to me as soon as possible, I will be able to tell you which numbers I need blocked. I should have the abstract written within the next hour. How do I get it to you?"

"Email it to me."

"I only have work email. I don't have internet service at my apartment, either."

"The phone you are holding is a wi-fi hot spot, and the laptop I sent with you is already linked to it. I took the liberty of setting up an email account for you to use. It will come up automatically. The email to use for me is also programmed as 'Maxwell.' Send me an email as soon as you have the computer set up. My people will likely have the list for you by then."

"Okay." He hung up, feeling slightly silly. They were just pulling up to his apartment.

* * *

Once inside, he set up the computer, plugged the phone charger into the wall socket, and opened up the browser. Indeed, he had service. He opened the mail server, then sent an email to Maxwell. In return, he received an email with the call schedule attached. Our Lady of Salubrious Penitence had four complete teams on call, with another four on back up. He scanned the names. Of the eight techs, three were problems, as well as two of the nurses. He sent their names to Maxwell, with the instruction to disable their phones before two a.m. He then thought about it some more, and sent him the names of every other neuro nurse and tech, whether on call or not, just in case some well-meaning do-gooder tried to help him by calling in someone special.

He then opened Word and began to write his abstract. *"Reduction in Re-do Post Craniotomy Edema Using Microfibrillar Cortical Mesh and Di-Electric Pulsed Stimulation." That was a mouthful,* he thought. The abstract described how, in patients that had had previous brain surgery, there was less fluid pressure build-up using a new device that sealed the surface of the brain and stimulated it via an externally connected device. *I hope that's adequate.*

He mailed the abstract to Maxwell, with instructions to insert it into *Neurosurgical Review* from the prior July. Overbridge received all his journals in paper form, but he accessed them at work occasionally on line, and knew that particular journal made abstracts available to everyone, whereas the articles themselves could only be purchased by members of the neurosurgery association. If the anesthesiologist became curious or suspicious, Overbridge would simply reference the article, and explain that he had received a new prototype that was perfect for this case.

He then mocked up an emergency encounter form from a small hospital in southern New Jersey, which gave an imaginary history for Luis Martinez, and a report of the CT angio showing that his previously clipped aneurysm was leaking. In reality, he would normally require much more imaging than that to go back to the OR with an aneurysm, but he only had to satisfy the OR desk, not a neurosurgeon. He emailed it to Maxwell, and told him to have Luis arrive at Our Lady via ambulance as close to six a.m. as possible. He, Overbridge, would be waiting in the ambulance bay.

All of this took almost three hours, and his own brain was pounding as he finished. He set an alarm for two a.m., and went to bed.

At two, he called the operating room, explained that he had an emergency redo coming in from New Jersey, and told them to have the neurosurgery OR open and ready by six. There was a little grumbling, which he ignored. He also called admitting and told them the same thing. They were able to pull up Mr. Martinez' fake record from New Jersey easily enough, and gave him no trouble. No trouble at all. He went back to sleep until five. It would be a long day.

Chapter 35

The ambulance arrived at Our Lady at 6:03. Dr. Overbridge was waiting, and walked with the patient in through the Emergency Room to the after-hours admission desk. They had all the information from the imaginary prior admission in New Jersey, and Luis was up to pre-op in less than a half hour. The anesthesiologist walked in. Michelle Fujami. Perfect. She never showed more than a cursory interest in the procedures. *I should have slept instead of spending so much time on that fake abstract,* Overbridge thought. *Better use of resources.*

"Hi, Dr. Overbridge," Fujami extended her hand. "Any idea how long this will be?"

"I really don't know. There are some special considerations. I would guess about ten hours."

Fujami stopped and turned. "*Ten* hours? I've never heard of you going longer than four."

"As I said, there are special considerations. His prior surgery was performed by, shall we say, one of my less proficient colleagues. I will be using a new cortical implant, and it will require some extra work. This patient is at particularly high risk for hydrocephalus." He then introduced Maxwell as the equipment company rep, who had been so kind as to bring in the new implant, and who would be observing the procedure.

"Okay, whatever." Everyone knew that arguing with Overbridge would be an exercise in futility. She checked the chart, and went over to talk to the patient. When she was told the patient was both deaf and blind, she just listened to his lungs and heart, and headed off to the operating room to get things ready.

When they got to the operating room, Overbridge walked over to the sterile back table and opened the sterile pack containing the mesh. He pointed to it and said to the tech, a middle-aged portly man he had never met, "Do not touch this implant. I don't want any water or saline anywhere near it. Just leave it there. I will get it myself when it is time.

255

Got that?" The tech nodded.

Once the patient was anesthetized, Dr. Overbridge quickly affixed the rigid circular titanium halo to the skull just over the ears and eyebrows with six pointed screw grips, which then allowed him to fix the head firmly in place at the correct angle, the bed configured so that the head was upright, giving him easy access all around the top of the skull. The actual surgery began with an incision from just behind the left ear, over the top of the head to just behind the right ear. Dr. Overbridge took it smoothly and expertly down all the way to the bone. He clamped the scalp edge with a series of clamps that resembled small bull-dog clips with teeth, preventing any bleeding. The skin of the scalp and forehead was then separated from the skull, and turned inside out over the face, out of the way. The back side was also raised off the skull and flipped down. At this point the entire top half of the skull was bare, glistening white in the strong OR lights. He used a bone saw to cut all the way around, just above where the halo was attached, his depth perfect and precise, with the whole surgery to that point having cost less than a teaspoon of blood loss. The entire top of the skull was lifted off in one piece, peeling with a sucking sound from the underlying dura, which itself was a dull white, like a thin leather. He incised the dura by making a small cut with a scalpel, then used scissors to make an H-shaped opening, which he peeled back to expose the cerebral cortex.

He stopped for a moment to admire the brain. He had never exposed it completely like this in a living patient, and, as always, touching the brain was almost a religious experience. The tissue pulsed with each heartbeat. *Today I re-attach this brain to the world*, he thought reverently.

Things were going well. He commenced his act, working under the microscope, carefully exposing the area of the supposed aneurysm, and expertly applying a clip adjacent to the perfectly normal artery. *A successful placebo operation*, he thought to himself. All of that would have looked entirely normal to anyone who could not actually see through the microscope, which no one could. He had surreptitiously dripped a drop of superglue onto the lens of the camera, which made it look like the focus was broken. With the limited tech support on the weekend, there was no one to fix it.

So far, so good.

* * *

It took them the better part of an hour to fully bring SAC Crawley up to date on everything. He was not a happy man.

"So, what you are telling me is that you two killed a man in Manhattan Friday, and fled the scene. And you," he said, pointing at Mitzi, "are not even an Agent. You're essentially a lab tech. You can't even legally carry a weapon." Crawley threw up his hands.

"Actually, that's not correct, sir. I am a Special Agent, did the whole Quantico thing after medical school, then the Bureau was enthusiastic when I went back to train as a pathologist. Check with H.R." She pulled out her credentials. "I am just not currently *functioning* as a field agent."

Crawley stared at her. "Okay, so I just suspend you instead of arrest you? Where's the gun." She handed it over. "Not a service piece," he noted.

"No," she acknowledged. "Burner gun to go with my burner phone." She attempted a smile.

Kevin Crawley drummed his fingers on the desk. "What a mess. On the one hand, they attacked you, so it would normally be a righteous kill, but you fled. What were you thinking?"

"That NYPD is not the right entity to follow this through," Cameron replied. "This is a terrorist organization, falls under ATU authority."

"So, what do you think I should do?"

"We were hoping you could help us get some Agents to push through investigating ServCorp to try and establish a firm link with Perez."

"Tell you what. Both of you give me your credentials and guns. I assume you have an actual service piece in that purse?" Mitzi nodded and they both handed over the items as requested. "Be back here tomorrow morning at eight. I need to give this some thought. Do you have somewhere safe to stay?"

"Yes, sir," Cameron replied.

"Go there. See you tomorrow. Try not to kill anyone." He waved them out.

* * *

Overbridge went over to the back table, and carefully removed the plastic packaging from the mesh, which allowed it to spring open to the shape of the brain. He carried it carefully over to his patient, and lined it up so that the connector was around on the back. He paused, about to place it on the brain, when the scrub tech reached in and squirted the implant with saline. It promptly melted into a mass resembling wet toilet paper. His heart nearly stopped. He turned to the tech. "Did I not tell you to keep water away from the device?"

His face behind his mask must have looked frightening, for the tech visibly quailed and managed to croak out "I thought you would need to moisten it. I'm so sorry."

He tried to spread the mesh between his fingers, but it was useless. There would be no possibility of placing it correctly. Overbridge's chest felt tight. He looked toward Maxwell, who simply smiled and said, "Don't worry doctor, I brought an extra implant."

Overbridge had them get him a fresh set of dry gloves, and accepted the mesh directly from Maxwell, instructing the hapless tech to keep his distance. He carefully started on the front of the brain on the left, and manipulated the mesh onto that side, then the other, and finally around to the back. It fit perfectly. He then irrigated with saline, and watched with satisfaction as the mesh disappeared onto the surface of the brain.

He started to close. At this point, the surgery had been going for about seven hours. And a new presence was in the operating room. *Felix. What was Felix doing here?*

"Afternoon, Augie," he almost bellowed. "What on earth got the Great Man here on a Sunday? Trying to keep from burying your mistakes?"

Overbridge just blinked at him, as Dr. Fujami gave the report to Felix, then turned to him. "Sorry to leave you," she said, "but I am on Alitalia to Rome at 7:30, gotta get home and meet my husband. Felix is relieving me."

Felix, unlike Michelle Fujami, had always taken a keen interest in every procedure, particularly neurosurgery. He watched as Overbridge closed the dura, then with increasing interest as he cut a groove in the back of the skull and re-positioned the bone so that the connector fit precisely in the groove. "What is *that?*" he demanded.

Maxwell piped up. "The stimulator for the new microfibrillar mesh anti-edema implant."

"Never heard of it." Felix sounded suspicious. "I try to keep up to date."

"Then you should have seen the article in July's *Neurosurgical Review*," put in Overbridge. "Now kindly keep it down as I try to get some work done here."

Felix busily looked up the abstract on the OR computer. He was interested, and more so as he tried to search for more information on line. There was none. He went over to the trash and started poking around.

"What'cha doing?" It was Susie, the circulating nurse. They had a history.

"I think Fujami accidentally threw away a bottle of Fentanyl. I can't balance the narcotic log without it." Susie offered to help, and he asked her to check the other garbage bag. He found what he was actually looking for, the sterile wrapper from the mesh packaging. There were no markings. No corporate logos, no instructions, no warnings.

"Found it," he said, holding up the narcotics bottle he had palmed earlier. Susie came back over and managed to brush her chest against his arm as she looked at the bottle in his hand.

"Oh good." Her eyes wrinkled in the corners as she clearly smiled at him from behind her mask. He went back to his machine and sat down, as the tech asked for some more sponges.

Felix was more than a little troubled. He was no fool, and had been watching surgery for many years. Neurosurgical anesthesia had been his particular interest. *This whole procedure made no sense. This should have been a routine, two-hour case, no reason to expose the whole brain. None. Shouldn't have needed a shunt, and if it had, then a standard V-P shunt would have been fine. And Overbridge was behaving strangely. Even for him. He had actually been chatting with the nurse and the tech, for goodness sake. Telling stories.* Not at all the silent aloof surgeon Felix was used to seeing. *Like a magician's patter,* he muttered to himself. *What could possibly really be going on?*

When Dr. Overbridge flipped the front of scalp back into place, Felix became even more confused. It was a face he recognized. He looked at the chart. *Luis Martinez.* He looked at the patient. *Juan Carlos Perez. What was going on?* He started to say something, but decided to wait until a more private time. *If Perez is involved, appearing to know more than I should would definitely be dangerous.*

* * *

Overbridge finished just before three p.m., eight hours after starting the case. After accompanying Luis to recovery, he walked back through the OR towards the changing room. Maxwell stayed in recovery, ostensibly filling out a report on his laptop, but actually to watch and listen to the recovery room nurses.

Felix was waiting for Overbridge in the corridor.

259

"What just happened?"

"I have concluded another successful operation." He turned and started away.

"What is going on with you and Juan Carlos Perez?"

Overbridge started at the name. He stared at Felix for a long minute. It was possible, he realized, that he would need help to get out of this situation. *Why not Felix? Because he was an oafish buffoon?* Despite his inappropriate demeanor, Overbridge knew he was competent, and, he had to admit, brilliant.

"Come on," Felix insisted. "What gives?"

Overbridge decided to risk it. "Let's go over to the lounge." He strode briskly down the corridor to the surgeons' lounge. Felix followed, and they sat on the ratty old sofa near the vending machines. They were alone.

"I'm waiting," Felix stated.

Dr. Overbridge hesitated, then took a deep breath, and told Felix about the mesh interface, the lab in Queens, the amazing rehabilitation of Pierre LeMieux, the possibilities for thousands of other paraplegics and quadriplegics, the opportunity to change the world.

Felix listened, then asked, "So, tell me about what you did today."

Overbridge explained about Martinez' industrial accident, the paralysis plus the blindness and deafness suffered by their patient, and how the whole-brain mesh would allow not only walking, but seeing and hearing.

"So, *who* do you think this patient is?"

"Luis Martinez."

"Wrong." Felix was emphatic. "First, he is not blind. Totally normal pupillary reactions coming out of anesthesia, and the eyes tracked normally. Second, he is not deaf. Fujami had told me he was, but when I saw that the eyes were normal, I intentionally dropped a clipboard. He jumped. Third, he is not Luis Martinez. He is Juan Carlos Perez."

Overbridge reared back slightly as if he had been slapped. "No, I met Perez. This is his uncle. There is certainly some resemblance, but you are mistaken."

"I am *not* mistaken. Perez and his thugs have destroyed the whole section of Mexico where my people are from, and two of my cousins were killed by his men." He pulled out his phone and did a Google search for pictures. Something Overbridge had not thought of doing. "Look!"

Overbridge looked, and as Felix swiped through picture after picture, he saw the face of the man he knew as Luis Martinez.

Overbridge got up and pulled the book on Perez he had read on Friday off a pile of worn paperbacks in the corner. "I had dinner with the Tuckers last week."

Felix interrupted. "YOU had dinner with the Tuckers last week?" He thought back to the day he had seen Jack in the OR a couple of weeks previously. "Oh, yeah, I heard you say something about that when he was here."

"Actually, that was in reference to a prior dinner engagement. We had a second engagement. Dr. Tucker had helped me with a personal issue. In any case, I was at this dinner, and Perez's name came up, not very favorably. So, I did some research and acquired this book. I didn't know how much to credit this author, but I became concerned enough to arrange to do this surgery here, instead of in Mexico. Everything else I saw was extolling him as a successful businessman and humanitarian, and I chose to believe that this book was exaggerating."

Felix was annoyed and confused. "Okay, so you are an idiot. I suspected as much. But *why* would Perez choose to have this procedure, which is not only experimental, but very dangerous, even in your very competent hands. What is the point? If he wanted to walk, the small mesh you described earlier would have done the trick. Advancement of society, science, and humanity? Not this butcher. This is a man who has caused the deaths of dozens, maybe hundreds, of people who stood in his way, who cares no more for humanity than he does for a mosquito. Tell me about anything else you saw."

He thought back. He remembered Blaylock saying something about "fourteen terabytes of memory." He also remembered that, while they were doing the programming work on Pierre, there had been some discussion about how the memories in the brain were diffusely held.

Felix was shaking his head. "Could it be more obvious?"

Overbridge looked at him blankly.

"He means to transfer his consciousness to the machines. He wants to become immortal, omnipotent, omniscient. He means to become God."

"What do you mean, transfer his consciousness? I don't follow."

"It's an old idea. If you can create a computer or computer system which is analogous to the brain, and then embed all of a person's memories and thought patterns, the machine would BE the person thus transferred. The computer would in theory have all of the thought attributes of that person. The question would be whether the person's essence, his *soul,* would also follow the knowledge and memories, but for anyone on the outside, the computer would *be* the person. Immortality would be a strong impetus for a man like Perez. Not only that, but, resident in cyberspace, his ability to manipulate data would be extraordinary, and he could add additional speed and memory at will. Heck, he could export himself into the internet, and it would be impossible for anyone to stop him."

Dr. Overbridge was silent. He was trying to piece it all together in his mind. It certainly would explain some things. Such as the discussion about memory storage. And teaching Pierre to talk through the machine. And spending untold millions on a secret project – which could easily have been done legitimately, albeit more slowly. He considered what Felix, and Cathy, and Miguel, and that book had said about Perez. Suddenly, it all made perfect sense. His eyes focused on Felix. "We cannot let that man's essence join with the machines," he said softly. "That would create a dictator with no conscience." He paused for a long moment. "People die after surgery all the time. Perhaps I need to simply kill him."

Felix had not responded, and had stared at him. *Wow,* he thought. *Talk about cold-blooded.* "Why not turn him over to the FBI or Homeland Security or something? Or maybe stop the upload in some way? You're scaring me."

"Of course, you are right. I'll think of something else. We should assume that I am almost certainly under surveillance, and I would recommend that you not be seen with me. Thank you for listening."

Felix was about to say more, but just at that moment Maxwell came in through the door. "Ah, Dr. Overbridge, I'm glad I found you. They are asking for you in recovery." He turned to Felix. "You were the anesthesiologist, right? I did not catch your name."

"I am Felix," Felix replied automatically, "and Felix means lucky."

"Nice to meet you," he smiled, "I am Bill Martin, from the equipment company." He motioned for Overbridge. "Please, doctor, they said it was urgent."

As they walked down the hall to Recovery, Overbridge was feeling a clarity that had been lacking in his mind for years. He had a mission. There were no ghosts, no voices telling him to count, just an overwhelming, all-consuming drive to find a solution.

Everything was going well in Recovery, and Overbridge and Maxwell accompanied "Luis" to the Neuro ICU. By the time things were squared around, Overbridge was completely exhausted, and he was more than willing to accept a ride home from Maxwell. The man he now knew to be Perez would be in his ICU for several days, so he figured he had plenty of time to figure something out.

* * *

After dropping off Overbridge, Maxwell called Santiago and reported that everything was progressing according to plan. He gave instructions for the next steps, and hung up, a satisfied smile on his lips.

He was well on his way to earning his bonus. Half a billion dollars. Billion. With a B.

Chapter 36

Monday, November 7
New York

Felix had not gone home after finishing his shift at Our Lady. He spent the evening drinking at one of his regular clubs, and when he passed out, the manager had him carried to the back office couch. It was not the first time. He awoke at four a.m. with a splitting headache, and a knot in his stomach that had nothing to do with his drinking. He headed uptown to his Westside apartment. As he approached the building, he was greeted by a scene of fire engines and other emergency vehicles. He paid the cabby and got out. There was someone from the Fox News affiliate standing around, and he asked what was going on.

"Gas explosion. Took out a whole floor. Four apartments completely destroyed, they're just starting to figure out how many dead. At least a dozen. Everyone on the other floors got out. Looks like there was a leak in 703, the family was away on vacation, and it blew a couple of hours ago."

Felix immediately turned and walked over to Broadway, where he dove into the subway and took the first train to anywhere. That turned out to be downtown. He got out at Times Square, and went into an all-night diner, where he had breakfast, and thought. His apartment was 702. He did not believe in coincidences, and when your building blows up after you have just learned something you are not supposed to know about Juan Carlos Perez, you disappear.

* * *

Santiago had had a long night. Maxwell had been very clear about loose ends, and wanted to make sure to include anyone who could have seen anything important. Santiago had waited outside the hospital and followed the scrub tech into the subway, riding north into the Bronx. His neighborhood was dark and deserted, and Santiago's thin knife dropped him without a sound. He took his wallet, phone, and watch, and hopped back downtown on the next train.

He had then gone to the home of the circulating nurse in Queens. She lived on the top floor of a five-story walk-up. He waited patiently until first her lights and then the blue glow of the TV had been extinguished for an hour. He crept upstairs, quietly picked her lock, and smothered her with a pillow. He turned the window air conditioning unit to high, and closed the radiator valves. He was careful to lock her door on the way out. Blaylock had determined she lived alone, and social media did not show any evidence of a current relationship. It would likely be a week, maybe more, before there was enough of an odor to draw anyone's attention.

His final stop had been the anesthesiologist's building. Everything had been dark and quiet there, and it was child's play to set up the gasoline bomb in the apartment next door, right against the common wall with the bedroom. Blaylock had ascertained that the neighbors had conveniently put a vacation hold on their *New York Times*, and had also been able to open the electric door remotely by hacking the building's system. Just for fun, he had emptied their bank accounts and opened a fire claim for the explosion barely fifteen minutes after it occurred.

The other anesthesiologist was en route to Italy for a month-long vacation, which was good enough. In a month, everything would be complete.

* * *

Felix had been staring, glazed, at the TV in the diner when a story came on that caught his attention. Just a routine mugging-and-murder in the Bronx, the victim identified as "a surgical tech on his way home from Our Lady of Salubrious Penitence." He was suddenly wide awake. He berated himself for not having thought of it earlier. He was not the only witness. He felt a chill. He pulled out his phone, then cursed his own stupidity and turned it to airplane mode. *I'll be safer if they think I'm dead.* He looked up Susie's number and dialed it from the pay phone by the kitchen, surprised to find one still in service. It rang until it went to voice mail. *Of course, five in the morning, lots of people's phones were off. She's probably fine.* That thought lasted about a minute, and then he decided to go to her apartment. He remembered it well.

After he had pounded on her door for several minutes, a bleary-eyed apartment manager shouted up the stairwell. "Hey, what's going on!"

"My friend Susie just broke up with her boyfriend, and when I got up this morning there was a text from her threatening to kill herself. I ran right over to check on her, but she doesn't answer."

The manager looked worried, and ducked back into his apartment, coming back out with his pass key. He puffed up the stairs, gasping a little with the effort. When he got the door open, frigid air poured out, and Felix rushed in. Susie was very dead, and her skin was very cold.

"Better call the police – do it from your phone, don't touch anything here."

"Right," he said, and rushed back down the stairs, glad to escape the scene.

Felix waited until he disappeared into his apartment, then quietly hurried down the stairs, ran out into the street. He ducked into the subway, and was away.

* * *

At 5:30, Augustus Overbridge awoke as usual, and turned off his alarm. Cognizant of his probable watchers, he followed his usual morning routine, with the exception that his need to count was now non-existent. He was a man on a mission. *No way is Perez leaving my hospital alive,* he thought. He strode briskly up to OLSP.

He went directly to the Neuro ICU. It was oddly quiet. Last night, in addition to Luis, there had been three other patients, and he had expected it to be a hive of activity. No one was there. He called the nursing supervisor.

"Oh, the census was low, so they moved the patients to the regular surgical ICU to save money."

"When did that happen?"

"About two. There was a call from Dr. Lyman." Lyman was the hospital medical director.

It was not the first time that something like this had occurred, and therefore more annoying than shocking. He rode the elevator up to the next floor, and entered the surgical ICU. There were seven patients. None of them were Luis Martinez. Puzzled, he went to the computer and searched for his patient. There was no record of him in the hospital. He checked the surgical log file. No neurosurgery had been done the day before. The record had been hacked and deleted. He felt a pit in his stomach. He went up to Dr. Lyman's office.

Lyman was in his mid-sixties, and his weight was in the mid three hundreds. He looked like what he was – an apathetic, mediocre functionary in a sub-par ghetto hospital.

"Why did you feel compelled to move the Neuro ICU patients in the middle of the night?"

"What are you talking about? I didn't do any such thing."

Why did I even bother? Overbridge thought. He shook his head. "Never mind." He strode out the door. Lyman blinked a couple of times, then went back to contemplating the stain on his tie.

So, the transfer phone call had not come from Lyman. He went to his office, where there was a pink phone memo. "Call Maxwell." He retrieved the phone Maxwell had given been him from his overcoat, and pressed one. A voice answered that he recognized as Blaylock, the head programmer.

"Sorry to surprise you, but we decided to move Mr. Martinez to the medical facility here at the lab. He is doing fine, we have excellent nursing, but it would be good if you could come check on him. The car will pick you up at noon." The line went dead.

* * *

Felix had ridden the trains for a couple of hours, thinking. He could try and contact Overbridge at the hospital, but probably not until eight. He did not know where he lived, and had no phone number.

He went into a CVS and bought a burner phone. At eight sharp, he called OLSP. Overbridge was not in his office, so he had him paged overhead. No response. He hung up, planning to try again every fifteen minutes.

* * *

Overbridge could think of three general options. He could involve the governmental agencies in some way. He could stop the upload by destroying the device. He could kill Perez. While distasteful, he thought that killing him might be the best. After all, he was no longer in the hospital, and so there would be no inconvenient autopsies or paperwork. He would need some way that was not instant, and would not be obviously due to his attentions. It was a little tricky to kill someone in an ICU-type setting. Paralytics and sedatives would not work, since he would be on a ventilator. There were things that would stop the heart, but most of them would lead to awkward questions if he tried to acquire them in sufficient quantities. Plus, they would be bulky and hard to conceal. He had a thought. *Digoxin.* It would be easy enough to get what would normally be a one-month supply of pills, and then if he crushed them and dissolved them, a syringe-full injected into Perez's IV bag would fairly reliably do the trick. He wrote a prescription for himself and sent it to the hospital pharmacy.

To disable the device was Plan B. *Maybe destroy the connector? That would also perhaps make them want to keep me alive for a revision or replacement. I'd need to avoid being noticed.* The connector was external, and could be accessed directly. It would be easy enough to bend some of the little prongs. *No, the techs could repair that too easily.* He had a sudden inspiration. *Perfect.*

He went down to the pharmacy, picked up his prescription, and a pill-crusher. He returned to his office, and retrieved one of his most treasured possessions from his desk drawer. He then went down to the pathology lab. *Not likely Perez has surveillance down here.*

After carefully crushing the entire bottle of the tiny pills, he added water drop by drop until he had them dissolved in the minimum amount possible. He then pulled out the item he had taken from his desk. It had belonged to his grandfather. It was a 1920's era Mont Blanc fountain pen, sterling silver with gold inlay. It had a reservoir that was filled by unscrewing the top, and was perfect for holding the digoxin solution. He removed the nib, and mounted a short needle in its place, then replaced the nib. It would certainly pass a quick look. He filled the reservoir with the poison, and put the pen back together. He clipped it in his pocket, and headed back upstairs. As he was walking across the lobby, he heard his name paged overhead. He went to the nearest phone.

"Dr. Overbridge," he announced into the receiver.

"This is Felix. They tried to kill me. They killed Susie. They killed Peter. We need to get the police."

Overbridge was silent for a moment. "The patient is not here. He is at the facility in Queens. I will solve the problem myself." He hung up.

* * *

Felix stared at the phone, barely able to comprehend the arrogance of the man. He did not know what to do next, when suddenly he had a thought. *Jack Tucker.* Jack had been in the OR for the first mesh implant, and had seen Overbridge at least twice more in the past two weeks. *Maybe Jack knows something.* Then another thought. *Maybe Jack is a target.*

He called LexMed and asked for Jack's nurse. She was in, and he asked her to please get Jack, and have him talk on her phone, not transfer it into his. She thought that was a little odd, but he had a way of being very convincing, so she complied. Jack came on the line in a minute.

"What's going on, 'Dr. Felix?'"

"Something truly, truly bad. I need you to meet me. You are in danger. Cathy, too."

"What are you talking about? Danger from what?"

"I'll explain it all, but you have to leave work now, and meet me at the deli on 40th and Madison as soon as you can. It has to do with Overbridge. Over a dozen people have been killed already. It will be better for you to get out of your office NOW. Find your wife and get her, too. Turn off your cell phones, make sure no one follows you. Trust me, Jack, go NOW." He hung up.

Jack stared at the phone in his hand. *This is insane,* he thought, *I can't just leave.* But there was something in Felix' voice. He stood for a minute, then decided. He grabbed his coat and ran down the stairs and out the fire exit on the alley. He hailed a cab on Madison, and was just coming around the corner on his street as Cathy was walking towards the cab stand on Fifth. He yelled out the window at her, and she slid in when they pulled up.

"What's up, sweetie?" She kissed him on the mouth.

"40th and Madison," he said to the cabby, and then to Cathy, "I really don't know. We are meeting Felix. He thinks we are in danger. And I believe him."

Felix was waiting when they got to the deli. He looked around, then pulled them to a booth in the back.

"Overbridge is mixed up in something that may get us all killed."

"Why us? We really just met him. We've only seen him a few times in the past month."

"Maybe, but that is practically the sum total of his entire decade of social interaction. Plus, you are a neurosurgeon, and you were there. I was there, twice. They won't know what you know, or what he may have told you. Or what he DID tell me. I know they have already tried to kill me once, and Overbridge is getting ready to try something desperate."

"What on earth are you talking about?" Jack was getting impatient.

Felix started going through what Overbridge had told him.

"That was Pierre LeMieux? The poet? I didn't see Overbridge do anything unusual."

"You left before he closed. He knocked out the video monitor and so I didn't see it either. Was there anything unusual that you DID see?"

"Well, the bone window was much larger than I would have thought necessary. Nothing other than that, but that would make sense if he were putting in this mesh you are describing."

Felix went on to describe the experiments that had been taking place. Jack was fascinated. "That kind of interface could be the key to solving untold problems in brain science. This is incredible."

Felix went on, "That would all be great, but the memory experiments have only one clear goal. He wants to transfer his consciousness to a computer system. If successful, that kind of sentient machine would be able to control every system linked to the internet. And he is NOT the kind of guy you want running the planet."

"Is that really possible," asked Cathy? "Seems very far-fetched."

Jack was thoughtful. "I really don't know. I don't believe his soul would follow into a machine, but if this did lead to a self-aware machine, it would potentially be completely amoral and therefore just as dangerous. Short term, as long as he is still alive, if he was completely integrated with the servers, he would have the same power of control even without the transfer of the ability to think."

"Well," Cathy looked grim, "I agree with Felix that Perez is a really bad actor. I haven't talked that much about him before, but he seems to be the power manipulating both the governments and the gangs in Central America. I want to get in touch with a guy I know at CIA who may be able to help." She pulled out her phone.

Felix snatched it out of her hand and turned it to airplane mode. "Are you nuts? This guy is the telecommunications king! If that phone is transmitting, he can know where you are!"

Jack sheepishly pulled out his phone and turned it to airplane mode as well.

"Let's go." They left the deli, hailed a cab, and headed downtown. Felix handed Cathy his burner. Cathy looked up the number of her contact at CIA and dialed.

* * *

Detective Terrence was typing on his computer in the squad room when an email popped up from the lab. It was the enhanced version of the witness' video. He still could not really make out features, but as the two figures were running down the street, he could see that the man had a rather distinctive gait. A slight limp. Like the one he had noticed on Agent

Cameron Hansen. He picked up the phone to call over to the ATU, then thought better of it, and decided to take a drive. He was a big believer in surprise in-person questioning. Always so much more satisfying.

Chapter 37

Perez had finally awakened around three a.m. The nurse immediately called to Blaylock's room down the hall. He came at once.

"How are you feeling, Boss?"

Perez was semi-reclined, the ventilator was making its rhythmic hum, but his eyes were alert. He motioned for paper.

"Get this tube out of my throat," he wrote.

"Sorry, Boss," replied Blaylock. "I think we better wait for the doc. Maxwell will be bringing him around noon."

"I don't want to wait until noon to get started," Perez wrote in response.

"No need to wait," Blaylock assured him. He left the room, and came back in a few minutes rolling a tower mounted with computers and a large screen, which he positioned so it was easily visible to Perez. He uncoiled a cable, which he carefully plugged into the connector protruding from the back of Perez's scalp. Then he taped a small chip camera just above each eye, and microphones next to both ears.

"Okay," he said, "we did analytics on the contours of your brain and that of the boy's, and used a sophisticated algorithm to predict the positions of the motor and sensory areas, including speech, vision, and hearing. The dogs were fairly consistent from one subject to another, and if humans are the same, we should be pretty close. More a matter of calibrating than actual programming. Let's start with vision and hearing. Focus on the screen, try to look exactly at the center, don't move your head or eyes around, so the camera will see exactly what you see." He stuck a round white sticker in the exact center of the screen. "Just look at the dot."

Perez focused on the screen. The entire screen was red, which slowly faded through orange to yellow to green to blue to purple, then back to red. After that, a series of lines and geometric shapes were shown, then multiple people and faces, then several animals, flowers, and trees, and finally cars, airplanes, and buildings.

At the same time, the room was filled with sounds, first simple tones, then musical scales, then sounds of nature, then speech.

Blaylock was at a console on the side of the tower, and was watching with satisfaction as the superimposed images from the cameras and the mesh cortex slowly became more and more similar. After about twenty minutes, they were indistinguishable.

"Okay," he instructed, "now close your eyes."

The screen now was showing a movie, and Blaylock was watching the same film on his monitor, taking the feed from Perez's cortex. It was slightly grainy, but otherwise the same, with the exception that some of the colors were slightly off.

Perez opened his eyes and picked up the clipboard. "It is like a TV with bad reception," he scrawled. As he wrote, a garbled noise came out of the speaker on the tower.

Blaylock winced. "The resolution will improve over time, but even as good as the mesh is, we still only have about ten percent of the effective neural density as the actual visual cortex. You will get to the equivalent of standard def TV, but probably never HD. Let's put on the goggles and get eye movements."

The goggles were adapted from those used to study eye movements in dizzy patients, tracking the eyes with infrared light, and those movements were used to control cameras mounted with tiny motors. He peeled the sticker off the screen and encouraged Perez to continue to watch the screen, but also to look at different parts of the screen and around the room.

All the while, the sounds in the room were being tracked as waveforms on another monitor, with the actual sounds in blue, the sounds detected from the cortex in yellow. By the time they had finished with the vision, the two waveforms had completely superimposed into green. Blaylock put earplugs into Perez's ears, and spoke quietly into the microphone.

"How is the sound reception?"

Perez wrote again. "Fine. Get this tube out or give me speech." Once again, garbled noise came from the speaker.

Blaylock typed a command, and words started to scroll down the screen. "Read these out loud to yourself, and try to only think of what you are reading, nothing else," he instructed, "I'll listen on headphones so you won't have to hear that noise." He turned off the room speaker, and sat listening as he also watched the words scroll. The process was slow, and it was an hour before he turned on the speaker, and a completely intelligible voice filled the room.

Perez stopped reading. "Good work," the robotic voice said. Then some more garbled sounds. "That was me speaking Spanish. Maybe not such good work."

"No worries, Boss," replied Blaylock. "We have Spanish calibration text as well." The screen started to scroll again. "This should go quicker." Which, indeed, it did, and a half-hour later, Perez was able to converse fluently in both languages, despite the tube in his windpipe.

By then, it was nearly seven a.m., and Perez was showing signs of fatigue. "How about taking a rest before we do the sensory calibration," suggested Blaylock. Perez was adamant.

"No, I am fine.

"The next part," Blaylock told Perez, "is where we calibrate feeling, including touch, heat, cold. And pain."

"I watched with the boy," Perez reminded him. "I know what's coming."

"Fortunately for you, again it is really more a matter of calibration. My plan is to do one area, say the left forearm, for calibration, then let the program predict the remainder of the skin surface. If the other arm matches, then, with just a few confirmatory touches on the face and chest we should be good. Probably less than an hour. We should be all done by eight, and then I will insist on a nap."

Perez was puzzled. "You told me that you needed twenty-four hours of consciousness, and that it would be torture."

Blaylock looked at him. "It is running the memory acquisition that will be the hard part. I have designed a process of rapid stimulation and recording, which should do it, but the experience will be very unpleasant. The good news is that everything so far has been going faster than expected."

"Let's move it along."

The sensory calibration went smoothly, and although the burning, freezing and stabbing were painful, it was, as promised, brief.

Blaylock turned out the lights and left the room. Perez fell into a fitful sleep, and woke up after less than an hour, rang his buzzer, and insisted that the nurse bring Blaylock back.

The memory acquisition program was more than a little

uncomfortable. Images, sounds, feelings, even smells, pulsed through his brain, first every few seconds, then faster and faster until it seemed like they were coming a dozen a second. It was overwhelming, disorienting. It was horrible. Perez stood it as long as he could, then waved his arms and said, "Stop." Just over an hour.

Blaylock stopped the program.

"Let me analyze what we have so far while you take a break," he said.

Perez took a break. He was exhausted, although, in fact, his body had been resting comfortably in his bed the entire time. After letting his mind settle for a few minutes, he asked for a report.

"Actually, going very well," reported Blaylock enthusiastically. "The process is working. What the computer has so far is random bits from throughout your brain. Like a large mosaic where only five percent of the tiles are in place. Try remembering something specific. Let's say when you first met me."

Perez complied, and Blaylock was able to see and hear the sounds and images detected on his cortex. He then ran a comparison program with what had been stored in the system memory to that point.

"Yes," Blaylock said, "I can access that memory using the pathway detected. It is just very incomplete. We need to continue acquiring. Are you up for more?"

"Resume," he responded simply.

This time, he was able to tolerate it a little longer, and, in fact, it was Blaylock who called a time out, as he said the data was getting a little fuzzy.

* * *

Cameron and Mitzi arrived at the Anti-Terrorism Unit as planned, and sat down with SAC Crawley in his office. "I spoke with your DDO yesterday," he started, pointing at Cameron. "He tells me that you are probably right about all this insanity, but that you have nothing like legally useful proof of any of it."

"That's why we need to get more manpower on this." Cameron leaned forward. "We just have to get a firm link between Perez and ServCorp, and the rest will unravel."

"Perhaps, but I still need something to tell the NYPD about firefights in Morningside Heights. They hate that."

"Terrorists, national security, classified operations. You know, the usual," suggested Mitzi. He gave her a pained look. He was just about to blast her, when an aide tapped on the door.

"What?" Crawley snapped.

"I have a woman asking for agent Hansen, says she has urgent information about Juan Carlos Perez. Says her name is Cathy Holland."

Crawley turned to Cameron. "And who is Cathy Holland?"

"A woman I knew back in the day. Ran Alexander Lake's foundation in Central America. Perez blocked one of their humanitarian projects. She actually provided a lot of the information I used when I went undercover."

"Another one of your conquests?" Crawley raised his eyebrows.

"Not likely. Not that I would have objected. She just never showed interest. I haven't heard from her for years. She is someone I would consider *extremely* reliable."

"Put her through," Crawley directed, punching the button to put her on speaker.

"Agent Hansen here. How are you Cathy? Long time, no see."

"No time for chit chat. Perez is in New York, he just had surgery to implant something in his brain that will allow him to take control of cyberspace. He has killed two OR workers in the past twelve hours, tried to kill another, and I believe my husband and I are in personal danger as well."

Crawley broke in. "Where are you? This is Special Agent in Charge Kevin Crawley. You need to come in. Meet Agent Hansen at this address." He rattled off a street address in lower Manhattan. "Get there as soon as you can."

"On our way," Cathy said, disconnecting.

Crawley turned towards Cameron. "This better not be someone you set up to convince me about your crazy ideas," he growled. He pulled open his drawer and handed Cameron and Mitzi their credentials and weapons. "We'll get back to the suspensions later."

Mitzi was quiet. It was all making far too much sense.

* * *

As Cameron, Mitzi, and Crawley were walking down the steps to their car, Arthur Terrence blocked their path. "Agent Hansen, I have some questions for you."

The SAC stepped in front of him. "That will have to wait. We have a situation here."

"Indeed we do," agreed Terrence. "I have one homicide at Agent Hansen's apartment, and video of him fleeing the scene of a second homicide."

Cameron started to say something, when Terrence shot out his hand and gave him a friendly tap on the shoulder. The wounded shoulder. Cameron almost collapsed with the sudden pain. Terrence smiled.

"Bring him with us," Mitzi snapped, "there's no time, and he seems like a sharp guy. We may need backup from NYPD."

Terrence turned her way. "You look just the right size and shape to be my shooter."

"*Of course* I'm your shooter. Let's go!"

Intrigued, Detective Terrence decided he would indeed go with the federal agents.

* * *

"So, Overbridge did not tell you where this lab was located?" Cameron, Crawley, Mitzi, and Terrence had listened to the whole story.

"A veterinary hospital in Queens. Sorry, that's all I've got," said Felix.

It was about 10:30. Hansen showed them a bag of cell phones. "With this guy, we will only use one-time phones for calls to numbers he may be monitoring. And we will use the special feature of the apartment." He took them to the back. The window overlooked a UPS facility, and a steady stream of trucks was going up the alley behind the building. There was a box full of what looked like bags of gelatin."After you make a call, leave the phone on, put it in the gelatin, and drop it on a truck. It will stick for about fifteen minutes, then fall off. That will keep anyone monitoring the phones confused about our whereabouts." He laughed. "Just like in the movies."

He then had Jack call Overbridge's office. The nurse said he was there, but could not be disturbed. Jack insisted, and she went to pull him out. She came back, apologetic. "I'm sorry, but he says he can't talk to you, and that he wishes you the best. It was very odd."

Jack disposed of the phone.

"Well, at least we know where he is. I'll talk to the boss." There was a secure scrambled land line. Hansen went through a series of codes, then arranged for satellite surveillance of Our Lady, and got a mobile team on the way. "Follow him," he instructed the dispatcher, "find out where the lab is, but remember he is probably under surveillance. Make sure they don't spot you."

"It's on the list," Mitzi broke in.

"What do you mean? What list?" asked Crawley.

"The FBI list of sites with unusual power and broadband service. A veterinary hospital in Queens. I had sorted it to the pile to check out, but by the time we got to Queens, we were concentrating on the ServCorp locations." She jumped up. "Come on, let's go!"

"Go and do what?"

"Take them out! They are killing people and pose an imminent cyberthreat! We can't let this madman take over the world!"

Terrence tilted his head. "Actually, YOU are the one I have proof is killing people. All we really have is a bunch of hearsay and circumstantial evidence. You need a lot more to send an assault team into a veterinary hospital."

A conference call was set up with the DDO, an Assistant FBI Director, and an NYPD Deputy Chief. The DDO reminded Cameron that the last time they went in, guns blazing, they lost almost twenty men, and had nothing to show for it except a crater where a facility had been.

They got plans from the city on the veterinary hospital. It was a large building, four stories above ground, an underground parking, and two deeper basement levels. Phone, power, and cable were from a common conduit with an access tunnel off of the street, but, like most hospitals, it also had a large backup generator. Interestingly, the plans also showed a cremation oven for disposing of animal remains. "Convenient," commented Mitzi.

Google Earth had a nice view of the roof, which showed that two thirds of the top floor was covered in glass.

"Must be a swimming pool," remarked Cameron. "All of Perez's places have a pool. That nails it."

"CIA clearly has a different standard of proof than the rest of us," said Crawley, shaking his head. "This is not some third-world country where we can slip in and out and do whatever we want. We need more."

In the end, the Deputy Chief agreed that they could set up a team in the tunnel, ready to interrupt the utilities, and set up radio jammers on surrounding structures so as to be able to isolate the building from cell service, and have a SWAT team at the ready two blocks away. IF Overbridge did go to that building, THEN someone could knock on the

279

door and investigate, but there was still no hard evidence of a crime.

"I'll go," Cameron said. "They know me. They hate me. If I show up, I am sure that enough criminal activity will ensue to give you all probable cause."

"I'll go with you," Terrence added, "to represent NYPD. I'd like to keep this as legal as possible."

"Me, too," said Mitzi, "FBI."

"No," replied Crawley, "that would be me. You can join us after things are secure. That's when your expertise is likely to be needed."

They staged to a vacant apartment a block away from the veterinary hospital, and settled in to wait. The team at Our Lady checked in. "We are set up in the neighborhood watching all the hospital's exits. They have people at all the exits, too. Amateurs. Effective for soft targets like Overbridge, but easily identified. We'll let you know as soon as they move."

Chapter 38

Monday, November 7
New York

A black town car pulled up at 11:55, and Overbridge emerged precisely at noon. They picked him up on satellite coverage, and as the car moved east, the tail team trailed them as they headed onto the Triborough Bridge.

Inside the car, Overbridge was wondering exactly why Jack had tried to call him. He could not imagine. *Probably inviting him to dinner or something to do with that church of his*, he thought. He put that out of his mind. *Time to focus.* He let his mind go to the place where it had lived month after long month in Vietnam. *He was the warrior. This was his mission.* He was going to accomplish it, or die trying. *Perhaps AND die trying.*

They pulled up underneath the lab building and went in. There was a new feature, a metal detector. Overbridge was glad he had not obtained a gun. The Mont Blanc passed scrutiny, the guard remarking on its beauty. Maxwell met them, and escorted him to a room on the third floor that exactly mimicked any first-class ICU. Except that, in addition to the patient and the nurse, there were two very fit-looking, very alert men with AR-15's slung over their shoulders. They stood at the doorway. Blaylock was also there, manning a workstation on the side of a tower with several large monitors, the largest facing the bed in view of the supposedly blind patient.

The man who Overbridge now knew was Perez was awake. He did not LOOK awake, to be sure, as he still had a breathing tube in his throat, and his eyes were closed. However, a small video camera over the head of the bed turned towards him as he entered the room. From a speaker on the ceiling, the same voice that had spoken for Pierre called out, "Hello, you must be Dr. Overbridge. I am so happy to finally see you. Please take this tube out of my windpipe." Despite his mission, he could not help but be both surprised and even thrilled that the mesh connection was working so well. A part of him was arguing that this work was important enough that it needed to continue. He gave a tiny physical shrug, and cleared his mind. He was a marine on a mission.

"How are you feeling?" he asked.

"Other than my splitting headache," said the voice, "remarkably well. It is such a pleasure to see and hear again." The camera panned around the room, finally coming back to rest on Overbridge. "I can never repay you."

Overbridge checked the scalp incision carefully. It was healing beautifully, no sign of infection, no fluid leak. Likewise the connector exit point on the back of the skull. He was more than a little self-impressed. Despite the long surgery, and having been moved across town, his patient was awake, alert, and looking generally far better than would be expected.

The nurse turned towards him and gave the report. "Vitals have been stable, oxygenating well, no problems with urine output, everything's smooth as silk."

This was going to complicate matters. Overbridge had counted on a heavily sedated patient. He was, however, definitely willing to remove the tube. His patient would be far easier to kill off of the machine.

With Perez awake, his original idea of simply disconnecting the EKG to simulate a cardiac arrest would clearly not work. He had hoped to simulate the arrest, and then destroy the interface by "accidentally" catching the cable under one of the paddles delivering the shock from the defibrillator. Then they would have needed to keep him alive for the eventual implant repair. There was also the chance that the shock would have not only damaged the mesh, but the cortex itself. Which was also acceptable.

That option was now gone. The kill option would be needed. Overbridge checked out the configuration of the IV. There was an injection port just at the level of the head of the bed.

"It would seem like you could be extubated. Let me just make a few calculations." He pulled out his pen and tried to write on the clipboard hanging from the ventilator. He turned to Blaylock. "My pen doesn't work. Could I borrow yours?"

Blaylock didn't have much use for such archaic instruments, and said so. He went out to get one from the desk in the next room.

As soon as he left, Overbridge pulled off the nib, and injected the digoxin into the IV line. The port was behind the head of the bed, not within the view of Perez, the camera, the nurse, or the guards. He slowed the IV rate down to a trickle, and figured that it would take about twenty minutes for enough to get into Perez's bloodstream to cause what he hoped would be a fatal arrhythmia.

Blaylock returned with the pen and Overbridge feigned some calculations. "Everything looks good." He suctioned the breathing tube, deflated the cuff, and pulled it smoothly out.

Perez coughed, and then said hoarsely, "Ah, that's much better. I'm starving." The voice from the speaker said the same thing. There was about a quarter second delay, which was most annoying. Blaylock turned off the speaker.

"How long to upload my entire memory?"

Blaylock studied his screen. "Hard to say. Can you sense the difference between your brain memory and the machine? Can you recall them for us independently?"

"I think so." The main display monitor showed what was clearly a child's birthday party. The resolution was excellent. "This is from my brain," said Perez, "and this," he continued, as the screen showed the same scene but grainy, almost pixelated," is from the computer."

"Perfect!" enthused Blaylock, typing rapidly. "It tests out as nearly ninety percent concordance. We should get to the limits of the mesh's resolution in about another twenty to thirty minutes of stimulation."

"I still do not sense thoughts from the machine side," remarked Perez. "That is really the essence. Without my consciousness moving, all of this will be for naught. Resume."

Overbridge watched, enthralled despite himself, as the screen flashed through images far too quickly to be recognized, more like a colorful, muddy, flowing river. Perez was twitching slightly, his pulse and blood pressure elevated, his breathing labored.

"What is happening?" Overbridge asked Blaylock.

Blaylock smiled. "We are uploading his memory. I have created an algorithm to simultaneously stimulate and record from the cortex. It is an accelerating process. The first hour, we only got through about two percent of the stored memories, as the machine learning calibrated and verified, then another ten percent the second hour, then another forty percent the third hour. The screen is showing the feed from the visual cortex, but the LCD monitor has a refresh rate of only six hundred screens per second, whereas, at this point, we are processing data at about a million times that speed. And your eye can only resolve a tiny fraction of what the display shows. I just like to watch. For him, of course, the psychic strain is immense."

* * *

Hansen, Terrence, and Crawley entered the lobby of the facility. It was clearly a veterinary hospital. There were fifteen or twenty dogs and cats with their owners in a large waiting area, a long reception counter, and a door leading behind the counter. "Take a number," called a young woman from behind the counter, waving towards a dispenser. Cameron took a number. While doing so, he looked up at the security camera and stuck out his tongue. They sat down. Terrence sent a text to the men in the utility van. "Ready?"

The response came back immediately. "Negative – wrong equipment. ETA 20 minutes. Hold." He showed the text to Crawley and Cameron.

"It would have been good to have seen that before I rattled their chain," Cameron remarked.

* * *

After about ten minutes, with Perez's heart rate at 180 and his blood pressure 240/145, Blaylock shut it down. Perez was limp for a half minute, and his pulse slowed back to something approaching normal.

"Why did you stop? I can take it." His voice was strangled, gasping. He was drenched in sweat, and pale.

"We don't succeed if we kill you," Blaylock replied. "Take a break. We have plenty of time."

They went through the exercise of recall of an event, this time a reception at the White House when Perez had been given an award for "humanitarian contributions." "Ninety-five percent!" Blaylock enthused.

"I still don't sense thoughts from the machine."

Blaylock was studying the monitors. "I don't know why not. It worked for the boy. Worst case we will just leave you connected. That should accomplish most of your goals, anyway."

"Until I am dead. Which is not acceptable. Resume."

Santiago ran in, a radio pressed to his ear. "Hansen's here, in the lobby," he said to Maxwell. He motioned to one of the guards, and they went over to the elevator. He ignored Overbridge, no longer concerned with the masquerade.

* * *

As the program resumed, Overbridge felt hopeful. As long as the digoxin worked, which should be any minute now, the process could be stopped. The EKG started showing some irregularity in the rapid heart rate, then suddenly Perez went into ventricular fibrillation, and slumped over.

Overbridge rushed to the bedside. "Get the crash cart!" he yelled. He had seen one in the corner. The nurse wheeled it over. He tore the gown off Perez's chest, grabbed the shock paddles, switched the defibrillator from automatic to manual, and charged it up to 360 joules. He then placed one paddle on the right side of Perez's chest, and the other under the left armpit, being careful to catch the thick cable under the paddle as it ran down the side of the bed.

"CLEAR!" he shouted, and pushed the button. Perez's back arched, and the heart rate returned to normal. Perez opened his eyes, staring blankly into space.

Blaylock was frantically pounding on his keyboard, but the monitor above him was blank. "What do you think you are doing, you idiot!" he screamed at Overbridge. "You fried the computer!" He powered it down, then restarted it. While it was booting up, he shook Perez, trying to get a response. Perez was breathing fitfully, staring into space, and drooling slightly. He was completely unresponsive. "And his brain!"

Overbridge remained calm. "He was in arrest. I saved his life." Internally, he was extremely gratified. It would appear he had successfully destroyed both the man and the machine. He was just beginning to try to figure out his next move when Perez went back into ventricular tachycardia. Overbridge grabbed the paddles again, and shocked Perez again. No good. The nurse was doing chest compressions. Overbridge intubated the patient, and the ventilator was turned on. They worked furiously.

As they were working, the computer was restarting. Suddenly, the camera turned and pointed first down at the bed, then at the EKG monitor. A voice came from the room speaker.

"Let my body go. I am safe. I am here."

Overbridge stopped. Perez was in the machine.

* * *

The elevator door opened, and Santiago and his man burst out, sweeping the waiting room with their rifles. One of the dog owners screamed, and all the animals were instantly in an uproar. Cameron dove behind a pillar as Santiago opened fire, just as a giant Rottweiler clamped his jaws on the guard's gun arm. Crawley and Cameron returned fire, and

Terrence screamed into his phone, "Kill the power, send in SWAT!"

"You're lucky, just got ready. Killing power and jamming in three, two, one. . ."

The power went off briefly, then came back on as the generator kicked in. The servers all had battery backup, but the battery on Blaylock's workstation failed, due to the prior shock. Overbridge watched the monitor as it moved through the restart screens. Blaylock raced down the hall, returning with a spare battery backup, and replaced the fried unit, which caused the computer to restart once again.

Santiago retreated into the stairwell, and sprinted up the stairs, his injured man following more slowly. Staff, patients, and their owners all ran for the door, pouring into the street. Cameron started up the stairs, but Terrence grabbed him. "Wait for SWAT. You don't know what they have up there."

They arrived forthwith, a dozen men, heavily armed.

"Okay," Crawley said, "I'll take six men and go down to clear the basement and take out the generator." He pointed at Cameron. "You take the other six and head upstairs. Detective Terrence, you stay here in case there were any remaining guards in the back." They all checked their tactical radios, and deployed.

Cameron's team headed up the stairs, with him at the rear. There were cameras mounted at every corner. "Careful," he whispered, "they could be watching us."

"Thanks for the tip." the SWAT leader replied sarcastically. As he was nearly to the second floor fire-door, it burst open, and he and the two men behind him were taken down by automatic gunfire, the door swinging shut before they were able to return fire. The three men sprawled on the landing, two of them groaning with pain as their vests had taken the impacts, the leader screaming as blood sprayed from a wound in his neck, his blood spreading rapidly to cover the floor. Another officer was trying to apply pressure to the gaping wound, but the screams rapidly became gurgles, then silence. Cameron thumbed his radio.

"Red team to blue team, come in Crawley," he whispered urgently. "We're taking fire here, one dead, two down, vests took it, they should be okay, but I'm looking at a steel door with unknown number of unfriendlies behind it."

"Roger that," Crawley replied. "No resistance on floor A. The whole floor is filled with computers. About a hundred machines, maybe thirty geeks, all looking confused. Gimme a minute, I should be able to get into the security system and access the cameras. Looks to me like every inch of the building is covered. The generator access is in here, I can shut it down at any time. Yep, looks like you have four guards on the second floor, looking at a monitor. I don't see anyone one except Terrence on the ground floor. All the civilians are gone. Third floor has a hospital room with a man in bed, a nurse, three armed men, one holding a bleeding arm, an old guy that must be Overbridge, a computer geek, and a guy in a suit. There is also a man in another room, lying on the floor next to a treadmill. No one on four, no one in the sub-basement below us."

* * *

Santiago burst into the ICU, glancing towards Overbridge, then spoke to Maxwell. "We're trapped. Looks like at least a dozen men - they control the stairs and are coming up."

Just then, the computer finished its reboot, and the camera panned around the room. "I don't have internet access," the voice said. "If you can get me access, I can escape and you can simply surrender. I will easily free you from cyberspace."

Santiago started, then looked at Perez's limp body, and back to Blaylock. "It worked!" he shouted.

"I can see all the cameras," intoned the voice. "They have taken over the server room. I am sealing the building and activating the Halon."

"What about my techs!" Blaylock was aghast.

Down in the server room, the Halon fire-suppression gas alarm went off, but as the policemen and techs rushed to the doors, the locks activated, trapping them in the room. As he started to feel light-headed, Crawley was able to get to the electrical panel, killing the generator and plunging the building into darkness. The automatic locks remained engaged, however, and his men's gunfire was having no effect. With his last breath, Crawley transmitted, "Suffocating here."

The servers, all attached to their battery backups, hummed along.

Blaylock was trembling, the thought of his twenty-eight techs dead in the server room unnerving him. He pressed the power button, shutting down the work station.

The speaker crackled, "Too late, Mr. Blaylock, I am safely in the servers. And that room is sterilized. I can hear, but I am blind. The video surveillance server must not have battery backup. Now, find a way for me to get internet access so I can escape from this building. My first action will be to transfer your bonus."

The room was light enough from the large windows, and Overbridge looked around, helplessly.

Blaylock was back at his workstation, typing furiously. "Santiago," he called, "get the travel bag from the conference room and bring me the satellite phone. It works on a different frequency, maybe it is not being jammed."

Santiago ran from the room. He returned a few minutes later with the bag. Blaylock opened the sat phone, and it powered up. "Weak signal. I can make a call, but there is no way to transmit any significant data."

* * *

The stairwell was dark, the emergency lights only dimly illuminating the space. At least the cameras were no longer glowing red, so Cameron knew they were not being watched. He got no response as he tried to contact Crawley. His two downed men had caught their breath. He thumbed the radio. His men's radios crackled, but the only other response was from Terrence, who reported that the exit doors had locked down and metal shutters closed over the windows and doors. He tried his cell phone, but realized that the jammers were also isolating him. He had no way to call for reinforcements. He had his five remaining men, Terrence, and himself. He stared at the fire door, which from this side was locked. He pointed at the two wounded men. "You two keep this door covered, you're not very mobile. You other three, come with me." He thumbed his radio. "Terrence, get up here. All the bad guys are upstairs. I need help."

There was a clattering from the stairs, and Detective Terrence shouted "Terrence," as he came around the turn back. The five of them headed up.

* * *

Maxwell was arguing with Perez. "We can't hold here, we need to let it go and activate you again at the backup facility. Everything should be there, just as it was here, it was transmitted automatically and simultaneously. It will be up-to-date for the moment prior to the power loss. All we have to do is execute the program."

"No," the machine answered, "there can only be one, and it will be me. And you will all be in prison."

"There will be no prison. We can call one of the server techs at the site and have them start the program. YOU will be able to manipulate the system in your new state. I'm sure you can make prison go away."

Perez was silent for a few seconds. "Yes, you are correct. Blaylock, make the call, then you can surrender."

The floor shook as Cameron blew the stairwell door at the end of the hallway, killing the guard who had been standing near it. Santiago had only himself and his soldier with the mauled arm, but they had defensible positions that would be difficult to take. To Overbridge's surprise, the nurse also pulled an automatic weapon out of a cabinet on the wall, and joined the men in the hall, leaving just Blaylock and Maxwell with him in the room with Perez's body.

"Make the call, Blaylock," the voice repeated. "Put it on speakerphone, please."

Blaylock punched in the number, and waited until the tech picked up on the other end. "I am calling for service on account 17J3669," Blaylock began.

"Yes, sir," said the tech on the line. "PIN?"

"2-12-1-25."

"Yes, sir. How may I help you? It sure is noisy there."

"Yes, we are at a construction site. Type in 'Execute resurrection'."

"Very good, sir. It is asking for a password."

Blaylock was just getting out his first syllable, "Ha. . . ," when the heavy base of an IV pole slammed against his temple, and he dropped as if shot. The phone skittered across the floor, as Overbridge twisted hard the other direction, swinging the pole the other way and hitting Maxwell full in the chest. He lay on the ground, blood streaming out of his mouth, his crushed chest heaving ineffectually. Overbridge walked calmly over to the phone and hit the red button, disconnecting the call.

Out in the corridor, Santiago was oblivious, the gunfire drowning out all sounds from within the room. His man and the nurse were down, as were the three SWAT officers, and he was alone facing Cameron on his left, while Terrence was working around from the right. He spun right, got off a shot that hit Terrence in the forearm, the big slug nearly blowing off his gun hand at the wrist. He then spun left, and hit Cameron in the thigh, knocking him down and sending his gun skittering down the corridor. Suddenly it was quiet, and he walked slowly towards Cameron, who was now unarmed and bleeding. Smiling broadly, he raised his gun, pointed it at Cameron's head, and said, "I have been waiting a long time to kill you."

Cameron was staring at the barrel of Santiago's Beretta, bracing for the impact. *Stupid,* he thought, *I'll be dead before I feel it.* But he did feel it, felt the warm spray as Santiago's head exploded. Overbridge had come out of the ICU room, carrying another rifle from the cabinet, and dispatched Santiago. 79 Brains. He walked back into the room, and found Blaylock was dead. 80 brains. He went over to Maxwell, watched as his last shuddering breath gasped out. 55 bodies. He looked at Perez's body. 56 bodies. Except not yet. Perez was still alive. He went over to the workstation and started pulling cables out of the back.

The room was eerily quiet. "What is going on?" asked the voice.

Overbridge realized that the workstation was no longer relevant. He did not answer, but instead went back into the corridor. Cameron had strapped a belt to his thigh, and was dragging himself towards Overbridge, who checked his leg, and then went about checking the other bodies littered around the floor. The only other man still living was the now-one-handed Arthur Terrence, who was gripping his stump tightly, and rocking slowly. Overbridge placed a tourniquet, then went back to Cameron.

"Perez is alive and well and living in the computers downstairs," Overbridge started. "If he gets internet access or even a telephone, he will get into the web and be unimaginably powerful."

"I get it. I have two men downstairs. We need to clear the rest of the building, then get back into the server room and destroy it."

"Can't you call in more men?"

"Not from inside the building. The frequencies are jammed. More cops will show up eventually, I'm sure."

Overbridge nodded, and ducked back into Perez's room. He stared at the satellite phone for a minute, then played with the buttons until he figured out how to retrieve the last number dialed. He memorized it, then smashed the phone repeatedly with the stock of his rifle, splintering it into pieces.

"Blaylock! Maxwell! What is going on up there," came the voice.

"I'm afraid they are unable to answer," responded Overbridge. "Sad, really. This process had so much to offer the world. At least we helped my son. Now I am tired of listening to you." He unplugged the microphone, and used his rifle to destroy the overhead speaker.

Down in the server room, the machine that was Perez was now cut off from all outside stimuli.

Overbridge went down the hall to Pierre's room. He was lying on the floor, groggy, bleeding from a gash on his scalp. He was tethered to his workstation, which had battery backup, but had crashed when Pierre knocked it over as he lurched awkwardly off the Stair-Master with the loss of power. Overbridge found the portable unit on its charger, and helped Pierre attach the cables. He dressed the scalp wound, and picked up the charging unit. Terrence and Cameron were sitting in the hall. Terrence was pale, staring at his mutilated arm. Cameron had radioed one of his men to go to the main floor and figure out how to get help. "I am worried about the four guards we have trapped on the second floor," he said.

"I would be delighted to cover the door," Overbridge said grimly, "Delighted."

Chapter 39

Monday, November 7
Queens

In the end, it took the Fire Department over an hour to break into the building, which had clearly been designed with assault defense in mind. Assistant NYPD Chief Cranston had arrived with the second wave of SWAT, and took charge of the scene. The HazMat team used the jaws of life to pry open the server room, and then vent the Halon. Crawley, six policemen, and twenty-eight techs were dead. The servers were running on battery power, but the monitoring screens were all blank. "Don't restore internet service," Overbridge warned them. "Perez is in the servers. If he gets out, he will control the world."

Not sure they understood, the techs checked with Chief Cranston. He was not sure he believed in any of that, but could see no advantage to restoring the connection in any case. "Get the power back on, but leave the internet disconnected," he had finally answered. *Better to not take the chance*, he thought, *at least until I get some answers.*

Upstairs, four more SWAT officers had been killed, along with Maxwell, Blaylock, Santiago and his men, the nurse, and, of course, Perez. The remaining guards on the second floor had eventually surrendered without a fight, and were being held, handcuffed to empty dog cages. The dogs had not stopped barking for even a second since the shooting started. Cranston established a command center in Perez's luxury fourth floor apartment, where Dr. Overbridge was confined to a small guest room. Terrence was rushed to the nearby Elmhurst Hospital, as were the two policemen who had taken rounds to their ballistic vests. Cameron's leg was re-dressed by the paramedics, but he was cleared to remain on site. Pierre was also cleared to be kept at the facility, and was taken upstairs to be interviewed. Soon the DDO and the FBI Assistant Directer arrived together from Washington, both looking haggard.

"Okay, gentlemen, where should we start?" The DDO looked around the room.

"Jurisdiction," began the Assistant Director. "Clearly the FBI will be taking the lead on this."

"Wait a minute," Cranston was red-faced. "You're not pushing us out. I've got ten dead SWAT officers, one maimed detective, and dozens of homicide victims."

"This is part of an international terrorist incident, and everything in this entire building is going to be classified," continued the AD. "No one is pushing you out, but the fact remains this is under my jurisdiction. We lost the ATU SAC here today as well."

"Tell you what," offered the DDO. "Let's get Agents Hansen and Lenz in here, see what we can put together, and go from there."

"I think," said the AD, "that it is likely this Dr. Overbridge who can give us the most information. We already got Hansen and Lenz's report of what they knew."

"Okay, get Overbridge, Hansen, and Lenz in here. What a total mess," Chief Cranston said.

Once they were all assembled, Dr. Overbridge was invited to tell them what he knew.

"Certainly," he offered, "just as soon as my immunity paperwork arrives. Until then, I have nothing to say other than 'do not connect the internet'."

"Why would we grant you immunity?" the AD was intrigued.

"First, because I have critical information that you need. Second, because all of my actions today were necessary and justified. And third, because the President will insist. Call him."

They all stared at him. Finally, the DDO spoke up. "I'll call that bluff." He called the Director, gave a brief explanation, and then said, "We'll be right here."

Ten minutes later, his secure mobile rang. "Hello," he said.

"Please hold for the President," came the voice.

After a brief pause, the familiar tones of the President came on the line. "Who is in the room, Deputy Director?"

"Chief Cranston, Assistant FBI Director Jenkins, CIA Agent Hansen, FBI Agent Lenz, and Dr. Overbridge."

"Put me on speaker." When that was confirmed, he continued. "Please listen carefully. Dr. Overbridge has my full confidence. He is to be granted not just immunity, but I am issuing him a blanket pardon for any and all actions. Is that understood?"

"Yes, sir," everyone responded.

"Very good," said the President. "I would like a full report of this incident once it is wrapped up." The line went dead.

"What just happened?" asked Cranston, looking around the room.

"Never underestimate the gratitude of a father," replied Overbridge.

* * *

It took over two hours for him to tell what he knew, interrupted by field trips to the clinical areas of the third floor, the dog lab on the second floor, and a walking and mind-talking demonstration by Pierre. The sub-basement had an MRI machine, an elaborate 3-D printer, and a complex machine which appeared to be the mesh-spinning device.

Mitzi convinced the Assistant Director to declare Perez's body a matter of national security, so it would be autopsied by the ATU, meaning her. The other forty-some bodies would be processed by the New York Coroner's Office. They were loaded in their body bags into a plain brown truck in the underground garage, and escaped the notice of the massed press which had assembled outside the building.

"How will we ever figure it all out?" Cameron asked. "I don't know if there are any of Perez's people left that know anything."

"Well, we have the dogs, and several examples of the mesh, and the computers. Surely with enough geeks from the Bureau, we'll get there." Mitzi was thoughtful. "I hope so, anyway. Think of all the paraplegics who could be helped. Maybe make the whole mess worth it."

* * *

As he rode in the back of an NYPD cruiser into Manhattan with Pierre, Overbridge was ruminating. He was not sure what to do with the information he had NOT shared. He knew the telephone number, the program name, the codes. He had been paying careful attention. And for some reason he was absolutely certain that the password Blaylock had been about to say was "Happy Birthday." His thoughts were interrupted by Pierre.

"Was she beautiful when she was young?" he asked. "I mostly remember a woman devastated by cancer."

"You know?"

"I read everything I could find about you. There were a lot of coincidences. I assumed. I hoped."

Thoughts of Perez receded. "Yes, she was very beautiful." Pierre put

295

his strong arm around Overbridge's shoulder, and they rode on in silence.

THE END

Acknowledgements

I began this novel as a part of the NaNoWriMo challenge to write a novel from start to finish in the month of November. I was inspired to make the attempt by my girlfriend Candy's roommate, Camille. The result was a 50,000 page book that was unreadable, but had the kernel of a story.

In the six years since then, I wrote the novel, married my girlfriend, re-wrote the novel, got sidetracked by taking on two pre-teen foster children, re-wrote the novel, and re-wrote the novel. It was not until the third or fourth re-write that I realized that I had named my hero after Camille, who had started me down this path.

I want to thank my friends and family who read early versions, and particularly Candy, who put up with her surgeon-husband taking enormous chunks of limited leisure time on the project.

Thanks also to my editor, Stephanie Lundeen, for her advice and insight, as well as her patience with the unruly commas.

If you want to be a writer, I strongly suggest you write. There is nothing else.

Jaq Wright
December, 2019

About the Author

Jaq Wright is the pen name of John Burgoyne, MD, a practicing Otolaryngologist-Head and Neck Surgeon in Seattle, Washington. He is the author of numerous scientific papers, and his book on obesity and emotional eating (co-authored with his wife, Candy Wright Burgoyne under his real name) will be released this winter.

John and Candy enjoy walking, reading, theater and cinema.

Brains is his first novel. For more information visit his website, visit **Jaq-Wright.com**, or his Facebook page, **Jaq Wright Author**.

Made in the USA
Columbia, SC
23 December 2019